CHRISTINE FEEHAN

Air Bound

A SEA HAVEN NOVEL

piatkus

PIATKUS

First published in the US in 2014 by The Berkley Publishing Group,
A division of Penguin Group (USA) Inc., New York
First published in Great Britain in 2014 by Piatkus

A CIP catalogue record for this book
is available from the British Library.

ISBN 978-0-349-40186-7

Printed and bound in Great Britain by
Clays Ltd, St Ives plc

Papers used by Piatkus are from well-managed forests
and other responsible sources.

MIX
Paper from
responsible sources
FSC
FSC® C104740

For my niece, Samantha Goodacre . . . with love

ACKNOWLEDGMENTS

As always, I have many people to thank. Domini Stottsberry, for keeping up with me, and Brian Feehan, for always being there when I need to talk fight scenes. My writing group, for calling me at seven A.M. to get me going. Andrew Mowery is owed a huge debt of gratitude for his immediate help on disabling a helicopter. If there are any mistakes or errors, they are solely mine, and not that of my expert! Thanks so much, Andrew.

Air Bound

1

THE taxi dropped Airi off just one house over from her own, something she always did just to allow herself a little time to prepare for going home. Five days out of the week she lived in a dorm—well, a small apartment—and going home took some adjustment. Sometimes it was absolutely wonderful and other times it was awful.

She walked slowly, counting her steps. Breathing. In and out. She was able to quiet her mind and not look at the patterns around her. Counting was obnoxious, but she had to give her mind something to occupy it or chaos reigned.

Wind teased her face. Once. Twice. Like the feeling of fingers brushing lightly but persistently over her skin to get her attention. She promised herself she wouldn't look, but she couldn't stop the compulsion. She glanced up at the clouds above her head. They swirled around, seemingly at random, but her mind pieced those puzzles together. Click. Click. The patterns fell into place and left her gasping. Sick. She pressed a hand to her stomach and shook her head, refusing to believe what she saw.

She was normal. Not at all like her mother. She wasn't being eaten alive from the inside, her mind slowly turning in on itself. She refused to believe that could happen.

Patterns in the clouds, or a lake or even on the walls of their home were figments of her imagination and nothing else. She wanted to believe that, but her body didn't, and it took effort to force one foot in front of the other to proceed up the walkway to her home.

Music blared. Sounds poured out of the windows and through every crack. Loud, brass, a cacophony of noise that shook the panes and filled her mind until she was afraid it would bleed. Her footsteps slowed. Music that loud meant bad things. Very bad things. Her mother's mind, like hers, refused to quiet sometimes and when counting or any of the other tricks didn't work, she resorted to drinking to self-medicate. And when Marina was drinking . . .

Letting out her breath, Airiana reluctantly opened the front door. The music blasted her in the face, nearly pushing her back out of the house.

"For God's sake, Airi, make your mom turn that off. It's been going on for hours now," Wanda, their neighbor, called. "I pounded on the door but she didn't answer—as usual." She paused, her expression turning compassionate. "Come over later if you want. I'll have dinner. You can take some to your mother."

Even the neighbors knew about Marina's drinking. How could they not? The music was atrocious, and more often than not, Airi slept outside where it was safe. Sometimes, when her mother's drinking was really bad, she had to take knives away from her to prevent her from doing harm to herself. Those were the worst times. She was careful never to tell anyone, especially where she lived and went to school. They would take her away from her mother if they knew just how bad it had gotten at home.

"Thanks, Wanda. I'll probably take you up on that." She liked Wanda. The woman didn't have a mean bone in her body and she was particularly good to Airi and Marina. Although nearly seventeen, Airi still looked twelve. Her young looks might have contributed to Wanda's compassion, but whatever the reason, Airi was glad Wanda was close by. She had moved into the neighborhood about four years earlier and Airi was grateful she had. She was a friend when times were particularly bad—one she could confide in when things were really awful and she needed someone safe to talk to.

Taking a deep breath, her stomach lurching, Airi walked into the living room. In spite of the music, the feel of the house was still and ominous, as if she'd just walked onto a horror set. She had taken four steps inside when the odor hit. Blood. Lots of it.

"Mom," she whispered softly, her hand going to her throat. Her blood roared a warning in her ears. She didn't want to move, wanted to stay frozen in time right there, no going back and no going forward. Just not move and nothing would be wrong. Her mother had threatened to kill herself many times, when she was drunk, but Airiana hadn't believed she'd really do it.

The house creaked. The music blared. Her heart slammed a terrible rhythm of dread in her chest. She tried not to breathe in the coppery scent. She absently waved a hand toward the player, and the music abruptly ceased. Air circulated, but it didn't relieve that appalling, frightening odor.

Pressing her lips together, she forced herself to walk into the kitchen. Dark coffee swirled in another pattern across the cheerful blue and white tiles, looking like a river of mud. Broken pieces of her mother's favorite mug lay scattered like white islands through the dark spill. A drawer, wide open, tipped precariously downward and a chair lay overturned beside the kitchen table. Her mother was a neat freak. She would never, under any circumstances, have left such a disaster behind, not even if she was very drunk—or suicidal. Airi's heart pounded harder than ever.

"Mom," she called again, this time a little louder. Pain edged her voice. Fear. It was a child's voice seeking reassurance, when lately she'd often had to be the adult.

There was no answer. She shook her head and forced her feet to move one step at a time down the hallway toward her mother's bedroom. She pushed open the door slowly. It was empty and as perfectly pristine as her mother always kept it. The duvet was white lace, along with the abundance of pillows and shams. Marina loved white, that pure background that soothed her mind and allowed her to rest.

Airi leaned against the wall and closed her eyes. The scent of blood was overpowering now. Much stronger in the hallway. When she turned her head just slightly, she could see a thin line of red leaking out from under the door of her bedroom. Her body, of its own volition, turned away from the sight, a full flight response, but her feet remained frozen in place. She couldn't move. She couldn't leave.

If her mother was alive in that room, she needed help. There had been no bottles of alcohol out on the sink in a single line in the way her mother liked to arrange them. There was no blender plugged in to make the drinks her mother chose to inhale by the gallon when her mind was too chaotic and she needed a respite. There had been coffee—coffee—on the floor.

Airi bit her lip so hard blood welled up. She had to check. She couldn't run like a coward to her neighbor's house and beg her to look first. Holding her breath, she made it down the hall to her bedroom door. It was slightly ajar, but she couldn't see inside. Very slowly, using her fingertips, she pushed the door open so she could look into her room.

She screamed. And screamed. And screamed. Her throat was raw and she felt blood vessels break, but she screamed on and on because nothing was going to save her mother—or what was left of her.

She knew it was her mother only by the dress she wore, her favorite dress. The one she wore when she wanted to do something fun with Airi. When she tried to make up for the times she had a bad time. When she was sober and determined to start all over again and this time, stay sober.

"Airiana. Airiana." Hands shook her shoulders. Gentle hands.

"They killed her. They tortured her, and they killed her."

Airiana Ridell covered her face with her hands, sobbing like that teenager.

"I know, honey. I'm here. You're safe. She's in a place where they can't hurt her anymore."

The calm, soothing voice broke through the web of her nightmare. The memories in such vivid detail were horrifying, as if it had just happened, as if she had just entered her bedroom and found her mother. She could still smell the blood. She would never get the odor out of her mind. Her stomach cramped and heaved and her throat hurt so bad she could barely swallow.

"Lissa," she gasped, pushing herself into a sitting position. "I'm sorry. Did I scream again?"

Lissa Pinar sat on the side of the bed, pushing back the heavy fall of hair from Airiana's forehead. Tiny beads of perspiration dotted Airiana's brow, and her thin sweats were damp as well. Lissa looked her sister of the heart over. Airiana was short, with a slender, almost boyish figure. Everything about her was fragile. A good wind might blow her over. Her eyes were deep blue, almost cobalt, fringed with golden lashes, and her hair—damp at the moment—was a true platinum blond. Natural streaks of silver and gold ran through the thick pelt of platinum hair, which, to Lissa, lent Airiana the ethereal appearance of a fairy. Right now there were dark circles under her eyes and she looked more fragile than ever.

Lissa nodded in answer to Airiana's question. "You've screamed two nights in a row now. What's bringing these nightmares back? You haven't had them in quite a while." Lissa's five acres bordered Airiana's within the large acreage of the farm, so it wasn't as if their homes were close, yet the wind had carried Airiana's cries to her.

Airiana glanced toward her windows. They were open as usual. She never closed them, not even in the rain.

Lissa might not be a blood relative, but she was family to Airiana, a sister, every bit as loved as one born to her mother.

"I don't know why the nightmares are coming back so strong," Airiana admitted, but there was a nagging feeling in the back of her mind, one that told her the nightmares were heralding of disaster.

Each of her chosen sisters had gone through something similar in their pasts—having a loved one murdered and feeling responsible—so she knew Lissa would understand exactly how she felt.

Airiana pressed her palm to her mouth, feeling sick. "I'm beginning to see patterns in everything, like I'm losing control again." That frightened her. The thought that she'd go down the same path of madness as her mother was terrifying.

"Maybe we should call Debra Jems. I could go with you to Monterey for a consult," Lissa offered immediately. "There's nothing terribly pressing that I can't put off at work."

Debra had been the amazing counselor who had brought six women together in group therapy. Each of them was a victim of a violent past, and each believed she was responsible for the murder of a family member she loved. All had been at the very end of their ability to survive when they had gone, as a last resort, to Debra, in the hopes that she could help them.

"Do you ever wonder why or how we were each drawn to Debra's group?" Airiana asked. "Each of us has a gift, we're bound to an element, and somehow we found one another just when each of us wanted to give up."

The six women had formed a bond so strong they had decided they were better off together and had pooled their money to buy a large farm. Eventually they were able to build a separate home for each of them. Although each had a designated space of five acres, they ran a communal farm and donated a portion of their outside businesses to the running, care and expansion of the farm.

"That's the part that has amazed me," Lissa agreed. "That we all came with special gifts and didn't even realize it. It's no wonder Sea Haven called to us. I think there's magic in our little village and we just responded to it."

"Do you know what's really bad?" Airiana blinked away the tears on her lashes and sent Lissa a small scowl, deliberately changing the subject to give herself a little respite. "Ilya Prakenskii married Joley Drake and settled here. Levi is really Lev Prakenskii. That's two of the brothers here in Sea Haven. And then who comes along to marry our Judith? Another *bossy* Prakenskii—Stefan."

Lissa nodded. "He can call himself Thomas Vincent, or anything else he wants, but he's a Prakenskii all the way with his domineering attitude."

Airiana held up three fingers. "And that's three of the seven Prakenskii brothers right here in Sea Haven. What are the odds of that? They're here, and somehow our sisters are attracted to them, drawn like magnets, when both professed to never want to be with a man. And that, my sister, is a very scary fact."

"What are you saying?" Lissa frowned at her. "Don't even be thinking the other brothers are going to show up here. Thinking it might make it happen."

Airiana nodded. "Right?"

The nightmare faded a bit, just enough to take the edge off, now that they were talking about the Prakenskii brothers. The seven brothers were Russian by birth, taken from their parents and trained as agents for their government in a secret program. She was fascinated by their past because it was very close to her own, without all the brutality—until her mother's murder; but the brothers had seen their parents murdered as well—and they'd been separated from each other.

"You have to admit they're darned hot," Airiana said. "But dangerous as hell and just plain bossy."

"I do agree with them on self-defense training. Stefan and Lev know so much more than I do and are very good teachers," Lissa admitted. "I'm grateful you're all learning. I tried, but I wasn't tough enough on you."

Airiana chewed on her nail. "You did just fine, Lissa. Aren't you just a teeny bit worried that the other brothers will show up and somehow we'll be . . ." She frowned, trying to think of the right word. "Trapped? They have their own gifts, and we seem to just fall right under their spell. Judith was never going to marry. And Rikki? Who would have thought she would allow someone in her home, let alone on her boat? That's a miracle in itself."

Lissa slipped off the bed. "*Don't* say it. Things happen in Sea Haven that can't be explained, and I'm not tying myself to any man, let alone one of those Prakenskii brothers. Can you imagine my personality with a man like that? So domineering. I'd shove him off a cliff. You just can't put something like that out into the universe and not have it come back and bite you in the butt."

"My butt's pretty small," Airiana pointed out. She swept both hands through her thick hair, breathing deeply. She was beginning to feel normal again, although a residue of the nightmare had lodged in the pit of her stomach, leaving her with a vague uneasiness.

"Yes, it is. But I'm kind of curvy. Which means my butt is just big enough for fate to laugh its head off while it bites me. I'm not taking any chances."

Airiana found herself laughing. That was the beauty of having sisters. It might not be her biggest laugh, but at least she was thinking of something other than portents of danger. She sighed softly. "Thanks for coming over. I'm sorry if my screaming scared you. I should have closed my windows."

She never slept with the windows closed. *Never.* She needed fresh air touching her face even when she slept. Maybe especially when she slept, but the wind had sought help for her, carrying her cries to Lissa, and she should have realized that it would always happen after the first few times.

"I wasn't afraid, Airiana, just worried about you. I'll make tea. You're supposed to help Lexi this morning in the greenhouse, right?" Lissa said, pausing to look over her shoulder at Airiana.

"I forgot about promising Lex I'd work this morning. Sheesh, that's two mornings in a row I'll be late. I don't have time for tea."

"You have time. Lexi won't care. Take a shower and get dressed. I'll have tea waiting for you. In fact, I'll give Lex a call and see if she'll join us." Which was code for "I'm telling Lexi all about your nightmare."

Airiana sighed. Every single sister would know very quickly that she'd been having nightmares again, which was both good and bad. She didn't like worrying them, but on the other hand, she wanted the support. When all six women were together, the strength they had was empowering. Airiana always came away from a family get-together feeling strong and vibrant. Right now was a good time to get a little family boost.

"Maybe we could have a dinner together," Airiana suggested. A slow, wicked grin came over her face. "We could ask Levi to cook for us. He's actually gotten really good at it."

"You are mean. It's a dive day. Rikki and Levi headed out early this morning to go after sea urchin," Lissa reminded. "The sea is calm today and they've been waiting all week for a day like today."

Airiana nodded. "How could I have forgotten? Rikki was very excited last night. You know how she loves to be out on the ocean."

"Or, more precisely, in it," Lissa corrected.

Rikki was another sister, recently married to Levi Hammond, or rather Lev Prakenskii—although he could never use his given name and be safe. Rikki was autistic, and the sea helped her find balance. For Rikki, any day she could dive in the ocean was a good day.

"I'm glad she's so happy," Airiana said. "Although she still won't let Levi captain the boat."

They both laughed. Rikki was fiercely protective over her boat and Levi had somehow managed to worm his way aboard. All five of Rikki's sisters of the heart were very grateful that he was watching over her when she dove for sea urchins. She'd always been a loner and went out to sea by herself. None of them liked it, but they hadn't been able to stop her until Levi had come along.

"Go take your shower"—Lissa made a shooing motion with her hand—"I'll put on the tea and call Lexi in. She's determined to start on the greenhouse beds today, but right now it's very cold outside. The fog's rolled in."

Airiana waited until Lissa left the room before she slowly pushed back her covers and padded on bare feet over to the window. The fog had come in dense, so thick she could barely make out the trees in the distance. A light breeze came up from the ocean, swirling the fog into giant pinwheels.

She went very still, staring out the glass, half mesmerized by the spinning mist. There were the patterns she tried so hard not to see. Right there in the fog itself. As plain as day—and she'd seen them before. She knew if she called Lissa and pointed them out, Lissa wouldn't be able to see them. She would try, but the wind would snatch them away and Lissa would think Airiana was really losing her mind.

She pressed her forehead to the cool glass. Her gift was a blessing and a curse. Being bound to air had advantages, but not when her mind was so demanding. She didn't want to ever think about her childhood, the love she had of learning, of doing, the need and hunger that grew every day and filled her life until there was barely room for relationships. Until there was barely room for her own mother.

She jammed her fist into her mouth to keep silent when she wanted to cry loud and long for the selfish child who didn't understand that her mother needed her as much as she needed those amazing patterns and all that incredible knowledge just pouring into her brain.

Child prodigies were hailed as something unique and wonderful. In reality, gifts such as hers could be a curse for everyone around her. Sometimes, when she was alone too long and not occupied with the day-to-day running of the farm and the books for each of the businesses, her mind began to work out complex mathematical problems right there on the walls of her home. It always terrified her. She had actually turned her basement into a secret laboratory, one she never told anyone about.

Was she going crazy? Was her mind finally eating through her sanity and demanding more than she was willing to give to it? Her mother had been older than Airiana was now when she began resorting to drinking to calm her brilliant mind. She hadn't wanted to end up in an asylum, or worse, a government laboratory. Marina had tried to kill her brilliance; Airiana tried to run from it.

There in the swirling fog Airiana could see the portents of evil. How did one explain it to anyone? Worse, something bad was definitely going to happen to someone close to her. She had never told a single soul, not even Debra Jems, her counselor, but she had seen the swirling patterns in the clouds above her home before she'd ever walked inside.

She leaned her forehead against the glass and wept. She'd had a chance here, with these wonderful women who had accepted her as a sister, as family, when she had none. Now there was only madness, and if she was reading the fog correctly, some horrible fate for one or all of them.

"Airiana?" Blythe's gentle voice brought on another flood of tears.

Blythe was the oldest of the women and all deferred to her when there was any kind of conflict. Blythe was tall and athletic, with very dark chocolate eyes and blond hair. Right now it was pulled back in a ponytail and she wore her running clothes. Her features were soft and her voice gentle and soothing. She was a cousin to the Drakes, the most powerful magical family in the town of Sea Haven.

Airiana allowed Blythe to turn her into her arms, and she cried for everything she'd lost long ago and everything she was about to lose. Blythe held her in silence, allowing the storm of tears to pass before she said anything. When Airiana finally looked up, Lissa was in the room, settling the tea tray on her bureau, and Lexi stood in the doorway with tears running down her own face.

"Lexi, you're so sweet," Airiana said, feeling a burst of love for her youngest sister. "You can't stand to see anyone cry."

Lexi attempted a smile. "I know, it's silly, but if any of you is upset and I can't fix it, I have to cry too."

"Well, let's sit down and have a cup of tea," Blythe said briskly. "When we're together, we always manage to resolve whatever is wrong. Perhaps we should sit in the sitting room rather than in here."

"I'm in my jammies," Airiana pointed out.

"They look like sweats to me," Blythe answered cheerfully, tugging on Airiana's arm.

She allowed Blythe to lead them all down the stairs into the soothing colors of her largest room. Comfortable chairs made a semicircle, with low tables allowing for conversation. She knew Blythe had deliberately had them come into the sitting room because everything about and in the room relaxed Airiana.

Light yellow provided a backdrop and paintings of golden sunbursts and sunsets adorned the walls. The overstuffed chairs were covered in splotches of yellow and gold with every shade in between. A few brushstrokes of burnt orange lent ambience to the soft materials. Her sister Judith had been her interior decorator and as always, Judith knew exactly what colors would be best for each of them.

Lissa placed the tea tray in the center of the low coffee table and poured each of them a cup. She handed one with milk to Airiana and settled in the chair across from her, leaving Blythe and Lexi to sit close.

"I don't think I can explain adequately," Airiana said and took a cautious sip of tea. She was beginning to shake and feared her tea would spill, but she didn't want to put the cup down. It gave her something to do with her hands.

"All of us have a past," Lissa said gently. "And all of us keep secrets. If yours is beginning to consume you, Airiana, then you need to tell us and let us help."

Airiana had to put the teacup down. If she didn't, she knew it would end up on her floor and she didn't want that.

In more ways than she wanted to admit, she was like her mother. She preferred neat and tidy and everything in its place.

"I think I'm losing my mind." She blurted her fear out fast, wanting to get it over.

Lexi shook her head and Lissa frowned. Blythe leaned toward her, looking into her eyes and gently sweeping back the mane of wild hair Airiana hadn't yet brushed into some semblance of order.

"Why do you think that, honey?" Blythe asked, all practical and interested like she managed to sound. *Sane.* She always sounded grounded and sane. That was the reason the rest of them always relied on her.

"My mind won't stop seeing patterns everywhere. I can't stop doing mathematical theories and I see them in my head. I was like this before when I was a child, but for a time it stopped and I thought I'd be all right. But it's come back worse than ever. I'm devouring books. Textbooks. Anything I can get my hands on. I stay up all night on the Internet and read hundreds of articles," Airiana confessed quickly, wringing her hands together, terrified that she was already so much worse than her mother had been. She ducked her head. "I even set up a small laboratory for myself."

"Your mind was traumatized by finding your mother tortured in your own bedroom," Blythe said softly. "You know you need to stay occupied . . ."

Airiana shook her head. "Not like this. This is different. This is . . . madness. I can't make it stop. When I was young, I soaked up everything, absorbed knowledge, anything I could find or read. It was fun and exciting and I never considered the consequences of having a mind that couldn't be satisfied. But my mother . . ."

"You aren't your mother," Lissa said firmly. "And you have all of us to help you through this. When you were young, did it help to keep learning?"

Airiana nodded slowly. "Yes. My mind would be quiet in the evenings, and on the weekends when I went home to see Mom, I didn't have the chaos going on. The continual demand to keep working and learning abated a bit, although, when my mother wasn't drinking, we discussed theories. She was wicked smart."

"So there was balance," Blythe said.

"Yes. I could talk to people who were as excited as I was about all the discoveries we were making. Before Mom drank, I could always share with her, but once she began, half the time it was just impossible. The breakthroughs in . . ." She trailed off, shaking her head, pressing her palm over her mouth, her large eyes growing enormous. "There are things I can't talk about. For your safety as well as my own."

Blythe nodded. "We understand. My cousin Sarah's husband, Damon, works for the Defense Department. There's never a discussion about his work."

Airiana's heart jerked hard. Blythe was far too shrewd not to know why Airiana's mother had been tortured, not simply killed outright. In their group sessions, she had admitted to the others that she was responsible, but she had never said why. She'd never told them the kind of work she'd done back then.

She had explained that she lived in a dorm house that was really small apartments in a building the government provided for her and a few other remarkable students attending a special type of school. She couldn't tell them the type of things they were all working on. She wanted them safe.

She hadn't been able to keep her mother safe. Her mother, who resorted to drinking too much to still her brilliant mind and had talked to the wrong people—people who wanted her daughter's work. Marina had taken money, or at least the frightening agents investigating her death had claimed she had. When she didn't deliver the goods to the foreign agents, she had been tortured for the information and then killed. Airiana didn't believe them.

Airiana had been whisked away, back to the school in protective custody. The story didn't add up. Marina couldn't possibly have known enough about Airiana's work to sell it to a foreign government. In the beginning, she had chattered to her mother incessantly, but when her mother started drinking, she had stopped talking about her project so much. When she turned fourteen, she had taken an oath to keep her research secret, and she'd taken that very seriously. She had never so much as whispered about her work to her mother, even on Marina's good days. Sadly, that had been the wedge that had slowly driven them apart.

Airiana nodded her head slowly to acknowledge Blythe's revelation about Damon Wilder. The truth was, she had recognized Damon the moment she laid eyes on him when he'd first come to Sea Haven, only a couple of years earlier. She had studiously avoided close contact.

Damon had been aware of her, of course, but he hadn't approached her, and she knew he wouldn't. It had been years earlier that they'd met, and she'd been a child, but still, he couldn't fail to recognize her. She had a very distinctive look. At the time, he'd come to brainstorm her project with her, but until he'd shown up in Sea Haven, she hadn't seen him again.

"So what can I do to keep from going insane?" Airiana asked. She felt calmer now that she'd told them. She picked up her cup of tea, and this time her hands weren't shaking nearly as much.

"You said you see patterns," Lexi said. "What did you mean by that?"

"The day my mother died, I felt the wind on my face and I looked up at the clouds. I could see this amazing pattern forming, always moving, but immediately I knew something was very wrong. It was there, right in front of me. Who sees forecasts of danger or death in clouds?" Airiana pressed her fingers to her eyes. She had the beginnings of a wicked headache.

"You do, obviously," Lissa said. "And why wouldn't you? Why doesn't that make sense to you? You said you felt the wind on your face just before you looked up. Airiana, everyone knows you're an air element. You're bound to air. Air is bound to you. Wouldn't it try to warn you of danger?

You communicate with air. Could it be that it communicates with you?"

"Well of course, Lissa, but not in patterns. I just know things when I'm outside, I feel things in the wind. But the patterns are different."

"Warnings?" Lissa guessed. "Air warning you of danger, trying to tell you what is going to happen, or what has happened?"

Airiana frowned at her. "What are you saying?"

"I can read fire," Lissa shrugged, looking a little embarrassed. "The way it moves speaks to me. I can tell if the flames are angry or joyous. I can manipulate fire. I just presumed you could do the same with air."

Airiana shook her head.

"But you do," Lexi leaned forward. "A hundred times a day. You blow out candles without being close to them. I've seen you lift your shoes and bring them over to you from across a room without even looking up. You manipulate air. You read air all the time. You know before anyone if a storm is approaching. You know if it's going to rain. You always let me know days in advance what the weather will be like and I listen to you, not the weatherman. I plan my work around what you tell me. So if you're communicating with air, how come it can't communicate back?"

Airiana frowned. "I don't know."

"Think about what the element of air actually is, what it represents," Lissa said. "Isn't it the manifestation of communication? Of intelligence? Along with a lot of other very powerful things, air is definitely about intelligence and communication. You've got one of those incredible minds, Airiana. And air communicates with you."

Airiana shook her head slowly, trying to process what her sisters were saying to her. How could they know and not her? She'd been afraid her entire life of going insane because Marina had told her that her mind would eventually devour her.

"You read patterns. You see things in patterns others can't. It doesn't make sense to us, but it would to you. That isn't going insane, Airiana, it's your element manifesting itself in a larger, more complicated way," Blythe explained. "Because you're so highly intelligent, your brain needs continual work to keep it satisfied. But first and foremost, you're bound to air. You simply mistook your brain's ability to see patterns in mathematics for your element's need to communicate with you. Two different things are going on."

"But . . ." Airiana trailed off. Could it really be that simple? She was smart. "If that's the case, why couldn't I figure it out?"

Lexi shrugged. "When we're too close to a problem, sometimes the answer's right in front of us but we can't see it. And sometimes the answer is just too simple when we're used to dealing with something much more complex."

"So you think the patterns I see on the walls, in the ground, in the waves of the ocean are air's communication with me." She wanted to believe them, believe that answer was so simple, but her mother . . . She couldn't help but doubt them. She'd seen her mother's slow deterioration.

Blythe and Lissa both nodded.

Lexi shrugged. "It's possible, isn't it? The ground communicates with me. I know what it needs at all times for my plants. If air is the source of communication, of course it would want to find a way to speak with the person bound to it. Your mind sees in patterns. What better way?"

Airiana felt stunned. Absolutely stunned. She had always thought she would eventually go insane. Everything pointed to that. She had all the same signs her mother had. Marina had given her the signs to watch out for, and she had every one. Had her mother been bound to air and didn't realize, like Airiana, that her mind was seeing mathematical problems in patterns but her element was communicating as well?

Was it really her element trying to warn her when danger was close? She could feed her mind data and keep it happy, but seeing patterns everywhere that no one else could see made her certain she was mentally ill and would eventually succumb to the illness.

"What did you see today that upset you?" Blythe asked, using her gentlest tone.

"In the fog, when I looked out the window, I could see danger coming at us. I know it's coming, just as I knew when I walked up the steps to my house when I was a teenager. I didn't know my mother would be dead, but I knew something was dreadfully wrong."

Lexi and Lissa exchanged a long, alarmed look. "Rikki and Levi are diving today. And Judith and Thomas went to an art show in New York. They were flying out this morning from San Francisco."

Airiana shook her head. "No, it's here. On the farm. I could see the layout of the farm, but it doesn't make sense."

"No tractors today, Lexi," Blythe said decisively.

"So you don't think I'm crazy because I see patterns all around me?" Airiana asked, drawing her knees up to rest her chin on top of them.

"No, I think you're perfectly sane," Blythe said. "A little mixed up, but that's to be expected given what you've been through."

"Let's not go that far," Lissa teased. "She's got it in her head that we're all going to find ourselves with a Prakenskii man in our laps."

Lexi nearly spewed her tea across the room. "*Don't* say that. Good grief, Lissa. This is Sea Haven. You can't put something like that out into the universe and not expect repercussions."

"It wasn't me," Lissa denied, holding up both hands. "Airiana said it first, and I told her the exact same thing."

Blythe kept her head down, her thumb pressed into her palm, not entering the banter.

"Well don't even think it," Lexi reprimanded. "I love Levi and Thomas, I really do, but seriously, they're both a force to be reckoned with. Did you know that even though we warned them we might have to move once Elle Drake and Jackson return, they put in a bid on the property neighboring ours?"

Airiana could hear the secret pleasure in her voice. None of them wanted to sell the farm and move, least of all Lexi, who had poured her heart and soul into it. Unfortunately, Lev Prakenskii, working undercover, had been unable to help Elle Drake escape from a human trafficking ring. The leader, Stavros Gratsos, had held her prisoner for some time before her sisters and husband, Jackson, had been able to mount a rescue operation.

All of them worried that when Elle and Jackson returned from their honeymoon and trip to Europe, Jackson would object to Lev's presence on Elle's behalf. There was no way to hide who he was from Jackson and Elle, nor did Lev want to hide from them.

Blythe sighed. "Levi made it very clear that he would not uproot Rikki. She's happy here and functioning well. He said he'd find a way to make his peace with Elle and Jackson and the other Drakes. Naturally his brother is going to support him."

"So they really put in a bid on the piece of property we've been salivating over for the last four years?" Airiana asked. "Well, Lexi's been salivating over. I presume they plan on joining the two properties."

"That's the plan," Lexi said. She couldn't hide her smile and this time she didn't try. "The soil is really good. There's a very large section of forest that is just awesome as well. I've been talking to Thomas about possibly getting a few llamas. The manure is excellent for plants."

Airiana groaned. "It's too early in the morning to be talking about manure, Lexi, especially in such an enthusiastic tone."

In spite of the fear gnawing at her, she couldn't help but be happy when she looked at her youngest sister. Lexi's wild mass of auburn hair was pulled back haphazardly in a ponytail. She looked a little like a pixie, with her large green eyes and pale oval face. She nearly always wore faded and often holey jeans and a flannel plaid shirt, but she managed to look adorable—at least Airiana thought so.

Lexi smirked. "What do you think we're going to be doing in the greenhouse today, Airiana? Make certain you wear old clothes."

"That's my cue to leave," Blythe said. "If you're all right, Airiana. We'll talk about your concerns with seeing patterns . . ."

"Going insane," Airiana corrected.

Blythe smiled at her. "That too. This evening. I'm certain you'll see that the patterns are all about you being bound to an element and not because you're losing your mind. Think about it logically and try to set aside childhood fears. You're intelligent and you like to learn about things, start reading everything you can about the element of air."

Lissa gave a little sniff of disdain. "Really? On the Internet? Do you think she's going to find a lot of really good data on elements on the Internet? Do we put things on the Internet that we know about our gifts? We don't acknowledge them to ourselves half the time."

"There might be something pertinent," Blythe ventured. "You never know."

Airiana blew Blythe a kiss. "Thanks. You think it will help to keep my mind occupied."

"I do," Blythe conceded.

The phone rang, a loud intrusion in the soothing colors of Airiana's safe retreat. Everyone else looked toward the instrument. Airiana found herself drawn to the center of the room, where the sound took on ominous patterns. Her heart nearly stopped and then began to pound.

"It's Damon. Damon Wilder," she whispered. "And it's for me."

2

AIRIANA placed her teacup carefully on the table in front of her. Her mouth had gone dry. She watched as Blythe casually picked up the phone and greeted the caller in her usual gentle, cheerful voice.

Lexi slipped her hand into Airiana's. "Damon's always been nice, Airiana. Why are you afraid?"

Airiana shook her head when Blythe held out the phone to her. Blythe frowned but resigned herself to being the go-between.

"Damon wants to come out this morning and have a meeting with you."

"I'm working in the greenhouse this morning with Lexi and I won't be able to schedule anything for several hours." It would give her time to think. Damon and Sarah were supposed to be on their honeymoon. What would be so important that they would suddenly return and Damon would want to schedule a meeting with her? Whatever it was, it wasn't good—for her.

"He says he'll come by around twelve-thirty. That it's important." Blythe had a little note of warning in her voice.

Airiana nodded. That would give her sufficient time to gather her defenses around her and ensure Damon—or anyone else with him because he wouldn't come alone—couldn't convince her to do anything she didn't want to do. "That's fine," she murmured, and looked down at Lexi's hand, shocked that she'd been squeezing it so hard. "I'm sorry, Lex," she added.

Lexi shrugged, flashing a teasing grin. "I'm better off without that hand this morning; after all, you're helping me with the compost."

Airiana found herself smiling again. That was the beauty of family, especially a family as close as hers. One moment she could be completely terrified, and the next, one of her sisters could make her laugh.

"You wish. I'll pull all the beds, but you and that nasty smelling concoction you love so much will be all alone when you start shoveling."

Lexi made a show of rubbing her hand. "I'm injured and the compost has to be mixed in those beds this morning. At least you're capable of sending the odor away, although, really, it isn't that bad."

Airiana and Lissa both laughed.

"Of course you wouldn't think it was bad, you're a little farmer and it probably smells good to you," Lissa said.

Blythe was silent and Airiana was very aware she was watching her carefully. Airiana sighed. "I know. I should have talked to him, but I need a little time," she admitted, the smile fading from her face.

"He said he came back early. There was an emergency of some kind at his work," Blythe reported, her shrewd chocolate eyes never leaving Airiana's face.

"I wouldn't know about that," Airiana assured. "I wouldn't, Blythe."

"He works for the government in some capacity for defense," Blythe said. "You all know he was injured a few years ago when someone tried to steal his work. They tortured his assistant, Dan Treadway, and killed him."

Airiana's stomach lurched. She pressed her hand tight against it, nodding her head. "I know. I heard the story from Inez at the grocery store."

Inez Nelson knew just about everyone and everything about them here in Sea Haven, where she owned the local grocery store.

"Airiana, if this is a matter of national security . . ." Blythe began.

"*Don't*. Don't say it. I don't work in that field and I haven't for a very long time. I have no idea why Damon would want to talk to me. He's never so much as acknowledged me. My mother was killed almost ten years ago. Damon was targeted much more recently. One has nothing to do with the other. And I certainly wouldn't know anything at this point that could help him. They investigated my mother's death and said all sorts of things, but no one proved anything to me."

"But you did, as a teenager, work for the Defense Department," Blythe clarified.

Airiana sighed. "You know I never talk about that."

"Well, maybe it's time you did," Blythe said. "You're safe here. You need to talk about things, Airiana. If you don't, you're going to keep having nightmares and keep thinking you're going to lose your mind."

"We were told never to discuss our work. I took an oath."

"And no one is asking you to discuss your actual projects," Blythe pointed out.

Airiana took a deep breath and let it out. Lissa looked at her expectantly. Lexi gave her a tentative smile of encouragement, but she clearly only wanted Airiana to do what made her comfortable. She was such an empath that already she looked close to tears. Airiana found herself wanting to comfort Lexi.

"When I was about seven years old, some men came to my home and asked my mother if they could do special testing on me. I was already well into high school and even studying some college-level mathematics. My mother agreed. We were struggling financially, and they told her if I qualified for their special program there would be a lot of money involved for us."

"You never talk about your father," Lissa said. "Where was he?"

Airiana shook her head. "My mother never spoke about my father. If I brought the subject up, she would start crying like her heart was broken. I don't even know his name. Marina gave me her last name."

"These men who came to visit you and your mother were from our government?" Blythe asked, determined, obviously, to keep her on track.

Airiana nodded. "It was a new program they'd developed for children like me."

"Crazy smart," Lexi said, flashing an admiring smile.

Some of the tension drained out of her. She found herself smiling back at her youngest sister. "*Crazy smart* is a good term for me," she agreed. "They set up little apartments there at the school. It wasn't really a school like most schools. We were in a government very secure building, and we had teachers of course, but each of us worked on our own projects. We were educated as fast or as slow as the individual could handle, but clearly the projects were why they wanted us."

"But they didn't want parents living there with you?" Lissa asked, frowning.

Airiana shook her head. "They told my mother it was best for someone like me to learn without distraction, and honestly, I loved it, especially after Mom began to drink. I could have spent all day in school and in fact, I often worked late into the night. That was encouraged, and I've always been a bit of a night owl. I missed my mother, of course, and they allowed me to go home on weekends."

"You worked for them until you were sixteen or seventeen?" Blythe asked.

"I was nearly seventeen. It was ten days before my birthday when someone murdered my mother. So really, about ten years."

Lexi suddenly sat back, her eyes enormous. "Airiana, you can't suspect that the people running the school actually had something to do with your mother's death. You don't think that, do you?"

"They lied about her, Lex. She wasn't selling my work to another government. She wasn't spying for another country or leaking information. When I was little, we discussed my work, but once she began drinking, I rarely tried to talk to her about it, and once I turned fourteen, I never did."

"Why fourteen?" Blythe asked.

"I took an oath not to discuss my work with anyone. Mom had helped at first with the project, you know, brainstorming with me when I was little, but she'd begun to drink and I was going to her less and less." She shrugged. "We had a rule, and she was the one who made the rule. When we were together, it was just us. Not the school and not my projects. She wanted me to be a girl and go to the mall and the movies and learn to have fun. She wanted to teach me how to have fun. I was very serious and she was afraid that by allowing me to go to that school I wouldn't be a normal teen."

It was the first time Airiana could really defend her mother. She had tried, but no one had listened to her. Her sisters were listening. They believed her. She could feel it, see their understanding on their faces. After her mother's death, with the help of these women in the room with her, she had learned to have fun just as her mother wanted.

"Why would they lie about her? Why would they smear her name and act as if she was capable of betraying her country when she wasn't? What was the point?"

"Perhaps they thought it would make you more loyal to them," Blythe ventured.

"It had the opposite effect," Airiana said. "I detested them. I wanted out of their program but I had no relatives, nowhere to go and no one to advocate for me."

"And you blamed yourself for your mother's death," Lissa added.

Airiana nodded, tears burning behind her eyes. "I know intellectually I'm not to blame. Debra and the rest of you did a good job convincing me, but that child, that teenager, she believes that if she'd stayed home and never went to school, never was crazy smart, her mother would still be alive."

"Your mother made the decision for you to go to that school, Airiana," Blythe said gently. "A seven-year-old could not make such a choice. You both needed the money to make ends meet, and I suspect your mother was already beginning her downward spiral into alcoholism."

"Her mind wouldn't stay quiet." Airiana found herself defending her mother. "Alcohol was her only relief."

"That's the child talking," Lissa said. "You know that."

Airiana nodded, a little appalled that she still blurted out a defense for her mother, even when she knew better. "I know Marina should have gotten help, but she didn't, she turned to alcohol instead. Still, if I'd gone home several times a week instead of just weekends, she might have tried harder for me. She didn't start really drinking until I was already into my teens. I didn't even ask to go home more often because the more uncomfortable it got there, the easier it was to bury myself in my work. If I'd just noticed how hard it was on Marina and was even a little bit more compassionate . . ."

"You were a child, Airiana. A teenager with a mind that was demanding more knowledge every moment of the day," Blythe said.

"Now, looking back, I never said anything to my teachers about what my mother was doing because I was afraid they would keep me from seeing her—but they must have known. Right? They wouldn't have me working on the kinds of things I was without continually vetting my mother."

"Which is why you believe there was some kind of conspiracy and your own government murdered your mother," Lissa said.

Airiana nodded, biting at her fingernail. "I know it sounds insane. Maybe I think too much. I rarely sleep that well and I told you, my mind works on problems all the time. My mother's murder never added up for me. Even if a foreign agent came in contact with her—and how would they know I was at that top secret school—wouldn't it make more sense to wait for me to come home and then grab me? I would have told them anything they wanted to know to protect her."

Lexi nodded in understanding, tears welling up. "We do anything we can to protect the people we love."

Airiana put her hand gently over Lexi's. "I'm sorry, baby. I don't mean to bring up bad memories."

"I'm upset for you, Airiana," Lexi insisted. "You're right. It doesn't make sense to murder your mother over money for your work when they could just as easily have grabbed you."

"So what happened?" Blythe said. "With your project?"

"I wasn't finished, not nearly finished. They took me back to the school and essentially I was 'locked down' for my own protection. They didn't let me see anyone other than a psychiatrist they brought in. I didn't talk to her. I stopped working, and everyone was upset and in an uproar. The psychiatrist tried to tell me throwing myself back into my work would be good for me, but I told her I couldn't think, that the trauma of finding my mother like that had done something to my mind. I just couldn't cope.

"At first they thought I was being stubborn, you know, a teen trying to outwit them, but in the end, after endless cajoling, threats and talks, they gave up. I don't know if they were convinced I really no longer could do the work, or if I just was too much trouble, but they released me just before my twentieth birthday."

"And we found you," Lissa said with great satisfaction. "You and Lexi are our little sisters and we'll protect both of you. This is a safe place."

Their farm had always felt safe—until now. Airiana hugged herself tightly. Fear clawed at her belly and bit at her throat until it swelled and she felt as if she was choking. She needed to get to work, to smell the compost and feel the morning fog on her face just to block out the feeling of trepidation growing in her.

There was no real way to convey the feeling of danger to the others. They believed no one in their government would commit such a horrendous act—torturing and murdering a woman so they could keep the daughter isolated and alone, working on a project that could change the world.

In spite of the excellent counseling she received, there was no way to ever get the sight of her mother lying on her bedroom floor covered in blood from her mind. That image was stamped there for all time and no one had ever been caught. As far as she knew, the investigation had been dropped once she was back at the school. She'd asked numerous times, but they simply told her that Marina had been selling information and it was best Airiana not be involved for her own safety.

"Do you think the murder of your mother had anything to do with the murder of Damon's assistant?" Lissa asked.

Blythe shot her a look that told her to back off, but Airiana was grateful to Lissa. At least someone wanted to try to piece together the puzzle with her even though it might hurt. She knew Blythe wanted to protect her emotions, but Airiana wanted to know who had killed her mother and why.

"As far as I know, Damon's assistant died nearly two years ago. My mother's death occurred a good six years before that. Nearly seven. So how could they be related?" Airiana asked aloud, but her brain was already working. Click. Click. She could feel and hear the pieces of the puzzle being put together.

Why would Damon Wilder suddenly want to talk to her? There could only be one reason. He had been given her project all those years ago to work on. That was the only answer. He had come to her school once. He must have been one of the people who had knowledge of what she was working on. She had refused to continue with her project, and the government wasn't about to let something that promising go by the wayside. Damon had to have been given her work.

She closed her eyes. Her project had been worth killing for. Worth torturing other human beings over. *She*
had created it, or rather the beginnings of it, and most
likely Damon—and maybe a few others—had finished her
work . . . or . . .

She bit her lip hard. Or maybe they couldn't finish it and
Damon wanted to talk to her about it. Why else would he
suddenly be interested in her after two years of knowing
she was living close by? Had he come to Sea Haven because he'd known? Now her mind was really going crazy
with the possibilities.

"Airiana?" Blythe said her name gently, calling her back
to them. "What is it?"

"I don't want to talk to him, or to anyone else, about
anything having to do with what I used to do. It isn't that
I'm unhappy because I didn't have a childhood, I wanted to
be there. I loved learning. I loved what I was doing. But I
know that whatever my brain was conceiving turned from
something good to something horrific."

"This is our home," Lissa reminded. "You aren't a child.
No one can force you to do anything. You're safe here.
Spend the morning with Lexi in the greenhouse. I've got
two appointments this morning in the shop. I've got to finish the glass chandelier for the hotel in France and two
other metal pieces as well for their gardens, but I'll be
home before Damon gets here, even if I have to reschedule
the two appointments."

Blythe nodded and glanced at her watch. "I'm heading to the village to take over Judith's shop this morning.
I promised her I'd keep it open while they were gone.
They closed the gallery part time. Frank Warner, Inez's
fiancé, agreed to help them out and keep the gallery open
four hours a day during the week, which was good of him.
I won't be able to be here, but Lexi and Lissa will be. Unless you want me to close for a couple of hours in the
afternoon?"

Airiana found she could breathe much easier. There it
was. Love surrounding her. Keeping her sane when the

world around her seemed to be caving in. Three women who would stand by her and believe in her even if she couldn't always believe in herself. She knew if she called Judith she would immediately fly home from New York, from her important art show, to be with her. Rikki would leave her beloved sea and join her without question.

"I love you all," Airiana said. "Lexi will take good care of me while you're both gone and no, Blythe, you don't need to be here when Damon comes. We can handle it."

Blythe smiled at her. "Of course you can, but call me if you need me for anything at all." She stood up. "I still have to shower and change before I open the shop, so I'd better get moving, but . . ." She trailed off when Airiana shook her head.

"I really will be fine, Blythe," Airiana assured. Her stomach was still in knots, but her mind had settled and she wanted to examine the theory that the patterns she'd always considered part of the walking-on-the-edge-of-madness might actually be air communicating with her.

Lissa stood up as well, gathering up the teacups to put back on the tray. "I will come home before he gets here, so no worries."

Lissa was small, but fierce. She was definitely their warrior woman and she had no compunctions about going up against an enemy three times her size if need be. Anyone threatening her family was considered an enemy. Even her red hair crackled around her with her fierce energy.

Airiana caught her breath. She could see patterns in the air around Lissa's silky red hair. It gleamed like living flames with every movement Lissa made. She knew exactly what those patterns were and what they meant, which had never been the problem. Now, she could study them intently instead of fearing them, believing air was giving her information, trying to convey something important.

She had always known Lissa loved her and she could see that love clearly in the fierce patterns of determination surrounding Lissa's red head. There were no dire warnings of impending doom. Only her sister's deep resolution that she would protect Airiana and Lexi with her life if need be.

Lissa sent her a small smile. "Stop looking at me with that mushy, goofy look. You know I don't cry and I'm not in the least bit girly. I refuse to get all teary-eyed with you." She picked up the tray and turned toward the kitchen.

Lexi burst out laughing. "Lissa, you're the most girly-girl I know. You can try to hide in your most excellent baggy jeans and tees, but there's no hiding the way you walk. Just because you refuse to be a sympathy crier like me doesn't mean the tears aren't there. That's why you're running away to the kitchen."

"I can pound you into the ground, little sister," Lissa reminded. "We have self-defense class tonight."

"You can try," Lexi said with a little sniff, "but I've been improving. Working on my moves." She made chopping motions in the air with her hands.

Airiana found herself laughing. The image of little Lexi, who had trouble killing snails, fighting warrior woman Lissa was just too funny. "I want to believe you could take her, Lex, but seriously? Lissa can score on Levi and Thomas occasionally."

"I wish," Lissa said, and left the room.

"I'll take a shower, get dressed and meet you in the greenhouse," Airiana promised Lexi.

Lexi nodded. "Take your time, eat something. I'll have everything ready for us. You do know we're really working with compost, right? And you're going to shower first?"

"Yes, I am. I *am* a girly-girl and I'm not going outside without a shower and clean clothes," Airiana declared with a small laugh.

Lexi shrugged. "You'll want another one when we're finished."

"Llamas? Really, Lex? For their manure?" Airiana asked as Lexi headed toward the door. "You weren't kidding, were you?"

"There are studies done about concocting a sort of tea with their manure and using it on the plants . . ."

Airiana held up her hand. "Don't use 'tea' and 'manure' in the same sentence or I'll have to pound you into the ground."

"You're such a baby," Lexi said. "It's science. You're supposed to love science."

"I draw the line at foul-smelling llama-manure tea."

Airiana watched Lexi leave laughing before she got up and made her way to the kitchen. Lissa had most of the teacups washed. Airiana leaned her hip against the doorway and watched her for a long moment.

"I love you, Lissa. If anything happens, I want you to know that you and the others mean the world to me. Being in our family has changed me, made me a better person. You've instilled confidence in me that I never had, and I appreciate you more than I can ever say."

Lissa spun around, holding the dripping teapot against her chest. "*Nothing* is going to happen to you. Rikki got through her crisis and came out stronger than ever. So has Judith. This is your time, Airiana. I'm not going to dismiss your fears and tell you everything is going to be fine when you're feeling like something terrible is coming. I say, if it is, let it come. We'll face it together. We're strong together, whether we're all physically present or not. You'll get through this and you'll be happier for it."

Airiana nodded. "I know. I don't want to go the way of my mother. My mind can be very demanding and chaotic if I'm not continually learning and the last thing I want to do is start drinking to numb myself."

Lissa smiled at her. "Crazy girl, you don't drink alcohol. I can't see you suddenly swilling the stuff."

Airiana laughed. "Keep an eye on me. If you see me suddenly hitting the alcohol cabinet, hit me over the head or something."

Lissa rinsed the teapot again and set it aside with the rest of the clean dishes. "I am coming back, Airiana. If Damon gets here before me, just stall."

"I will, I promise." Airiana blew Lissa a kiss and turned to go back to her bedroom.

"Airiana? I love you right back," Lissa said, her voice tight.

When Airiana turned around, Lissa was already ducking out of the kitchen through the arched doorway on the other side of the room.

Airiana found herself smiling as she took her shower. She was afraid of what Damon was going to say to her, but it didn't matter, because she had her family and they were already closing ranks around her.

She pulled clean underwear from her drawer, hurriedly donned them and shimmied into her oldest pair of comfortable jeans. She ran her hand lovingly down her thigh. The jeans were soft and just perfect after several years of wear, but they also had a few holes in them and she couldn't wear them too many places outside the farm. Sighing, she found a T-shirt that was somewhat threadbare and could be sacrificed to the cause.

Airiana brushed her teeth fast, shoved her feet into her oldest, *very* cute combat boots and with hair still damp, ran down the stairs of her home, slamming the door closed behind her. The fog continued to roll in off the ocean, bringing a wet, cool feel to the air.

She ran along the path in the direction of the greenhouse. It was a good distance away, but all of them had resolved to walk as much as possible to help stay fit. She was nearly there when she had to stop. She couldn't help herself, she spun around in a circle, arms wide open, welcoming the sea air. She felt as if she was completely free when she was in the open air. She thought it might be a leftover need from those last couple of years in the government school.

As she turned in her circle, celebrating her freedom, it happened again, patterns moving in the dense fog. At once a heavy dread fell over her and she ceased moving abruptly. She lifted her hands and shoved. Nothing happened. Always when she gave a little push, the fog opened for her, but this time, the mist seemed locked in tight. Her heart gave a startled jerk.

She began to run again, along the path leading to the

greenhouse. The trail was familiar and well-worn, but in the thick fog, she found it slow going. Her heart rate increased, her mouth going dry. Something was wrong, but she couldn't put her finger on what it was.

"Lexi," she called.

Sound was muffled in the fog when it was so thick, and she couldn't see much in front of her. For one moment she thought she heard the sound of male voices, and she stopped moving, holding herself very still to listen.

"I'm here. This fog is strange, it was thinning nicely and then all of a sudden it got like this again. It's weird, but I thought I heard a helicopter and then the sound was gone," Lexi added. She came out of the veil of gray mist and handed Airiana a thick sweater. "I knew you'd forget to wear one, you always do."

Airiana took it gratefully. Her body was shivering, but not so much from the cold, more from the muted voices swirling in the fog. Those voices were not a figment of her imagination—or in her head. She was certain. She caught Lexi's arm when her youngest sister would have turned toward the greenhouse.

"Let's get back inside," she whispered. "Into my house. Something's not right. Has Lissa already left?"

Lexi didn't argue. All of them had known danger and even if whatever Airiana felt was a false alarm, it was far better to be safe than sorry.

"I saw her car leave," Lexi said, dropping her voice to a low thread of sound.

Airiana tugged on Lexi's arm to keep her following. They moved in silence, trying to stay on the path leading back to Airiana's house. With each step they took, the fog seemed to grow thicker, almost as if it were deliberately slowing them down.

Airiana lifted her hand and waved it toward the fog in an effort to clear a space so they could see better and wouldn't have to move like snails. Her body was in full flight mode, fear clawing at her.

She could hear Lexi breathing behind her and knew she

had to be terrified. Lexi had been through so much, and terror was never very far from her. She stayed on the farm because she felt safe there. Airiana felt the edge of anger, a slow boiling that started somewhere in the pit of her stomach. She might be afraid herself, but she was getting angry on Lexi's behalf. The farm was their refuge and whatever threatened Airiana had no business coming to their home— and she was certain the threat was to her.

Something moved off to her left, something large. Her breath caught in her throat, and she tugged at Lexi's hand hard.

"Move fast. Run."

She began to sprint, veering away from the left side but angling toward her porch. She couldn't even make out the house in the thick fog.

"This isn't natural," Lexi said as she kept pace.

No, it wasn't. The fog definitely pressed back at them, as if something drove it, commanded it to slow them down or stop them altogether. Her brain screamed at her to stop panicking and think rationally. Airiana took a deep breath and stopped running, dragging Lexi to a halt beside her. She leaned in close to her sister and put her mouth to her ear.

"Someone is influencing the fog. We've got to get off this path and then stay very still. We can't hear them, but that means they can't hear us either. They're expecting us to run for the house. If the air communicates with me, whoever is manipulating this fog is listening to it too. We can't make noise or disturb it too much."

Lexi nodded in understanding. They stayed very low to the ground, trying to slip through the dense veil as slowly and carefully as possible. Lexi touched her shoulder and indicated she would lead the way. She knew the farm better than anyone else, and she could find the best places to hide. She wouldn't get lost no matter how thick the fog became.

Airiana allowed Lexi to crawl past her and they stayed close together, crawling low to the ground until they came to a series of bushes that ringed Airiana's home. Where Judith's property was mainly flowers and carefully cultivated plants and Rikki's was all about fire safety, Airiana's property reflected her personality. She had wild bushes and grasses growing everywhere, a virtual sea of color waving madly in the winds coming off the sea.

Lexi moved confidently between the large willowy bushes, weaving in and out between low branches. The leaves caught in their hair, and vines slapped their faces, but they kept inching forward as quietly as possible.

It was impossible not to disturb the fog. Airiana whispered to the air, asking for aid in keeping the dense mass of vapor as still as possible. She knew how to manipulate fog and even hold it still in one place, but whoever commanded the dense vapor was far more experienced than she was. Still, she kept the tiny droplets from displacing too much, enough, she hoped, that whoever was hunting them wouldn't find them, not without first thinning the fog.

Someone cursed, the male voice muffled, but his foul words still discernable. Beside her, Lexi winced and sat very still, pressing her hand to her mouth to cover her ragged breathing.

Airiana put her arm around her and pulled her close. Lexi trembled continuously. She had been taken as a child from her home, snatched right out of her bed at the age of eight, kidnapped and systematically abused emotionally, physically and sexually by a cult leader and his followers. She had worked on their farm by day and been forced into slavery at night by the male members. Airiana knew she had to be terrified. She pushed aside her own fears to try to wordlessly comfort Lexi. She felt if she conveyed absolute confidence, Lexi might not break down.

"Where the hell is she?"

Lexi shuddered and Airiana turned her into her arms. Lexi buried her face against Airiana's shoulder. She'd spent nine years in captivity, living under the threat that her captors would kill her family if she ever tried to leave. This had to be hell for her. She had finally found a way to escape the cult and had made it back to her family. Airiana imagined that Lexi had to hide many times on that farm out in the middle of nowhere.

Anger welled up that anyone would hunt them this way. She felt like prey for a large predator, huddled there with her terrified sister. Damon Wilder was coming around noon. There were far too many hours between now and when he would show up, and everyone else was out for the day.

"Stop whining." The voice cut like a knife. Hard. Merciless. An authority.

Airiana closed her eyes and inhaled slowly, concentrating on slowing her breathing, not wanting to take any chances that she could be heard. It helped to slow the wild beating of her heart and hopefully that would keep Lexi from a full-blown panic attack.

Her younger sister rarely left the farm unless it was for business, and then she never went alone. She still suffered panic attacks, and their counselor had said it was possible she always would, but that Lexi would find the tools to better handle them. Hiding in the bushes with men hunting them was not going to help.

Footsteps drew closer. Lexi pushed her palm into the ground. She was bound to earth, and Airiana had noticed that often, when Lexi was agitated, she would press her palms into the soil and that simple action seemed to soothe her, just as she spun in a circle with her arms wide and embraced the open air.

Lexi's teeth began to chatter. Airiana couldn't blame her. The footsteps were getting closer. She could hear the one who had been swearing. She couldn't hear the second man, and it was that man who scared her the most. She felt his power in the air around her, in the dense fog surrounding them.

She lifted Lexi's face, framing it with both hands, love welling up. "Listen to me, little sister. I believe these men only want me." She whispered the words, let the scant inch of air separating their faces carry the thread of sound to her sister. "I want you to stay right here. Don't move. Stay here until Lissa comes for you. Don't even come out for Damon. Just Lissa. She'll find you. Do you understand me?"

Lexi frowned and pressed her forehead against Airiana's, shaking her head slightly as if she knew what Airiana was going to say.

"I'm going to lead them away from you. I'll make a run for Judith's house. Thomas has all kinds of weapons there. I've gotten pretty good with a gun."

Lexi shook her head adamantly and clutched at Airiana's arm.

"I can't let them take you, Lexi. I can't. I wouldn't survive it. And they could use you against me. This is for me too. If they get me, Judith can unite all of your gifts and you'll find me. But if they have you too, I'll do whatever they ask me to do and they'll kill us both faster."

Her project. That horrible, wonderful project she'd begun all those years ago. Someone knew about it and they wanted it. There was no other explanation. Her mother had died over that project. Damon's assistant had most likely been killed over it and Damon's legs had been crushed. How many more people had been affected? She had no idea, but Lexi wasn't going to be one of them.

"Do you understand? I'm *not* abandoning you. I can't let them take you," she repeated fiercely. They'd talked too much. Even though she'd been careful, whoever had the power to manipulate air the way this man did would probably feel that slight disturbance eventually.

Airiana leaned forward and kissed Lexi's cheek, squeezed her hand and put her mouth up against her ear. "I love you. I love all of you."

She leapt up and ran for the path leading to Judith's house. Twigs snapped, vines slapped at her legs and leaves crunched beneath her feet. She ran as if her life depended upon it, and it probably did.

Behind her, she heard running footsteps slamming into the ground. He was following her, the one who had done the swearing, Lexi was safe if the other followed as well.

She hit something hard, so hard she thought she ran into a tree. There was no give in the trunk and her breath left her lungs in a long, painful gasp. Arms closed around her—strong arms—the kind that didn't feel when she punched and kicked and struggled, trying to execute just one of the self-defense moves she had learned. He simply lifted her off the ground, slung her over his shoulder without a word and strode through the already thinning fog.

3

AIRIANA would not go with him. Screaming would only draw Lexi out of her hiding spot, so there was little point in indulging her fear. There was no one to hear her but these men—and Lexi—everyone else was away. She would not bring her younger sister into danger she was certain was hers.

She made up her mind she wasn't going with this man. Wherever he was taking her was definitely a place she didn't want to go. She forced her mind to calm. To think. Her brain was her best defense, at least both Levi and Thomas insisted it was. To make her assailant continue to think she was panicked she kept struggling, but her mind was already laying out the farm in grids for her.

She began to weave the fog, binding it into long ropes as she pounded on his back with her fists. She timed his steps and threw a loop over his back foot as he raised it. He stumbled, nearly dropping her, forced to catch himself. Quickly she looped the fog around his neck and head, dropping it over him like a hood. She kicked hard, driving backward, using her legs and arms for momentum as well as his forward fall to throw herself off.

She hit the ground hard and rolled away from him,

scrambling on all fours in an effort to make it into the brush. He threw out his hand blindly, but unerringly, probably feeling, as she could now, exactly the position of everyone around him in the fog.

He shackled her ankle with his hand—a big hand. He was a big man and incredibly strong. Once his fingers circled her ankle, she felt not only his strength, but his will surrounding her flesh and bones. She also felt his shock at her fight—and his amusement. Well, he wouldn't be amused for long. She turned over as he dragged her back to him, and kicked his knee hard, once again using his own force against him, driving hard with her combat boot.

He grunted and the amusement vanished. He hung on to her, knocking her leg down when she came in for a second kick. Her leg went numb with the force of his blow. She felt the burn of tears, an automatic reaction. That just made her even angrier.

Fighting him physically was impossible and his hold on her ankle seemed unbreakable. She forced her body to relax while she went back to what she was most familiar with. She could manipulate air. Sitting up fast as he crouched down, his upper body coming toward her, she shoved air at him with both hands, a burst of wind at a frightening rate of speed. Honestly, she hadn't meant to push so hard, but she was terrified, angry and determined.

The wind caught him square in the chest, lifted him and threw him back. She was up and running again, pretending she was a gazelle and could run fast. Running had never been her thing. Blythe and Lissa could run forever and enjoy it, but she had always considered it a waste of time. Now, she called on air to keep her lungs filled, to move through her body and aid her as she sprinted as fast as she could.

She hit a barrier, soft this time, and knew it was a net of woven fog. The moment she encountered it, skin to fog, it wrapped around her like a sticky spiderweb. The more she struggled, the tighter it got. She closed her eyes and pushed down a sob as she once again found the control to stop moving her body when she wanted to scream and tear wildly at the bonds holding her prisoner.

Taking a breath, she tested the ropes, trying to find a weak strand. He was adept, extremely skilled, but he had to work fast and that meant his weave wasn't perfect. She tried not to admire his work, but his will was iron and somehow he embedded sheer determination within his weave of air. She tested several strands and realized he was so certain he had won that he wasn't running to catch up with her, he was walking. Once again she could feel his amusement.

Airiana turned her attention to her assailant. With every movement he made, he displaced air and transmitted information to her. He was well over six feet with very broad shoulders and a thick chest. His body felt mainly muscle. He was a machine, she realized, a fighting machine. He was purposeful and confident. He knew she was small and he felt completely in control.

She tilted her chin, holding herself still so once again she appeared resigned to her fate. Very slowly, so as not to disturb the air around her, she began to weave a thin chain going from one tree to the other just in front of her, the trees he would have to pass to get to her if he continued in a straight line. It was a long, very thin strand, neck high, impossible to see in the surrounding fog.

She concentrated on defiance and fear as her uppermost emotions, knowing he could read both just as she could feel his amusement at her pitting herself against him. He didn't seem the least inclined to call to his partner to help him. Both things told her he was arrogant and definitely felt in charge.

Once again she began to test the strands holding her prisoner. She would only have seconds to loosen the ropes of fog if her plan worked. She had to have a place to start. Up around her shoulder was a thinner strand and she concentrated on it. She felt the exact moment that the man hit the "clothesline" she'd fashioned.

For one small second the bonds loosened and she struck at the weak link, lightning fast. He went down hard, and this time he swore—in Russian. Her heart contracted pain-fully in her chest. She backed away from him and turned to run. She had taken four steps when he tackled her and brought her down just as hard. She hit the ground, his body over hers, both of his arms wrapped around her waist and the considerable weight of him slamming her to the ground.

She cried out, the force of the blow driving the air from her lungs. She couldn't have moved if she wanted to. Her body went slack and her lungs burned painfully. She gasped, a fish out of water, desperate to breathe, her dia-phragm spasming.

He turned her over, surprisingly gentle, his hands going around to the back of her waist, lifting her slightly to ease the cramping. "Just breathe. You'll be all right."

Intellectually she knew he was right, but the reality of not being able to catch her breath left her panic-stricken.

He lifted her again, and the breath slipped back into her lungs. The air around them shifted and she could see his face now. A man's face. Purely masculine, except, perhaps, for the long lashes framing his glacier-blue eyes. He had the coldest eyes she'd ever seen. She shivered, terror pushing at the edges of her control. He looked invincible. He felt in-vincible.

"I'm not going to hurt you unless you make me. We have to get you out of here and I don't have much time to explain to you. Your father sent me. I'm not with the others, and you'll need to stick close to me so I can help you."

He pushed the words into the small space of air between them, using the technique she had used with Lexi. It was a thread of sound that couldn't go anywhere other than straight where the thread was directed.

"I don't have a father."

"You do, and he wants you safe."

"If you were trying to help me, you'd let me go," she pointed out.

He lifted her into his arms. His strength and the sheer hardness of his body were overwhelming, making her feel as though it would be impossible to defeat him.

"You are no longer safe here. These men with me want you for a very different reason than me. Follow my lead and I'll see to your safety."

He was covering ground fast with long strides. Never once did she hear his breath hitch. He moved with fluid steps, with a strange grace for a man his size. He seemed to flow over the ground rather than step, never once jarring her.

"Let me go." Airiana tried to keep the plea from her voice, but it was there. That quiver of fear she couldn't quite suppress.

"I'm not going to let anything happen to you. Once I get you to safety, your father wants a few words with you. Then you're free to do as you wish, once the threat has been taken care of."

"I told you, I don't have a father."

"His name is Theodotus Solovyov." He waited a moment as if she might have heard the name.

The fog thinned more, allowing her to make out the helicopter sitting in the middle of Lexi's carefully planted field.

She gasped. "You ruined Lexi's lettuce."

It was now or never. Once he had her in that helicopter, he could take her anywhere. She felt him startle at her words, the beginnings of amusement—it was always nice to have information on one's enemy—and she knew he had a sense of humor.

She hit him hard with her fist right under his chin and leapt out of his arms—or tried to. He caught her before she actually touched ground, yanking her none too gently back against his chest as if she was a rag doll.

"Stop it," he hissed between his teeth. "You keep it up and I'm going to knock you out. It's for your own good. You're in danger."

She knew she wasn't going to get away, that she had no real chance. The knowledge hit her hard. She'd been certain with her gifts she would manage her freedom, but this man was far more knowledgeable than she was when it came to manipulating air. She wasn't going to make it out of this. No one was going to get there in time to save her, and she couldn't save herself.

Visions of her mother, cut to pieces on her bedroom floor, rose up. She would rather die right there. She had nothing to give these people. She hadn't worked on the project in close to eight years. What could she possibly tell them even if they tortured her? She fought back burning tears. The lump in her throat burned as they approached the helicopter.

There were two others beside the pilot inside the helicopter and a third, probably the man who had hunted with her captor, stood outside of it. Her heart sank. They were heavily armed. She couldn't stop her body from shivering and the man carrying her drew her closer to his body as if sheltering her with his heat.

"Maxim, you got her," the man on the ground greeted.

"Of course," her captor snapped briskly. "Was there any doubt? Let's get out of here. This took longer than expected."

He didn't hand her into the helicopter although one of the men inside reached for her. Maxim leveled a look at him and the stranger stepped back. Slinging her over his shoulder, he crouched and jumped, landing softly on the soles of his feet inside the helicopter. He swept past the others, slipping her back in front of him, almost hiding her from the others as he made his way to the back of their transportation.

The moment he set her in a seat, she shrank away from him. He acted as if he didn't notice, but snapped a seat belt around her. "Don't give me any trouble," he said, once again using that thread of sound. "Our lives depend on your cooperation."

The men kidnapping her were definitely Greek. Well, not Maxim, she was fairly certain he was Russian. The men were talking back and forth rather abruptly and she recognized the Greek language. The other man leapt into the helicopter, his weapon in a ready position, as if he was prepared for combat. She was grateful that Levi and Thomas were away from the farm.

She bit her lip hard, not looking at any of the men, knowing that would terrify her more. She kept her eyes glued to her safe haven, the farm where she had finally managed to feel happy and alive.

She couldn't go with them. That was a certainty. Wherever they were taking her would only end in torture and death anyway. She had nothing to exchange for her life, and she wouldn't want to anyway. These men could very well have been the ones who had murdered her mother.

Airiana couldn't prevent the delicate shudder that ran through her body. She hadn't made a sound, but beside her, Maxim turned his head abruptly to look at her, as if without looking, he had still felt the tremor running through her.

"I'll keep you safe," he promised, the sound clear in her ear.

His voice should have instilled confidence. It was strong and commanding, just like the man himself, almost bordering on arrogance, but that only added to her belief that there was no hope of escaping him. The helicopter lifted from the lettuce field, banked sharply and began to fly toward the sea. They had left the doors open so the gunners had a clear shot should they be interrupted.

She doubted they would be. The sound of the helicopter itself seemed to be muffled, rather than the loud ones she was familiar with. Whoever had hired these men to kidnap her had money. Lots of it.

She closed her eyes and concentrated on the air outside. Not the fog this time. A heavy wind could wreak havoc with a helicopter. She knew from the sea rescues performed by the forestry department that it was dangerous to fly in winds, especially when near the cliffs. And they were moving fast toward those cliffs.

She waited in silence, allowing herself to look through her long tangle of eyelashes at the scenery as they passed over Sea Haven. She tried to reach out to her sisters, to at least encompass them with her love. They meant the world to her. They'd given her back her life.

She built the storm slowly, carefully, not wanting Maxim to notice the difference in the clouds forming just ahead of them. Of course the pilot noticed. He grunted and said something under his breath she couldn't hear.

"Don't do anything stupid," Maxim warned.

She didn't look at him. She didn't look anywhere at all, holding herself still. Waiting. Airiana was a patient person, and there was no need to engage with any of them. She doubted if any of them would make it out of the helicopter alive.

Airiana waited until they were over the ocean, close to the cliffs, and she lifted her arms and called the wind. Using every bit of force and determination in her, she drew the wind from the sea, from the air, from the upper atmosphere. Waterspouts erupted from the ocean, climbing high, spinning like giant fingers reaching for them. The wind slammed into the helicopter and sent it spinning out of control, straight for the jutting bluffs and the sea-stacks.

For the first time, she felt Maxim's anger. It radiated from him, a dark, monstrous entity that enveloped her, swallowing her whole. He slammed his palm into her arm, knocking it down, giving her a dead arm. She thought he might have broken it. His shoulder hit her next, shoving her hard against the wall of the helicopter as it spun madly.

Maxim threw his own hands into the air and wove a pattern quickly, overshadowing her command, taking back control. The helicopter slowly righted itself, although not before the men were thrown around and one nearly was pitched into the sea.

"What the hell, Roman?" one called to the pilot. He was a swarthy man with a dark complexion, the one who had run after her with Maxim in the fog.

"Shut the hell up, Cyreck," the pilot snapped back, clearly still fighting to keep them from crashing into the water below. "Is everyone all right back there? Did we lose anyone?"

"Istvan nearly went out the door," Cyreck reported, "but Deke managed to hang on to him. All of us got thrown around."

"What about the prisoner?" Roman demanded.

"Maxim has her pinned up against the wall and seat. She's not going anywhere," Cyreck said. "The storm came in fast."

"Just our luck," Roman snapped.

Already the wind had died down, much more slowly and naturally than Airïana would have thought, and she knew Maxim was responsible.

"Are you crazy?" Maxim hissed in her ear, his breath coming from between strong, white teeth. "You'll kill us."

Her arm hurt so bad she couldn't think for a moment. He had her pinned tightly against the wall of the craft, so that she hadn't moved at all when the force of the wind hit. She hadn't been thrown around like the men, but her entire body felt bruised and battered.

"That was the point," she hissed back, not certain why she continued with their private conversation.

Her body had begun to shiver uncontrollably, stress and pain taking their toll. Maxim sighed softly and eased his weight off of her, but was careful not to give her any room.

"Don't do it again or I'll knock you out. Do you understand me?"

She forced herself to turn her head and look at him. Straight into his eyes. Their gazes collided. She was caught there. Held there. A prisoner of his sheer iron will. If anything, his eyes were colder than ever. Like beautiful, untouchable glaciers. A startling blue, like a great pool of ice she fell into and froze there, unable to get out. The shivering increased until her teeth chattered, but she couldn't look away from him.

"I asked you if you understood?" he persisted, each word distinct.

Airïana nodded her head. If she tried to speak she knew she would cry. No one could defeat this man. No one. He was a born killer. She could see it in the cold, dispassionate expression on his face and the deadly quiet of his eyes. He would hit her if she tried anything else and knock her out and not think twice about it.

There was temptation in the idea. She might not wake up. If she provoked him . . . he had a temper. A really dangerous one. But he hadn't lost control.

"Whatever is going on in that brilliant mind of yours, just stop now."

Her stomach lurched. Brilliant mind. He knew. They had come after her for that horrible project she'd conceived when she was a child. It wouldn't go away, no matter how hard she tried to make it.

"Airiana, just for a few minutes, trust me. Nothing is going to happen to you."

Somehow the way he said her name, almost as if he was familiar with her, twisted her up more inside. Of course he knew her name. He had to know whom to kidnap, didn't he? But calling her by name made her resistance seem even more futile than ever.

She detested that he used that low, almost velvet voice, as if he brushed his fingers over her skin to soothe her—or caress her. There was no way not to be affected. She was absolutely certain this was the most lethal man she'd ever come across—and that included both Levi and Thomas.

Tears burned in spite of her violent blinking to prevent them. Her lashes grew wet and spiky just before she managed to pull her gaze away from his.

"I need to take a look at your arm," he said, reaching for her.

There was not a single soft note in his voice, yet he still managed to send her the strange sensation of brushstrokes over her skin. He sounded commanding, clearly not asking, but his touch was gentle when he wrapped his fingers around her wrist and tugged.

She bit her lip hard, suppressing a cry of pain as he straightened her arm. He hadn't hit her in the shoulder, but just above her elbow, a short, straight blow with the heel of his hand that packed a lethal dose of power. She shook her head but didn't attempt to pull away from him. Instinctively she knew he didn't much care what she wanted, and she also was very aware that any movement hurt.

Tears tracked down her cheeks, but at least she remained steadfastly silent, not giving him the satisfaction of having her fall apart. What was all the crap about her father, anyway? Some new psychological warfare to make her think he was on her side? If he'd been on her side, he wouldn't have kidnapped her for these men.

It was difficult, so close to him, not to let his scent surround her. He smelled surprisingly good. Worse, he had gorgeous hair. Thick and black, and it fell around his face in a shaggy cut as if he'd taken scissors to it himself, and she found herself totally caught up in the patterns she saw there.

Her breath caught in her throat and she closed her eyes briefly, resolutely turning her face away from Maxim to stare out the open doorway of the helicopter. They were headed out to sea. Helicopters didn't get far without fuel, so there had to be a boat, a ship, a yacht, something big waiting. Her heart pounded harder than ever at the thought. There would be no escaping, not this far from land with no boat, even if she did manage to slip away from them. She would drown before she got to shore.

"I have to take off your sweater," Maxim said. He touched her wild hair, brushing silken strands from her face. "It's going to hurt for just a moment, but then I can help take the pain away. Do you understand?"

That just plain irritated her. "Of course I understand. I'm brilliant, remember?" It would have been a lovely comeback but for the hiccup in her voice.

"You have the mind of your father. You know that's why they want you, right? To force him to give them what they want." He slipped the sweater from her arm as he gave the piece of information.

Her heart jerked. She turned her head to stare at him. Shook it. He nodded as he pulled the sleeve from her arm. It hurt, but she was so distracted by his revelation she barely noticed.

"He is a great man, brilliant beyond any other in my country. He was attacked some time ago for his work. They were able to steal a microchip but it was taken from them, apparently sat in oil for five years and all the data was destroyed. Theodotus told everyone it didn't matter, just as long as no one else could get the information off of it. Theodotus believes the only way they have a chance of persuading him to do their bidding is to take you prisoner. You're the only Achilles' heel he has."

Hope flared for the first time. *They didn't know.* If what Maxim was telling her was true, they didn't know anything at all about her project. This kidnapping had to do with her birth father—a man she'd never met in her life. She still didn't altogether believe Maxim, but what could he possibly get out of lying to her?

His fingers touched her bare skin. Heat flared. Sparks bit at her arm, like little fireflies lighting all over her and leaping away. The air crackled between them. He gasped and removed his hands from her skin, leaning back away from her, his eyes glittering with menace.

She couldn't look away, not even if her life depended on it. His eyes were a clear deep blue, and so icy she should have been shivering with both fear and cold, but instead her blood had caught fire and rushed through her veins with the searing heat of a fireball.

"You're Maxim Prakenskii, aren't you?" she whispered, shocked. Horrified. Terrified. She touched her tongue to suddenly dry lips in an effort to moisten them, to get some balance.

Of course he was one of the Prakenskii brothers. She should have known by those eyes. She was more afraid than when she thought he was a stranger kidnapping her. Of course he was a stranger . . . but . . . he was *Prakenskii*. She knew three of his brothers, and every one of them was dangerous. Potentially he could be dangerous on a personal level as well.

His fingers tightened hard around her arm—her injured arm—to the point of bruising. "Don't use that name. Do you hear me? Anyone who knows that name doesn't live very long. Do you understand what I'm saying to you?"

"That you'll kill me if I reveal your true identity." She didn't look away.

"You've never heard of me or my family. Especially my family."

The grip on her arm was fierce and it was beginning to draw the attention of some of the other passengers.

"Is she giving you trouble, Maxim?" Cyreck called. "I'll be glad to come and help you tame that little wildcat."

The man who had nearly fallen from the helicopter, Istvan, laughed nervously, but the other one, Deke, looked down at the ground. That told her a lot about Maxim Prakenskii. He was considered a man not to mess with. Cyreck had been careful to use a playful tone, one he hoped to garner an atmosphere of camaraderie with.

Airiana nodded her head ever so slightly. Prakenskii was clearly not part of this group, yet they wanted him to be. Like his brothers, he'd been taken at birth and trained to be used as a tool for the government—and she knew the brothers were highly skilled in weapons, hand-to-hand combat, even sexual practices. More, they were all gifted with psychic abilities.

She knew the brothers were used for assassinations and undercover work. They all spoke multiple languages. Maxim wasn't hiding the fact that he was Russian, so whatever cover he had included his own nationality. The Prakenskiis were true operatives, able to shed one skin and easily slip into another.

Just because she knew his brothers—his family—didn't mean he was any less dangerous to her. If anything, he might decide to kill her outright to protect their new identities. She was positive she was right about him, yet not enough that she would ever mention Levi, who was supposed to be dead, or Thomas, who had changed his identity.

The third brother, Ilya, lived openly and comfortably with his own name. He had been an Interpol agent and had much more easily transferred his life to the States—to

Sea Haven more precisely, and it would stand to reason that she would know him since the village was quite small. Maybe that would keep her alive. She couldn't help but know of the man married to such a famous singer as Joley Drake. Everyone knew of Ilya Prakenskii.

Maxim looked across the helicopter at Cyreck, and the Greek shrugged his shoulders the moment those icy blue eyes stared a hole through him. Maxim wasn't the friendly type, that much was made clear.

Once again, Maxim took her arm, the pads of his fingers moving over her bruised skin. Each stroke seemed to ease the pain, but her heart only pounded harder. She should never have tipped him off that she knew his identity. Of course he would kill her. How could he not? So far she hadn't seen a single real expression cross his face. Had she not caught that brief glimpse of his temper, she would never know he could be human. She swallowed hard, fighting back tears all over again.

Her gaze was drawn to his fingers against her skin. His hand was large enough to wrap around her arm and then some, yet he didn't seem disproportionately large. She guessed it was the way he moved that made him seem leaner. He looked rough, scary even, although she suspected much of that was because she was terrified. She had made a terrible mistake blurting out that he had to be a Prakenskii.

"Please, please believe me, I don't have a father. I've never met anyone, spoken to or received even a single piece of mail from someone claiming to be my father," she whispered, remembering at the last moment to keep the thread of sound between them.

"Your mother—her birth name is Marinochka Venediktov—was a student at the Moscow Institute of Physics and Technology when she encountered Theodotus Solovyov. He had gone there to consult with a distinguished professor and friend who happened to have Marina in his classroom."

"My last name is Ridell. I don't know any Theodotus

Solovyov, or for that matter Marinochka Venediktov. You have the wrong person."

Her arm had gone from a throbbing pain deep in her bone to a dull ache, like a nagging, sore tooth. When he released her, he took the warmth of his touch with him. Who would have suspected that a man so cold could radiate so much heat?

"He said, if you were truly his daughter you would deny it without proof. I saw his proof, and he's waiting to show it to you. There's a Greek ship out at sea and the helicopter is heading for that. The Gratsos family owns that particular line of cargo ships. I'll keep you close to me. Don't make a run for it. Don't draw undo attention to yourself. Just stay quiet and let me handle things."

So far, no one else had come near her, and he wasn't asking her questions she couldn't answer. He wasn't asking her any questions at all. Maybe they really did have the wrong person. It was possible the woman Marinochka he was talking about wasn't her mother and someone had simply mixed things up.

She nodded her head that she understood as he carefully eased her sweater—Lexi's sweater—back over her arm. The thick, familiar sweater gave her comfort and she pulled it closer around her. She put her nose against the threads and inhaled Lexi's scent to drive away Maxim's.

"Solovyov was married to a very wealthy woman with friends in high places. She enjoyed being the wife of the most intelligent physicist in Russia. She wasn't a particularly nice woman and he was gone a lot working, which was just fine by her. She liked drinking and parties and men. Mostly she liked her status, and nothing was going to change that. Certainly not a young college student, no matter how bright and promising she was."

Airiana felt eyes on her and she glanced up to see Cyreck staring at them. Something in the way he looked at her sickened her. This was not a man who would treat an injury gently on any woman, let alone one he'd kidnapped. She drew closer to Maxim without realizing she did, sliding her much smaller body nearly behind his in an effort to get away from Cyreck's leering gaze.

Maxim flicked Cyreck a singular look from his glacier-cold eyes. "Is there something you want?"

There wasn't an ounce of friendship in his authoritative voice. More like a challenge, daring the other man to cross him, even hoping he might.

"Just hoping you're going to share the goods," Cyreck said. "Mr. Shackler-Gratsos said he didn't care what shape she was in as long as she was alive." He stroked his crotch suggestively. "I want her after you."

"I don't share," Maxim replied in a low, slashing voice. "I will cut you into little pieces and throw you to the sharks if you attempt to lay one finger on anything that belongs to me. I brought her out. She's mine. When I'm finished with her, I'll take her to Mr. Shackler-Gratsos myself. That was the deal I made with him."

Cyreck swore in Greek, and turned away. Again none of the other men looked up, unwilling to go against Maxim.

Airiana let out her breath slowly. Maxim sounded like he was standing up for her, but he certainly had made some kind of deal with Mr. Shackler-Gratsos. She recognized the name. How could she not? Stavros Gratsos had drowned off the coast of Sea Haven the very day that Rikki had pulled Lev Prakenskii out of the sea and saved his life.

Gratsos had been a billionaire, a shipping magnate, and he had a brother. She didn't recall the brother's name, he was far less well known, but he had to have inherited everything. This helicopter and the ship they were taking her to were owned by the Gratsos shipping company.

What had been far less known about the playboy shipping magnate was that he operated a human trafficking ring as well as running arms to terrorists and anyone else who could afford his prices. Her heart began to pound as she tried to recall the facts she knew about the Greek brothers. It wasn't much, but she knew Elle Drake had suffered terribly at their hands.

Maxim put a hand on her thigh and she nearly jumped

out of her skin. His touch was completely nonsexual, but it didn't matter, not with the memories of what Elle had suffered uppermost in her mind.

"Evan Shackler-Gratsos will not get his hands on you," he said. "I'm taking you to your father."

She didn't look at him. That implacable, merciless face. Those ice-cold eyes. It didn't matter that his voice was low and persuasive. Or that his touch could be gentle. She didn't trust him. She knew that as a Prakenskii, he'd been trained in the art of seduction as well as killing. He probably knew how to charm the birds out of the trees and a dozen different ways to kill each of them as they flew to him.

She kept her head down, refusing to acknowledge him anymore. The only thing left to her was to wait until she boarded the ship and hope there was a chance to find a way to escape. She should have paid more attention when Rikki talked about her boat. There had to be lifeboats. Her mind began to try to formulate a plan.

"Airiana, look at me."

Maxim's voice was so compelling her gaze jumped to his. It was a mistake. She found herself drowning in his eyes. Her breath caught in her throat, and something deep inside her, something feminine and rebellious, connected with his penetrating stare.

"I will take care of you."

"I don't trust you."

He nodded his head slowly. "I don't blame you. How could you? I'm the man who put you on this helicopter and took you from your home. But you weren't safe there and there was no other way to get to you. You have to trust me. You don't have anyone else."

4

AIRIANA kept her head down and her body close to Maxim Prakenskii as they walked past the leering men on the cargo ship. Maxim had a firm grip on her arm, so tight she knew she would bear the mark of his fingers for several days or weeks to come. He gave her no chance at all to leap overboard or beckon the wind.

She felt the contempt and apathy of the sailors as they walked past. No one tried to stop Maxim or ask him questions, and part of her was very grateful for the fact that he appeared so scary. She wasn't the only one who didn't want to have anything to do with the man. Still, in spite of everything, he made her feel safe in an unsafe situation.

The ship creaked and swayed in the swells of the ocean, and she knew it was only Maxim's tight hold on her that kept her from falling on her face in front of everyone. The men working aboard the ship seemed suspiciously used to prisoners being brought aboard. She couldn't help but think about Elle Drake and how scared she must have been.

Maxim took her right past the crew and down to a second level into a narrow hallway. They'd gone only a couple of steps when a man wrapped in a velvet robe blocked their way. Maxim pulled her up short. Her breath caught in her throat, in her lungs, until she wanted to scream in fear.

"Maxim. What delicious little morsel have you brought to me?"

Her heart sank. The man looked to be easily fifty, perhaps sixty, and was certainly of Middle Eastern origin. He reeked of money, a man used to getting exactly what he wanted at all times.

"Prince Saeed, I had no idea you were aboard."

The prince looked her over, his gaze greedy, bright, like a child staring at a new toy. Airiana knew she looked far younger than she actually was, and this man was looking for young.

"Is she still a virgin?" The prince licked his lips. "I prefer virgins."

"This one is already taken, I'm afraid," Maxim said. "Bought and paid for, I'm told. I'm just the deliveryman. I don't deal in women. You know that."

"But she's so perfect for me," the prince insisted. "You know I can pay. Double what you're already getting. I'll have the money wired to your account."

"She's not a gun—or a target." Amusement took the sting from his refusal. "I deal in weapons. I'm sure the captain has someone else for you."

The prince's eyes narrowed. "She's the one I want." He reached to touch Airiana's hair.

Maxim thrust her behind him, all friendliness vanishing instantly. He gave off the feeling of absolute danger. "It would not be in your best interest to put your hands on this woman. I gave my word to deliver her safely, and as you know, I am a man of my word."

Airiana tangled her fingers in the back of Maxim's shirt, terrified that the prince might persuade Maxim or the captain to hand her over.

The prince stood utterly still. "I am not a man you want for an enemy."

Maxim shrugged. "Move aside. We can continue this

discussion at a later date if you desire. You know how to get in touch with me."

Saeed shoved open the door to his luxury cabin, and Airiana glanced inside. There was blood on the sheets. A small girl lay across the bed sideways, her head hanging over the edge, eyes wide open and glassy.

Maxim caught Airiana and yanked her to the other side of his body, beneath his shoulder, keeping his bulk firmly between her and the sight of the broken child. Her heart stuttered and a tremor seized her body. She couldn't stop shaking once she started.

Maxim glanced down at the top of her head. "You can do this. Be strong for a few more minutes. Keep walking."

She wasn't certain she could. Her legs felt like spaghetti, weak and wobbly and nearly impossible to control. Pride—and his death grip on her arm—kept her moving more than anything else. Her stomach lurched and she feared she might throw up.

"Airiana, these men won't touch you."

It was a decree. A promise. Even if it was true that he was somehow on her side, how could one man fight his way through all those men with her in tow? Again, where would they go? They couldn't fling themselves into the sea. But she went with him. What else was there to do? She couldn't stand the sight of all those smug men with their disgusting leers and snide smiles.

"This ship is used to traffic women, isn't it?"

"One of the two that I know of. That's why they have the luxury cabins on board. Not for eccentric, rich travelers who want to 'rough it' on cargo ships, but for clients who pay large sums of money to do as they wish for their time at sea. Bodies are easily disposed of here." His voice was grim. "The women and children brought aboard these ships never live long. Evan Shackler-Gratsos owns both. He and his brother conceived the idea some years ago. Business is brisk."

There was no mistaking the stark honesty in his voice.

He was either the best actor in the world or he really despised those on board. Still, the information, honest or not, didn't make her feel any easier. She was now a prisoner on board a vessel at sea where women and children were given to men to do as they pleased and then murdered and thrown overboard. This had been the information Elle Drake had gone undercover in order to find.

Airiana bit her lip hard and tried to fight back the burn of tears. It did no good to cry. She had to think, to not give up hope, but right now, all she wanted to do was get away from the horrible stares as they continued to make their way through the ship.

He took her down another set of steps, through a narrow path and thrust her into a small room. The cargo ship might have a few luxury cabins for nefarious reasons, but thankfully, this wasn't one of them. She stumbled to the cot and sank down on it the moment he let her go. For one terrible moment she couldn't breathe. Her lungs burned, her throat, her eyes. She covered her face with her hands and allowed herself to crumble into a tiny ball, pulling in her knees to her chest, fighting panic.

She understood Lexi's panic attacks so much better. She was helpless. Entirely at someone else's mercy. Surrounded by enemies, she knew life would never be the same again even if she survived. She'd been taken from her home, and she'd never feel entirely safe again—just like her youngest sister.

Maxim Prakenskii sighed as he stood with his back to the hatch, observing the young woman as her emotions overcame her. He much preferred her anger to her tears. He could take her defiance far better than her breaking down. He knew it was momentary, Airiana Solovyov—and whether she liked it or not, that was her legal name—had backbone. She wasn't going to stay down long.

She was . . . unexpected. Clearly she was an element, bound to air as he was. He had a plan for getting her off the ship—but she wasn't going to like it. She didn't believe that her father had sent for her, and he couldn't really blame her.

It didn't much matter if she believed him or not—he would take her to Solovyov and be done with it.

But damn it all. Just damn it. He hadn't expected to like the woman. Or feel like a first-class bastard for hitting her. He had done so for her own safety, and yet he still felt like a bully. She would have killed all of them, which was a gutsy move he admired. And why the hell did she have to be so small? She was a toothpick. Barely there. Which made striking her equivalent to hitting a child.

"Damn it, woman," he snapped. "Stop crying. Are you hysterical?"

"Maybe." Her voice was muffled by the pillow and her hands. "What if I am? Are you going to offer to slap me for my own sake?"

He winced. The woman knew how to strike a death blow. Or at least go for the jugular. "If you keep it up," he threatened, knowing it was an empty threat. In his entire life he'd never had the inclination to gather a woman up, cradle her against his chest and rock her just to soothe her—until now. He wasn't that kind of man, and he never would be, so why was he fighting to stay leaning his hip casually against the door?

She lifted her head just an inch or so out of her hands and glared at him through the wild tangle of her hair. "You're a real bastard, did you know that?"

"Well, pull yourself together and I won't have to be. I'm risking my life to save your very fine ass. The least you could do is help me out."

She sat up slowly, pushing the heavy fall of hair from her face, all the while giving him the death stare. "You kidnapped me, in case you've forgotten. I was doing quite well until you came along."

His eyebrow shot up. There in the close confines of the small room, all he could do was smell the faint peaches and vanilla scent her skin and hair seemed to give off. He'd noticed it the first time he'd slung her over his shoulder and again in the helicopter, sitting beside her.

He swore to himself. What the hell was wrong with

him? He'd agreed to help Theodotus Solovyov because his brother Gavriil had asked him to. Gavriil had risked his life to save the physicist and in fact had been stabbed seven times during the attack on the man who had designed Russia's defense system. The attack had effectively ended Gavriil's career and put him on a hit list now that he was no longer of use.

Gavriil actually liked Solovyov, and Maxim had come to understand why. When the physicist had gotten word to Gavriil, the only man he trusted, that he was in trouble, Gavriil had sent for Maxim. Maxim had gone in his older brother's place. Gavriil was still recovering from his horrendous wounds, and in any case, he was a marked man. He didn't dare go anywhere near Solovyov.

The Prakenskii brothers had learned to trust no one outside of each other. There was always the chance that Solovyov might help set Gavriil up for the kill. Maxim had no compunction about killing Solovyov if the man had betrayed Gavriil, but instead, he found himself on a mission to save the physicist's daughter—a daughter who had no idea who she was.

"Do you really believe that if I hadn't been with the others you would have gotten away from them?" Maxim asked.

She sat up straighter. It didn't help. She looked small, fragile and bruised. Beautiful. Ethereal. He swore to himself again. His fingers itched to push those few stray strands of hair she'd missed from her face.

What the hell was wrong with him? He didn't notice every detail about a woman the way he did her. Somehow, maybe their common element or the fog had bound them together, because he felt her inside of him. Stamped into his bones. Just like the air filled his lungs and seeped into his pores, she had come with it, twisting her way inside his brain and his body.

"Yes. I think I could have eluded them," Airiana said truthfully. "They couldn't have manipulated the fog. Or read it. They wouldn't have known where we were."

"And what then, Airiana? What do you think they would have done next?"

She frowned at him, tilting her head so that her hair fell around her face like a living silken cloak. He couldn't take it one second longer. He stalked across the room and pushed those silky strands of platinum hair from her face with his fingers. Silver. Gold. Platinum. Her hair was the most unique color he'd ever seen.

"I don't know what you mean. What next? They would have left." She didn't pull away from him, but held herself very still.

The moment those silken strands slid through the pads of his fingers and whispered against his palm, he knew it was a mistake to touch her. His fingers closed around the strands, holding them in the exact center of his palm. He felt her heart beat. Contract. Pound. He felt the air catching in her lungs. In his. He stared into her eyes—eyes so blue he felt as if he might be pulled into them and be lost soaring through the skies.

A frisson of awareness—of alarm—traveled down his spine. Abruptly, Maxim opened his hand, allowing her hair to drop away. He stepped away from her, dark suspicion rising. He didn't feel for others, emotion had been taken from him long ago. He was a machine, not flesh and blood. He couldn't be hurt. Couldn't feel compassion. He suppressed even the flashes of anger that had never quite been beaten out of him when he was a child.

This . . . this made no sense, and anything that wasn't logical to him was dangerous. "You can't believe that. They would go into town, snatch one of the women sharing your farm and hurt them until you begged them to come get you."

His voice was harsh, far crueler than he meant it to be. He knew she had found her mother cut into pieces, tortured and left on her bed for her to discover. He had just conjured that vivid nightmare up for her all over again. He could see it on her face.

Maxim was disgusted with his behavior. Nothing threw

him, and yet this small slip of a woman had done so without even trying. She hadn't acted seductive or flirtatious. She had fought valiantly, even managing to score a couple of times against him. He found himself inexplicitly drawn to her. Worse, when he was close to her, like now, he could barely think straight.

He stepped backward until he was once again resting his hip against the door. He knew he wouldn't give himself away with his facial expression. He looked confident, cool and casual leaning there, but every instinct he had was on full alert. Every cell in his body was coiled and ready for a fight.

Tears swam in her sky blue eyes and his heart squeezed down like a vise. It took every ounce of discipline he possessed not to press his palm over his chest. "Damn it," he swore at her between clenched teeth. "Stop with the tears." She had to stop. He felt a little desperate. Tears weren't supposed to affect him in the least. They never had before.

Airiana blinked rapidly and drew back further into herself, but her chin went up, and he felt the breath ease in his lungs.

"I didn't think about that," she said in small voice.

"You deliberately led us away from the other woman with you," he said, his tone much more gentle. "I knew she was there, but you felt protective of her. You didn't want anyone to get their hands on her. I'm guessing it was the younger one. She manages the farm. Lexi Thompson."

He'd done his homework as soon as he became aware Ilya, his youngest brother, had settled in Sea Haven, and then Lev, his second to youngest brother, had supposedly drowned there. The Prakenskii brothers had a way to get word to one another. It wasn't used often because they didn't dare chance that their communication could be compromised, but Lev had checked in using that route. He was alive and married to one of the women who owned the farm with Airiana. One of Maxim's older brothers, Stefan, had also let the others know he was alive and married to another of the women owning the farm.

Maxim had immediately done extensive research on the farm and the women who owned it. He knew more about Airiana than she appeared to know about herself.

"Lexi's very fragile," Airiana said, her voice tight with emotion, but she didn't allow tears to spill over. "Thank you for not grabbing her as well."

"It's going to be a tough job getting you off this ship, let alone two of you. I knew I could protect you, but you see how these men are. You know what this ship is all about. Bringing a second woman on board would only double the danger." As it was, knowing Prince Saeed was there had already compromised everything, because he had no intention of leaving the man alive.

Airiana let her breath out slowly. She nodded, twisting her fingers together so tightly her knuckles turned white. He had to resist the urge to lay his hand gently over hers to quiet that telltale movement of distress.

"Why do you think I'm this Theodotus Solovyov's daughter?"

"He told me. He has pictures of you from the time you were born as well as a box of letters from your mother. Hundreds of letters. He treasures every one."

"You expect me to believe my mother had a secret life, one I didn't know about? She didn't take trips to Russia, and believe me, when I say our family was investigated thoroughly, I mean by the United States government. They would have found a connection to Russia."

"They did find it eventually, but they already had you in their school and they didn't want to give you up. Marina Ridell was born Marinochka Venediktov. She had an incredible mind, and I suspect she was also bound to an element, probably air as you are. She had no brothers or sisters and her parents were killed in an accident when she was eighteen. She was attending Moscow Institute of Physics and Technology and she met Theodotus Solovyov there when she was at her most vulnerable."

Airiana pressed her lips together and blinked several times. He held his breath, afraid the fresh flood of tears on her lashes would fall, but she controlled herself, and he exhaled. She didn't belong in his world, she was far too sensitive.

"She was young and grieving and was drawn to him probably because he had such a brilliant mind and could discuss subjects she was interested in intelligently. He was older and very taken with her. The combination was . . . impossible to resist."

Maxim kept his gaze burning over her to catch every nuance. Body language told him a lot about his opponent. She wasn't adept at hiding her feelings. She wasn't even trying. She didn't want to believe him, but she was beginning to in spite of herself.

"He was married." Airiana made it a statement.

"Yes, he was married," Maxim admitted. "His wife, Elena, was not a nice woman, and he was lonely. Your mother and Theodotus met at the wrong time for both of them. They fell in love. Elena had no desire to carry on a conversation with Theodotus, she could barely understand what he did, but Marina was just the opposite. She cared nothing for money but craved conversation and closeness with him."

Maxim heard footsteps coming down the narrow corridor. At once he was on Airiana, nearly leaping across the small space, slamming her back on the mattress. "Scream. Scream loud." He kept his voice a thread of sound between them, hoping she would understand.

She stared up at him in horror, those sky blue eyes shocked and bruised. Deliberately he caught the wealth of wild blond hair in his fist, pulling her head back so that he stared down into her terrified eyes. "Scream," he instructed again. His voice was harsh, his grip brutal. He was afraid he would have to go further.

Airiana obeyed, her cries very real, terror so close he could feel it coming off of her in waves. The footsteps had stopped outside the door to the cabin.

His mouth came down on hers, effectively cutting off her scream in midcry so there could be no mistaking what was happening inside the room. One part of him remained on alert, listening for the sound of receding footsteps—or a stealthy entry. Another part of him was caught in a firestorm of pure feeling. Her mouth was soft and tasted as good as she smelled.

Like his brothers, he'd been trained in the art of seduction and how to please a woman, but he was too rough, too distant to ever be effective at that particular skill. Kissing Airiana was different, and he felt that difference immediately. His mouth gentled, his hands relaxed a bit. Sadly, for both of them, it wasn't all show.

His teeth nipped at her lower lip. "Struggle," he instructed, keeping the thread of sound between them. "Struggle hard enough that they can hear you."

She nodded, some of the panic receding. She kicked out, punched at him, the sounds of the blows audible in the small confines of the room. He amplified them a bit, added a grunt and slapped his own thigh hard. She cried out, and he stopped the sound again in midcry, his mouth covering hers.

Her hands went to his shoulders, holding on, anchoring herself there. He couldn't say she responded—she didn't—but she didn't pull away either. He kept kissing her over and over until the footsteps receded.

The moment he was certain the intruder had retreated down the corridor, he lifted his head and gently pulled her into a sitting position. "Are you hurt?"

She touched the back of her hand to her mouth and shook her head, her sky blue eyes enormous. "No. But you scared me. You move so fast, and when you do, you look terrifying."

His smile was slow in coming. Hers was even slower in answer. Her smile was tentative, but genuine. He brushed her hair back with gentle fingers. "Thank you for trusting me."

"I didn't have much choice." Her smile widened, lighting up her eyes. "I did think about bringing my knee up very hard into your groin, but then I realized you could have attacked me the moment we entered this room."

"Good girl. Keep thinking like that. We may need your fighting skills before we're out of here."

The powerful engines vibrated throughout the ship as they cut through the waters fast, taking them farther from all help.

"That little girl was dead, wasn't she?" Airiana asked, sobering. "The one in Prince Saeed's room. She was dead."

Maxim nodded his head slowly. "I'm sorry you had to see that. Saeed's been a problem for everyone, and unfortunately he has enough money to buy several countries as well as just about anything else he wants. There's always going to be someone willing to get children for him as long as he pays what they want."

"That's sick."

"Yes, but men like Saeed find places like this ship and men like the owner who provide for him."

"How does he know you?"

"I'm an arms dealer and he buys weapons and ammunition from me."

She rolled her eyes. "I see."

"There are very few things our countries are in agreement on, and Saeed as well as those providing for his proclivities is one of them. We sent the U.S. information in the hopes that they could shut down this operation, but sadly it failed."

Airiana was certain she knew why. Elle Drake had gone undercover in an effort to find out just who was behind the human trafficking ring, and she'd been taken prisoner. Elle's family and fiancé had rescued her, but Stavros Gratsos had wanted her back.

Maxim's brother had also been working undercover as well, as a bodyguard to Stavros. He had been unable to keep Elle from being taken the first time. Eventually the yacht he was on with Stavros had sunk off the northern California coast.

Maxim was no arms dealer. Well, he might be. But if so, his reason was not money.

She scooted across the bed to lean her back against the

wall, drawing her knees up tight. Her heart still pounded a little too fast. Her breath still burned in her lungs. She had to struggle to stay cool. No one had ever kissed her in her life. She didn't have boyfriends. She didn't date. Did everyone react to kisses the way she'd wanted to?

She didn't want to think about how she forgot, just for a moment, that his kisses were fake and that he might be an enemy. She was ashamed of herself, but still, fake or not, it was her first kiss. She couldn't imagine what he thought. She was totally inexperienced and probably had been awful, while he'd been . . . enough to sweep her away from this horrible ship and the circumstances she faced.

She took a deep breath and lifted her head to look at him again. She was beginning to trust him and that might be the biggest mistake of her life. Still, he was all that she had. "When you get me off this ship, is there a way to get the other women and children off as well?"

Maxim couldn't look into those blue eyes and lie. Or maybe he didn't want to. "No. It would be impossible. I will, however, do my best to have someone standing by to rescue them."

"How can we just leave them here?"

At least she'd said "we," not "you," and he was grateful she was identifying with him. "It's called not having a choice. My first priority has to be you."

He had plans. Saeed had been a target for a long time. Twice he'd met with the man in the hopes of creating an opportunity to kill him, but Saeed surrounded himself with too many bodyguards to make a clean exit possible.

Saeed's presence aboard ship was unexpected and Maxim was not going to pass up the opportunity to execute him, especially after seeing the young girl dead in his room. No doubt he already had another one. The thought was sickening.

"The way we're leaving the ship it would be impossible to take anyone else with us. We're diving and meeting a small sub."

Her head jerked up. Both hands went to her hair, shoving

it from her face, horror in her eyes. She began to shake her head. "No. No way. I can't dive. I don't know how to dive. Rikki dives. I just sit and admire the ocean from shore. Water is not my friend."

He found himself smiling again at the absolute resolution in her voice. "Water is not your friend? Did you just say that?"

"I really don't swim." She shook her head adamantly. "I'm afraid of the water."

He could tell the confession was difficult for her. The words sounded strangled and she blushed admitting it to him.

"I never learned," she added. "I was in a boarding school and they didn't have luxuries like swimming pools. We certainly never had one at home. My mother didn't swim. She was afraid I'd drown."

"You won't drown. You'll be with me."

Her eyebrows shot up. "Do you have any idea how arrogant you sound? Of course I'll drown. What part of 'I can't swim' don't you get?"

He shrugged. "I'll tuck you under one arm and do the swimming."

"Do you expect me to use a tank to breathe?"

"We could do mouth-to-mouth if you prefer."

She glared at him and then reluctantly began to smile. "You're really impossible to argue with. You have an answer for everything."

"That's our only exit. We have no choice. When you have no choice and it's life or death, you do it," he pointed out.

"I suppose so." She was silent a moment, rubbing her chin back and forth on top of her knees. "Do you know who tortured and killed my mother?" She looked up, her gaze colliding with his.

He shouldn't have been surprised that she would just come out and ask, but he was. Solovyov had quietly investigated Marinochka's murder. Solovyov had confided in Gavriil that he had his suspicions that it had been his wife,

Elena, who had tipped off the U.S. government that Marina Ridell was not who she claimed, and then when the young woman hadn't been arrested, Elena had arranged for her murder. Solovyov wanted proof before he confronted Elena. No proof had ever been established, but Elena had betrayed her husband and arranged for him to be murdered as well and his work stolen. Fortunately, Gavriil had saved Theodotus's life, but Gavriil had nearly died. Stefan, another Prakenskii brother, had found Elena. There was no asking her questions now.

"There was no proof, but your father's wife was suspected. She sewed a microchip containing his work into his coat and then arranged for him to be ambushed."

"Did anyone question her about this?"

"She's dead."

Airiana twisted her fingers in one of the many holes in her jeans while she thought that over. "Why didn't he contact me after his wife died? Why wait until now?"

Of course she would ask the pertinent questions—she was too intelligent not to, but she was very nervous. She had to have a lot of questions running through her mind, and he doubted if he could answer most of them.

"He was tipped off that you were in danger and he asked me to come and get you." He watched her face carefully. Her fingers continued to pluck nervously at the white strings around the holes in her jeans.

"I want to go home."

He nodded. "That's understandable."

"But you won't take me there."

"I promised your father I'd take you to him first. He wants to meet with you."

She brought the pad of her thumb to her mouth and bit down with her small white teeth. He wished he could read her mind. The middle of his palm itched and he rubbed his hand down his thigh to rid himself of the persistent and very annoying irritation.

"So my father—and you—believe my mother was tortured and killed because my father's wife was jealous?" A storm gathered in her sky blue eyes. "That's what the two of you want me to believe."

Damn. Why did she have to be a smart woman? He shrugged, keeping his features expressionless. "As I said, there was no proof, but certainly Elena was capable of such a thing. Theodotus was devastated both for himself and for you." Everything he said was absolutely the truth. He used a low voice filled with conviction.

"You said Theodotus Solovyov was a physicist?"

Solovyov's career was public knowledge. Maxim didn't have to make up anything at all. Now he felt he was walking on eggshells with her. He nodded his head slowly, trying to figure out where she was going with her questions. "Yes, he's a very brilliant physicist."

"He wasn't, by any chance, developing a brand-new defense system, was he?" Her voice was innocent. Too innocent. "Was that on the microchip? The stolen one? The one that ended up with Jean Claude La Roux?"

His heart jerked in his chest. "How the hell would you know something like that?" He stepped closer to her, feigning anger. He knew exactly how she had gotten that information. Stefan had sent the chip back to his handlers before he disappeared, and had become Thomas Vincent, the art dealer. Stefan was married to one of the women on the farm. Information like that could get her killed.

Her lashes fluttered. She shrugged. "This man, Solovyov, he kept no other records, did he? He wiped out everything to protect his work. It was too important. And now it's gone."

"What are you implying?"

"You know exactly what I'm implying. This whole thing is an elaborate setup. Do you really think I'm so stupid I'd buy into it all? My father suddenly surfaces after all these years and sends you to protect me. Wow. His jealous wife, after waiting sixteen years, hunts down my mother and murders her. Why wait all that time? She woke up one morning and decided, hey, today might be a good day to murder my cheating husband's mistress from sixteen years ago even though she's in America and hasn't seen my husband in all those years. How very neat and tidy for you and dear old dad."

She had a sharp tongue on her, but he still couldn't help but admire her. "It didn't happen quite like that."

"No, of course it didn't."

"Marina was brilliant, as is Theodotus. Their daughter inherited their intelligence. It's well documented. Marina was proud of you and she sent your accomplishments to your father. What mother wouldn't? He has pictures of you from every year of your life as well as various letters from universities anxious for you to attend their school."

"Don't you dare accuse my mother of betraying her country." Now the storm clouds swirled turbulently. "She would never take money from anyone. She wasn't like that, and you'll never, not in a million years get me to believe she did. She wasn't a traitor. There was never any money."

"She was a citizen of Russia, not the United States. Her loyalty was to Russia. You're right, Airiana, there was never any money in exchange for information. She sent your work to your father for love. Loving you. Loving him. For pride. Her pride in you. She wanted him to feel that same pride. She didn't believe she was doing anything wrong. She was a mother who loved her daughter and her daughter's father. That same father who sent me to protect you from Evan Shackler-Gratsos."

She closed her eyes, but not before he saw the blow he'd struck her. She had been convinced Marina had never sent her work to Russia. If he was telling the truth, then Marina had betrayed the United States.

"So who murdered her?" Airiana asked again in a low voice.

5

THERE was a long silence. Maxim sank down onto the bed beside Airiana. He reached out and covered her nervous fingers with his palm, unable to stop himself. He knew each time his skin touched hers, he was going down a path there might not be recovery from, but he couldn't stand the way she seemed so alone and frightened. He was systematically destroying her world.

Airiana didn't pull her hand away. Instead, she lifted her long, spiked, tear-wet lashes. "I'm crying again."

"I know. I'm not happy about it either."

"Neither am I," she admitted. "I can't seem to stop."

He slid across the bed, his back to the wall and drew up his knees as well. He kept close, his shoulder and thigh tight against hers. "That's all right. This one time I'll let it go."

"Thanks." She turned her face toward him and rested her head on her knees. "Is Theodotus really my father?"

"I have proof."

"I happen to know what family you come from, although I know I'm not supposed to know, and I'm certain you can manufacture proof of anything you want."

"That's true. I can. But I didn't. You're really his daughter. And you really are in danger. I give you my word, once you speak with him, I'll take you back to your home if you really want to go back." That was a promise he would probably regret making, but he'd keep it.

"When are we getting out of here?"

"We'll leave the ship around three in the morning." He felt the small shudder that ran through her body and resisted the urge to put his arm around her. The less physical contact he had with her the better.

"Don't sharks feed at night?"

"You really do have a thing about swimming, don't you?" He kept his voice gentle. She was holding on by a thread. The tears still streamed down her face, but she was weeping quietly.

"Yes. I know it's weird when I live on the coast, and I actually love the sea, but I don't even put my feet in it."

He sighed. "Baby, if you don't stop crying, I'm going to have to hold you. That could be bad for both of us."

She kept looking at him with her eyes that reminded him of the sky at night during a summer rain.

"All right then." He surrendered to the inevitable. "I'm not going to be responsible for anything strange that happens between us." He simply picked her up. She didn't weigh much and it was easy enough to pull her onto his lap. She fit nicely into the shelter of his chest.

Airiana's head rested against his chest, right over his heart. He was fairly certain his heart was pounding hard enough for her to hear. How the hell did a woman so small, and weepy at that, affect him the way she did? He'd shut off his emotions far too many years earlier. There was no other way to survive in his business.

"Go to sleep. At least rest. I'll hear if anyone tries to come into the cabin," he advised, one hand going to the nape of her neck, his fingers massaging the tight muscles.

"You think someone will, don't you?" Her lashes fluttered, dropped down, and some of the tension eased out of her under the soothing pressure.

"Prince Saeed doesn't like to be told no. I suspect no one

has ever done it before and lived. He'll send his body-guards." He didn't bother to keep the satisfaction out of his voice.

"You want him to send them."

"He won't have brought very many aboard ship. When you're killing children, I don't care how much money you have, you don't advertise it much. He'll keep his guards to a minimum."

She lifted her head to look up at him. "You're going to kill him."

"Damn right I am." There was no apology in his voice. He didn't feel particularly apologetic. He'd missed the bastard twice. How many young women had suffered at the hands of a monster because he'd been unable to get the job done?

She was silent a moment. He held himself still, telling himself it didn't matter what she thought of him. She was a package to be delivered, nothing more. Her opinion of him didn't—couldn't—matter. His life, from the time he was a child, had been this—killing, serving his country, remov-ing men like Saeed from the face of the earth. She couldn't possibly understand the filth and depravity he'd witnessed. The cruelty.

Maxim didn't want Airiana to ever know such things. It had been bad enough that she'd seen that young girl dead in Saeed's room while the prince had drooled over Airiana. Maxim had wanted to kill the monster right there in the passageway, even knowing his bodyguards were close. Had he actually laid his hands on Airiana, Maxim knew he wouldn't have been able to stop himself.

"How can I help?"

His fingers ceased giving that slow massage to her neck and shoulders. It was the last thing he expected her to say.

"Airiana, I'm going to kill him," he repeated.

"I'm scared, Maxim, not hard of hearing." There was resolution in her voice. "He tortured and killed that girl, and he's probably doing the same to another one right now. I sat here thinking that could have been me, or Lexi. It could be any child he takes a fancy to. I don't want to give him that chance, not ever again. Maybe it's wrong, but I don't care if it is. She was like a broken toy to him, nothing at all. He'd already dismissed her and was looking for the next one."

He allowed himself a breath. A deep inhale, taking her scent into his lungs, feeling it fill him, spread through his system, penetrating every cell in his body. He was making the effort to console her, and in some strange way, she was comforting him.

She'd found a way of getting inside of him. She'd slipped in when he wasn't prepared, breaching his every defense before he knew he even had chinks in his armor. He hadn't realized he was vulnerable. She actually made him feel naked, completely exposed. It was an uncomfortable feeling and one he didn't like.

"Killing someone isn't easy, Airiana." His voice was gruff. Harsh, even.

"I can't imagine it would be, nor is it supposed to be."

She lifted her head to look him directly in the eyes and he felt the jerk of his heart in response. Her tears were gone. Her eyes were dark blue now, like a midnight sky. Steady. Soft. She turned him inside out with that look of complete understanding.

He damned well didn't need her understanding—or approval. Still, there was no getting away from her eyes. He'd lost his soul a long time ago, forgotten he even had one, but she found it there inside of him, the last little piece he'd thought long gone and she'd claimed it for her own. Somehow, those blue eyes in her perfect face looked right inside of him and found—Maxim Prakenskii.

"I'm going to kiss you."

She blinked. Frowned. "Why?"

"Because I need to, and the first time I was just being a bastard. I am, you know. A complete and utter bastard with no redeeming qualities."

She smiled a slow, beautiful smile that could steal a man's breath. "I think you have a few, Maxim. Don't sell yourself short. You're capable of ridding the world of a monster like the prince. I'd say that was a redeeming quality right there."

He framed her face with both hands and leaned down to take possession of her mouth. She should have pulled away from him. Didn't the woman have a single ounce of self-preservation? More to the point, didn't he?

Her lips were just as soft as he remembered. Angel lips. So perfect they couldn't be human. He wanted to feel something real. Just for a moment—for this small stolen instance of time they shared.

Kissing her was absolutely inexcusable and inappropriate. He was taking advantage of her vulnerability, but damn it all, once wasn't enough. He hadn't kissed her properly. Or nearly long enough. He had every intention of rectifying that situation.

His tongue traced the seam of her lips, demanding entrance, and she opened her mouth for him. His breath moved through her, through him as his tongue swept inside to taste her. To claim her. Or was she claiming him? He felt himself falling into her.

Her kiss swept him away, far away from his past. From himself. From the ugliness of his life. She took him to a place that he'd never even imagined or fantasized about. One touch. So tentative, her tongue tangling with his.

He hadn't known he could be gentle. Not like this. Not bordering on tender. He was a rough man, so much so that he'd never really been asked to seduce a woman, when he knew every trick there was.

Emotion burst through him, as if somewhere deep inside a dam had burst. She was small, inexperienced, yet he felt as if she'd taken a battering ram to his heart. He was actually shaken by her touch. In that moment, with his mouth devouring hers, he felt as if no one in the world could possibly feel such intensity of emotion as he did. She was building a firestorm in him—and that was dangerous to both of them.

Reluctantly he lifted his head, knowing he had to stop.

He stared down into her face for a long time, fighting to find that place of stillness in him. His heart raced. His breathing was ragged. She affected him as no one else had ever done—or could ever do. He was certain of that.

"Why did you let me kiss you?" he asked, still shaken.

A small, mischievous smile curved her lower lip, the one he was far too intrigued with. Her blue eyes had gone smoky. Sexy. A little glazed from his kisses.

"Well, we're probably going to die trying to kill Saeed and his friends. Or if we make it off the ship and into the ocean, the sharks will finish us off. Even if you survive, my chances are fairly slim. I'm sure you noticed I don't have a lot of experience, in fact, you're the first man to ever kiss me, so since we're going to die, it just seemed like a good idea."

He stared down into the amusement in her amazing blue eyes. He found himself smiling with her. "I'm your first?"

She nodded. "Yep. Probably my last as well. As kisses go, it rocked. Just in case you wanted to know." She pulled back, slipping off his lap, hugging her knees to her again, back against the wall. "I suppose if I have to die, at least I can check that off my list."

His eyebrow shot up. "What else can I help you with on that list? Surely a kiss isn't the only thing you're looking forward to doing before you die."

A small laugh escaped her throat. Soft. Amused. A thread of sound, no more, but his insides did a crazy slow somersault and his palm itched like hell. She was killing him without trying. For a moment he entertained the idea that she was the enemy agent trained in the art of seduction, because he was the one being seduced.

"I think we'll leave it at a kiss."

"Have you forgotten those sharks? Great whites feed here."

"Really? I thought they fed in coastal waters mainly. We're far from coastal waters and moving fast."

He sighed. He had to do something about that. He glanced at his watch, surprised Saeed hadn't made his move yet. The man had been furious that Maxim, a lowly arms dealer, would dare deny him a woman he wanted. "They'll be along any minute. They'll be coming in hard and fast, trying to kill me to take you. I'm going to give you a rifle, an MP-5. It's a semiautomatic and shoots nine millimeter cartridges so it has a low recoil. That means you're going to fire one round at a time if necessary to save your life. Only if absolutely necessary. We don't want to draw attention to ourselves and bring the crew down here. The magazine has the standard thirty rounds, but if we need it, we have more."

"I'm familiar with the weapon," Airiana said. "I've been working with various firearms. Thomas and Levi, my brothers-in-law, have insisted all of us know how to shoot. I'm fairly decent." She tried to look innocent and wide-eyed when she mentioned his brothers.

He ignored the reference. "Aim for the middle of the body if you're a fairly decent shot. Don't get creative and go for the head shot. You don't want to miss. Remember, shooting at a human being is different than shooting a target and you can't hesitate."

Airiana nodded, watching as Maxim opened a locker and pulled out a fairly large war bag. He handed her a small stack of neatly folded clothes. She took them reluctantly. They were all black, thin, but warm. A turtleneck, long sleeve sweater, as well as form-fitting pants. "These are my size. I suppose you went shopping?"

"You'll need to change right now," he instructed, his voice once more brisk and impersonal, as if he still wasn't reeling from his close contact with her. He kept his back to her. He didn't need to see bare skin—and he wasn't about to answer her loaded question. "I've got soft-soled shoes for you and a wet suit. You won't need the wet suit until later, but get changed."

He could hear the whisper of clothing and was grateful she didn't argue with him. She was aware of the danger and definitely had made up her mind to aid him. Maybe the fact that she knew he was a Prakenskii was an advantage. She seemed to accept her two brothers-in-law. He did have to consider her family, the only thing he was truly loyal to and fiercely protective of, so his behavior couldn't possibly be as bizarre as he first thought.

"Okay," she said softly, "you can turn around now."

He took her folded clothes from her hand, resisting the urge to inhale their scent, and stowed them in his waterproof bag. He'd noticed the old sweater seemed to mean a lot to her. He exchanged the clothes for new shoes. Her combat boots would be too loud, too heavy and clumsy where they were going.

He didn't dare leave her behind in their room while he took care of Saeed as he'd intended. It was too risky. He'd seen the way Cyreck had looked at her and knew it was only a matter of time before the man got stupid and came demanding he get his turn. In any case, he doubted if Airiana would have been satisfied being left behind now that she'd thrown her lot in with his.

Knowing that the cargo vessel was really part of the Gratsos floating sex trade made his mission far more encompassing then he'd first thought. He had to make certain what was on the ship came to light.

"We're going to have to do something about your hair. It's too—blond." The color was highly unusual. "Does it glow in the dark?"

"Ha, ha, and I'm not dyeing my hair black."

She looked a little hurt, although he'd been attempting a joke. She was frightened, but standing with him, giving her his trust when he hadn't really earned it, and that nearly broke him right there. He wasn't a man anyone trusted. He caught strands of her wild, bedroom hair in between his fingers. Pure silk. "A man would give his life to feel your hair on his body, moving over his chest and thighs. It's beautiful. Truly beautiful. But we'll have to cover it up so you're safer."

She blinked at him, a little shocked, but she nodded.

He hadn't really intended to say what was in his mind, but it was there, a little bit of the erotic fantasy already playing in his head when he didn't have such things. "A hat. A scarf. Something," he added briskly. He ripped a piece from a dark shirt from his pack and handed it to her. "Do that thing women do when they want to cover their hair."

She rolled her eyes at him, but obediently tied back her hair and wrapped it with the strip of material. "Seriously, do you know how chauvinistic you can sound?"

"Yes." He made up a small pack for her, with a knife and extra ammo, just in case, before handing her the rifle. "Don't be tempted to shoot me."

"You'll have to take it back before we enter the water," she cautioned, her smile tight. Frightened. Not lighting her incredible eyes. "That's the only way you'll really be safe."

He shook his head, wanting to smile when he could feel his muscles beginning to grow loose and relaxed, while deep inside he coiled tighter and tighter like a snake, just waiting. His alarm system had begun shrieking at him and there was no time left. He caught her hand and tugged her toward the locker.

"Get behind my bag and lay on the floor of the locker just in case they come in with guns blazing." He kept his voice a thread of sound between them, allowing the air to create their own private communication system. "I doubt they'll do that because they won't want any undue attention drawn to them any more than we do."

Airiana glanced at the locker. It was very small. She could fit, but she didn't much care for closed-in spaces. "Where will you be?"

"Where I can see them coming at us, but they can't see me," he said. "No matter what happens, Airiana, you can't make a sound. Do you understand?"

"How will I know it's you when I hear someone trying to open the locker door?"

The fearful note in her voice turned his heart over. "You'll know it's me." He reached out his hand to her. "Get in now." Instincts were kicking in, his radar warning him the enemy was close.

"If you really stop them from taking me," Airiana

ventured, "won't the crew try to kill you as well? And if they think you'll tell someone about what really happens aboard this vessel, won't they just kill the women and children immediately?"

He cursed her intelligence under his breath, but he wasn't going to lie about it. There were too many other things he had to lie—or at least mislead her—about. "Yes." His voice was grim. "Now get in the damned locker."

She placed her hand in his. Small. Soft. Not the hand of a woman used to fighting for her life—or the lives of others. She looked him straight in the eye. There it was again. That trust. To a man like him that was pure gold. A treasure beyond any price. She had no idea what she was gifting him with, and that made it all the sweeter.

He kept his eyes on hers, holding her gaze captive while she stepped inside. Her face was stark white, and her mouth trembled, but she slowly knelt and then lay behind his heavy, waterproof bag.

"They're coming." He kept the thread of his voice between them. "Don't make a sound."

She nodded, and he closed the locker door, muffling the sound so the men sneaking down the passageway couldn't possibly hear. Opening the grate over the window, he called in the fog, beckoning long gray fingers toward the ship and into the small cabin before leaping up to catch the ventilation screen above his head. He lowered the metal grate carefully and swung into the small space.

For a big man, he was flexible and used to closed-in compartments. He was also very patient and could remain still for hours if necessary. He didn't know about Airiana. She had looked very fragile and vulnerable as she slipped behind his war bag. The damned thing was bigger than she was.

The hatch swung open abruptly and four men spilled inside. He recognized them. Prince Saeed didn't go far without them. Conley and Shamar Dover were brothers, mercenaries with a sizable reputation. Saeed considered them the best in the business. Maxim had run across many others far better. They were loyal to Saeed because he paid them massive amounts of money and kept them supplied with women and all the weapons they could possibly want to play with.

Yosuf and Jamel had grown up with Prince Saeed and entertained him as boys. They were used to his savage, brutal need for blood and death. He enjoyed hurting others, and they had learned if they didn't want to be one of his victims, they had to continue supplying him with warm bodies. Over the years they had become accustomed to disposing of the dead and covering for him. He compensated them and considered them true friends.

Yosuf approached the locker, reaching a hand to open it. Before he could touch it, Maxim slammed the heavy metal grate into his head, driving him back into Jamel. Both men staggered, Jamel trying to catch Yosuf before he fell. Blood streamed down Yosuf's face from the wicked cut to his temple.

Maxim swung down from the small, cramped space in the ceiling, using his momentum to kick Conley with both boots right in the face. He dropped in front of Shamar, his knife slicing deep into the inner thigh, up high to sever the artery. He turned and threw the knife at Jamel, the blade sinking deep into the carotid in his neck. As Jamel fell, Maxim caught Shamar's wrist with biting fingers, digging deep into the pressure point to open his fist and remove the bodyguard's knife.

Jamel was dead, and Shamar wasn't far behind him. Maxim threw himself forward onto the floor, using a scissor kick to weave his legs between Yosuf's legs as the bodyguard came at him. He rolled, taking Yosuf hard to the floor. Slamming Shamar's knife into Yosuf's throat hard, he kicked the body off of him and rose, facing Conley.

Conley spat blood and teeth onto the floor. He brought his knife in close, protecting his possession of it. Maxim pulled another knife from the sheath at the small of his back. They stared at each another, two warriors who had performed this dance too many times.

"You son of a bitch, you killed my brother," Conley hissed between his broken teeth. His eyes glittered with anger and the need for revenge.

"He was a first-class, pompous asshole and a rapist and murderer. No one's going to miss him much." Maxim kept his voice pleasant. "Your own mother put out a hit on the two of you. She knew you were scum."

He had no idea if the woman kept in contact with her sons, but she'd certainly come under investigation and she seemed decent enough. Conley had a temper. He liked to beat his opponents to death with his hands. He held a couple of boxing titles and had competed in martial art events when he was young. Riling him up shouldn't be too difficult.

Conley spat more blood on the floor, aiming for the toe of Maxim's boots. "I'm going to cut you into little pieces and feed you to the sharks," he snapped.

The bodyguard followed his threat with action, coming in hard and fast. He was good with a knife, but not nearly as fast as his brother had been. Maxim had disposed of the most dangerous threats as quickly as possible. Maxim met Conley halfway, their hands moving with blurring speed. Deliberately Maxim blocked several attacks and cut small slices into Conley's arms and chest.

Swearing, Conley kept coming. "You always did think you were better than us."

"I've always known it," Maxim replied softly.

He sidestepped the bodyguard, shoving at the man as he went past. The hard push sent Conley stumbling, and Maxim was on him like a large jungle cat, thrusting his knife deep into the right kidney and twisting to get the maximum damage possible as he pulled out to do the same to the left kidney.

Conley dropped hard, choking. Maxim kicked the knife out of the fallen man's hand and crouched down beside him. "Go to hell, Conley. It's where the two of you belong." He cut the man's throat.

Shamar held up his hand as Maxim approached. "Just let me die in peace."

"Like all those children you let your boss rape and murder? Did they die in peace?" Maxim asked, his voice low, keeping the words between them. "What's his body count, Shamar? Five hundred? More? He's been raping and killing for years. Little children, and you helped him. You're just as guilty as he is."

"So just let me die. What difference does it make?"

Maxim's radar went off. He forced a smile. "Stall tactics and not very good ones at that."

He watched Shamar's eyes, and sure enough the "tell" was there. A small narrowing, just enough to let Maxim know he was right in his assumption that the four men hadn't come alone. Shamar didn't want to die in peace, he wanted to make certain the bastard who killed him died as well. There was at least one other in the passageway waiting to ambush Maxim should he come out alive.

He cut Shamar's throat without another word. Very carefully he moved toward the hatch, blowing softly into the middle of the room so that more fog began to swirl around. He took up a position just to the side of the hatch, staying low, prepared to wait while the fog built in density.

He pressed his thumb into the very center of his palm where it itched. He knew the meaning, and knew what he had to do to give himself some relief, but if he put his mark on Airiana, his claim bound him just as it did her.

That face. Those eyes. The trust she'd given him when he'd ruthlessly taken her from the sanctuary of her home. He didn't know women like Airiana existed. Certainly they didn't in his world. She didn't belong with him, no matter what his body or his head said. It would be impossible.

Men like him didn't have wives or families. Loved ones were liabilities and could be used against him. He'd learned that rule when he'd been a boy and his parents had been murdered in front of him.

He directed the fog in small tiny fingers to slip through the slightly open door, just a touch, enough to pique the curiosity of whoever waited for him. Into the silence, he "threw" Shamar's voice. "You weren't so tough after all, were you?"

Out in the passageway, someone heavy moved. A second pair of footsteps, much lighter than the first, moved closer to the cabin. The heavier man took the left side of the hatch while the lighter man took the right.

"We're clear," Maxim called out, sounding annoyed, his voice the exact pitch of Shamar's. "He hid the girl."

"He can't have hidden her too well," the heavier man began, walking into the cabin. He halted when he saw the density of the fog. "What the hell is this?"

"He had the vent to the outside open," Shamar's voice came from across the room. "I think he pushed her into the cubbyhole up above. She could fit there."

Maxim waited for the man with the lighter footsteps to enter, but he didn't even come to the hatch. If anything, he'd shifted away from the cabin. Maxim didn't wait. If this man's partner was becoming suspicious, he needed to kill them both and be done with it.

He came up behind the heavyset man fast, his arm locking around his throat, his knife stabbing him deep in the chest, right in the heart. He used the same twisting motion as he withdrew, the one ensuring as much damage as possible, but just for good measure, he lowered the body silently to the floor and cut his throat.

Using the fog to guide him, he somersaulted out of the room right to the feet of the last bodyguard, slashing across his thighs fast and deep, coming to his feet as he slammed his knife under the man's arm then he brought his weapon up high to slash down across his neck.

The bodyguard staggered back, gurgled and toppled before Maxim could catch him. The last thing he wanted was for anyone else to come down to the cabin and discover a pool of blood—not before he was ready for them.

He dragged the fallen man into his cabin and hurried to the locker. "Airiana, don't shoot. And don't look. Just stand up and look only at me." He pulled the door open, blocking the view in the room with his body and the fog.

"How many?" she asked.

"Saeed sent six. He meant business," Maxim said, reaching for his bag. He shouldered it easily and then caught her up with one hand, swinging her around to his back. "Hang on. And close your eyes until we're out of here."

Airiana clung to him, burying her face against his back. He was grateful she didn't struggle. He stepped over two of the bodies and skirted a third. He felt her sudden inhale, a kind of gasping shock, and knew she had seen the two bodies nearest the hatch.

"I said not to look," he snapped. "Just do as I say. You need to obey me when I tell you to do something. I don't just say it to hear myself talk."

She pressed her face into his back without speaking, and he found himself sighing softly. Once into the corridor he closed the hatch, took her a few more feet away from the blood splatter and set her down.

"Are you all right?"

She didn't look at him. "Yes. I'm sorry, I didn't try to look, not like you think. I wasn't curious, it was more confirmation."

It cost her to admit the truth. She needed to see a body to know he had actually fought off Saeed's men and it wasn't some kind of elaborate game he was playing with her. She was actually embarrassed that she had doubted him for a moment.

"No harm done. I would have done the same thing." Of course, he was a skeptical man and didn't believe a third of what anyone said to him.

"The weird thing is, I trust you. And that scares me. I don't trust so easily and it's hard for me to get to know anyone or even talk very much to outsiders, but the more I'm in your company, the more I feel comfortable and that's just so strange."

He saw that she kept a grip on her assault rifle. "I understand. I'm having those same strange feelings. It's the situation. We only have one another to rely on." Which was a great line of bullshit, but he delivered it in a reasonable tone.

Some of the panic left her eyes, and she nodded. "I guess you're right. The situation certainly is unusual and very intense. Where are we going now?"

"I'm killing Saeed. I've been after him for over five years and I've never had a better chance. I'm not missing the opportunity." He'd be damned if he made apologies either. She said she wanted to help him, but she'd seen the blood on the floor and bodies lying in the cabin.

"Are there others on board? Others like Saeed?" She stayed right behind him as they moved toward the stairs.

"I studied the layout before coming aboard. There are seven luxury cabins, so potentially, that could be six other sexual predators aboard. They will all have bodyguards, although I suspect not quite as many as Saeed."

"Did you know this was a floating human trafficking vessel?"

"I suspected. There was no way to know until I actually got aboard ship. I wasn't told about any special passengers, only that sometimes the rich and famous are bored enough to pay lots of money for the privilege of traveling on a cargo vessel."

They kept their voices projecting only to each other, that thin thread of sound that connected them. He found he wanted that connection with her, even there, in the middle of a very dangerous situation.

"How many crew?"

"Including the cooks, twenty-one, and there is a security force that Evan keeps aboard. There're eight of them."

"Great. We might be a little outnumbered."

"No problem, baby, that's my specialty."

She touched the back of his shirt. He knew she didn't mean for him to feel the barely there brush of her fingers, but he did. He felt the impact all the way to his bones. She was seeking reassurance, that was all, nothing more, but he felt as if she belonged to him. She had been under his protection for her father's sake, but he knew that was no longer the reason he watched over her. Selfishly, he wanted her alive in the same world with him.

"I wish I could be more of a help to you," Airiana said. "This isn't my specialty, but I'm good at following orders."

He glanced over his shoulder at her, one eyebrow raised.

"When I want to," Airiana corrected.

He put his hand on the railing of the stairs. "We go up slow and easy. Stay directly behind me and try to step where I step. Don't make a sound."

Airiana twisted her fingers into his shirt, bunching the material into her fist. He wanted to give her that much. It would be a small comfort, but he knew he had to be able to move fast when necessary.

"Honey, you're going to have to let go. I'll watch out for you. I will, but . . ."

She dropped her hand away as if he'd slapped her. He cursed under his breath in his own language. He wasn't suave or sophisticated. All the training, all the beatings had never made him into someone different. He could pass himself off as those things, but he was a rough, dominant man whose every instinct was that of a killer.

Airiana needed reassurance, and he found himself baffled by her. She followed him closely, but she didn't touch him again. Her shoes whispered on the metal stairs, but she contained the sound, every bit as adept in that gift as he was.

It didn't surprise him that no one came to challenge them—this was Saeed's luxury cabin and as paranoid as he was, he wouldn't want anyone, not even a crew member, disturbing him. He brought his own security with him and they would keep everyone away.

He signaled to Airiana to move up to his side.

6

KNOWING a depraved monster was just on the other side of the hatch kept Airiana's stomach churning. She pressed her hand over the knots and took a deep calming breath. She didn't know why she believed in Maxim Prakenskii, but she did. He exuded absolute confidence, and somehow, that gave her the strength to stay by his side.

Maxim took the MP-5 from her hand and laid it on top of his war bag, just to one side of the hatch, so when the door opened, no one could see it.

She let out her breath and twisted her fingers together, feeling naked and vulnerable without the weapon.

Maxim caught her hand for the briefest of moments. Her fingers trembled inside of his, and he pressed his thumb into the exact center of her palm. She felt the touch over her heart. Startled, she looked up at him, her gaze colliding with his. He had amazing eyes, brooding and hooded. Sexy. Dangerous. He was all those things and more.

He lifted one eyebrow. "Are you ready for this?"

She nodded her head. Who could ever really be ready to face a monster?

Maxim called on the air surrounding them. He blew out his breath in a circle around their bodies. Instantly she felt the difference, as if the air was heavier, much denser in the passageway. She actually could see it shimmering between them, distorting his features until he looked a little shorter, more compact and his shaggy, wild hair was glossy and polished.

He tapped on the hatch, a one-two signal repeated four times in rapid succession. Clearly he knew the right code, because the hatch began to creak and groan as someone inside slowly opened it. Maxim didn't move aside, but stood firmly in the center of the opening, transferring his hold from her hand to her arm.

"The others are dead, Saeed, but I brought her to you." Maxim spoke in a perfect replica of Shamar's voice.

Saeed's robed figure filled the doorway. The robe was open and his bloated body gleamed with oil. He rubbed his hands together gleefully, leering at Airiana, not even looking at his bodyguard or acknowledging that the men who had served him for years were dead.

She shuddered and forced herself not to move closer to Maxim for protection. Bile rose. The prince was disgusting, his face pure evil. She was afraid if she looked at him too long, she'd throw up. She gave her brain another problem to work on, pushing out fear to try to mathematically understand how Maxim had managed to distort the air until his own features resembled those of another human being. The voice was easy enough, but to be able to change appearances, that was exceptional.

She kept her head resolutely down, working the probabilities in her mind, trying to find a theory that would explain how he'd done such an incredible feat, anything to keep her mind away from what might happen to her if Saeed actually got his hands on her.

Chuckling, pleased with his victory, the prince turned his head to look over his shoulder. "All is well, Sasha. You can have that little used one and leave me alone for a few hours." He sounded smug and magnanimous.

Maxim thrust Airiana behind him and struck fast, a blur

of movement, whipping a garrote around Saeed's throat as he spun him around to face the inside of the cabin. He twisted the thin wire mercilessly while the prince thrashed and fought.

Sasha rushed to his aid, dragging a naked child of about ten in front of him, holding a gun to her head. She cried continually, terror on her face and bruises on her body. There were thin knife cuts across her small torso.

"I'll kill her, Maxim, let him go."

The child called out in Italian, "Let him kill me. Don't let that pig go."

Airiana felt the breath leave her lungs in a burning rush, terrified for the little girl. The garrote continued to cut off the prince's airway, his wild struggles only making it tighter. Maxim never moved. His face was set in hard, implacable lines. His ice-blue eyes had gone dark, a turbulent storm of absolute resolve.

He whispered in Italian, the thread of sound going straight to the child. "This pig will never harm you again."

Saeed made horrible gurgling sounds, his face purple and his eyes bulging. His efforts to escape became feeble as the garrote tightened relentlessly. Maxim continued to look at the man he obviously recognized, his gaze unblinking while he strangled the prince in front of the bodyguard.

"You know I'll kill her," Sasha warned.

Airiana was standing almost directly behind Maxim. He moved so fast she didn't actually catch the blurring motion as he whipped his hand behind him and withdrew a pistol, pulling it forward around the prince's body and aiming all in one movement. The bullet hissed out of the chamber and smacked into Sasha's forehead. A hole blossomed there, bright red and ugly.

The child screamed and twisted out of the Sasha's slackening grip. His gun fell to the floor. The prince was entirely limp now and Maxim allowed his body to fall as well. Grimly, he bent down to ensure Saeed was dead, using his knife to finish the job.

To Airiana's horror, the child picked up Sasha's weapon and turned it on herself, putting the gun to her head. "No! No! You're safe. Don't."

Maxim was only a foot from the girl, crouched on the floor by the prince's dead body. He reached out slowly, his hand closing over the child's, his finger preventing the gun from firing. He was extremely gentle, every movement easy and unhurried.

"He is dead. Both of them. They can't touch you again."

His voice was so gentle, so compassionate, Airiana's eyes burned with tears. In his company, she knew him as a lethal, dangerous and mostly rough man. He could be kind, but this was an entirely new side she hadn't experienced.

"Find her something to wear. I've got a couple of shirts in my bag," Maxim said, without turning his head toward her. "A dark color."

Airiana hastened to do so. When she turned back, Maxim had the child in his arms. She sobbed against his chest, her black mop of long curls hiding her face. Maxim took the shirt from Airiana and pulled it over the little girl's head.

"Tell us your name," he encouraged.

"Nicia." The girl's voice was muffled. She didn't lift her head, her arms around Maxim's neck.

He picked her up and rolled the prince's body completely into his opulent cabin with his foot and then closed the hatch firmly. "Nicia, we have to be very quiet. There are other men on board like Saeed. Bad men. Is there a place with other women or children where they kept you?"

Nicia nodded.

"How many women? How many children?" Maxim asked.

The terrible shaking that threatened to break the little girl's bones apart had lessened, but she clung to Maxim as if he was the only thing in her world. "My sister Lucia, my little sister Siena and my brother Benito. I think Sofia, my twin sister, is dead. Sasha and another man came and got her last night and she never came back." She began to sob all over again.

They both had seen the body of the child Saeed had killed. Maxim stroked the child's hair and rocked her gently.

"I'm sorry I didn't get here in time to save her, Nicia," Maxim said. "But we're going to do our best, all three of us, to save the others. Will you help us?"

Nicia nodded without speaking. She was so small, a little girl who should have been playing with dolls, not serving as entertainment for a depraved monster.

"The young girls had to be kept for Saeed. He had an insatiable appetite, and they would have brought more than one child aboard for him. Eventually he would have murdered all the girls."

"Could they have brought the boy and the teen for him as well? He was looking at me, and while I might look young, I don't look Nicia's age," Airiana said.

"He might want the teen as well, if she's a virgin," Maxim said. "But not the boy. There has to be another predator aboard. At least one more, possibly two."

"How do we find them?" Airiana asked. She picked up the assault rifle and the web of ammo and weapons, slinging it over her shoulder.

"First we're going to find the other children. I need Nicia in a safe place. We'll move them to one of the cabins not in use. They can barricade themselves inside while we take care of the others."

That made sense to Airiana. They couldn't very well sneak around the ship with children in tow. She was certain Maxim was unhappy about having to take her along with him. More than ever, after seeing what was happening aboard the ship, she wanted to help find a way to stop whoever was running the trafficking ring. She understood Elle Drake's need to put herself in harm's way in order to stop it.

She also understood Lev Prakenskii's need to try to find the source. Even if they stopped what was happening aboard this vessel, there had to be others, both on land and sea, where other children were being harmed.

"Don't cry," Maxim said, his voice firm. "I mean it, Airiana. I've already got this little one weeping, I can't have both of you doing it. Nicia, tell me where you and the others are being held."

"It was very dark. There were big containers everywhere. We were inside one of the containers. It was hard to breathe sometimes."

Maxim swore under his breath. "Let's find an empty cabin. Airiana, I'll leave you with Nicia while I get the others."

Airiana caught her breath, stopping herself from protesting. She didn't want Maxim out of her sight, but she wasn't going to complain. She knew too much time had passed. Saeed had been occupied with Nicia and the other child he'd murdered, so while the teen and the youngest child were probably safe, the boy wasn't. Maxim was going to go after the boy. She wasn't going to whine because she was afraid. He'd given her an assault rifle and she knew, deep in her heart, that she would protect Nicia against anyone trying to harm them.

Airiana's gaze clung to his. Maxim wanted to comfort her, but he needed her strong. When planning his escape from the boat, he knew he had to stop the engine to allow him to get Airiana into the water, but he hadn't planned on rescuing children or having to leave dead bodies behind.

He couldn't take the children with him, and he couldn't leave the crew alive to kill them, which they would. The crew of the ship would have to destroy all evidence of human trafficking in case they were boarded. Airiana didn't have a clue as to the extent of their problem. He glanced at his watch. He was under a time constraint as well. The sub was going to rendezvous with him at night, the best chance for him to get Airiana away without anyone noticing. Now . . .

He put Nicia down, but she clung to his leg, terrified all over again.

"He needs his hands free to protect us," Airiana said, in

perfect Italian. "Stay with me, behind him. It's the safest place."

Nicia studied her face for a long time. "Does he belong to you?" She spoke in English, a little halting, but she'd clearly been raised using both languages.

"Yes," Maxim answered her firmly. "I belong to her. I won't ever let anything happen to her—or you. Just stay close and be as quiet as you can."

Maxim followed the passageway down the corridor to the next hatch. No bodyguards were present. There were four luxury cabins on this floor. Saeed would have wanted complete privacy, so the odds that the cabin on each side of his was empty were very good. There would have been some activity already, but no one was moving around at all. Still . . . he wasn't going to take chances.

Maxim signaled Airiana and Nicia to move to the far side against the wall, out of sight of the hatch. He noted that Airiana pushed Nicia behind her and brought up her weapon in a very businesslike manner. It was difficult not to feel admiration for her.

She looked darned cute in her black pants and makeshift scarf covering her bright hair, with a MP-5 cradled in her arms and a webbing of weapons and ammunition slung over her shoulder. He sent her a small salute before banging with his fist on the hatch. Silence met his demand for entry. He quickly spun the lock and stepped back to swing the door open. The cabin was empty.

Relieved, he signaled to Airiana. She took Nicia's hand and they went inside. The room was equipped with a large bed, mirrors, a closet, and drawers that locked in place. There was a private bathroom. Along the walls and on the floor were bolts to loop chains and cuffs through. An array of devices was displayed in cabinets locked onto the wall. Everything from whips and floggers to canes.

"I'm sorry, honey, I can't do anything about the room," Maxim said. "But you'll be safe in here. No one will know you're here. I'm going to leave some extra ammo, a knife and a couple of grenades, just in case. I should be back soon."

Airiana nodded her head but she didn't speak. Tears were already welling up in Nicia's eyes and he had the feeling that Airiana wanted to cry right along with her. Nicia took the nearest chair, sinking into its luxury and drawing up her knees beneath Maxim's shirt, unable to control the shivering in her body. He knew it wasn't from the cold, she was terrified of him leaving. Airiana immediately tucked a blanket around her.

Maxim turned to go, but couldn't do it. Not like this. Not without giving her something. "Come here, Airiana," he ordered softly without turning around. He stood facing the hatch, away from the room.

Puzzled, she stepped around him to stand directly in front of him, tilting her head to look up at him. Her eyes caught him like they always did. Sky blue eyes that could signal sunshine or rain, a coming storm or a hurricane.

He caught her wrist and lifted her palm straight up facing him. "In my family there is a small thing a man does when he belongs to a woman—when the woman belongs to us. We have to feel it, not with our bodies, but deep in our soul. Mine was ripped to shreds a long time ago and there isn't much left. But whatever remains belongs to you. I'll come back for you. No matter what, I'll come back."

He pushed air at her palm. More than air. Something deep inside him rose to rush toward her. He felt it rise, a connection that would be unbreakable. He was giving himself to this woman not knowing if she could accept him as he was, rough and scarred and very lost. He didn't know if he would even come out of this alive, but he had to do this one thing. The need—the compulsion—overcame everything else. He belonged—somewhere. With someone. Airiana Solovyov was his someone.

He heard the sound of the air hitting her palm, an electrical charge that actually zapped her. Two intertwined circles flared into life, a brand. A tattoo. The rings blazed a bright gold and then slowly faded into her skin, disappearing entirely.

Airiana yelped and tried to jerk her hand away, but he held her wrist firmly and brought the injured palm to the warmth of his mouth. His tongue stroked over the exact spot where the two rings had sunk beneath her skin. He traced each one, feeling the brand of Prakenskii, knowing it was on his own hand, trying to soothe the ache she felt. Her eyes widened and she gasped, heat flaring between them.

"What have you done?" she whispered.

He allowed her hand to slip away from him. She rubbed it down her thigh, her gaze clinging to his. "I gave myself to you. What you do with me is up to you. But I don't lie to children, and I won't lie to you. I'm coming back, Airiana." He stepped closer and framed her face with his hands. "I'm coming back for you."

She opened her mouth to answer him, to protest or to plead. He didn't know. He didn't care. He stopped all words with his own mouth, kissing her like a man drowning. Hot. Passionate. Pouring himself into her. Just this one time he took what he wanted from her, dragging her response from her, kissing her again and again, unable to stop himself from sinking further under her spell.

Abruptly he jerked away, and without another word, left her there. He swung his war bag over his shoulder and stalked out, closing the hatch behind him. His body was on fire. Crazy in the situation he was in, but still, he felt alive for the first time in more years than he cared to count.

He checked the other two cabins and both were empty. That meant the boy was on the next level down. There would be more bodyguards and probably a crew member or two. There would also be a despicable deviant who would torture and kill a small boy just because he could.

He had no compassion for any member of the crew who had signed on to work this cargo vessel. There were no secrets on a ship this size out to sea for long weeks. Every man who worked on board the ship was aware of what took place in the cabins.

He went down the stairs using extreme caution. Without Airiana he could move much faster, using his stealthy, silent mode. Air cushioned his sound, preventing any spills so, although he was large, he could move easily through the ship and never be heard. He kept his image distorted so a quick glance from someone passing at the end of the passageway wouldn't be enough to spot him.

His gifts allowed advantages, and as a covert operative, he needed—and used—every one of them. As he neared the bottom of the stairs, he waited a moment to allow the air to speak to him, delivering vital information. Being bound to air was a part of him, natural, like breathing, and he read every nuance in the displacement like a map.

There were two men in the passageway, down toward the end. No others seemed to be around, but it was a long way to get to them without being seen. He slipped down the last two steps and into the shadows just beneath the stairwell, studying the situation.

Two bodyguards—he recognized them both. They were mercenaries out of Italy. Both had belonged to the mob, worked as contract killers, and when it got too hot, they left the country to hire out until things cooled down. He had an entire dossier on both and wasn't surprised in the least that they were on board this particular type of vessel, because the last he'd heard, Evan Shackler-Gratsos had hired them.

Leone Marciante was a brutal killer. He had grown up a bully and had continued to be one. His uncle was embedded deep in the mob in Italy and he had naturally gravitated toward his uncle's work. He rose fast, a ruthless, dangerous man who had no problem killing anyone, even when he was a boy.

His partner, Ricco D'Amato, had grown up down the street from Leone. He'd been wild from the beginning, beating up his mother often and raising hell at school. The two stayed close, probably because their similar personalities allowed them to feel safe tormenting schoolmates and families. It was a natural progression for Ricco to join the mob with his longtime partner.

Leone had a penchant for women. He thought of himself as a charming ladies' man, and often bragged about what a lady-killer he was. He laughed heartily at the intended pun.

Ricco preferred men. Not men, younger boys. Teens as a rule, but it was rumored he sometimes preyed on street boys even younger. He generally garnered their loyalty, using his street teams for information, spending money on them and setting them to be drug runners, even occasionally using them for other crimes. He was far more careful than Leone, making certain no trail ever led back to him. Where Leone loved to brag about his prowess with women and his work, Ricco rarely spoke. Maxim considered him the far more dangerous of the two.

He always found it interesting how criminals found one another so easily. They formed packs when they came across one another, especially child abusers. They exchanged pictures, stories and even children, aiding one another across countries.

These two men had left Italy, but they found the very man, Shackler-Gratsos, who would allow them to continue their lifestyle. Maxim slipped his gun into his belt and loosened his knife. He breathed into the air, blowing out a steady flow from under the stairwell. The surrounding air turned warm as it streamed along the narrow corridor, filling it from floor to ceiling, slowly elevating the temperature.

Evan must have provided the bodyguards for whoever was in that room. The man probably wanted to torture and kill a child in private, far from anyone who would know him—including his own bodyguards. There were a few, like Saeed, who thought themselves so powerful it didn't matter, but most didn't want their sins out in the open where they might be blackmailed.

He waited a short time until he knew the two men would be feeling the rise in temperature and then blew more air, increasing the heat until it was much hotter in the passageway. Both men took off their jackets, exposing the harnesses their weapons were housed in.

Leone swore loudly and walked over to tap on a vent. "What the hell? The air down here is stifling," he snapped, wiping at the beads of sweat forming on his forehead.

"It's happened before," Ricco said, his voice low and calm.

"Not like this. It's bullshit. I'll bet Galati's room is plenty cool for him and his little friend." He laughed. "That kid looked like a scared little rabbit. He thinks you're going to save him. I love that look of utter devotion they give you. They do anything you want them to, don't they?"

Ricco shrugged. "He's a smart kid. He could be of use to me, but once they're aboard this ship, there's nothing to be done but get rid of them. I tried to steer Galati to another boy, but he chose Benito." Ricco turned cool eyes on his partner. "We were given orders to give Galati whatever he wanted so . . ." He shrugged.

"Too bad. Are you in love with him?" Leone taunted. "Maybe you want to take him home with you?"

He sounded jealous, which again, didn't surprise Maxim. Leone might appear the dominant in the relationship, but it was actually Ricco. Leone had no one else in his life and he didn't share well with others. Maxim would bet his last dollar that Leone had helped Galati choose Benito out of Evan's special catalogue of young children, probably from a video recording.

"What I want doesn't much matter. Galati has his hands on him now. He'll be brutal with the kid and ruin him. The kid's straight and needs to be handled with care, but Galati plans to kill him so he's not going to bother with finesse." Again Ricco shrugged, but his eyes were watchful on Leone's face.

"You're the one who killed his family," Leone pointed out. "Just so you could cultivate him. I wonder how he'll feel when Galati whispers that to him right before he kills him, or maybe he's already done it. He likes the kids to know ahead of time what he plans to do to them. He said the terror increases the fun. He strangles them and lets them come back just so he can do it all again."

Maxim increased the temperature again, this time the heat rising fast, as if fires had broken out all around them. The metal on the walls of the passageway nearly glowed. Both men's shirts were damp, sweat running in rivers and pooling on the floor. They began to look uneasy, tempers increasing along with the heat.

"This is bullshit," Leone said, kicking at the wall.

Ricco said nothing, but he tested the temperature of the wall, using the flat of his hand. It was hot, but not excessively so despite the fact that it nearly glowed, a trick, maybe, to the eye. "I think the ventilation system stopped working is all," he said.

"I don't give a damn what happened," Leone snapped. "Someone needs to fix it."

Maxim added a whisper of condensation, so fine it could barely be seen, but the water in the air increased, hot now, turning the passageway slowly into a steam room. Again it was a slow process to fill up the corridor, and at first neither noticed until the long fingers of haze began to creep around them as if they were in a sauna.

"I'll go check and see what's going on," Ricco said abruptly.

"The hell with that. I'm not staying here to burn to death," Leone protested. "I'm going too. No one's going to disturb Galati and if it's getting hot in there, he can boil for all I care."

Ricco shrugged and started down the passageway toward the staircase. Leone followed, grumbling every step of the way. Maxim let them come within several feet of him before he fired two rapid shots, aiming for the kill, a bullet right in the middle of the forehead, his signature shot. Both went down simultaneously. Neither ever saw Maxim and probably didn't know what hit him.

Maxim used a silencer, but still, he remained beneath the stairwell, in the shadows, in case Galati or anyone else heard the shots. He was patient, taking his time, ignoring the two bodies lying on the floor. He allowed the temperature in the passageway to cool just a little, although it didn't affect him. He kept a bubble of cooler air surrounding him, but he didn't want Galati to get spooked and maybe kill the boy.

He found it difficult to think about the boy locked in a room with a man who intended to use him and then kill him. He couldn't allow his mind to go there, not and be of any use to the kid. He'd been taken from his home and become a prisoner of the state, beaten and trained, shaped into a killing machine, so he knew, more than most, what it was like. He could identify in many ways with the boy.

Maxim was grateful Airiana wasn't with him. He had no idea what he'd do to Galati, or what condition he'd find the boy in. Like little Nicia, the boy would be traumatized for life. To have a woman witness such a humiliating and degrading circumstance would only make it worse.

Nothing moved. No one came to investigate. He slipped out of the shadows, nudged Leone's body aside with the edge of his foot and padded silently down the passageway. The hatch to the luxury cabin was sealed. He couldn't go in with guns blazing, he needed Galati to voluntarily open the door, so that he was away from the boy.

He had to heat the room through the ventilation system. Doing so could spread the heat throughout the ship, but still, even if the crew became alarmed, they wouldn't think to come to the cabin as the source. They'd be checking the engine room first.

He located the shaft in the passageway and manipulated the air once again, sending both hot air and condensation into the cabin. The room, although good-sized for a cabin on a cargo vessel, was small in comparison to the passageway and it warmed fast. He could feel the heat radiating from the hatch. He stayed to one side of it, pressed against the wall, allowing the air around him to distort his image.

The lock spun and the hatch swung open. Galati, naked, sweat dripping from his body leaned out to take a breath. Maxim yanked him into the corridor and threw him up against the wall. Galati's head hit first, Maxim's strength was enormous enough to nearly knock him out. Only self-preservation kept Galati from falling, although he staggered and grabbed his head, trying to focus.

"What the hell?"

"Hell has come for you," Maxim snapped and slammed the knife deep into Galati's throat to shut him up and get it over with fast. He twisted the blade, withdrew it and then stabbed into the carotid artery for good measure.

His temper had surged forward, a volcano erupting when he'd been taught to stay in control. He was tempted to do a little torture of his own, and he knew more ways to cause pain than Galati had ever thought of, but he never wanted to be that man. He wanted to execute fast and dispassionately. The problem was, he detested men like Saeed and Galati who preyed on children.

Maxim let the man drop to the floor and left him there, sprawled out naked and dirty, lying in his own pool of blood. Stepping over the body he hesitated at the doorway, steeling himself for what he might find.

The boy looked to be about twelve or thirteen. He was tied over a rack in a kneeling position. His body was covered in whip marks and bruises. Tears ran down his face, leaving tracks, but his eyes were defiant, furious, filled with hatred, which told Maxim the kid had a chance at recovery.

"He's dead," he announced. "I've come to get you out of here. Nicia is alive and I've left her with my woman in a safe place. I'll take you there and get the others." He spoke softly, seeing the distrust on the boy's face.

He cut the ropes digging into the boy's wrists. His hands were swollen and bruised, nearly purple. Galati had deliberately used a harsh rope to hurt the boy more.

"Flex your fingers to get the blood back into your hands," Maxim instructed over his shoulder as he went to the hatch to watch down the corridor. "Shake your arms out. When you can hold the knife, I want you to cut your ankles free. We could have company any minute."

He wanted to give the kid something to do to help himself and at the same time, by giving him a weapon, show he was no threat. Still, he kept an eye on the boy.

"He has two bodyguards," the boy said. He spat onto the bed several times and then reached for the knife. "They'll kill you for him."

"He's dead and so are they," Maxim said. "And we have to get the hell out of here. Do you have any clothes?"

"My name's Benito," the boy said and tried to stand. He groaned and nearly fell.

Maxim didn't make the mistake of trying to help him. "When we get to the safety zone, remind me. I have some ointment that will help in my bag."

"My clothes are on the sink. He said he likes to keep them for a memento." The boy turned too-old eyes on him. "He was going to kill me."

"I know. He's dead," Maxim reiterated for the third time. The boy was in shock but trying to fight his way back. His alarm system nagged at him. They weren't going to get a clean exit, the boy could barely walk.

Benito staggered over to the sink and turned on the water, rinsing his mouth repeatedly and spitting. Maxim pretended not to notice the tears still tracking down the boy's face. He wanted to kill Galati all over again. He thought of himself as a monster until he ran across men like Saeed and Galati and those who supplied them.

"We're going to have company in a minute. Get dressed," Maxim repeated, keeping his voice low and confident. "Keep that knife close, you may need it, but don't do anything unless I give the okay. Do you understand? We still have to get the others free. I need you to stay quiet and obey me."

For the first time he looked the boy in the eye to show he meant business. Benito dragged on his clothes, or tried to. Clearly every movement caused pain. Maxim had no idea how long the boy had been tied in that position, but judging by the swollen purple bands around his ankles and wrists, it had been awhile. The boy had been caned and whipped, the cuts deep. Pins and needles had to be horrendous, but he valiantly struggled into his clothes.

Maxim nodded approvingly when he picked up the knife. "You'll do, Benito. Stay close to me no matter what happens. Behind me," he added. "We'll get out of this alive, but I might have to kill a few people for that to happen."

Benito nodded. "All right by me," he said. "Kill as many as you'd like."

Maxim entered the passageway first and headed toward the opposite end where the stairs would lead down to the next floor. That was the engine room, and below that was the cargo hold where he was certain the other two girls were being held.

Movement behind him had him spinning around, his gun tracking. The boy bent over Galati, stabbing down with the knife several times, his face a mask of hatred.

Maxim remembered rage. Deep down he still felt it and in certain situations, such as this one, it welled up like a volcano, impossible to suppress. He understood rage. He moved up behind the boy and gently caught his wrist, stopping the movement.

"He's dead."

"Not dead enough," Benito said, and spat on the body.

"Dead is dead. You're indulging yourself," Maxim kept his voice harsh. "I need you one hundred percent if we're going to get those girls free. If you can't control yourself, you're of no use to me—or them."

Benito straightened up slowly, wincing as he did so. "I'm with you."

Maxim nodded and slowed his pace. They were going to get caught. The air was moving again and sending him all kinds of messages, none of them good. He had planned to take the boy to Airiana and leave him in the relative safety of the empty luxury cabin, but Benito needed action to bring him back.

"Good. We're about to have company. They're coming down the stairs now and we don't have time to reach the stairwell. Hug the side of the wall and let's make it to that passageway just ahead."

Benito tried but there was no way he could double-time it. Maxim glanced toward their destination, saw they wouldn't make it, and he signaled Benito to halt, waving him against the wall. Maxim took up position in the center of the passageway, once more distorting his image to look vaguely like Ricco. The two crew members ascending the stairs would see who they were prepared to see, at least until they got close.

He walked fast, covering the distance quickly now, bending air continuously so that it shimmered in waves, the distortion all around him.

He needed to kill these men silently. They were from the engine room. He could smell the heavy fuel oil on them. The air carried the scent of sulfur clinging to their clothes. Evan Shackler-Gratsos didn't believe in saving the environment, just in adding more money to his coffers.

Evan had complete deniability of course. He owned the ships, he didn't run them. He'd recently inherited them from his brother. Nothing Maxim had found could tie Evan to the human trafficking ring—not yet.

Maxim continued toward the stairs and the two men coming up them.

7

MAXIM had scoped out the engine room the moment he'd come aboard, knowing he would have to stop the ship. Both men had been working there. The blond, sounding Swedish, had talked incessantly about having the captain provide a woman for them to use on their journeys. The other, who looked as if he might be from Indonesia, hadn't spoken much.

It was the Indonesian man who spotted him at the top of the stairs. The Swede was still talking and hadn't even looked where he was going. Maxim kicked the Indonesian hard in the face and as he went down, he shot the Swede. The Swede fell hard, rolling on the metal stairway, landing on the Indonesian.

Maxim followed up his advantage, shooting rapidly to prevent the Indonesian from calling out for help. He dragged both bodies down the stairs and shoved them out of sight in a small storage closet. He didn't bother wiping up the blood, but called the boy down to him, using a thread of sound.

They passed the engine room and went straight for the cargo area. It was huge, with containers everywhere. Benito took the lead, hurrying up to one of the containers and thumping on it, anxiety on his face. A heavy lock on the door prevented them from opening it. Maxim smashed the lock and pulled back the heavy door.

Heat blasted him and with it an appalling stench. It didn't stop Benito from rushing inside and flinging himself into the arms of a girl no more than fourteen. She hugged him hard and reached down for the younger child, a little girl of about six or seven. She pushed the child behind her.

"It's okay, Lucia," Benito assured. "He killed them all. I saw him do it. And Nicia is safe. She's still alive."

Lucia stared at him with too-old eyes. She was the oldest of the children and she'd taken the role of the adult. The family resemblance was strong between them—they had the same features.

Maxim beckoned them out of the box. "Bring whatever is important to you. I'm going to stash you in a much nicer and safer place."

"We don't have anything important," Lucia said. "They made it very clear to us that we wouldn't ever leave the ship." There was disbelief in her voice.

Maxim couldn't blame her, but time was slipping away. "If you're coming with me, we have to go now. I need my hands free, so if the little one can't keep up, you'll have to carry her. And you need to be absolutely quiet. Do you understand?"

He used his most commanding, intimidating voice.

The children nodded. Benito took the hand of the youngest child. "This is Siena. She's six. We were all taken together. They're my sisters."

The child had Benito's huge dark eyes, as did Lucia. Siena's hair was long and thick and hung in curls and waves. Maxim could see why the three children had been targeted. All of them were beautiful and would catch the eye of predators like Saeed and Galati. He knew that the children and women chosen for the high-end "special" clients had to be disposable, which meant no one would come looking for them.

They were often runaways or had no other family once

their parents met an untimely death. A long-lost uncle might come forward and claim them. It was easy enough, with the amount of money exchanging hands, to forge the necessary papers. Once the child or children were in the "uncle's" possession, no one would ever look again. Scoring five children at once would be cheap and easy and a huge boon for the seller.

Lucia hung back. "The man who came to get us after our parents were killed in an accident said he was our uncle. His name was Ricco. He brought us here."

"Ricco's dead," Maxim said grimly. "He wasn't your uncle. It's a ploy often used by human trafficking rings."

Siena began to cry at the mention of her parents.

"Are you afraid, Siena?" Maxim asked, crouching down so he was level with her and would be less intimidating.

Siena nodded, tears tracking down her cheeks and curls bobbing around her face. She clung tighter to Lucia's leg.

"I'll get you out of here, but you have to be very quiet for me. When I tell you to, I want you to close your eyes and let Lucia carry you. Can you do that for me?"

The little girl gave a sniff, looked from her older brother to her sister and then gave a nod.

He felt like the pied piper. He was a loner and always worked solo. More than three people were a crowd to him. He didn't deal with children—he didn't know how. He was too gruff and far too rough, yet all three were beginning to look at him as if he were a hero, their savior. He was uncomfortable in that role. He didn't want any of them admiring him—especially Benito.

"Let's move. Stay right behind me, single file. Lucia, when I tell you, pick Siena up and carry her, but only until we're past whatever obstacle we find."

"He means the dead bodies," Benito said.

Maxim pinned him with a steely eye. "Your little sister doesn't need to be any more traumatized than she already is. Right?"

Benito ducked his head, but he didn't look remorseful. Maxim couldn't blame him. The kid was purple from head to toe and had a few open wounds. His clothes might cover up what had been done to him, but nothing was going to ever take it away.

Maxim couldn't do more than see to it that they were safe. It was going to cost him this time. The body count would be high. If he left a single person aboard alive, the first thing they would do would be to hunt down the children, kill them and throw their bodies overboard to remove all evidence. He would have to leave a ghost ship behind.

He signaled to Lucia to pick up Siena when they approached the stairs where the bodies of the two men who worked in the engine room were. "Keep your eyes closed very tight, Siena," he instructed.

He tried not to notice Benito kicking the body of the one of the men as they stepped around them. Lucia hissed a reprimand at her brother, but the boy shrugged, unrepentant. Maxim remembered that feeling of rage. Of helplessness. Of knowing a bigger, stronger and much more ruthless man could do anything and get away with it. He'd been beaten and caned. He still carried the scars from whips and even a chain.

He took them up the stairs past the floor where Galati had held Benito, wanting to avoid that particular place. Lucia would know what happened there. She might guess, but seeing the bodies of Galati and his bodyguards would only make Benito's shame and embarrassment deepen.

He stopped the little parade at the top of the stairs. This was the floor where he'd left Airiana and Nicia. He pushed air down the passageway and circulated it back to him, needing information. Pressing his thumb into the center of his palm, he reached for Airiana.

Are you okay? Has anyone disturbed you?

He felt Airiana's shock. He should have warned her they would have a telepathic connection, but he had other things to worry about. Now he had the children. He still wasn't certain what he was going to do with them all.

It's been quiet. Nicia is very worried about her sisters and brother.

Maxim wanted to curse. Ricco had killed their parents to acquire the children for the sex trade. He must have received a fortune from Evan Shackler-Gratsos, who had to be the head of the organization. He was a billionaire and little ever touched him.

I'm bringing them in. Don't shoot us.

He almost wished she would. What in the hell was he doing with these kids? He sighed again and signaled them to follow him. They made it down the passageway without incident, and he opened the hatch, blocking the entrance, just in case. He was like that. Always wary, ready for anything.

Well—almost anything. Airiana was an exception. Her sky blue eyes jumped to his. He'd never had anyone look at him like that—welcoming. Happy. She jumped up and flung her arms around him. His hand of its own volition came up to cup the back of her head beneath the scarf as she pressed her face against his chest. The silk of her hair slid over that sensitive spot in the middle of his palm, teasing his senses.

"I'm glad you're safe," she whispered.

He could hear the truth in her voice. He was bound to air, and one of the many gifts was the ability to read sound. She was truly happy he was safe—not for herself but for him. He leaned down and brushed a kiss on top of the silly scarf made from his own shirt, feeling a little foolish under Benito's smirk.

He gave the kid a glare and waved them all inside before closing the hatch. "Airiana, this is Lucia, Siena and Benito. Kids, this is Airiana."

The children nodded at her shyly. She gave them a smile of reassurance.

Ricco killed their parents and posed as their uncle, their only living relative, to acquire them. He sent Airiana the information privately.

You mean they really have no other family? She had no trouble using their telepathic connection to communicate. It was simply another form of sound and air.

No, they would have been thoroughly investigated before they took them. It was easy enough to orphan them and then step forward to claim them. Who would question papers that appeared to be legitimate?

Bastards. Airiana poured loathing into the word.

Maxim turned to the children. "This is your new home until the rescue boat comes. I don't want any of you to leave this room for any reason. You have a bathroom and water. There's a small cooler with food. You'll be safe here."

Lucia and Siena had rushed to Nicia, gathering her in their arms and hugging her tight. At Maxim's order the children all turned to him, shaking heads and protesting.

Siena looked around the room. "Where's Sofia? Why isn't she here?" Her trusting eyes jumped to Maxim's face.

Maxim slowly stepped away from Airiana, feeling helpless. He didn't much care for the feeling, he'd experienced it too many times as a child and he'd vowed never to be that way again. All the training in the world didn't prepare him for this situation. He killed people and was comfortable in his role. He didn't tell little girls with big eyes that he hadn't saved their sister.

Lucia held out her hand to her younger sister. "Sofia is Nicia's twin."

Maxim went still inside, hating the position he was in with these children. He couldn't fix it, couldn't take away the trauma and hurt. He wanted to kill Ricco all over again. And after he killed him, he would like another chance at Saeed, this time a long, slow death. He'd change his position on torture just for that deviant.

Maxim sank down on the bed. Airiana moved up behind him, laying her hands on his shoulder, connecting them, trying to comfort him.

Siena stood in front of Maxim, ignoring her sister's outstretched hand as if she knew only Maxim had the answers. "Where is she?"

Maxim took her hands in his. "I'm so sorry, little one. I didn't board the ship in time to save her. There was a very bad man on board, and he killed her." Did one tell a child the truth when it was so ugly? He didn't know any other way. He couldn't soft-soap it. Hell, children weren't his forte and never would be.

Tears welled up. Siena turned to Lucia, who gathered her close and rocked her gently. Nicia burst into tears all over again. She was every bit as traumatized as Benito. Maxim thought about punching a wall, but doubted if that would help comfort the children. He needed to get out of there.

"I'm sorry," he repeated lamely, floundering.

Airiana circled his neck with her hands. "Maxim tried, Siena, but we found her that way. As soon as he could, Maxim went to save Nicia, Benito and then you and Lucia. We're so sorry about Sofia."

"Mommy died too," Siena said. "And Daddy. Now Sofia. Where are we going to go? I don't want any more uncles."

"We're not going to any uncles," Benito said, his eyes catching fire. "We're staying with Maxim."

Nicia broke out into a smile, nodding her head vigorously.

Maxim hoped the horror didn't show on his face. He was trained to stay expressionless, but what the hell? He could just see himself going across countries, assassinating criminals with four children in tow. He had the good sense not to shake his head. The next thing he knew he'd have a house with a white picket fence and a dog.

"We'll see," he said.

"That means we'll never see you again," Lucia said. "We've heard it a hundred times. Come on," she gathered the younger ones to her. She looked so old, so motherly— and a little lost—struggling against tears.

He grit his teeth together. "It doesn't mean that at all. It means we'll see. I have to make certain there's no one on board who can find you children and harm you. I can't give guarantees. I'm not going to lie to you."

"But you will come back for us," Benito said.

"I've got business with Airiana, making certain she's safe. I gave her my word."

"But *then* you'll come back for us," the boy insisted.

Maxim could barely stand looking at their hopeful faces. They had no one and he represented hope to them. Survival. He was the hero, and they needed something to hold on to while they waited on a ship of horrors all alone.

He was no hero, and if there was anyone on the planet who knew less than he did about kids, he wasn't aware of them. They were waiting for his answer. He could actually feel Airiana willing him to answer in the affirmative.

He resisted the urge to swear at her. At them. At all of them. He cleared his throat. "Look. I'm not exactly a nice man. I know I seem like it in comparison to men like Galati and Saeed, but you don't want to rely on me."

Nicia slipped her hand in his. His heart stuttered when she turned her dark, Italian eyes on him with a child's trust. "I feel safe with you."

The others nodded. He closed his eyes. *This is your fault. You look at me all trusting and these poor traumatized children get the idea that I'm trustworthy.*

You are. And they need to know you'll see them through this. Can you imagine them sitting here waiting for someone to come and being scared out of their minds? They need to know you're coming back, that you'll check on them. They have to believe in something, Maxim, and they believe in you. That's not a bad thing.

You don't know what the hell you're talking about. He stared down into the child's eyes and then looked at Benito. The boy was trying hard to keep it together.

He yanked open his war bag and took out ointment, tossing it to Benito. "Yeah. Fine. I'll ask some people to keep you close until I can come back for you. They'll have to take you off this ship, but we'll find a place . . ."

The farm. Have them sent to my farm, Airiana said. *My sisters will look after them and they'll be safe. Try to arrange that. At the same time you can get word to them that I'm safe and I'll be coming home as soon as possible. They'll be worried sick.*

He didn't want to think about taking Airiana back to her home.

Airiana, these children are never going to be normal. They'll need special care. The trauma they've been through . . .

Everyone on that farm will understand. Trust me, Maxim, I know what I'm talking about. Can you find a way to get them transported there when they're taken off the ship? My brothers-in-law are very good at arranging papers if there's need, she reminded. He would know that Lev and Stefan Prakenskii would be every bit as adept as he was at creating new identities.

Maxim sighed, feeling as if his life was spinning out of control when he was all about control.

Lucia's gaze had jumped to Maxim's face. "There are four of us and we want to stay together." Siena began to cry, and Lucia put her arms around the younger child.

No one at the farm would try to break them up. I have plenty of room at my house and if necessary, we can figure out legal papers to keep them in the country if they want to stay. The point is, I know a wonderful counselor and she can help them.

"Airiana has a farm," Maxim said aloud. "It may be a *temporary* solution, just until I can figure something else out."

"It's a little isolated. No big city close, but it's near the ocean and the redwoods and is absolutely beautiful," Airiana offered. "You might hate it, but you'd be safe. My sisters live there as well, and each of us has our own home. I have a fairly big house, enough bedrooms if the two younger girls can share."

"And he'll come?" Benito asked, indicating Maxim with his chin.

This was too much. Airiana was already arranging a future for the children, ignoring all the laws and trapping him into something he didn't want. He wasn't that man. "I'll come. Now all of you settle down. It's going to be a long wait. At some point the ship will stop. You'll hear the engines stop. Stay in this room. I'll let the rescue crew know which cabin you're in."

"But you'll be gone," Lucia guessed shrewdly. "That's why you're stopping the ship. You're getting off."

He nodded. "I have to protect Airiana. Some very bad men are after her as well."

"Why can't we go with you?" Benito asked.

"I can't take all of you with me while I clear this ship, it would be too dangerous," Maxim explained. "And then I have to get Airiana to someplace else fast. That's dangerous as well, and there's no way you children could make the journey. But I keep my word, and I said I'd come back for you, to make certain you're safe and in a good place. I have a couple of men I trust who will come for you. They'll say 'nutmeg grows in odd places.' If they don't say that, Benito is going to shoot them."

Are you crazy?

They need that, it helps to make them believe they're safe.

But giving Benito a gun? He's a child.

Not anymore. Galanti made certain of that.

Lucia clutched the blanket on the bed so hard her knuckles turned white. "There is no safe place." Tears welled up in her eyes.

Nicia and Siena crying was one thing, but Lucia had been struggling so hard to be grown up and take care of her siblings. Seeing the tears spilling down her face was too much. He took both of her hands, gently prying open her fingers.

"You have no reason to trust anyone, least of all me, Lucia, but we don't have too many choices left. I'm running out of time. If I want to clear the ship for you, I have to do it now. I'm on a time schedule. Airiana's farm is the best we can think of. Otherwise, the authorities will ship you back to Italy. I'll look for you, but I have far less control over what happens to all of you once you're there."

"You'll be safe," Airiana added. "Everyone on the farm has been through . . ." She trailed off, searching for the right word. "Horrific circumstances. They'll help you with the younger ones."

Maxim looked at his watch. Time was slipping away. He had to get to the engine room. "We have to go now, Airiana."

Lucia straightened her shoulders, her gaze clinging to Airiana's. "You'll come back? Both of you?"

Airiana nodded. "If we're alive after all of this, we'll meet you on the farm. If not, you'll be in good hands. Lexi, my youngest sister, will be particularly understanding. She'll help all of you. We'll come back as soon as possible."

Maxim stood, reaching for Airiana's hand. "We have to go now, honey, we're running out of time." He tugged until she went with him across the room.

Airiana looked back at the four children huddled together. "Be patient. Stay strong. And don't leave this room."

She tightened her fingers around Maxim's, just as reluctant to leave the children as he was. He opened the hatch and resolutely stepped through into the passageway. Airiana glanced back, but she didn't say a word.

Maxim's eyes met Benito. The boy was holding himself very still, but his body vibrated with fear. "I'm coming back for you, kid," Maxim promised again before he could stop himself. "I know everything in your life has been turned upside down and you haven't been able to count on anyone else but one another. I'll find you. Do you understand me? Tell me the password."

"Nutmeg grows in odd places."

Maxim nodded. "Shoot anyone else who tries to come in. You keep your sisters safe and together."

Benito nodded, his gaze still clinging to Maxim. Maxim swore and slammed the hatch closed.

"I want to kill those bastards all over again," he admitted to Airiana, pushing down the rage threatening to take over.

"I wish you could too," Airiana said. "We have to do something for those kids. I know you think I was being impetuous, but I really thought it through. All of them are traumatized. They'll need special help to see them through this. Just the murder of their parents would be enough to traumatize them, but their sister as well? At the hands of a sexual predator. And then Benito and Nicia, the things she told me Saeed did to her . . ."

"She talked to you about it?" Maxim asked. He led the way to the stairs. The engine room was his next target.

"I think she had to. She was so scared and so grateful that you found her. Benito looked as if he worships you."

"Lucia and Benito knew they were going to be killed probably the moment they were brought aboard the ship," Maxim said.

"Nicia said Lucia and Benito told her to do whatever the man said so he wouldn't hurt her. She did it, but he hurt her anyway."

Maxim heard the anger in Airiana's voice. Anger and despair. He stopped just at the top of the stairs and put his arm around her, pulling her into the shelter of his body. "We can't save them all, but we saved these four. For now, that has to be enough, honey, or you'll end up going crazy."

"When we moved to the farm," Airiana told him, "I thought we were done with violence. We live pretty simply and it's beautiful there, and so peaceful. It sickens me to know that this is still going on right under our noses."

Airiana had used the word *still*. He didn't question her, but he knew she was referring to her youngest sister, Lexi. Of course, the moment he knew Lev and Stefan were involved with two of the women living there, he'd investigated all of them.

"We'll take care of those kids. I don't know how, Airiana, but we'll get it done. Right now, I need you to put everything else aside and give me a hundred percent right here and now. What we're doing is dangerous. We have to disable the ship, but there are going to be men down in the engine room. If possible, we'll round them up and put them in the cargo container they put the kids in. If not, we'll have no choice but to kill them."

"Do we know they're a part of this?"

"They know what's going on aboard this ship. They're paid to keep quiet, and they have in spite of the fact that women, boys and children are brought here, used and murdered. They aren't innocent. In any case, once we're gone, those children will have no protection. If I don't get to everyone, they'll be in danger."

Airiana nodded her head several times. "Okay. I understand. I just wanted to be certain."

"I'm sorry about all this. It was supposed to be simple— snatch you out from under the noses of Evan's men and get you off ship to a waiting sub and to your father where you would be safe. The children complicated things."

"I would much rather have been here where you could help those kids," Airiana said firmly.

Her blue eyes were a little cloudy, but steady. His heart did some sort of curious melt, leaving him wondering at the power of women—especially the one he found himself drawn to. She was small, and seemingly fragile, but her looks were definitely deceiving. She could roar like a lion, and no matter how afraid she was, she moved forward, willing to help him.

He wanted to kiss her again. The urge was strong, but he resisted. This wasn't the time or place and they had work to do. "Stay behind me," he ordered, his voice once again all business.

She flashed a small, secretive smile that made his insides tighten, but she obediently dropped back to do as he said. She had the assault rifle and the webbing over her shoulder while he carried his war bag over his.

They moved down the stairs in silence. He muffled the sound, but realized she was automatically doing so as well. She learned fast and he appreciated that. Once more, he shifted into stealth mode. He couldn't afford his mind to be anywhere but on his mission. The flight of stairs led to the engine room, and below that was the cargo hold.

Airiana walked in his footsteps, directly behind him, so quietly he wouldn't have known she was there other than the fact that her scent was so alluring to him. Everything about her was and he damned well wasn't going to lose her.

Voices drifted to him.

"Damn that Swede. He was supposed to be right back here. I'm not taking his bullshit anymore. Go find him, Lance, and get him back here."

"He's probably in the galley. He spends more time there than in here. I swear he puts on twenty pounds every time we go to sea." Lance laughed. "Really, Cahill, you need to see the humor in the situation."

"I don't find it so funny," Cahill groused. "Not when we have to do his work."

"We have to do his work when he's here," Lance said. "He doesn't belong in the engine room. He doesn't know what the hell he's doing. I think he's a hired gun. Half the crew doesn't know what they're doing. But the pay's good, and we occasionally get a woman for a while. What more do you want?"

"Someone to help out with the work," Cahill snapped.

"It's never going to be the Swede." Lance laughed. "If you want to find him, go yourself. Maybe you'll come back in a better mood."

Maxim held his fist up, a signal for Airiana to stop moving. He slid his war bag from his shoulder to the floor. Stalking Lance was easy, he'd begun whistling, giving his position away. Cahill had fallen silent after his outburst, but air told Maxim he was moving through the machinery, heading straight for him.

Crouching in the shadows, he sent Airiana reassurance. *Just stay very still.*

I'm out in the open.

I know. He's going to spot you, but he won't believe what he's seeing.

I'm bait?

He smiled at the outrage in her voice. *He doesn't have a gun.*

How do you know? What happened to me being so important?

You saddled me with four kids. I'm not certain your worth outweighs that particular transgression.

Cahill rounded the long line of pipes and came to a halt, his mouth open, staring at Airiana. Before he could move, or make a sound, Maxim came up behind him and pressed a gun into the back of his neck.

"You've seen me before, Cahill," Maxim said softly, keeping the thread of sound between them. "You know I have no problem ending you. Call your friend. Be very careful what you say. I killed the Swede and his buddy, so no one's going to rescue you. Just keep your temper in check and you'll come out of this alive."

Cahill swallowed hard several times. His face had gone bright red and his fingers curled into two tight fists. "Lance." He raised his voice. "Lance, I need a little help over here."

"Can't you do anything yourself?" Lance called back. "I'm on a coffee break, like the Swede." He laughed heartily at his joke.

Cahill swung around, going for the gun, hoping to shove it away from his neck, shouting as he did so. Maxim shot him through the temple, muffling the silencer he used so that no sound escaped. His body fell hard, and Maxim didn't block that sound.

Open your eyes and get into that dark alcove right behind you, he instructed Airiana. She looked a little shell-shocked.

She obeyed quickly, her face very pale. From his position he could see she was distressed, but her hands were rock steady on the MP-5.

It's going to be all right, honey. Hang in there with me. He couldn't resist reassuring her.

Lance moved around the long row and stopped abruptly when he saw Cahill's fallen body. Blood seeped out around his head, creating a halo of red.

"What the hell?"

Lance ran to the fallen man, crouching down, or he started to. Recognizing the wound for what it was, he pulled out a gun and looked wildly around.

"Drop it, Lance. Right now. I tried to give Cahill his chance, but he didn't listen. Make your choice."

Lance dropped his gun.

"Put your hands behind your head and lock your fingers together."

Lance complied, and Maxim stepped behind and used a zip tie to secure his hands.

I'm taking him to the cargo hold. Stay right where you are. No one should come down here, but that doesn't mean they won't.

Maxim could feel her reluctance to be left alone, but she didn't object. He shoved Lance ahead of him, already regretting not killing him. He didn't like leaving Airiana alone either, but it would only take a couple of minutes to get Lance secured in the container the children had been locked in. He shoved Lance toward the stairs. The man was solid, although not particularly large, but clearly he was all muscle. A small alarm went off in Maxim's head.

Lance had indicated that the Swede was useless in the engine room—implying he was most likely a hired gun—but the Swede had been easy to dispose of. Too easy. He was no highly skilled mercenary, but Lance . . .

Maxim indicated the stairs and Lance went down them without question. The moment he hit the bottom, he crouched and swung around, using his head to butt Maxim in the chest with a hard blow. Prepared for the attack, Maxim moved his body back just inches enough to escape the assault.

Lance kept spinning around, hooking his ankle in Maxim's, his momentum pulling Maxim's foot out from under him. Maxim leapt over the man, kicking him hard in the head as he went down, somersaulting and coming back up on his feet. Lance's head hit the metal railing hard and he slumped down, shaken.

Maxim reached for his shoulder to yank him up and

Lance came up fast, a knife in his bound hands, ripping up Maxim's belly to his chest. The burn was fierce, but it was a shallow wound. He leapt back away from the grinning man. Lance spat on the floor and flicked the blade of the knife through the zip tie.

"Amateur hour," he snapped.

Maxim smiled. "Nice move."

Lance circled to the left, forcing Maxim to circle with him. He kept the knife in close, indicating he knew what he was doing. Maxim lifted his gun and shot him right through the middle of his forehead. Lance actually looked a little startled, as if he'd forgotten Maxim had a gun, not a knife. He toppled slowly to the floor.

Maxim sighed. The body count was climbing higher than he expected. He glanced at his watch again. He needed to disable the engine, forcing the crew to drop anchor. He still had to figure out what to do with the rest of the crew.

He made his way back to the engine room. As soon as he entered, he held his hand out to Airiana. She came to him instantly and he wrapped his arm around her, pulling her in close to him. It astonished him just how much she had taken over his thoughts. She'd found a way inside of him, creeping in when he wasn't expecting it.

"You're dangerous," he said, his tone harsher than he intended. She was just so insidious, slipping into his soul when he was so certain his every defense was in place and no one could ever find that last piece of himself that belonged only to him. There was no running from her.

He'd known her less than twenty-four hours. What would it be like in her company for a lifetime? She'd be so tightly wound inside of him that there'd never be an escape. Would he even want to?

Abruptly he caught up his war bag and stalked through the engine room with Airiana following. She didn't say anything at all and he kept his back to her, not wanting to see her face. He was giving too much of himself away. He wasn't a man to be out in the open, naked and vulnerable to a woman. He lived in the shadows and slipped easily from one skin to another. No one could know him. Not even Airiana.

He went to work, losing himself in the familiar process of building his devices and setting his timers. He took his time, not wanting to make a mistake. Everything depended on the ship stopping on time.

Airiana waited quietly until he straightened up and looked at her. "What next?" she asked, her voice quiet.

"Everything depends on stopping the ship. We've got a few hours before the engines start to go. The ship will slow and then they'll drop anchor. We'll suit up and get out of here. I'll call for help to rescue the kids. These couple of hours, waiting until dark, is our most dangerous time."

She made a face. "You know they landed that helicopter on the deck. It's still there. Why don't we just use the helicopter to get out of here? You can do everything else, I can't imagine that you don't pilot a helicopter as well."

He couldn't help but smile. "As a matter of fact, I can fly a copter, but that's not the plan. You're doing your best not to set foot in the ocean, aren't you?"

"It makes sense to fly."

He shook his head. "We're disabling the helicopter. I don't want it used for anyone's escape. Come on, we have a lot to do to keep those children safe."

8

AIRIANA made a face at Maxim's back. He was determined that she was going in the sea, with scuba gear no less. She didn't know how to breathe with a tank, and she didn't swim. Taking a chance with the helicopter seemed a much better idea.

"You're stubborn and bossy, did you know that?" she asked, exasperated with him. "I've done everything you've said, and given you the courtesy of listening to you. I can't swim. I'll drown in the ocean."

He moved up the stairs, past the deck with the empty luxury cabins and continuing toward the upper deck. "I always listen to you, Airiana," he said, over his shoulder. "The problem is, you keep repeating yourself. We have no choice, we have to use the water. I've gotten you this far; why don't you believe I'll get you the rest of the way?"

He sounded so reasonable she had an unexpected urge to kick him. His back was to her and she could probably get away with it, although she wouldn't be surprised if he had eyes in the back of his head.

"Maxim." She bit out his name between her clenched teeth. "I'm terrified of the water. I can't swim. What part of that don't you understand? I suppose you've never been afraid a day in your life, of anything, but I actually am a human being and the thought of water closing over my head and swimming in the dark is sheer madness. I don't think I can do it."

Maxim stopped abruptly and she found herself blinking up at him, a little ashamed that she couldn't conquer her fear when he was so omnipotent. He caught her chin in his hand and leaned down, his eyes drifting over her face with a kind of hard possession. No one had ever looked at her like that before. She found herself holding her breath, wishing he'd bend his head closer.

"Nothing is going to happen to you, Airiana. Not as long as I'm alive. We've gotten this far together, and I'll get you through the rest of it."

She understood why the children had clung to him so fast and so fiercely. Maxim seemed invincible. She knew he wasn't. There was a thin line of blood staining his shirt from his belly to this chest, but he hadn't said a word to her of how it had gotten there.

"You really don't like me very much, do you?" Airiana asked.

He was the most reluctant of heroes. He didn't want to tow the kids around, and she doubted if he was happy with being in her company. In spite of being physically attracted to her, there were times when he seemed annoyed with her presence. Still, he had something reliable and steady in him, an absolute conviction that he could get through anything—and take her with him.

"You're very unexpected, Airiana," he said softly. "I've never met a woman like you. It doesn't seem to matter how frightened you are, you're still ready for business. I find myself intrigued—and distracted by you. Neither is a good thing for either of us."

She rubbed her palm down her thigh. "You marked me. I've seen Rikki and Judith rubbing their palms just the way I am right now, so I know you've somehow connected us. But the reality is, you don't really want to have anything to do with me."

To his credit, he didn't back away from the conversation—or deny it. "I have a difficult time trusting something I don't understand. The way you make me feel—I don't understand. I've never wanted a woman the way I want you. I've never kissed a woman and then couldn't get the taste and feel of her out of my mouth. You're like a drug in my system, and the craving just gets worse the longer we spend time together. I made you a promise to keep you safe. Now I have to wonder if your greatest threat is me."

Airiana frowned. She could hear the ring of honesty in his voice. "Maxim, I'm not afraid of you." She touched his mouth with the pads of her fingers. "I'm just as drawn to you, just as vulnerable. It could be because we're both air elements, or that you're incredible and you're saving my life, but I can't help it either."

"We're not alike, Airiana. Never make the mistake of thinking we are. I'm utterly ruthless when I have to be. If you belonged to me . . ." He broke off, shaking his head. "I'm not doing that to you . . . I hope."

"I'm just saying that you don't have to be afraid of me either. Or *for* me when it comes to you. I make my own decisions regarding my life. I have since I was about fourteen. I make my own choices and my own mistakes. Don't think I'm so easily pushed around that you can walk on me. We're in life-or-death circumstances and this isn't the way life is on a daily basis . . ."

"That's where you're wrong, Airiana. I live in a life-or-death reality every day. I have for most of my life. I don't want that for you."

"Then walk away from it. Don't tell me it isn't possible. I know a couple of people who have managed."

His hand circled her throat. "Don't put temptation in my path." The pad of his thumb slid back and forth in a mesmerizing rhythm. "It was a mistake to put my claim on you—a compulsion I couldn't resist—and that should tell you something right there. I have to be in control, and you somehow manage to throw all my discipline and control out the window. It isn't safe for either of us."

Airiana did her best not to be hurt, which was absolutely ridiculous. She knew nothing about this man, but at the same time, she'd never been so drawn to another human being. From what she'd witnessed with Rikki and Judith as well as Joley Drake, the Prakenskiis had practically thrown themselves at their women. If this particular Prakenskii was really the man who should have been hers, he wasn't exactly chomping at the bit—and that hurt.

She blinked several times and pulled away from him. "I get it. Let's just get this finished. I really want to go home."

Maxim stood for a long moment staring down at her, not releasing her, and her heart pounded in spite of every effort not to be affected by him. She was close to the women on her farm, but she didn't trust anyone else, and she couldn't put her trust in this man, he'd just told her that. He was taking her to her father—if Theodotus Solovyov was her father. She had to step back from the situation she was in and stop relying on Maxim to save her. She had a brain. She was intelligent. She needed to think for herself.

Maxim knew the moment he told Airiana he'd made a mistake in connecting them together that he'd just blown it big-time. He watched her shut down and draw inward. Those beautiful trusting eyes became shuttered, and her aura changed. She used her air element to hide herself from him, changing who she was, what she was, in the blink of an eye.

Like Maxim, Airiana could be a chameleon, blending into her surroundings and hiding herself in plain sight. She looked amenable and even smiled at him, but it was empty and wrong. All wrong. He cursed under his breath and turned away from her, heading back up the stairs.

After all these years, why would she suddenly cross his path? Why would the other women on the farm be the women his brothers were connected to? What had drawn them all together?

When he was a child he understood very little about politics, but now his life was completely entangled with men who schemed for power and money. The man who had managed to make and then collect orphans for his special training schools had been overthrown, but his son was still very much in power—and he wanted all evidence of those schools buried. The Prakenskiis were part of that evidence.

Right now, Maxim was of use to his country, but the moment his assignment was over, he would be placed on the hit list along with the rest of his brothers. He was an embarrassment, a stain on their past. There was no place in his world for a woman. His brothers might think they were safe, appearing dead to the world, assuming new identities, but they had put every woman on that farm in jeopardy—including Airiana.

He wanted her. Maybe was becoming obsessed with her. When a man had nothing at all, no one at all, when he met that one person, regardless of how long he spent with her, he knew. Maxim knew. She was the one who could live with him. She fit. No matter how much he wanted her, he was not going to tie her life to his and watch his enemies kill her.

He heard the whisper of movement above him, on the upper deck. He needed to keep his mind on his business and not worry about a mythical relationship that could never happen. Kissing her was all he was ever going to have and that had to be enough.

He put his fist up and Airiana froze. Very slowly he put the war bag down and signaled to her to pick it up. It was heavy, but she could manage.

I need to stash you in a safe place while I do a little recon. We need intel.

What does that mean?

Her voice was tight with nerves, but she offered no objection. He almost wished she had. It was another indication that she'd accepted the limitations he had put on them. What had he expected? She might throw herself at him? Tell him she had to be with him or she couldn't go on? He mentally shook his head at the idea, rejecting it. If she'd been that kind of woman, he wouldn't be attracted to her.

No, she'd go on all right. She'd live her life and she'd

find a way to be happy. Just as she'd gone on after her mother's murder. She was the kind of woman who protected her younger sister and offered to take four traumatized children into her home so they could stay together and get help.

Airiana Solovyov was a woman who would stand in a crisis, even if she was terrified. She wasn't going to pine over a man who roamed the world at the whim of his puppet masters.

I'm going to talk to a few of the men.

You're going to do what? Do you have a death wish? What if they know about Saeed and the other one?

At least she had genuine concern in her voice. He waited until he was certain they had a clear path to the lifeboats where he intended to stash her. Containers were stacked on the upper deck and he used them for cover. He went first, moving easily across the ship's deck to the nearest container. He looked around the corner as well as up, just to be certain there were no roving guards. He beckoned Airiana to his side.

She was weighed down with the war bag and her assault rifle, but she moved almost as easily as he did, certainly as silent.

Are you ignoring my question on purpose?

If they knew, there would be much more activity than this. Men with guns would be rushing to the lower decks. My guess is the customers pay for privacy and no one goes there unless invited. I'm more worried about the men from the engine room being discovered than Saeed or Galati.

Maxim was considered one of Evan's men. He'd been brought aboard because the "boss" insisted he come along to collect the package and personally deliver her unharmed. The "boss" owned the shipping company, and he had enough money to buy his way to one of the best mercenaries out of Russia he could get.

Evan Shackler-Gratsos had inherited billions from his brother as well as his empire of crime. He would claim, if challenged, of course, that he had no idea what his cargo ships were being used for, and he never gave orders personally.

Gavriil Prakenskii had gotten word to Theodotus Solovyov that his daughter was in danger—that one of the greatest criminal minds had fixated on her. A few years earlier, Solovyov's wife, Elena, had told her lover, a man working for Evan's brother, Stavros, that Theodotus hadn't been the one originally to think up the platform for his work, that his daughter had done so. She had tried to give the data to her latest conquest, but the microchip had been lost for years and then destroyed.

Evan Shackler-Gratsos had been part of his brother's criminal empire all along, and privy to all information Stavros had. Maxim was certain of it, but he had no real proof. He'd been on his trail now for a while, trying to unravel the threads leading back to Evan Shackler-Gratsos without breaking them, or letting the spider realize he was being watched.

Maxim made certain to be available for work, and he wasn't at all surprised when he received the request through unofficial channels. He'd built up his mercenary persona over many years and he had a certain reputation. He'd named an outrageous sum for his work, but the Greek billionaire apparently hadn't even quibbled. Half the money had already been transferred into a numbered account not even Maxim's Russian handlers knew of.

Immediately Maxim had contacted Solovyov to let him know Gavriil had been correct and Airiana Solovyov was in danger. His employment had gotten him aboard the helicopter and assured that he would be the man looking after Airiana. She was a valued commodity, not at all disposable like the young children aboard.

Evan Shackler-Gratsos's orders had made it very clear to Maxim that Airiana was to be kept in excellent health and if he didn't deliver, he would be hunted down and killed. Maxim had wanted to tell them to get in line. It wasn't like he hadn't been threatened many times before—it was a fairly common occurrence.

Airiana basically thought most people were fundamentally good. That wasn't his experience and he doubted if he would ever reach a place where he could think like her. She didn't jump in the deep end and trust people automatically, but she didn't think or expect the worst of them either. He thought it was amazing that she could believe in him. He'd thrown that carelessly away with his idiotic statement about making a mistake by putting the Prakenskii brand on her.

He moved to the next container, peered around it and signaled her to hurry. The air around them indicated others were close by, but he couldn't see them. The moment Airiana was behind him he rounded the corner of the container with her following close. The lifeboat he wanted to stash her in was close.

The sound of a woman's laughter cut through the air. At once the wind shifted subtly and her scent lingered. Maxim glanced over his shoulder. One moment Airiana had been following him, subdued and determined to get through the entire ordeal without incident, and the next she had abandoned him and was going back along the wall of the last container. *She* had been the one to shift the wind.

What the hell are you doing? We're very exposed out here and there are far more crew members here than below.

I recognize that laugh. Her voice was tight.

Maxim caught up with her, one hand on her wrist, slowing her down. She had remembered to muffle all sound around her, but she had no idea what danger they were in. Any moment they could be spotted and his careful planning would go out the window.

I know that laugh. Her name is Wanda Payne. When I was growing up she lived next door to us. She was there at least four years. I'd know her laugh anywhere. Why would she be here?

His heart sank. There was only one reason for a neighbor of Airiana's to be aboard the ship. Maxim let his breath out slowly. This was a betrayal. Undercover operatives sometimes went deep. Very deep. She had to have been put in

place by the Russian government—or the United States—
and if it was the U.S. why would she be aboard this vessel?

*We're going to do this slowly and the right way. Drop
back behind me.* He used his harshest voice more to distract
her and force compliance than anything else. He didn't
want to move forward and allow her to see this woman. She
already had to cope with too many things. Betrayal was
always an ugly one.

He peered around the corner of the next container. They
were on the ocean side now and the wind was cold. He
spotted Cyreck and a woman walking toward them. They
stopped to talk again, the woman laughing at something
Cyreck said.

Airiana's swift intake of breath alerted him. He spun
around and clapped his hand over her mouth, pulling her
body tight into his. *Don't make a sound.*

*That woman. The one with Cyreck. That is definitely
Wanda Payne. She moved in next door after Mr. Grayson
died unexpectedly. A heart attack, I think. Wanda was nice
to me. Mom started drinking just after Wanda moved into
the neighborhood, and Wanda helped me quite often.*

He could imagine how helpful Wanda was. Holding Airiana tight against him, he studied the woman's face. Plastic
surgery was often used when an agent assumed a long-term
undercover role, but he usually could identify them by the
way they moved. It was one of the most difficult things to
change.

It took a few minutes before he figured out who she was.
Wanda had gone to the same school as he had, although, at
the time, her name was different. She was Russian, and
she'd gone a completely different path. She'd gotten a taste
for the high life, and she broke away from her handlers.
She would take work from anyone as long as the paycheck
was fat.

Wanda looked up to Cyreck, laughing, flirting, clearly
enjoying herself. She wasn't a prisoner, more, he was certain, she helped get the children aboard. He shifted the
wind just enough that they could hear the conversation.

"Next time, Cy, I promise, I'll bring one just like her for you." Wanda laughed.

Cyreck grinned at her. "I'll hold you to it. You only brought two for the crew and they're getting used up. The captain is especially hard on them."

Wanda's smile faded. "He tossed one of them overboard a few minutes ago because she wouldn't cooperate with him. What did he expect? She's been working since the moment she came aboard."

Airiana stiffened. Maxim didn't let her go. The tension in her body told him she was already figuring out just what her old neighbor was doing on board the ship and whom she worked for.

Be still, he hissed into her mind when she began to struggle.

She had to have been planted there to spy on us, Airiana said, fury welling up.

I know, honey, but it won't do us any good if we're caught. Relax, we'll deal with Wanda, I promise. She's Russian and a traitor. I should have known she'd end up working for a man like Evan. She likes money and has no scruples.

You know her? You know that horrible woman?

He felt mist on the back of his hand, the one covering her mouth. Tiny drops—he glanced down to see tears on her lashes and tracking down her face.

I've kept every promise I've made to you, Airiana, he said, knowing he was a fool, but unable to help himself. *Wanda will not get off this ship alive.*

They're talking so casually about the captain throwing a woman overboard. There must be a second woman held somewhere close by.

He nodded his head slowly. He should have known that they would bring women aboard for the crew, particularly the captain. If they entertained other clients at sea, he would insist on some kind of compensation along with money.

I could send a wind and knock her overboard, Airiana

declared. *Maybe they'd stop the ship and try to get her back.*

You know they won't. No one is that important to them—unless it's you. I doubt that any of them wants to be the one to tell their boss that something happened to you.

He deals in weapons, human trafficking and top secret defense systems? He's a busy man.

He runs the shipping company, and his biker club runs drugs. They do it all.

He removed his hand from her mouth, but didn't let go of her. Cyreck and Wanda were once more on the move, heading toward a storage container just a few feet from the one they hid behind.

Wanda took out a key and unlocked the door. She swung it open and began swearing. Cyreck looked in. It was too much of an opportunity to pass up. Maxim released Airiana and put a finger to his lips. He moved in silence around the container, right out into the open, walking up to both parties as if he didn't have a care in the world.

Cyreck glanced over his shoulder and then turned back to look inside the container again. Maxim could see the dead woman inside. She'd slit her own wrists with a piece of glass. Wanda kicked at the woman's feet. Cyreck bent to get a closer look.

Maxim shoved his knife through the back of Wanda's neck hard, spun her around and slit her throat, throwing her body on top of the dead woman's all in one continuous movement. Cyreck jumped back as Wanda's body fell nearly on top of him.

"What the hell, Maxim. You can't just kill her because you don't like her. Sheesh. Now I've got to tell the captain we don't have any women available. He'll have to take the teenager, and he hates kids. He wants a woman that knows what she's doing."

Maxim palmed his knife and threw it, the blade penetrating Cyreck's chest and slicing deep into his heart. Cyreck's eyes went wide with shock and he looked down at the knife sticking out of his chest in total disbelief.

"No worries," Maxim assured. "I'll tell the captain my-self. You just rest here with your friends."

He shut the container door and locked it. Just to be on the safe side, he drew the air through the holes, so that Cyreck couldn't breathe if the knife wound hadn't killed him. He waited a few minutes before he joined Airiana.

Do you think she killed my mother? Was she capable of torturing her like that? Airiana asked. *Mom would have opened the door for her, let her in, asked her if she wanted coffee. Wanda knew what music my mother played when she was drinking. She could have set the scene easily.*

Every one of the operatives had been trained in torture. He was very skilled. He didn't use those skills, but he cer-tainly knew just about every possible way to hurt and then kill a human being. In his opinion, Wanda was a psycho-path. She didn't have any morals and it didn't bother her to inflict pain on others. He nodded his head slowly.

If she lived there for four years, what would have trig-gered her to suddenly go after your mother?

I stopped talking to my mother about my work when she began drinking so heavily. She had nothing to pass on to my father, if that's what she really was doing. Could that have something to do with it?

He heard the guilt in her voice. He hated this. Hated all of it. He wrapped his arms around her and pulled her into him, his hand cradling the back of her head.

That day, after you found your mother, what was the first thing you did?

I screamed and screamed. Then I ran outside. I couldn't stand the smell inside the house. I called Westwood at the school and told him what happened and that I was going over to my neighbor's. He said they'd be right there. They sent a helicopter, the police, an ambulance, everyone. I ran to Wanda's and told her how I found my mother. She said she'd go check, just to be certain.

She didn't know you'd called this person, Westwood, did she?

Airiana shook her head.

That's what saved you. She was gaining your trust by going into the house. She would have taken you away that day, but they got there too fast and they took you back to the school.

You're saying Wanda tortured and killed my mother.

I believe that's probably what happened, yes. And your mother's death wasn't sanctioned by the Russian government. Wanda was already working for someone else—most likely Evan's brother, Stavros.

They'd been out in the open too long. He had to stash her quickly and find out the lay of the land. He urged her back toward the lifeboat that was lashed up on deck. It was covered and had supplies in it. The captain made certain it was always well stocked and that the mechanical rigging was well-oiled and working perfectly. That was his escape should there be need.

Maxim pulled up one of the corners of the canvas to allow her to crawl inside. *Stay still. Don't make a sound. I'll be a while. Guard that bag, we'll need it to get out of here.*

What are you doing now?

I'm going to disable the helicopter and then go talk to the captain. The engines should begin to lose power soon and the ship will start slowing. He'll be barking orders at the engine room but no one is alive to hear him.

Her gaze clung to his, making it difficult to leave her. He leaned down and brushed his lips over hers. She blinked up at him, but she didn't pull away and she didn't kiss him back. She merely looked at him. He stepped back and yanked down the canvas, sending up a silent prayer no one discovered her.

He made his way to the helicopter, not bothering to hide his presence. He would draw more attention slinking around then just walking right out in the open. He was supposedly a member of Evan's mercenary army and few would consider interfering with him or questioning him.

Two men patrolling around the upper deck nodded to him and kept moving. They looked bored with their job and weren't paying much attention to anything but each other and the argument they appeared to be having. He waited until they had disappeared from sight and then strolled right up to the helicopter.

It wasn't difficult to slip inside without being seen. He moved quickly. Flying helicopters had been easy enough to learn; repairing them was something altogether different, but they had to learn just in case their ride went down. He crawled to the baggage bay and removed two of the avionics panels.

He worked fast, but meticulously. He took off the cover housing to the start solenoid and took out the contact. The engine wouldn't start without it and a few other systems wouldn't work either. He replaced the cover and then the panels before easing out of the baggage bay. He glanced at his watch. He'd disabled the helicopter in record time, but still, night had fallen fast and already the ship's engines sounded labored.

The ship was definitely slowing. He jumped from the helicopter and slipped under it, between the skids, waiting while the wind brought him information. The two guards were on the far side of the ship from him, but two men were hurrying toward the stairs, most likely to find out why no one was answering below in the engine room.

He moved into the shadows to follow them. He caught them just above the stairwell. "You'll need to remain quiet and come with me," he said softly, announcing his presence.

Both swung around to face him, eyes going wide with shock when they saw the gun. He handed the shorter of the two a zip tie. "Hands behind his back, put it on tight."

The taller of the two men glared at him as the shorter one complied. "You'll never get away with this."

"You're lucky I'm letting you live. Everyone below is already dead." He slapped tape over the man's mouth and then indicated for the shorter one to turn around. It took only seconds to tie and gag him with the tape and zip ties. The container that had held the women was a short distance from the stairs. He marched them to it, unlocked it and shoved them both inside.

The smell of death was overpowering. He slammed the door closed on the foul odor and inserted the lock. He strode across the deck again, heading toward the bridge. The ship shuddered and slowed more. Several crew members raced toward stations. He kept walking, ignoring the chaos breaking out on the deck. The captain was shouting into his radio, calling down to the engine room for an explanation, but clearly it was of no use.

"Captain Martsen?" Maxim said softly.

Martsen spun around, swearing as Maxim continued toward him. He waved the Russian off. "I've got no time right now," he snapped. "I've got problems."

"Of course you do," Maxim replied in a soothing voice. "You've had them for a while now, haven't you?"

"What are you talking about?" Martsen demanded.

The ship shuddered again and the roar of the engines quieted. The momentum of their speed kept them moving, but clearly they were no longer being powered.

"I suggest you drop anchor," Maxim advised.

"I know what to do with my own ship," Martsen proclaimed. "Get out of here before I call security to have you thrown out."

Maxim leaned his hip against the wall and looked coolly down his nose at Martsen. "It's a little too late for that, don't you think?"

Martsen turned back to give the order. "Drop anchor. Drop anchor now."

At once the sound of the huge chain vibrated through the bridge and sparks flew up into the night like a small fireworks show.

"That's all I needed from you," Maxim said. He pulled out his gun. "Keep in mind, Martsen, you're of no more use to me and I prefer to just kill you outright. Get moving. Walk toward the container where you keep those women prisoner."

The first officer and second officers raised their hands immediately and began to walk toward Maxim when he indicated to do so with his weapon.

The captain glanced through the glass, out onto the deck to see the two men running toward them with assault rifles. "Go fuck yourself, Maxim, this is my ship . . ."

Maxim shot Martsen dead center in the middle of his forehead and turned the gun on the two security men running toward the bridge. They fired at him, and he dropped low. The first and second officers went down as the sweep of bullets smashed equipment. Maxim took careful aim, using the wind for his map, and he fired one shot, taking out the closest of the two men.

He could hear more men running, and satisfaction moved through him. It was going to be easier killing them all in one place. They should have spread out and used available cover.

Airiana screamed. Loud. In pain. That hadn't been in his plan. His heart jerked hard in his chest and he called the wind, looking for her exact location and how many men surrounded her. Two in front of her and two on either side.

He rose and fired at the second security man, killing him instantly. Two men dragged Airiana toward the bridge while two others held their weapons at ready. Maxim slipped out of the control room and found the shadows. He was part of the night and could move in silence. He waited for the two men in the lead to reach him. He kicked the first one in the face hard, using a roundhouse kick, and caught the other by the neck, dragging him in front of him.

He rapid-fired two bullets, aiming for head shots, taking out the two men on either side of Airiana. She shoved one fist in her mouth, but reached down to recover her rifle as he shot the man he was holding in the head, shoved the body away and slapped at the gun of the second attacker, knocking it away. He caught the man's head in his bare hands, twisted as he spun his body around, lifting him over his shoulder by his head and neck. The crack was loud. He ran toward Airiana and caught her arm, taking her with him as he continued running back toward the lifeboat and his war bag.

Blood ran down her face from a wound in her hairline. The dark scrap of shirt that had been serving as a scarf to hold her hair was gone. The blood looked obscene running down her pale face and smeared in her wild, angel hair. He wiped at it with his shirt. "Get back in there and get dressed. Put the wet suit on fast. Put the oil on your body first and stash these clothes in the war bag."

She shook her head but complied. He had a couple more men to secure and then the children would be safe. The chief steward and cook, the boatswain and three more seamen. They would have heard the gunshots and they'd be expecting trouble. He didn't want Airiana anywhere on the deck when trouble came.

He slipped carefully through the containers, allowing the air around him to guide him. Someone had climbed up above for a better view. That was easy enough. He brought in the wind, a gale force directed at the man leaping from one container to the next. The wind hit the man square in the chest while he was in the air, blowing him backward. The man screamed and flailed in the air as he was picked up and thrown overboard.

He heard a whisper of movement coming from the stairwell. Maxim rolled from the shadows of the container to the small tucked-in alcove beside the stairs, coming up on one knee, his weapon trained on the second man coming up. The first passed him, assault rifle in hand, and the second, a dark-haired, swarthy, heavily muscled man moved stealthily into view.

The dark-haired male suddenly turned his head alertly, shifting on the balls of his feet and launching himself at Maxim. Maxim got two shots off before he was hit hard, knocking him backward, the breath rushing from his lungs. Both bullets hit the first man, but the noise of the large man tackling him brought four others running.

He rolled, came to his feet, and the man slammed a boot in his chest, driving him back to the stairwell. He nearly went over the railing, his weapon tangling in the metal frame. Another kick to the ribs nearly smashed his bones. His rifle stayed in the metal and he went flying.

He palmed a throwing knife as he hit the deck, rolled and threw with deadly accuracy. The big man went down, the knife buried in his neck. A bullet smashed right over his head and Maxim dove for cover. The four men formed a semicircle, blasting the entire area, keeping him pinned and putting dozens of holes in the bodies of their shipmates.

Behind them, he heard the sound of a gun and his heart nearly stopped. One of the men stumbled forward, went to his knees and toppled onto his face. A second did the same. He saw her then. Dressed in her wet suit, all in black, even her hair covered by the hood, she stood a distance away with the assault rifle steady in her hands.

He fell in love right there. As the others turned toward her, he pulled his weapon free and shot them just as she did.

"You were late," she said. "And I got scared."

"I know. I'm sorry."

Now that it was over, her hands trembled. He took the weapon from her. "We're getting out of here."

"I'm feeling a little light-headed."

She was definitely pale. "Just sit down. I'll be another minute."

It took a few minutes to strip, rub himself down with a little oil and slip into his scuba gear. He radioed the sub to make certain it was in position and waiting for them and then he called his brother and dumped the entire mess in his lap, making certain to give them the correct phrase so Benito wouldn't shoot anyone. Lev didn't sound happy, but he was cooperative, understanding, as no one else could be in the situation. He promised to get the children to safety and deal with the disaster aboard ship.

Maxim turned his attention to giving Airiana a crash course in breathing with a tank.

9

AIRIANA had never been so terrified in her life. She wanted to be back on the ship, fighting a dozen armed men rather than swimming in a dark, cold ocean in the dead of night. She wasn't a strong swimmer. She wasn't even a swimmer at all. She didn't go into the water. She'd never learned to swim. She might put her toes in the water, but never her face. And she didn't breathe into tanks. She didn't know how.

You're psyching yourself out again. Just breathe the way I showed you. There was a trace of amusement in his voice.

She didn't find anything funny about the situation at all. *This is insanity.*

It's an adventure. Just keep moving.

She didn't have a choice. He had tied them together, hooking a line from his belt to hers. He was a strong swimmer and was practically towing her through the water. She did her best not to panic, but every so often she couldn't remember how to breathe and he would stop and hold her, talking softly in her mind and showing her how until the panic subsided and she could use the equipment.

Are we almost there? She felt like a little child in the

family car asking every ten minutes when they'd arrive at their cross-country destination.

We've been in the water about ten minutes. You're asking me every ninety seconds. This time there was no mistaking the laughter.

There was no way that was true. She was certain they'd been *hours* in the water. She was so cold she couldn't stop shaking. And the terror didn't go away, it only increased the longer she was underwater.

I don't think you're funny. I want to surface. She knew she had a knife strapped to her suit and she was going to find the darn thing, cut herself loose and just swim without him to the surface.

She stopped kicking and felt her tool belt, searching for the knife. Instantly his hand clamped down on hers. She was always that little bit shocked at how strong he was. His arm circled her waist and he removed the knife from her hand.

Two more minutes, honey. That's it. I'm sorry I teased you. The sub's just ahead of us.

She clung to him for a moment, afraid she couldn't even last two more minutes. She just wanted to go home. To be in her house. Her bed. She wasn't the adventurous type.

Two minutes, Airiana. I promise.

She nodded her understanding and reluctantly let him go. He turned her in the direction they were swimming and set off again, using stronger strokes to cut through the water. She tried to do the same, mimicking his actions, struggling not to cry and to keep the air moving in her lungs. Her tendency was to try to hold her breath. It didn't help that tears clogged her throat and burned behind her eyes.

Can you see the lights just ahead?

She detested being such a baby. She should have learned to swim in spite of her mother's absolute panic every time they were near water. Marina had nearly drowned as a child and she'd never gotten over the fear. She'd never wanted Airiana to get even close to a large body of water.

I'm sorry, Maxim. I can't seem to overcome my fear of the water. She felt childish and silly beside a man who seemed to be able to do everything and do it well. *You don't seem to be afraid of anything.*

Of course I'm afraid. Maxim glanced at her.

She had no idea how afraid he was—of her, of what she was, of who she was. Meeting her and spending such an intense twenty-four hours with her had bound them together when already they had a strong connection. The thought of needing her, of craving her and becoming obsessed with her, was more terrifying to him than anything else he could imagine.

He could face anything, but caring about someone else to the extent he was beginning to care about Airiana was something so far out of his wheelhouse he wasn't certain what to do. She represented a home and family, and he had long ago, when he was a boy, lost those things.

Maxim?

Her voice was soft, brushing at the walls of his mind, finding its way into his heart. He knew weapons. He'd been shot and knifed and even tortured, but that soft voice was more powerful than any other threat he'd ever faced.

It's just ahead, honey. You can see the lights, he encouraged.

She stopped swimming abruptly, staring at the small submarine. *There's no air underwater, Maxim.*

That's not entirely true. There are gasses in the water and . . . He trailed off. She didn't need a science lesson and probably knew more than he did. *What's wrong?*

I can see patterns in the lights. There was fear in her voice. *You're an air element, can you see them?*

He could, and it didn't make him happy. *Yes. Stick close to me once we're on board. The sub will take us to rendezvous with a ship your father is on.*

The patterns suggest danger.

We're kind of used to that by now, aren't we? He kept his voice matter-of-fact.

He should have known that as an air element, she would

catch warnings as well. It was the last thing he wanted her to see. She'd been through too much, and she still had to meet her father and listen to his proposal.

All along Maxim had feared that Theodotus wouldn't take no for an answer from his daughter. He might love her in theory, in his mind, but he didn't know her, and when it came to his work, he could be utterly ruthless. Her father would have no qualms about taking her back to Russia with him. He wouldn't even consider it a betrayal. He'd convince himself it was best for her, that he could keep her safe. In reality, he'd be using her brilliance for his own gain.

That warning was for both of them. Keeping his promise to Airiana wasn't going to be easy. *We'll make it through this if you trust me. No matter what I do, trust me that I have your best interests at heart and that my goal is to get you back home, if that's your wish after speaking to your father.*

They were at the sub's hatch. He caught her wrist, holding her to him. Waiting. Her eyes searched his, there in the strange yellowish glow of the sub, behind the face mask. She nodded, slowly, almost reluctantly.

Maxim stayed very close to Airiana once aboard. They both stripped and he gave her the clothes he'd carried in the waterproof war bag that went with him nearly everywhere. She didn't protest that he didn't turn away from her as she tore the wet suit from her body. She didn't even look at him.

Airiana shook uncontrollably, and he took a towel and dried her body and hair as best he could before helping her into the soft sweats he'd brought along in her size, just for this purpose.

He dried himself off and then dressed, taking his time, giving her a chance to recover a bit before they faced anyone. When he was finished, he sank down onto the small built-in bench and pulled her into his arms, trying to warm her with his body heat.

"I'm exhausted," she admitted, and buried her face into his neck.

It was a sure sign of her weariness to actually allow him

to hold her again. She'd been withdrawn from him ever since he'd announced what a mistake he'd made connecting them together in the Prakenskii ritual. That was sacred, something they all knew one didn't ever do unless it was right and lasting.

He'd carelessly marked her, not ready for such a thing himself and uncertain of what would really happen. Now he knew. He just grew more obsessed with her. That—and caring more for her. He lifted her in his arms and took her through the hatch into the narrow passageway.

"Maxim." One of the few men he ever acknowledged he felt friendship toward greeted him. "Is she all right?"

Valentin Blatov was older than Maxim by a few years and he'd tried to look out for the younger boys in the training school. Maxim had learned to distrust anyone friendly very early on, but Valentin had proved to be the real thing, a rarity among those teaching or the older boys who were given orders to make the younger boys stronger.

"She doesn't swim, Valentin," Maxim admitted. "She needs a warm bed and maybe something hot to drink. A little food. She'll be good."

"We'll get under way immediately. Any trouble?"

"Nothing I couldn't handle." He liked Valentin, but that didn't mean he would trust those children to him—or to anyone else but his brothers.

Valentin took the war bag from his hand and led the way a short distance to another hatch. "It's as comfortable as we could make it. Quarters are small. We don't have much room."

"This is fine," Maxim said, and ducked a little to take Airiana inside. She hadn't lifted her head from where it was buried in his neck. He reached for the bag, blocking the hatch so Valentin couldn't step inside. "Thanks. If you could send us some hot drinks, Val, I'd really appreciate it."

Valentin nodded and turned to leave. Maxim closed the hatch and carried Airiana to the small bed. He only had to take three short steps. "Val wasn't kidding when he said there was little room. I hope you're not claustrophobic."

She sighed and lifted her head reluctantly. "If I am, I'll never admit it, not after you having to haul me through the water, with me forgetting how to use a tank every few minutes."

"You didn't forget, you panicked," he corrected.

"Yeah. Thanks for pointing that out. You don't have to be so literal." She scooted across the bed to the wall, drew up her knees and wrapped her arms around her legs, a position he was coming to know was comforting to her. She rested her chin on top of her knees and regarded him with her blue eyes.

"This can't be easy for you."

He shrugged. He didn't want her sympathy. He was the one who had kidnapped her from her home and taken her on a rather harrowing journey. He'd killed people in front of her and exposed her to a ruthless human trafficking ring. He'd even made her swim underwater when she was terrified.

"It's a job, Airiana. It's what I do."

"Quite frankly, Maxim, your job sucks." She kept her eyes glued to his. "Do you like what you do?"

"What the hell kind of question is that?" he snapped. He wanted to turn away, but it was impossible, he was already falling into all that blue.

"Aren't people supposed to like what they do?" She shrugged. "Is it so difficult to answer? You've obviously been doing this kind of work a long time, you're good at it, but is it what you want to do?"

"It's what I'm trained for. I'm more than good at it."

"That doesn't answer the question," she persisted.

"Damn it, Airiana, I don't have a choice. I'm not like other people, who can choose what they want to do. I was taken from my home as a child and trained to be a covert operative. I assassinate drug lords, heads of state, anyone my government wants out of their way. I kill people for a living. I seduce women and torture men. I climb into bed with the worst kind of depraved human beings in order to get close to my target. I turn a blind eye to victims, and when set on a path I don't stop until the job is done. That's my job, it's what I do, and it's who I am."

"Actually, it's not," Airiana said.

She didn't look in the least bit disturbed by his outburst. His voice had been low, but it was a whiplash, designed to stop all conversation. He couldn't believe he'd even admitted such things to her. By rights he should kill her and throw her in the sea to protect himself, his identity and his remaining brothers, who were still at risk.

She patted the spot on the bed beside her, those clear blue eyes beckoning him. "You're tired, Maxim. You may not recognize that you are, but I can see it. Come sit down and stop prowling like a caged tiger."

"You do realize that I kill people, Airiana. Being in the same room with me and baiting me isn't a very smart move."

She patted the bed again. "You're no danger to me and we both know it. Now you're the one being silly. Come sit down." She flashed a small, wan smile. "I won't bite you."

No, but she could see right through him, and that was far more dangerous than a bite. Fortunately someone banged on the hatch. He sent her one quelling look and pulled a pistol from his war bag. Standing to one side, he slowly opened the hatch, ready for anything.

"Don't shoot me, Max," Valentin said, and slowly stuck his head inside the cabin.

They had a code they always used. If they were alone and all was well, Maxim was "Max" and Valentin was "Val." Still, Maxim always remained cautious—and suspicious—it was what kept him alive.

Get the coffee, honey, and leave me a clear shot, just to be safe.

Airiana stood up without protest and took the two mugs of hot coffee from Valentin. "Thank you, I really need this," she said.

Valentin smiled at her and gave a small bow. "I'm Val, an old friend of Max's."

"Airiana," she said, and offered her hand.

Maxim's breath hissed out between his teeth. *Never let someone touch you like that. He could pull you into him and use you as a shield,* he reprimanded, his voice harsher than he intended. He'd forgotten how charming Valentin could be around women.

Valentin merely took Airiana's hand and raised it to his mouth. Maxim resisted pulling the trigger.

"You can leave any time, old friend," he snapped at Valentin.

The man grinned at him and held Airiana's hand a little bit too long—deliberately now that he knew he was getting to Maxim.

"I've got a gun," he felt compelled to point out.

Valentin burst out laughing, but he let go of Airiana and backed out of the room. Maxim resisted the urge to kick the hatch closed after him. Shoving the pistol in his belt at the small of his back, he took both coffee mugs from her and yanked her into his arms. She gave a startled little yelp. He didn't care. He bunched her thick hair in his fist and forced her to look up at him. Already his mouth was descending.

He kissed her long. Thoroughly. Over and over. Demanding compliance. He felt a bit like a drowning man going under for the last time, but it didn't matter. Nothing mattered but the feel of her slender body tight against him and the taste of her on his tongue, filling his body and soul with . . . her. Just her.

When he lifted his head, she blinked at him, her eyes a little glazed, her mouth swollen from his kisses, her breathing ragged. Both of her hands had found his shirt, clutching there for stability.

"What was that for?" she asked, touching her lips.

"For driving me mad. Get on the damn bed and drink your coffee."

She blinked again, those long feathery lashes that tempted him to start all over again, but she complied with his order, scooting back to the original position she favored. He handed her the coffee mug and sank down beside her, his back to the wall, his thigh pressed tight against hers.

She sipped at the hot liquid and leaned her head against his shoulder. "It's not who you are, Maxim, no matter what you say. Saying it doesn't make it so."

He turned his head to glare at her. She had her eyes closed, and she looked small and vulnerable, nestling into him for protection, if not comfort. He couldn't yell at her for wanting to save him. He could tell her it wasn't possible, but the truth was, he couldn't help the small thrill Airiana fighting for him gave him.

He took a drink of coffee to keep from kissing her. If he kissed her again, he wasn't going to stop and it wouldn't be fair to her. He would see this thing through and then he'd disappear.

"When you talk to me, mind to mind, I can see inside you. I also see the things you do and how those children affected you. You're not a killer, Maxim. Not at all. You kill, but that isn't who you are."

Her voice sounded drowsy, sexy. His body tightened. He wondered if he could be a rapist on top of all his other sins. "You're falling asleep."

"I don't want to. I have nightmares. Really bad nightmares. Do you?" She took another sip of coffee, more for warmth than the stimulant.

He wished he had nightmares. Maybe he'd feel more human. As it was he felt he'd lost all humanity years earlier and all that was left of him was a machine programmed to kill. "No." But he didn't sleep. And never with another person in the room with him. That would be far too dangerous.

"Just stop."

His eyebrow shot up. He looked down at her again. She hadn't opened her eyes. "Excuse me?"

"Your job. Just walk away from it. Levi and Thomas did. You could too. You don't need to do what they tell you if you don't like it—and clearly you don't. Everyone has a choice, Maxim, even you."

"Levi and Thomas disappeared because everyone believes them to be dead. If anyone realized they were still alive and living under an alias, ten hit men would show up and wipe out everyone on that farm. I can't very well add to the danger to everyone there, now can I?" And what would be the use of retiring if he didn't have a place to retire to—or someone to retire for?

As if she read his mind she turned her head and looked up at him. "You can do anything you want to do, Maxim." Her lashes fluttered again.

He took the mug from her hands and set it aside. At least she wasn't shaking anymore. "Lie down. You don't have to go to sleep, and I'll be here with you."

She simply shifted positions, using his thighs for her pillow, curling up into a little ball, her knees drawn up and her arms circling his thigh.

"What are you doing?"

"I'm making certain you're not going to leave me if I do fall asleep."

He stroked his hand through her hair, unable to stop himself. It was soft and silky and felt all too sensual against his bare palm. His entire body felt tight, hot and needy. He didn't mind in the least. It was a natural reaction to a woman—one that wasn't contrived or deliberate, but real— and that was the trouble with Airiana.

She was real to him. Flesh and blood. A person. He couldn't walk away from the emotions she stirred in him. He hadn't even realized he was capable of feeling the depths of positive emotions, or the intensity he did until he met her. He wanted to protect her, even from her own father. He was a patriot, and yet he wasn't going to allow his country to keep her prisoner.

He had a temper, boiling beneath the surface but held in check. That rage had never gone away. He closed his eyes, tangling his fingers in her hair, trying not to see the images of his mother's blood in the white snow, or hear the cries of the baby, Ilya, as the soldiers took him. He had told her the truth—he didn't have nightmares—but he slept lightly, and those memories of the soldiers tearing his family apart had never left him.

He knew each of them handled the loss in their own way. His way had been savage and relentless. Merciless. He found them, years later, when he was old enough and strong enough and trained enough. He cared little that they had been under orders. They had murdered his parents and taken his brothers from him.

That had been the first time he had ever run across his eldest brother, Viktor. Viktor had also hunted down the soldiers who had murdered their family, one by one, just as Maxim had done. Viktor had spent years finding each of the men and had systematically been killing them with accidents, nothing that could ever be traced back to the Prakenskii family or what had happened to them. He had bided his time, taking only a couple of them a year.

Viktor had been the one to teach him patience and how it didn't matter how long it took—if he was careful, he would triumph in the end. His brother hadn't wanted the men killed in a way that would point back to them, because more than anything, he wanted to find the man responsible for the orders. He wanted the man who had feared their father so much that he had ordered the murders for "political" reasons.

Maxim and Viktor were careful never to meet in person after that. The brothers had a way to get messages to one another, but the man behind their father's murder had so much power, they knew he would use them against one another given the opportunity.

"Who's Viktor?" Airiana murmured without opening her eyes.

The question startled Maxim. His hand paused the long, stroking caresses in her hair. "Why do you ask?" he said carefully.

"You were so deep in thought the name just appeared in my head." She hesitated, clearly weighing how much to tell him. "Along with images."

"What images?"

She turned her head and opened her eyes. "Your parents

were murdered just like my mother was. There was snow. A child was crying. You were boys and all of you fought, trying to get to the youngest, but they took him away."

His throat felt clogged for a moment. "They separated us. They feared us as individuals, so you can imagine how terrified they were of us being together. I think the original idea was to kill us, but then someone decided we could be useful if we were trained properly and our loyalties were to the man handing out the orders."

She lifted her head and pressed a kiss against his thigh before lying back down. His heart gave a peculiar leap and stuttered for just a moment as if that kiss had sent an electrical charge right through the material of his trousers, into his skin and through his bloodstream, straight to his beating heart.

The gesture wasn't in the least sensual—or meant to be flirtatious. She was offering him comfort. Caring. She offered him something he hadn't had before, not since his mother died. There was a part of him that wanted to push her away from him, the threat to him all too real. The other part wanted to gather her closer and hold her to him, to let himself believe his life could be different with her in it.

"Viktor was my oldest brother."

"Is he still alive?"

Her hand began a slow rub along his thigh. He'd never been so aware of another human being—or his own body—in his life.

"I don't know." It was true and yet not the truth. The last time he'd had contact with Viktor had been weeks earlier, but he was deep undercover and that meant he could be killed any time.

She sighed. "Your life is sad, Maxim. I thought my life was sad, and that I could never pick up the pieces and start fresh, but then I met these five wonderful women. They changed my life. They changed me."

She looked up at him with those startling blue eyes. Midnight blue now. Dark and mysterious. Eyes a man might get lost in forever.

"You could come home with me. Sea Haven is a magical place and people accept who you are. You can start fresh there."

"I'm not a puppy, Airiana. You can't just bring me home."

"Why not? Why can't I? You need a place to start over. You saved me from those awful men. You saved the children. Why can't I save you?"

"I would want a hell of a lot more from you than a puppy would want," he snapped. "Damn it, just go to sleep. You're driving me crazy. Do you realize the position you're in? You're here alone with me and you're all but offering yourself to me. At least that's how it looks from where I am. You can't do things like that."

The warning tumbled out before he could stop it. She really was driving him absolutely mad. What was she thinking, telling him he could come home with her? She didn't know a thing about him. She might be the most intelligent woman on the planet but she had no common sense at all.

"Maxim."

Just his name. Just like before. In that soft, velvet voice that suggested candlelight and silk. Or maybe it was all him and he just wanted to hear her that way.

"Don't, Airiana, I'm telling you it isn't safe."

"And I'm telling you that *you're* safe. No one is going to hurt you. Not like that. Not if I can help it." She sat up, coming up on her knees and framing his face with both hands. "I don't know why I feel this way about you. It's strong and real, and even if you don't feel the same way, that doesn't stop how I feel."

He started to pull away, but couldn't make himself do it. It was far too tempting to fall into her eyes even further.

"You don't want to be close to anyone or chance having a family because someone took it from you. I know that feeling. My sisters know that feeling. The pain. The rage. The fear of ever feeling such raw pain again. But I won't let it happen to you. I'll keep you safe there, Maxim. Don't go back to this life. Come home with me and just try to live. Find a way to live. It's a choice."

He drew in a breath when he was certain there was no more air in the room. "Do you know what you're offering? Airiana, you can't tempt a man like me."

"Why not? You deserve to live a life, a real one, Maxim."

"Because if you were mine, I'd never let you go. I'd hold on to you with the very last breath in my body. You're a free spirit, soaring high above me. You're wild, like the wind, and the wind can't be caged."

"Everything I do is a choice I make for myself. You're my choice."

He shook his head. "Don't you know anything at all about yourself? Or about men? Especially a man like me? You're that woman. The real thing, the kind a man dreams of, or in my case, doesn't dare let himself dream of. Men like me, we don't have families."

"Your father did. Your brothers do. Once I asked you what you were afraid of. What is it? Tell me?"

"I'm afraid of you. Of what you could do to me. I would be so afraid of losing you I'd hold on too tight and drive you away from me."

She laughed softly. "Listen to yourself. That isn't even logical. You fling yourself into the middle of a gun battle without wincing, but you're afraid to come home and just try living a quiet, peaceful life? Are you certain you're not making up excuses and you really do love what you do? My mother used to say, better the devil you know than the one you don't. I say if you're living with the devil, kick him out and find something different."

"Have you ever considered that I *am* the devil?"

She dropped her hands and shrugged. "Courage is reaching for something different, something unknown. One has to try, Maxim. If you don't, you'll never know what could have been."

That brought him up short. "Do you think I'm rejecting your offer because I'm afraid of a different life? If I came to that farm and stayed with you, you'd be in danger every minute of every day."

Airiana shrugged. "All of us on the farm have lived with danger. We're used to it. The thing is, Maxim, I'm only offering once. If you don't want to be with me, if taking the chance isn't worth it to you, then you don't belong with me."

"It isn't about that and you know it," he replied in a low tone. Why was he refusing when everything in him told him she could change his life, make him into a better man, make living worthwhile. "You can't just change who you are, Airiana. I've done things I can't take back."

"I used to think I was the worst person on the face of the earth—that I got my mother killed—and I still struggle with that at times. But I'm worth something, and I deserve a happy life. I've learned happiness is a choice. Only I can make that choice for myself. I am not going to allow the things I can't control to ruin my life. I choose to be happy, and no matter what life throws at me, that is always going to be my choice."

Maxim reached for her, settling his fingers around the nape of her neck, a neck he could break so easily. She made perfect sense and yet didn't. His life was complicated. The way he felt about her was even more so. She confused him, offering him a future he'd never considered.

He was used to protecting the small part of him that still recognized humanity. He had always protected his brothers. His every instinct told him to protect this woman—from herself if necessary.

"You're beautiful." She was physically beautiful, but it was more than that. She was bright on the inside, shining at him through her blue eyes. "I want you for myself." The admission was difficult for him, but if she was willing to put herself out there, he refused to be a coward. "I want to make certain you're always safe. I don't necessarily think those two things are mutually agreeable."

His thumb caressed the soft, silky skin along her neck.

She didn't pull away, but he saw the hurt of rejection in her eyes just before her lashes swept down.

"Don't, Airiana," he whispered, pulling her into his arms. "Don't feel like that. I'm not making excuses. My world is a reality."

She leaned into him, allowing him to enfold her in his arms. "Of course you're making excuses, Maxim. The sad thing is, you believe them. Love is risky. You can lose everything, there's no question about that. We barely know one another."

He closed his eyes and inhaled her. Images of her moving through the ship, the assault rifle steady in her hands, her bright hair tucked up in that silly strip of his shirt, went through his mind. She was risking everything telling him she wanted him, and he could give her . . . nothing. But he would never get her out of his mind or his heart.

"Don't feel sorry for me—I'm not going to wither and die because you choose to stay in this life. It's what you know, and obviously it's more comfortable for you. Who knows, you could be absolutely bored on the farm. It isn't like any of us lead wild lives."

He didn't reply, but stroked her thick platinum hair, allowing it to slide through his fingers. He wasn't feeling sorry for her, more like for himself. She seemed wild and free, a spirit soaring in the clouds not grounded on earth. Some man would come along . . .

His mind slammed that door shut fast and hard. The thought of her with another man made him feel— murderous. She snuggled into him, her head over his heart, her arm around his waist, holding him close to her.

There was no pouting. No protesting. No embarrassment. Airiana accepted that he felt he couldn't be with her, and that left him empty. Lonely. He'd never acknowledged either of those emotions before. He lived. He worked. His way of life just was. Suddenly, she'd changed everything, and now his life didn't seem much at all.

He listened to the sound of her breathing and knew the

exact moment when she fell asleep. He had to think about the things she'd said. He had never feared dying, in some ways it would have been a relief. He knew only pain. Heartache. He went through life alone. He faced death alone. It was easier that way.

But she had brought the unexpected. With her asleep he could admit to himself that the need to protect her, the overwhelming emotion he felt each time he looked at her, had to be love. He wouldn't know or recognize the emotion right away. He didn't remember love.

He was afraid Airiana had found her way inside of him and wrapped herself tightly around his heart. He was terribly afraid that love had taken hold and there was no way to remove it. He felt different around her, even in the midst of danger.

He thought to protect himself from pain by separating himself from her, but the feeling inside of him was so deep and strong it wasn't going to go away. It was there to stay. No matter how far he ran from her, where he traveled or what he did, she would be there with him.

Airiana was unexpected. She had exposed his weakness to him. A slip of a woman, and she'd shown more courage than he had. He'd known only loneliness, and he was comfortable in that world. He never wanted to feel the pain of losing a family again, and she'd exposed that as well. She made him vulnerable and he hadn't been able to accept that.

That was what love was. Being vulnerable. Airiana had showed him the way, left him a clear, marked path, and he'd just left her exposed. All along he had asked for her trust when she had no reason to give it to him—and she had. There was no way to hide from himself any longer. She had asked him to trust her, and he'd refused. What kind of man was he? He wanted to be that man for her. The one who would climb impossible mountains and face a future with her no matter what it held.

He bent his head and put his mouth against her ear. He

didn't say the words aloud. He couldn't. What he felt was too personal. Too strong. *Show me the way out, honey. Show me how to love you.*

Her breathing remained slow and even as it was meant to. There was a part of him that recognized he was angry with her for making him fall so hard, so fast. For offering him a way out, something he would think about endlessly. She had made certain he would feel every lonely moment without her for the rest of his life. Worse, she actually had made him question his motives.

10

THEODOTUS Solovyov was a big bear of a man with a bushy beard and piercing blue eyes behind glasses that sat low on his nose. He caught Airiana's face in his hands and kissed both cheeks before she could pull away. He didn't seem to notice her discomfort but turned to Maxim and pumped his hand enthusiastically.

"You did it. You brought my daughter to me. How can I ever thank you?"

How could I possibly be his daughter, Maxim? Look at him. Look at me.

Theodotus dwarfed Airiana. He made two of her easily.

Look at his eyes. Really look at them. You have your mother's build—and his mother's. But you have his eyes.

She didn't want it to be true. She felt nothing at all for Solovyov. If he had loved her mother so much, why didn't he leave his wife, who by all accounts was treacherous, and take care of Marina and his daughter? As Russian's top physicist, it stood to reason that even if his wife, Elena, had political clout, he would have even more. She didn't understand why Maxim and Gavriil didn't get that.

Theodotus reached for her again, and she stepped back,

slipping behind the long, ornate table. The yacht was a luxury vessel and equipped with every modern convenience.

"Why did you bring me here? I was kidnapped and taken from my home and family," Airiana said. "If you're my father as you claim, and I'm not convinced you are, why didn't you simply write to me or pick up a phone and say you're coming to visit?"

She didn't look at Maxim. She didn't want to see if he approved or didn't approve. He'd said to trust him no matter what happened, and she would, but she would also rely on herself—her own judgment. She had questions, and the answers had to be satisfactory or she was going to be the most uncooperative daughter Solovyov had ever met.

Theodotus smiled and nearly rubbed his hands together. "You're definitely my daughter. No one has ever dared push me around, other than your mother. So young. So sad. She had no direction in spite of her brilliance."

Airiana's chin went up. "My mother was a wonderful, intelligent person."

"Yes, yes, of course she was. I loved her very much. Her mind was . . . extraordinary." Theodotus turned to the liquor cabinet and pulled out a bottle of Scotch. He looked at Maxim and raised his eyebrow.

Maxim shook his head.

"Oh, surely this one time, you can dispense with your no drinking rule. We're safe now and my daughter is home. Have a drink with me."

"No thank you, sir," Maxim said, his voice firm.

Theodotus sighed. "You really must learn to have fun." He held up the bottle of Scotch. It was nearly empty. The physicist shoved that bottle beneath the bar and pulled out another full one to pour himself a drink and waved his hand at the two of them to take a seat.

Airiana took the chair facing the couch, not wanting to sit too close to either man. If Theodotus had loved her mother, he certainly hadn't felt deeply for her. "When was the last time you spoke to my mother? Or wrote to her? I didn't find any letters from you in her things."

"Well, of course not. We had to be careful. She burned them."

"She burned the letters from the man she loved all these years and remained faithful tò, but you didn't burn yours? Maxim informed me that you had letters from Marina. You had a wife who could find them. Why didn't you burn them?"

"I couldn't bear to let go of them. She had you. I had my letters." Theodotus took another drink of the Scotch. "Elena never came to my office or my laboratory. She preferred a far more luxurious environment. I have several photographs of you Marinochka sent as you were growing up."

"When did you last have contact with *Marina*?" Airiana persisted, emphasizing the name she knew her mother by.

Where is this going? I saw the letters and pictures. You were a teen, the last picture he showed me, although you looked very young. A mop of white hair and a long skirt and matching vest.

She'd been fourteen in that picture. She remembered the skirt. Marina had sewn it for her. She loved the fabric, and her mother had made the outfit for her birthday. She felt very elegant in it, and they'd gone out to dinner, a rare occurrence for them. It had been a wonderful night. They'd gone to the mall and had their pictures taken together in one of the machines. It had been a fun night she'd always remember. She still had the outfit her mother had made for her.

Airiana, what is it? Maxim asked.

She pulled her knees up to her chest and wrapped her arms around them tightly, setting her chin on top. She felt safer drawn in as she was. She kept her eyes glued to Solovyov's face.

He shrugged. "You were a teenager. A couple of years before she died."

"Before she was murdered," Airiana corrected.

He had nothing to do with that. You know your neighbor most likely killed her.

"Yes, of course." Theodotus shuddered visibly. "She was murdered. It was so terrible. We'd stopped communicating. We thought it was getting too dangerous."

She didn't bother to answer Maxim. What would be the point? He wanted to believe Solovyov, but certain things didn't add up.

"Why would you think it was dangerous after fourteen years of communication?"

Theodotus frowned. "I don't think you could possibly understand the politics and unrest in our country. There was turmoil and intrigue and everyone walked a fine line."

"I happen to be extremely intelligent," Airiana said, forcing herself to keep sarcasm from her tone. "I doubt if I have a problem comprehending anything. You could have left Elena, but you didn't. You can't pretend she would be more valued or powerful than you in your position."

"No," Theodotus admitted. "I've never said that, only that she was very dangerous, and had tentacles into the underworld she had no problem using. She tried to have me killed. She would have tried to kill Marinochka and you had she known about you."

"After all those years?"

"You didn't know Elena. She was extremely vindictive. She didn't want me as a man, but she wanted the prestige of being my wife. She had her parties and her friends, but she maintained her connections with unsavory people just so she could frighten anyone who crossed her. And yes, I was afraid of her. More than anyone, I knew the lengths she'd go to."

"And yet you dared to have an affair."

Theodotus pressed his fingers to his eyes as if his head was beginning to throb. "Yes. I couldn't help myself. As I said, Marinochka was extraordinary. We talked for hours. She always had a perspective on subjects I hadn't considered. She was young and enthusiastic. She made me more open-minded and expanded my thinking." He closed his eyes briefly. "She made me laugh. She had a wonderful sense of humor."

It was the first time Airiana believed him, and it made her uneasy. All along she hadn't really believed this man could be her father. She thought perhaps it was an elaborate setup to get her to defect, or to get information from her. No one was that good of an actor. Theodotus actually looked older, sad and regretful. He wasn't looking straight at her, but off across the room.

"She did have an exceptional sense of humor," Airiana conceded.

"She made me feel young and as if I could live again." Theodotus took a long swallow of the Scotch and shook his head. "We didn't expect a baby to come along. Marinochka had no family, and I asked a mutual friend to put an apartment for her in his name. She couldn't stay at the school."

Airiana was certain the things he was saying now were true. He had known her mother, and she probably was his daughter.

"We talked about what to do. Both of us knew you couldn't stay in the country, but it was important to us that you were born in our beloved country and bear my name. By that time, I'd talked to Marinochka about Elena and her family and she knew the danger to you. One of Elena's brothers was part of the Russian mob and another was very high in the ruling party."

She glanced sideways at Maxim. He would know the truth. His nod was nearly imperceptible. Knots formed in her stomach. More and more she was coming to believe that at least part of Solovyov's story was the truth. Wasn't that the best way to convince someone everything you said was true? To mix in portions of fact?

She looked around the opulent room. Theodotus could certainly afford to travel in style. Who had paid for the submarine? And Maxim didn't come cheap, she was certain of that. Did physicists in Russia make millions?

"Why didn't you just get in touch with me," she repeated, insisting on an answer.

Theodotus sighed. "I received word that you were in danger. Years ago, your mother sent to me the rudiments of a project you were working on. I recognized the brilliance and potential and it became the foundation for work that I was doing here. Unfortunately, Elena had her ways of getting information and she found out . . ."

"What ways?" Airiana demanded. *Was she trained to extract information using sex?* She couldn't help the small glare she shot Maxim. She had tried not to be hurt by his rejection, but still, he sat there, looking masculine and invincible, a man, not a boy, and everything in her responded to him. She didn't seem to affect him in the least.

Elena was no agent, Maxim denied, his voice even. *She was connected and she used everyone around her to get what she wanted.*

"She was able to seduce one of my assistants and he used hidden cameras to take information to her." Theodotus sighed again. "I understand your need to question me, I expected it, of course, but I didn't realize your refusal to believe me would hurt."

"It isn't that I don't believe you. I'm beginning to think I could possibly be your daughter and that what you've said about my mother and your relationship with her is true. But did you expect me to take this all at face value? Especially when my mother was murdered? The agents discovered that Mom was communicating with someone here in Russia and they believed her to be a traitor."

For the first time, Theodotus looked angry. *There he is. The real Theodotus Solovyov. He is not quite as easygoing about all this as he pretends. He doesn't like to be questioned.*

He is a man of great importance in our country. He has a certain stature and I'm certain few ever question him.

Exactly. If he went to his party and said his wife was a traitor and carrying on affairs and threatening him, they would have found a way to dispose of her. You know that. It's what you do. How many times has such a request been made from men with less political clout? And look around you, Maxim. Who is paying for all this?

Your father is a wealthy man.

*Surely you can see what Solovyov truly wants. He might
have been curious about me. He may have really had feelings for Marina. But ultimately, men like Solovyov are all
about work. They can't ever stop, even if they know a
weapon they're developing will destroy the entire world.
He's like that.*

"Marinochka was no traitor. She was a citizen of Russia,
just as you are. She committed no crime in telling me of
our daughter's school projects. No money exchanged hands.
She loved her country, and she loved me."

"Why did you really stop communicating with her then?
I was fourteen years old and my projects were really beginning to take off. What made you stop?"

"I told you. It was becoming far too dangerous."

She leaned toward him, looking him straight in the eye.
"It became dangerous because she was lonely and wanted
to go home to you. She wanted to be with you. When you
said no, she began drinking. That's what really happened,
isn't it?"

She'd taken a stab in the dark, but it wasn't that huge of
a leap. She knew her mother. Marina had been a romantic,
and if she had been rejected by the secret love of her life,
her illusions about him would have been shattered. She
truly was gifted. She was intelligent and she would have
come to realize that he'd been using her to gain information
on Airiana's work.

She'd stopped asking. Stopped discussing. She'd withdrawn from her daughter and begun drinking heavily. Airiana had always blamed herself, that she wasn't paying
enough attention, but it would be like her mother to punish
herself for believing in Solovyov for so many years. She
must have been devastated.

"Of course I couldn't allow her to return. Elena would
have had her killed immediately. Both of you. I couldn't
allow that to happen."

"You stopped communicating with her when I no longer
shared information on the project I was working on with
her, didn't you?" It was another shrewd guess. More than

anything, Marina would have wanted to protect Airiana, and her daughter had sworn an oath not to reveal to anyone the nature of her work when she'd turned fourteen. Marina had respected that oath, and had never asked her to discuss the work again.

"It was for your protection. Both of you. The timing had nothing to do with it. This is getting us nowhere." In a sudden fit of anger, Theodotus threw the crystal Scotch glass against the wall. It shattered into many pieces.

"I agree. I'd like to go home now," Airiana said, without looking at Maxim.

"I am taking you home. You're Russian, and no daughter of mine will be working for another country." Theodotus stood up and took a threatening step toward her as if that might intimidate her into submission.

Airiana didn't move, continuing to watch him the way a mouse might a snake—except she had a secret weapon, and she felt rather smug about it. Theodotus might *think* Maxim was on his side, but she *knew* he was on hers. He couldn't hide his aura from her, and he'd suddenly gone very dangerous, sitting there silently, coiled like a real cobra might be, watching his prey through narrow, hooded eyes. He hadn't taken his gaze from Theodotus, not once he'd stood up. He hadn't even blinked.

"I'm an adult, not a child," she reminded. "I have no intention of being bullied into working for any country, Russia or the United States. I haven't done that kind of work in years nor do I have any intention of doing so."

"How dare you throw away your mind. You were put here to serve a greater purpose. You don't just decide not to use the kind of genius you have because you don't want to anymore. That isn't your choice to make. Do you think I wanted to be Theodotus Solovyov?" His voice swelled, and he smashed his fist over his heart dramatically. "No. I wanted a simple life, but I was given genius and I use it for the good of my country."

Airiana nodded as if in agreement. "I can see that you're very passionate about your work, but I won't help you. I won't. I haven't worked on that project since my mother was killed."

"You live in the same vicinity as Damon Wilder. Did you think we wouldn't keep tabs on you?"

"As my father? Or as a physicist? And who is 'we'? The Russian government?"

"Both as your father and as a loyal patriot. I think you need to go rest. There isn't anything more to say, Airiana. I certainly hope you think about this and come to the right conclusion that you're better off with people who love you and can protect you."

Airiana let out her breath slowly. She was better off with people who loved her. Theodotus wasn't one of them. She honestly didn't think he was a bad person, but his work definitely consumed him and he had lost his research data. He needed her to help him recover his work. She was certain of that. This wasn't about saving her, although her father had certainly done that—she couldn't pretend he hadn't—but he had reasons other than paternal love.

"Why now, Theodotus? What's happening that I don't know about that has made everyone suddenly come looking for me? The man who owns that shipping company, the one who hired Maxim to kidnap me in the first place with his other goons, he really went to great lengths to acquire me. Damon Wilder was on his way to visit me for the first time. We've never so much as exchanged more than a hello. And you. After all these years, you've suddenly come looking. What is it you all think I can give you?"

Theodotus suddenly smiled, visibly relaxing. "You do have a superior brain, my little Airi. You inherited the best of your parents. I should have known that in spite of being under duress, you would still begin to figure things out."

He poured himself another drink, ignoring the shards of glass scattered across the Persian rug, and turned back to her, beaming. He saluted her with the glass. "You will be such an asset to me, my daughter. To my work. To our work. You are needed, and having you by my side, working with me, we'll be able to sort this problem out in no time."

"You haven't told me the problem," Airiana pointed out, infusing her voice with curiosity. The truth was, she couldn't help but wonder why all the sudden interest in her.

If she could read Theodotus, she was certain Maxim could as well, but still, she was certain her father wouldn't continue with Maxim in the room if he thought too much about it. His work was always shrouded in secrecy.

Right now he was trying to impress Airiana, and keep her interested, certain she really was like him and her brain would need to figure out whatever puzzle he had for her. Having Maxim close allowed him two things. First, he believed his daughter had bonded with her "savior" and was grateful to him to be alive. Second, should she continue to balk, Theodotus was certain he could rely on Maxim to keep her in line.

The very scary thing was—he was right. Already her mind was going over her old project, building on it, as it had for the last several years. She had stopped working on it with others, but there had been no real way to stop. She wasn't all that different from Solovyov—her brain demanded work and once set in a direction, she couldn't stop the need to continue.

Theodotus went to the bar again. "Is there something I can get you, Airi?"

She winced. No one had called her Airi but her mother. She didn't like Theodotus calling her by the name her mother did. Sometimes, on the farm, the others shortened her name to Airia, but never Airi. In some ways his calling her by her mother's preferred nickname reinforced the idea that he was her father—Marina would have referred to her that way.

"Water, if you don't mind. And if you can get it for me, a cup of hot tea with milk." She tried to sound friendlier. She didn't want to be locked up.

"Of course. Tea. Marinochka loved her tea. I should have remembered." Now that Airiana appeared more cooperative, Theodotus was in a jovial mood. He called for hot tea and poured her water.

Handing her the glass, he raised his own. "To us. May

we be the ones to solve this problem." She saluted him and took a small sip of water, watching him carefully.

Maxim hadn't moved a muscle, almost disappearing into the background. She realized it was a gift of his, fading his presence, using air to blur himself so that one could barely comprehend he was around. She was utterly aware of him at all times, even to the point that she knew every breath he drew. His gift didn't work on her, but she knew Theodotus had nearly forgotten his presence.

"Your wonderful idea, the saving of our planet using weather patterns, was quite brilliant, Airiana. Your study was mainly of the ice floes, but to be able to see a problem developing and stop it before the damage was too extensive had merit. You pointed out how it could be used against hurricanes and tornadoes, both caused by weather. Have you continued to work through your theories?"

"It's easy enough to see patterns developing," Airiana said. She hadn't spoken to anyone in years about her ideas and the temptation was nearly overwhelming. "I've thought about it, of course," she conceded, knowing he wouldn't believe her if she didn't admit at least that much, "but of course I stopped working on it long ago."

"I was able to take the rudiments of your earlier ideas and use them for a greater purpose. Can you imagine using the weather itself as a defense against an attack by other countries? You wouldn't need weapons of mass destruction that would ruin the planet for hundreds—perhaps thousands of years." Theodotus sank into his chair and leaned toward her eagerly.

Airiana closed her eyes briefly. She had known all along that both Russia and the United States had probably twisted what she considered changing the world for the better into some kind of weapon. She'd been a child with a giant's mind, playing in a playroom and believing she could make the world a better place. No matter what kinds of ideas she came up with to help the planet and help countries with droughts and severe weather, of course those things had been twisted to make them destructive.

"Why the sudden interest in me," she persisted. "If you completed your work, you don't need me."

"My work was stolen by my bitch of a wife when she tried to have me killed," Theodotus admitted. "I've re-created some of it."

Airiana's heart began to beat faster. "That's not the problem though, is it? With time you'd figure it out without me. Why am I here?"

"It didn't work. It never worked. And it should have."

She frowned. "Of course it worked. The patterns are so easy to spot. Anyone could see them and create new ones, it isn't at all difficult . . ." she trailed off when Theodotus's face grew dark and looked like thunder.

You're an air element, Maxim reminded. *Weather is part of air. You see the patterns easily because you're bound to air.*

It's all about numbers.

No, it's all about being bound to air, Maxim corrected. *He can study weather patterns and make an educated guess, just like everyone else, but he can't see them. There's a big difference.*

"We need you to figure out why this defense system isn't working," Theodotus said. "We've used computers to compile the data on the weather and we still can't make it work. There's been a threat to our country and we have to know we can defend ourselves from such an attack."

Airiana sat up straighter. "What do you mean, a threat? What kind of threat?"

"We received an impossible demand and with it a computer simulation of weather being used to destroy our cities. Hurricanes and tornadoes. Droughts."

"In other words, your defense system against other countries." It took great effort not to glance at Maxim. There was a bad taste in her mouth she couldn't get rid of. She was beginning to be very afraid. Damon Wilder had called to talk to her right before she'd been kidnapped. Had the United States received a similar threat?

A knock at the door sent her heart pounding. Theodotus

called out an order, and a man entered with a tray, carrying a small teapot and cup. As the door opened, from her line of vision, she caught a glimpse of three men, heavily armed. They looked nervous, and one glanced inside—not at her—and not at Theodotus. He seemed to be looking for someone else.

Click. Click. The pieces began to fall into place. She'd been wrong all along, thinking Theodotus had viewed Maxim as brainless muscle and was willing to talk in front of him. He was talking openly because Maxim wasn't going to leave the room alive. That bad taste in her mouth got worse. Theodotus had offered Maxim a drink, even insisted he drink. When he'd steadfastly refused, he'd taken the bottle of Scotch and placed it under the bar, taking a new bottle to pour himself a drink.

You're part of the deal, Maxim. All this, the yacht, the luxury, the submarine, it was all provided for him so he could use you to get to me and then kill you. There are three heavily armed men outside, maybe more, and they aren't there for me. Theodotus betrayed you and your brother.

The man, dressed all in white, set the tray carefully on the table beside her chair and poured the tea in the cup for her, adding milk. She couldn't help but notice that he looked around the room for Maxim. He had to look twice before he saw him standing just behind the chair she was sitting in.

I knew the moment I saw this yacht that there had to be someone else's hand in all of this, honey, he answered, his voice as steady as ever. *Sorbacov was very powerful when I was a child attending his schools, but his sins have caught up with him. His son wants his crimes swept under the carpet, so to speak. We're part of that shameful past. I knew they had already put hits out on some of my brothers. We're their biggest threat. It was only a matter of time. The moment Theodotus offered me a drink of Scotch and so cleverly switched bottles, I knew he was a part of it.*

Your brother saved Theodotus's life at a great cost to

himself. You came to help him when your brother passed on the threat to me, and yet he still betrayed you. I want to push him overboard.

She did. She really wanted to shove Theodotus into the cold seawater and just leave him there. He had strung her mother along for years, and dumped her when Marina was no longer passing him information he could use in his work. Now, after Maxim had helped him, he was willing to sacrifice him as well.

Theodotus waited until the waiter left the room and Airiana had taken her first few sips of hot tea before he began again. "This threat is very real, Airi. We know it can be done, because you did it."

"Did you actually get the defense system working even once?" Airiana asked. "Because if you did, perhaps these people have your work."

"In computer-generated models only. In theory it would function, but no matter how often I tried to test it in the field, I couldn't get it to work. It was very frustrating."

"And you used computer-generated patterns of weather?" She chewed on her bottom lip, trying to see the entire problem in her head. It should have been easy enough.

He nodded. "But there were always more variables we couldn't factor in until it was too late. The chaos theory at work."

"You think this person—this terrorist—has the ability to do what you couldn't? You're arguably one of the greatest minds alive today. Who has that ability?"

Theodotus looked pleased. Her compliment had been deliberately offhand as if she was simply stating a fact— which she was. There was no overlooking the fact that he had an amazing brain. Who could have completed his work? And how had they gotten the platform to begin with?

I believe there's a collective universal pool of ideas and that often it seems creative minds draw the same idea at the same time from that pool. In order to complete the weather weapon, and Theodotus failed because he couldn't do it with computer-generated patterns, whoever sent the threat would have to be an air element. How many can there be in the world? She forced herself not to look at Maxim.

If the threat is real.

What do you mean? That he's making it all up to get me to go with him? Damon Wilder made an appointment to see me and he's never even acknowledged me before. My guess is the United States received the same threat.

That still doesn't mean it's real. Solovyov believed he had the weapon wrapped up, but he couldn't make it work. My guess is it was the same for Wilder. What makes you think this terrorist can make it work?

We have to go on the premise that he can.

If he could, why would he need you?

"I have tried myself to think who would have the brilliance for such a thing, only a handful to be sure," Theodotus said, without a shred of modesty.

I was told the microchip containing Theodotus's work was destroyed.

But they had the rudiments already, didn't they? Wanda tortured your mother and extracted the information of your early beginnings from her. They had that much to go on.

Airiana tried not to wince when he reminded her of Wanda, a trusted neighbor, torturing her mother for information. *Who?*

I think Stavros Gratsos began the research and tried to get the more advanced work from Theodotus's wife. When that failed and he died when his yacht went down, his brother, Evan, inherited everything. If it's at all possible, he's far worse than Stavros. Imagine his shock when he discovered the ideas for such a weapon. He tried for the microchip, and when that failed, he went after you. That's why Wanda was in his employ, he found her through her connection to Stavros. She's the kind of person men like Evan and Stavros want to keep around them.

"Theodotus, is it possible the reason you were tipped off that I was in jeopardy is because whoever the terrorist is really can't use the weapon at all? That he believed he could kidnap me and force me to get it working?"

She kept her eyes on his face, watching him, waiting to see if he would lie to her. Of course he believed no one else had gotten the weather weapon to actually work. It wouldn't occur to him that another person could be smarter than him and figure out whatever element was missing—unless it was his own flesh and blood. He would glory in the fact that he'd created Airiana and ultimately had a hand in everything she accomplished.

"You may be right, Airi. That would make sense, wouldn't it? Or it is possible you are the threat to him, the only threat, and he wants you dead."

If he'd wanted you dead, that would have been his order, Maxim pointed out.

Clearly.

Airiana sipped at her tea, settling back in her chair, trying to look more relaxed. "I don't think he could figure it out, Theodotus, not if you couldn't." She yawned deliberately. "This tea is wonderful. I feel as if I can think again. I was so exhausted and freezing cold." She wanted to imply that earlier, when she'd argued with him, she hadn't been at her best. She wanted him relaxed, his guard down just enough that they could get the upper hand.

"Good. Good."

We're going to have to make our move soon, Maxim. He's going to call those men in as soon as he has me leave this room.

I'm figuring our best course of action.

I can bring in a hurricane at sea, she offered with a small inner smile.

I don't want to go down with the ship. We'll do it the old-fashioned way.

Kill everyone? She was beginning to feel a little bloodthirsty herself. How did people like Theodotus get away with everything? He felt superior and entitled. To make matters worse, he was treated as if he *was* both superior and entitled. Once in a great while, humanity crept in, but it was gone just as fast, because he considered his needs to be so much more important than anyone else's.

You're a woman after my own heart.

She ducked her head and took another drink of tea. She had no idea love could come so fast. She didn't know if it was the circumstances or the connection from her palm to his, but he owned her heart. She rarely felt even a tingle of arousal for men she met, yet just looking at Maxim could make erotic images play through her mind.

She accepted him the way he was. He wasn't the man to settle down in peace on a farm with her and four children who were scarred for life. He would need to roam, and she needed roots. Still, he was as bound to her as the air surrounding them was.

She felt a little smug about that. Theodotus had no idea, and perhaps Maxim didn't know to what extent they were attached, but she did. She had complete faith that he would always be on her side.

"Perhaps you did save my life," she conceded, lulling Theodotus further.

"A trusted friend tipped me off that you were targeted for kidnapping and he sent Maxim to me."

Airiana put her teacup down carefully. That had been her first real mistake. She'd drawn attention to Maxim, and they weren't ready to make their move. She couldn't allow Theodotus to call the armed men into the den. Maxim wouldn't endanger her, not in such close quarters.

On the other hand, Theodotus should never have mentioned his "trusted friend"—obviously Gavriil—the friend who had saved his life, the one he was betraying by conspiring to kill Maxim. She wasn't looking at Maxim, but she felt that rush of anger he kept hidden deep where no one else could ever see. It was more than anger, a rage against men like Solovyov who so easily could dispose of others when they were in his way.

Airiana stood up and stretched, keeping Theodotus looking at her. "Do you have any ideas at all who our enemy could be? It would be helpful if we knew him." She wandered around the room, casually picking up items and putting them back down, making her way toward the bar where Theodotus had broken his glass.

What are you doing?

There was a warning in Maxim's tone she ignored. Someone had to save him. She knew he would never fight them with her near, and she wasn't about to let Theodotus kill him. She was certain they would do so immediately. What would be the point of keeping him alive? He was far too dangerous.

Saving your ass. After all, you saved mine.

"There was a man, Dennet Laurent, he was French. He had an amazing mind, astounding in his abilities and thinking. He disappeared some years ago. Of course, we all thought him dead, but he definitely was one who could have completed the weapon, or taken it near to completion. He may have defected."

"Or was kidnapped," Airiana ventured.

She stepped close to the bar, her bare foot coming down right in the middle of the shards of glass. Blood spurted. She gave a little, startled cry. Theodotus whirled around and gave a shout for the men waiting behind the door.

11

MAXIM moved with blurring speed, clearing the couch to catch Airiana up, holding her body in front of his as a shield as he whipped out his pistol. He aimed it at Theodotus's head.

"Wait! Wait!" the Russian yelled as three men burst into the room.

Maxim gestured with his gun at the physicist. Theodotus reluctantly took the few steps to stand squarely in front of them.

"You don't understand," he said. "I had no choice. I had to cooperate." He glared at the three men. "Put your weapons down. You can't chance hitting my daughter or me. Russia needs us."

He sounded so pompous, Maxim wanted to hit him with the barrel of his weapon, but the three members of the security team—and Maxim was certain they were agents loyal to Sorbacov—obeyed.

"Step away from the door and get around behind the chairs. Kneel and put your hands behind your heads. Lock your fingers together. Do it fast."

Can you walk on your feet? Crazy woman, he added affectionately.

Yes. She hoped there would be time to take the glass out, but she wasn't going to mention that to him.

Maxim set her down and pulled several zip ties from his pocket. "Start with dear old dad. Bind his hands behind his back and then the others. They'd better be tight," he added for effect.

Airiana took the ties and pushed air beneath the soles of her feet to cushion them as she took the few steps necessary to get to Theodotus. She slid the ties over Theodotus's wrists and pulled them tight before making her way gingerly to the three men.

Stay out of the line of fire, Maxim cautioned.

She had been concentrating on not cringing when her feet touched the carpet, driving the glass deeper. She walked on the outside edges of her feet and kept the air flowing beneath them so that the glass couldn't push deeper into her flesh as she took the quickest route to the three men.

Damn it, Airiana, look what you did to yourself.

She glanced behind her and saw the bloody trail of her footprints on the carpet. *Let's just get these men taken care of and then you can pull the glass out of my feet.*

Maxim swore in Russian, a blistering attack on just what he thought of her diversion. She ignored him and used the zip ties on the three men.

"Pick up their weapons and step away from them," Maxim instructed next. Clearly he didn't want her walking around on her cut feet, but he kept the others thinking she was as much a prisoner as they were.

Maxim stalked across the room and slammed his gun into each man's head, sending him slumping to the floor. He wasn't gentle about it. Bending down, he patted down each man and removed several other weapons before taping their mouths closed. He turned his attention to Theodotus.

The physicist trembled visibly as Maxim approached him. "Don't hit my head. I'm not going to give you any trouble."

"I need to know how many soldiers you have on board.

How large of a security force did you bring with you? Don't be stupid and lie. I'll come back and kill. You know me. You know my brother. When I say something I mean it."

"I had no choice," Theodotus blurted out. "I'm telling the truth."

"How many, Solovyov?" Maxim was relentless.

"Eight altogether. But I'm telling you, I had no choice. You have to believe me. Uri Sorbacov approached me and told me he knew I was in touch with Gavriil Prakenskii. He wants Gavriil dead. He lent me this yacht. The men are under his orders. I'm as much a prisoner as you are."

Uri Sorbacov is the son of Kostya Sorbacov, the man who murdered my parents and forced us into the schools, Maxim told her.

"Who knew Gavriil passed on the tip that your daughter was in danger?" Maxim persisted. He lifted Airiana to the desktop and set her there, right in front of her father. Grasping her ankle, he lifted her left foot in order to see the sole.

Damn it, honey, this is a big chunk of glass and several small ones. Did you have to be so thorough?

It wasn't like I had time to figure out the best place to step.

"No one. The message came in by my phone. A text message. In code."

"So your phone is being monitored," Maxim said.

"They wouldn't dare." Theodotus scowled at him. "No one would dare."

"It's either that or you're lying to me. And if the message was in code, who wrote the code?"

"I did, of course. I use it for my work. No one knows it."

"Someone does. My guess would be Uri Sorbacov. He's having your phone monitored, and he knows your code. Is he the one that told you about the terrorist threat?"

Theodotus nodded his head slowly. "I knew Gavriil would send someone, but I didn't know it would be his brother. I thought I could have whoever he sent get my daughter for me, and then if he was killed and his body buried at sea, Sorbacov would be satisfied that Gavriil was dead and Gavriil could slip away and live out his life some-where. That's the truth."

"You were going to have the man who helped you killed?" Airiana asked.

Maxim extracted the largest chunk of glass from the bottom of her foot. She gasped and clutched at his shoulder.

Ouch. A very big ouch.

Serves you right. There will be no more of this. With bloody fingers he put the chunk of glass on the table and turned her foot up to the light to get the rest of the smaller pieces.

"You don't understand the politics in my country, Airiana. Uri Sorbacov wields a tremendous amount of power. It's rumored his father did some disgraceful, shameful things, and those rumors are true. Uri wants the presidency, and he has to clean up his father's image.

"I don't understand how this person wanting the presidency could possibly be a threat to a man of your stature, Theodotus," Airiana said and jerked her foot away from Maxim—or tried to. His fingers shackled her ankle, refusing to budge. *That hurts, you cretin,* she hissed at him.

"Those of us who remember such things about his father have to prove our loyalty to him. No matter how important we are, we could disappear just as easily as anyone else. He has assassins at his fingertips, men trained in schools . . ." He trailed off, looking at Maxim, his eyes going wide. "Of course. That's why he wants Gavriil dead. Gavriil was part of that program."

"In case you're wondering, and you're thinking of double-crossing me, so was I," Maxim said. "Trained in those schools. You don't want me coming after you." He picked two more small pieces of glass out of Airiana's foot.

"Ow." She glared at him. "Is that the last piece?"

"I hope so. I have to take a look at your other foot."

"I was trying to save your brother's life," Theodotus said. "You didn't introduce yourself as a Prakenskii. You said your name was Maxim Kamenev. I had no idea you were Gavriil's brother. Not," he added truthfully, "that I could have done anything to save you. Uri Sorbacov wanted a body and I had to give him one. If I didn't, I would be dead and so would my daughter."

"Not if the terrorist threat is real," Maxim said mildly, inspecting Airiana's right foot. "There's two more shards of glass that I can see," he added.

"No, he wouldn't have killed us outright, but we'd be imprisoned, still working for him, and we'd never see the light of day again. You know how ruthless his father was. Uri is every bit as much or more. He's as brutal behind closed doors as he is charming in his television interviews."

Is he telling the truth? Airiana asked.

Sadly, yes. Both Kostya and Uri Sorbacov can make people disappear. We're certain Uri's the one putting out the hits on our family and all the others his father created in those schools. In spite of the fact that we've always been assets to our country, they don't want the existence of the schools and the way the children who were taken there were orphaned to come to light. That would pretty much guarantee no presidency for him, and his father would be brought up on criminal charges.

Airiana sighed. *I can understand Theodotus trying to survive. It seems like every step could be the wrong one. Clearly these men want you dead as well.*

Clearly. He extracted the last two pieces of glass and drew a medical kit from the belt around his waist. "Hold still. I have to clean those wounds."

"Still, Theodotus," Airiana said, "you might have at least warned Maxim. He did save my life."

"I wanted to keep you alive," Theodotus insisted. "Both of us alive. And we have to have a decent place to work. If I can find the way to counter this threat and get the defense system up and running, Uri will think twice before he tries to make either of us disappear. It's possible even that I can align myself with his opponent, and we can get rid of the threat to us altogether."

"I'm not the least interested in political intrigue," Airiana said. "I don't want to live that way, or work that way. I want to go home and just work my farm and be with people I can trust. I can't live like you."

"You have no choice," Theodotus snapped, his brows drawing together in a black line. "You're part of this whether you like it or not. You started this all those years ago."

"I was a child, playing. Nothing more. I saw patterns in weather and duplicated them on a computer. The computer generated most of the data."

"And the computer-generated data was incorrect," Theodotus insisted. "You did something else, something you didn't tell anyone. That's why I need you in order to complete this weapon." His face had gone red and his voice had raised, as if she was still a child and did not understand the importance of his work.

"You just told the absolute truth," Airiana said. "You developed a weapon, not a defense, and certainly not what I had envisioned—something that would predict terrible storms and help calm those storms. Something that could stop global warming and keep our planet safe."

"A child's dream," Theodotus sneered. "Impractical."

"Maybe, but it was my goal. Not a weapon to cause drought and hunger in countries a government doesn't care for. Not to use as a threat. In any case, I can't reproduce material that I randomly put together so many years ago when I was a child playing with a computer program. If you can't remember what you did, why would you think I could?"

Maxim washed both of her feet while she was arguing with her father. He could have told her it was useless to quarrel with Solovyov. When it came to his work he was single-minded. Quite frankly, he didn't care who he worked for as long as they provided him with the materials he needed and the space to be comfortable. Theodotus needed to work, and he needed the admiration of the world around him.

"I know you can help me with this project, Airi," Theodotus insisted. He scowled at Maxim. "Get me out of these ties. This is ridiculous. We can find a way out of this without you dying."

"Thanks." Maxim couldn't help the sarcastic note creeping in. He covered the soles of Airiana's feet with an antibiotic cream.

"What are you going to do?" Theodotus asked, fear creeping into his voice, replacing some of the arrogance.

"I'm going to bandage your daughter's feet, and then put a muzzle on you." Maxim glanced over his shoulder at the physicist. "I know where you live. I can get to you anytime, anywhere. It won't matter what kind of guard you have. I'm a ghost. I've taken out heads of state, toppled governments and killed drug lords surrounded by their private armies. You won't be much trouble."

"*I'm* not a threat to you. It's Uri and his father," Theodotus hastened to explain. "I told you, I didn't know Gavriil would send his brother."

Airiana sighed as Maxim began to bandage her feet. "The point that you don't seem to be getting is, whoever Gavriil sent was *helping* you. They risked their own life to infiltrate a criminal group so they could keep me alive for you. Knowing they were doing that, you still were planning to repay them by having them murdered."

"It wasn't me. I didn't want that to happen, but I had no choice."

"You had a choice. There's always a choice," Airiana said, exasperated. "You can't shift all responsibility to someone else. You could have warned Maxim before you ever sent him after me."

"Then I would be dead," Theodotus said. "Uri or his father would have had me killed."

There is no point in arguing with him, Airiana, Maxim said. *He will not take responsibility for his own actions. I doubt he ever has. He certainly took no responsibility for you and your mother. I'm rather ashamed I brought you to him at all. I should have killed the extraction team and left you on the farm.*

Airiana wanted to agree, but she'd learned too much in the last couple of days. *He would have sent another team after me. And those children would be dead. Let's get out of here. I want to make certain the kids are all right. They must be so frightened and feel all alone.*

Maxim taped Theodotus's mouth closed. He leaned down to put his mouth close to the physicist's ear. "You won't have to worry about Uri coming after you. You know Gavriil better than nearly anyone. When he finds out you were going to have his brother murdered after he sent me to help you, no one is going to be able to stop him."

Theodotus's eyes went wide. Fear crept in. He began to kick the bar with his shoes, drumming out his alarm in hopes the other agents on board would hear him. Maxim knocked him out with the butt of his weapon.

Airiana winced at the casual way he took care of business, but she didn't protest. "What are we going to do? He said there were eight members of a security team on board." She gestured toward the three on the floor. "That means there are five more, just waiting outside that door."

He shrugged. He wasn't worried about the five agents on board, only about what waited for them when they reached their destination. He lifted her off the table and put her in a much more comfortable chair. "You're not going to be walking for a few days. Your feet will be tender."

"I can walk," she protested. "I'll use air to keep me from putting too much weight on the soles of my feet. But seawater is probably really bad for cuts," she added, giving him a quick look from under the sweep of long lashes.

Maxim laughed as he retrieved his war bag from the corner of the room where he'd stashed it when they first entered. He set it on the bar and poured himself a tall glass of water, taking his time drinking it while he figured out their next move. "It might be time to get creative, especially if you're not terribly keen on swimming."

She regarded him with suspicion. "What do you have in mind?"

"The yacht is headed to a harbor, someplace where they've got another form of transportation. Theodotus wasn't going to sail to Russia. He had a plane waiting."

"You aren't going to confiscate the plane?"

She didn't sound convinced that he wouldn't, and he found himself wanting to laugh again. Airiana sat in the luxury yacht, surrounded by men who had plotted to kill him, and she managed to look ready for adventure.

Her platinum hair was carelessly tousled and fell around her face, giving him far too many fantasies when he needed to keep his mind on business. The bruise around her eye, marring her soft skin, bothered him, but her eyes were as blue as ever, those eyes that seemed to look right into him. Her mouth curved into a smile.

"No. That might draw a little too much attention to us. But we definitely have to take over the yacht."

He was watching her eyes, trying not to fall into them, but waiting for that answering brightness, the storm clearing away to give him blue skies. She'd slept on the submersible, something he hadn't thought she would do, but she'd curled into him and managed to sleep with him holding her in his arms. He treasured those few hours, knowing it was ridiculous, but he would always remember her like that.

"We spent nineteen hours on the cargo ship and another twenty-four on the sub. The cargo ship had been heading to South America. The submersible rendezvoused with this yacht just off the coast of Cabo and we're somewhere near there. Theodotus supposedly has a plane waiting in Colombia to take you to Russia. He had planned to go up the coast to his waiting plane, using the time to persuade you to join him voluntarily. We're not that far from the United States. If we take over the yacht, we can pull into any number of harbors and hire a plane to take us back to Sea Haven."

"The big airports like San Francisco and Oakland are a good four hours' drive from Sea Haven. Santa Rosa about two, but the airport is small in comparison to San Francisco. There's a tiny airport, Little River, very close to Sea Haven, but we'd have to have a small, private plane," Airiana said.

He sent her a small grin. "I wasn't planning on

confiscating a jumbo jet. I don't want to steal one, just hire a private plane."

Airiana curled up in the chair again. "I'm exhausted. You must be too. I did get some sleep on the sub, but honestly, I was scared, and you didn't get any."

He sent her a sharp glance. "You don't need to be afraid when you're with me. I told you I wouldn't let anything happen to you."

"It was more the thought of meeting my father—if he really was my father."

"He is. I'm an excellent forger. I can put together a complete history for a new identity that will pass any investigation, so I know how complicated it is to do it. Those letters from Marinochka were very real. It was her handwriting, and the letters and photographs of you had begun when you were under a year."

"Please call her Marina. I know you love your country, but my country is the United States. I don't care if I was born in Russia. As far as I know, I've never been there. I don't remember anything but my childhood with my mother in the U.S." Airiana pressed her fingers to her eyes as if she had the beginnings of a headache. "I will accept that Theodotus Solovyov is my father. I will even accept that my mother lovingly sent my projects to him, unaware he would use them for anything. But that's the end of it. I live in Sea Haven with my sisters on a farm, and that's where I belong. Please just take me home."

He crossed the room to crouch down in front of her, still looking into her sky blue eyes. "I'm taking you home, honey. I'll get you there, but we may have a little more work to do before we're finished here."

"You can't kill my father. I want to kick him for being such a sorry excuse for a human being, but I don't want you to kill him—maybe dunk him in the ocean, but you just can't kill him."

"I hadn't planned on it. Russia needs his mind, although in all honesty, when he returns without you, Uri may try to dispose of him."

She took a breath and leaned her forehead into his. "I figured as much, but that's his choice, returning to Russia and facing this despicable man, knowing Uri is ordering the deaths of men and women his own father took from their homes and trained to be agents. Most of those people defended their country, and for his own gain, Uri wants them eliminated. How can Theodotus work for a man like that?"

He had to smile at the fierce tone. She was a little warrior at heart. In the back of his mind he'd been a little worried about the four children making their home with Airiana. She had said she'd take them in, but they would have problems and she was such a little thing. Now he knew better. She would fight for them, give them rules and standards and make them stick to them. She would see to it that they got any help they needed, and she was capable of loving them.

He tipped her chin up and kissed her, just because he had to. He didn't let himself think about why he had to, he just kissed her. She melted into him, sliding her slender arms around his neck and turning her mouth up to his. Her lips were soft and firm, her mouth the same paradise he'd remembered. He could lose himself so easily in her, but one of the agents was stirring and they had work to do. Regretfully he pulled back. Her blue eyes had gone midnight dark. Just for that he kissed her again, tenderness creeping in, shocking him.

He lifted his head and sank back onto his heels. "Woman, you're driving me crazy."

"You mentioned that once before."

His smile was slow in coming. "I did, didn't I? Well, it's the truth."

He dug around in the war bag and came up with a pouch filled with small, hollow darts. He filled several of them with a clear fluid from one of two bottles.

Her eyes widened. "What in the world is that?"

"If I remembered which bottle contained the knockout serum, we're golden." A teasing note crept into his voice.

"And the other bottle contains?" she prompted.

"That is much more lethal. Ten steps and you're dead. It really wouldn't be a good idea to mix them up."

"You really have a wicked sense of humor," she accused, her eyes laughing.

He had never considered that he had a sense of humor at all, but with her along, this mission was turning out to be far more fun than he'd ever imagined.

He inserted the little darts into a small gun and added the extra ones to a wide leather wristband.

"That is seriously cool. Where do you get all these toys? You're kind of like those agents in the movies with all your gadgets."

"My brother Gavriil likes inventing things, particularly weapons for the field. I test them out for him occasionally."

"I thought you never saw one another."

Maxim darted each of the three agents before answering. "We don't. But we leave things for one another on occasion. My work and Gavriil's overlapped a bit. He's like you, quite a genius."

She laughed. "He's definitely not like me. I'm kind of a nutcase." She watched him dart her father. "How are we going to take over the yacht? The moment you go out of this room, someone is going to shoot you. I'm surprised no one has tried to come in."

"They're out there," he said. "I can feel them." He indicated the west wall. "Two there. Two on the other side and one by the door."

"Do you know how many others are on board?" Airiana asked.

"A chef and steward and the captain and his mate. I don't think any others. I didn't get much of a chance to look around. I knew when we were brought here directly that there was something—or someone—on board I wasn't supposed to see. Otherwise they would have taken you to your cabin to rest, and Theodotus would have asked me for an update as to your state of mind."

"Show me how to use those darts," Airiana said. "No one is going to shoot me, and I can get close to them."

"I'm not letting you go out there alone."

She raised her eyebrow. "Since when do you get to tell me what to do?"

"I kidnapped you, remember? That puts me in charge."

"That puts you in jail. I'm making sense, and you're going all macho weird on me. What happened to all that survival training? Aren't you supposed to use every re-source available to you?"

He winced. She was right, but she wasn't a resource and he damn well wasn't using her. He detested that she'd walked on glass to give him the opportunity to get the upper hand just before the agents had come in. Granted, he was certain she hadn't planned on cutting herself so severely, but he didn't want a single injury to her body.

"I'm not going to argue with you."

Deliberately she misunderstood him. "Good. Teach me how to use the darts. I'll walk out the door and get close enough to the one standing right outside to dart him. You don't have near the chance I do, unless you're planning on killing them all. They're expecting you, not me."

He hated that she had a point. The agents were set to ambush him. Even knowing where they were, he'd be caught in the cross fire. "Suppose one of them is trigger-happy?"

"They're trained agents or they wouldn't have been sent here. I don't have to get to all of them, only the ones on one side. You can take the others without having someone shooting you in the back. If I feel I'm in danger, I'll bring in the wind."

"The last time you did that, there was nearly a hurricane."

She laughed. "True, my adrenaline was running a bit fast. I'm getting a feel for this type of work."

He leveled his gaze at her, doing his best to look intimidating. It worked on everyone else. She just raised her eyebrow.

"You know I'm right. Don't be all silly and macho. This will be a piece of cake. I'll take a little stroll around the deck. In fact, the smart way of doing it would be to go past the one at the door with a little cheery wave and stroll right up to the other two and dart them. The one guarding the door will get curious and look inside."

"Don't get clever, Airiana," he cautioned. "These are trained killers."

"Exactly. And they're expecting you, not me. I'm the merchandise, the reason we're heading for Russia as fast as possible. No one wants me dead. You, on the other hand, seem to be very popular with killers. You're the favorite on everyone's hit list."

The little snippy note in her voice made him laugh. "I'll give you a lesson, but if your aim is lousy, you're staying here and I'm going alone."

She rolled her eyes. "Have no worries, my aim has never been my problem. Until your undoubtedly dubious influence, I've never been an advocate of killing anyone."

"While I'm thinking about it," Maxim said, "keep your eye on Benito. That boy needs some guidance. He's a little too much like I was as a boy. I don't blame him, but I don't want him to have the opportunity to turn out like me. His anger issues and penchant for violence need to be cultivated into a much more positive channel."

Airiana's blue eyes fastened on his and he knew he shouldn't have said anything aloud. He kept forgetting she could see inside of him, in a place he thought was well hidden, the one that still worried about children whose lives had been shattered.

"I'll watch him," she said quietly, "no worries."

He winced. She was making it very clear she didn't need his help with the children. He'd said he was taking her to the farm and leaving her there. He'd rejected her offer to stay with her. She wasn't going to make it again, and he couldn't blame her, nor did he know what he'd do or say if she did. To distract her, he pulled out some empty darts and showed her how to load them in the small dart gun.

He made a small circular target and hung it on the cupboard. "They're light, but the velocity coming out of the gun keeps them from dropping too fast. You're a good shot with a pistol, so you should be good here."

She raised an eyebrow. "Do you want to play for points?"

"We've got killers waiting outside."

She shrugged. "If they come in, you have the advantage and they know it. Right now, they can't just spray the room with bullets because they'll hit Theodotus as well as me and their own men. We've got time . . . unless you're too chicken to lose to a woman."

"I won't lose."

"I hear you talk, but talk is cheap, buddy. I happen to be the champion dart player four years running at my school. No one could beat me."

He rolled his shoulders, loaded a smaller dart gun with empty darts and indicated the target. "You first. Let's see what you've got."

She stood up gingerly, but there was determination on her face. She lifted the gun and squeezed off three shots rapidly. It was a good grouping and he was impressed. There was no recoil on the small dart gun the way there was on a pistol and she had a steady hand, a good eye and true aim. He had no doubt that she'd hit what she was aiming at.

Maxim stepped back, crowding her so she couldn't accuse him of having any advantage. He took careful aim and slowly began to squeeze the trigger. Her hand slid up the back of his thigh to his buttocks, the lightest of brushes, but it nearly stopped his heart. His cock jumped and then swelled in response. He barely managed to stay his shot. The woman was one hell of a distraction. He'd spent months learning to condition his body against just such things and she blew his training out of the water. Training was everything.

"That was so unfair."

"I'm helping you," Airiana said, her smile just a little too complacent. "I wouldn't want anything to distract you when we're out on the deck fighting for our lives. I noticed you sometimes get a little sidetracked."

"You did, did you?" He turned fully to her, allowing his gaze to fall into hers. Distractions were bad in most cases, he'd learned that, but sometimes one just had to go with the flow.

He wrapped his free arm around her and dragged her into his body, his hand sliding down her back to shape her bottom, pressing her into him. She just seemed to melt, until he wasn't certain where he began and she left off. He wanted to be skin to skin. Inside her. Surrounded by her.

He brought his mouth down hard on hers, wanting to devour her. Needing the taste of her. There was such a brightness in her. She made him feel alive. Worse, happiness had found him. There was a part of him that was alarmed over her hold on him. She was making him more vulnerable by the moment. When he kissed her, he never wanted to let her go.

He kept kissing her, over and over, until neither of them could find air to draw into their lungs. Only then did he lift his head and look down at her face. She reached up with one hand, trembling fingers tracing his lips.

"I don't want you to die, Maxim," she said softly. "I know you've accepted death, but don't let it happen here. Or after you bring me home and go on your way. I think you're a good man, and the world needs you. Don't throw your life away because someone powerful decrees you're of no more use to them."

"Is that what you think I'm doing?"

She nodded slowly. "I don't think it's a conscious decision, but in your mind, you want to protect the people you love. In order to do that, you think you have to die. They made you believe that, right from the beginning. They separated you from your family and then held them over your head. To this day, after all that training, they're still doing it. All of you are lethal, and yet, to protect one another, you stay away from each other. Don't let them dictate to you anymore."

He studied her face. She believed what she said, and there was truth to her statement. He couldn't pretend there wasn't. He followed orders to keep his brothers safe. He refused to even consider the idea of staying with her in Sea Haven, no matter how strong the lure was, because he didn't want her in danger.

"Just please think about what I've said?" Airiana asked.

"I will."

"You know when I go home, this Evan Shackler-Gratsos will send someone else after me, don't you?"

He'd thought of that. But Lev and Stefan were there. They'd be alert to the danger now. He knew no one would get onto that farm without their knowledge. Still, if he was there as well, it would guarantee that no one would get to her. And there were the children.

"I've been giving that some thought. Staying until the threat has passed would also allow me to help you with those kids," he said.

She shook her head. "That's not what I was trying to say, Maxim. All four of those children have fixated on you as their safety net. If you come back to the farm and stay, even for a few days, they'll count on you more than ever. They've lost their parents and their sister. They've been abused and traumatized. I don't know if the best thing for them would be to think you'll always be there for them and then to lose you too."

She was basically telling him once he delivered her to the farm, he could leave. That anger, always buried deep, surged through him. She had awakened something in him he thought long dead, left him naked and vulnerable, and now she was going to decide whether or not he could be around her.

"I don't think you have a say in the matter of whether I decide to stay or not," he snapped, and turned away from her.

12

AIRIANA watched Maxim slam the loaded darts into the small gun before handing it to her. She could feel his anger seething just below the surface, but she knew he would never let it out. Still, she was right. The children had been through so much already, and if he stayed for a few days, even if it was to protect her, they would cling to him rather than transferring their dependence and trust to her.

"I have to do what's best for the children," Airiana said, slipping the gun beneath her shirt, into her belt.

"How the hell would you know what's best for them?" he demanded. "You have no idea, you just think that you do."

"Maybe you're right," Airiana admitted. "I haven't gone through the things they have, although my mother was murdered as their parents were, but there are others living at the farm who have had nearly the same experiences. They'll help. I also know an amazing counselor. I'll do my best to see them through this."

"You'd make a lifetime commitment to children you barely know?"

Airiana lifted her chin. There was disbelief in his voice. "You don't have to believe me, Maxim. Only they do. I was willing to give you a lifetime commitment, remember? I believe I can help those children. At the very least I can give them a safe place where people will love and protect them. I may have my issues, but I'm capable of real love and real commitment."

"Unlike me."

"I didn't say that. I didn't even think it. I'm not about to second-guess your motives. You saved my life and you've protected and taken care of me throughout this entire ordeal. You saved those children. You could have taken the easy way out, but you didn't. Clearly, when you give your word, it means something."

Airiana allowed herself a brief moment just to drink him in. She was walking out the door in a couple of minutes and putting her life on the line for this man. Didn't he see that she believed he was worth it? He didn't know he was—but she did.

She saw beyond the scars and his rough, unsmiling face. He was beautiful in a purely masculine way, a dark, brooding man with a perpetual five-o'clock shadow and shaggy hair she always wanted to tame. Mostly, he was lost. He didn't realize he was lost, but she saw that he was.

Maxim Prakenskii was so busy protecting everyone around him that he had given up on himself. He clearly felt he had sinned one too many times, and there was no redemption as far as he was concerned. She wanted to gather him into her arms and hold him close, just as she'd wanted to gather those children to her.

"Stop looking at me like that." He nearly growled the order, his eyes darkening, the heralding of a turbulent storm.

She sent him a small smile. "You can't stop me from looking at you, Maxim. You can't control everything around you, especially me. I look at you because I enjoy it. I see the man you refuse to see. I'm not afraid of either of you, because you're one and the same."

"Damn it, Airiana, you're messing me up."

"I can't help how you feel, Maxim, any more than I can

help how I feel." She watched him preparing for battle, shoving guns and knives and ammunition into loops on his belt. His features had gone grim and he looked lonely.

"Maxim." She said his name softly, insisting he look at her.

His breath hissed out in a long, irritated rush.

She met his stormy eyes. "Unlike you, I don't want to die and I'm very afraid. But I'd much rather go out there, knowing if I do, you have a chance to stay alive. You matter. If you don't to anyone else, you do to me."

He swore again, and took a threatening step toward her. She didn't move, but her heart accelerated. Not out of fear—she knew with every cell in her body that Maxim Prakenskii would never hurt her—but because she knew he was afraid. Not of the men with guns, or dying out there on the deck, but of her. Of wanting her so much. Of wanting the life she could give him that he no longer believed in.

"I won't hurt you," she said softly. "I'd never hurt you."

He caught the front of her shirt in his fist and yanked her close to him, his icy eyes suddenly blazing with fire, a blue flame of exquisite heat. "You have to stop. I can't do this, any of this, if I feel anything. You can't make me feel. If I loved you and then lost you . . ." He shook his head. "I can't do that."

"I know. I'm not asking you to," she replied patiently, refusing to look away from his stricken eyes. He didn't even see that he was too alone. Or that she already mattered far too much. "I just wanted you to know how I felt about you."

He kissed her hard. She tasted desperation. She tasted love—she knew she did. He could deny it all he wanted, but there, in his kiss, he was honest with both of them. She poured everything she felt for him into her answering kiss, giving herself up totally to him, without reservation. It might be the only time she ever gave herself that way, and she did it wholeheartedly, kissing him as if it were her last and only time with the man she loved.

Maxim's body trembled, a strong, invincible man. All muscle. All power. He trembled for her. She kissed him over and over, melting into him, wanting to let him know that once—one time in his life—someone had loved him. What she felt in that moment was absolute love. He was . . . extraordinary.

It was Airiana who pulled away from him, her heart beating too fast, the blood rushing through her veins, adrenaline pouring into her body. She turned away from him without looking at his face. She knew it already, every line, every plane, his masculine jaw that could be set so stubbornly.

She went barefoot, using air to cushion her feet. She pulled the door open slowly, knowing Maxim would fade into the background like he did, but would be in the precise location to see as much as possible when she pulled the door as wide as it could go.

A man stood to one side of the door and his assault rifle was pointed squarely at her head. She stopped, her eyes going wide with fear, her empty hands clutching at her heart. "What's wrong?" she asked, looking around her as if expecting to see pirates.

"Where are the others?" he asked, never wavering for a moment.

"With my father. He asked me to take a walk around the deck for a few minutes. Is something wrong? Should I get him?" She glanced at her watch. "He said he needed to talk to those other men and Maxim alone for about ten minutes." She half turned as if she would go back inside.

"No, your father's right. Take your walk." He lowered his weapon and indicated her feet. "What happened?"

"Maxim dropped a glass when those other men came in and I stepped on the shards. One of them helped me." She smiled at him and stepped around him with a little cheery wave.

Relief flooded her. He'd bought her story. It was plausible. The three agents entered, and of course her father would send her out before they killed Maxim. The guard probably figured they'd kill him and toss his body overboard while she was taking her little stroll. If she were lucky, he'd go in to help the others. She'd left the door cracked partway just to entice him.

You were born for this kind of work.

The grudging respect in Maxim's voice settled her churning stomach. She had been most careful not to block his line of fire to the guard, just in case.

My guardian angel, she replied back. Her palm itched and she rubbed her thigh absently. *Thank you. You gave me confidence.*

He gave a little cough of derision. *I've been called many things in my life, but* guardian angel *is not one of them.*

I guess no one's ever gotten the chance to know you. I'm coming up on the two on the west side. They're crouched low and both have their weapons trained on me.

She heard his curse echoing through her mind, but as she approached the two guards, she blocked out everything but her story, needing to believe it herself. Both men rose, looking around as if expecting an army with her.

"Hi. I'm Airiana, Theodotus's daughter." It was shocking to say the words aloud, almost as if just by saying such a thing she was betraying her country. "My father told me to take a stroll around the deck. Is it okay to come on this side?"

One of the men lowered his weapon, nodding his head. "Of course it is. Don't get too close to the rail. The ride is fairly smooth, but the ocean can act up at any time."

"What's your name?" She tried to look friendly as she took another couple of steps to get closer to them.

"I'm Akim and that's Feliks." He indicated his partner.

Feliks lowered his rifle as well, giving her a tentative smile, looking her over, not as a potential enemy, but as a woman. She widened her smile to include him.

"Do you know my father?"

Both shook their heads. Feliks stepped closer to her, into her personal space. He actually put a hand on her shoulder as if to steady her. She shot him in the neck with the dart gun and turned to fire the second shot at the other guard as Feliks went down, shock on his face.

Akim threw himself on the deck and kicked out at her, hooking his ankle around hers and bringing her to the ground hard. She retained her hold on the dart gun, and rolled over and over to try to put space between them. On the second roll she fired another dart at Akim. It hit his thigh, but fell to the deck.

Akim punched her hard in the eye. She actually saw stars. One moment the world was right and the next it was spinning like mad, the edges blurring and stars rushing at her from every direction. She went down, her legs turning to rubber, stomach churning, her vision blurring. She managed to raise the dart gun as he came at her again. Squeezing the trigger, she fell back, hitting the back of her head on the deck.

Akim's eyes filled with fury as he slapped at the small dart that had hit his arm. He swung his fist at her face a second time. She closed her eyes, but the blow never landed.

Akim flew backward, and Maxim was there, kicking the gun away and stepping in close to deliver three wicked punches to Akim's face. Each blow knocked the man backward until he was up against the railing. Maxim's elbow smashed into his face and then he reached down as if he might upend Akim over the railing into the water.

"Stop," she blurted out. "Just stop. He's done."

Maxim let go of Akim and the guard toppled to the deck, his legs no longer supporting him. He turned slowly to look down at her, sprawled as she was between the two downed agents.

She couldn't imagine what she looked like, but blood trickled down her face from the cut up by her eye. She wiped at it with her hand and managed to smear it.

Maxim winced visibly. "Don't. You do that again and I'm throwing the bastard into the sea." He crouched down beside her and touched the swelling around her eye with gentle fingers. "Remind me never to listen to you again."

"I distracted them," she pointed out, and tried to sit up.

He instantly swept his arm around her and helped her into a sitting position. For one moment her head seemed to explode and then it settled down again into a pounding rhythm. There was a roaring in her ears that hadn't been there before.

"Maybe I need to lie down," she said. She didn't want to throw up on him, not after trying to prove a point. No one had ever really hit her before. Not like that. She'd worked at self-defense in the gym, but neither Levi nor Thomas ever punched her in the face. When they broke through her guard, they pulled their punches.

Maxim gathered her up and lifted her right off the deck. "I'm going to put you in a lounge chair while I clean up this mess. The last thing we want is for the steward to see all the guards looking dead on his deck."

"They aren't dead, are they?" she asked suspiciously.

She didn't bother to look but laid her head against his shoulder and let him carry her to the forward deck. He felt solid, and she could feel his every muscle ripple subtly while he carried her.

"No, but I'm still considering killing them on principle alone," he warned. "Next time, don't let anyone punch you. It upsets me to see bruises on you."

"So next time I'll just let them know you'd be really unhappy if they decided to hit me." In spite of still feeling a little sick and her head wanting to explode, she couldn't help the laughter welling up. He wasn't finding anything humorous about it all, which made it all the funnier to her.

"Maxim, really, I'm all right. I wasn't fast enough getting off the second dart, that's all."

"You kept your head and your weapon," he said. "I'm proud of you."

She didn't point out that he didn't sound proud, he sounded surly. "Do you think you could find me something to drink after you take care of all the guards? What are you going to do with them?"

"Actually, they aren't technically guards, they're assassins. They were sent here to kill me, not guard you. Just to clarify." He settled her carefully on one of the plush loungers, in the shade on the owner's private deck.

"I didn't think of them like that," Airiana said. "I might change my mind and let you throw them overboard after all."

He did laugh then. It wasn't long or hearty, but he did give her a small laugh. "That's my girl. Let the bastard punch you in the face and we have to play nice, but someone threatens me and they can go overboard."

"Well, I do have my priorities," she answered.

He pulled out his first aid kit and broke open a gel pack. "Keep this over your eye until I get back. I won't be long." He put a cushion behind her head.

She stretched her legs out and took the cold pack gratefully. The instant cold took some of the sting from her swelling eye. "Don't be long. I feel vulnerable and a little exposed lying here. And I'm not certain I could get up if someone threatened me."

He put the dart gun next to her hand. "You can always get up if you need to, Airiana. It's a matter of will."

She knew he would always get up, even if it was with his very last breath. He was made that way. Or trained that way. She preferred lying on the lounger and waiting for him to bring her back a bottle of ice-cold water. She planned on fantasizing. She was on the yacht with him. No killer aboard. Lying in the sun and maybe dozing off.

Airiana waved him off and closed her eyes. She had a vivid imagination and was going to use it. Weren't they somewhere off the beautiful Mexican coast? She could get behind that. She needed a vacation . . .

Are you certain he didn't give you a concussion?

Don't rain on my parade. This yacht is the real deal. If we didn't have all those killers aboard, and we weren't heading to Colombia so they could fly me to Russia where I'd be a prisoner the rest of my life and probably tortured on a regular basis, I think I could make this a fun trip.

You're a little crazy, you know that?

She loved the amusement in his voice. She was in his mind and there was little that amused him. Little that mattered in his world at all. But she did. He hadn't meant to let her inside, but he had and now it was too late. She was there and she loved being that one. The only one.

Well. Yes. Probably. I might be a little crazy, but it's the only way to be in your company. Has it ever occurred to you that you attract the wrong kind of people?

I do what?

Attract the wrong kind of people. Take this yacht for example. We're not even going to mention the whack jobs aboard the container ship. Just this nice little yacht. On the surface, it all appears to be wonderful. Maybe it was when they were sailing around enjoying the sun and fun.

She paused to adjust the ice pack, looking at the ocean with her one good eye. He was dragging two men into the den and not being the least bit careful about it. She knew, not because she could see him through her physical vision, but because she was reading the air and knew the exact position of everyone on deck. Someone was coming up the stairs from below.

Then you came aboard, Maxim, and we discover that this isn't the nice yacht we thought it was. My father isn't the nice man you thought he was. Those men aren't the nice deck crew I thought they were. No one is nice at all. See, you attract the wrong people. When you think about the law of averages, this shouldn't be happening every-where you go.

The stairs were to her left. She shifted her position enough that she could see the top of the stairs. She could hear footsteps. No hurrying. Whoever was coming up the stairs didn't appear to be alarmed. She forced air through her lungs.

What is it? His voice was demanding.

She didn't want to answer him. She didn't want there to be any more trouble. She just wanted time to stop for a mo-ment and give her space to breathe. *Nothing. I don't know. Someone coming up the stairs.*

You should have told me immediately.

He's here. She smiled and waved at the man topping the stairs. He was dressed all in white.

"Miss Solovyov?" The man walked right up to the end of the lounger. "I'm Gorya, your steward. The chef is preparing lunch and wanted to know if there was anything you were allergic to or didn't care for."

"Tell him no allergies and I'm willing to try nearly anything. Please thank him for asking."

He frowned and moved closer. "Did you hurt yourself? I have some medical training. Perhaps I can help?"

"No, my father found me a cold pack. I was a little clumsy, broke a glass and stepped in the shards. It sounds crazy, but I fell and hit the side of my head on that little part of the bar that sticks out. I'm not used to the way the boat shifts out from under me."

"If you're feeling a little seasick I can get you something for that."

"I'm okay now." She knew Maxim was close. The middle of her palm itched horribly. She pressed her hand against her thigh, fingers feeling for the dart gun. Just the feel of it at her fingertips reduced her anxiety. "How many crew members? I've never been on a yacht this size before."

"There are eight of us who work full time. I have to find out what your father would like for lunch. For some reason the intercom wasn't working."

"He went to lie down. I think I gave him a headache." She gave a little laugh as if every daughter the world over could give headaches to their fathers. "Maxim is probably hungry though. He's around somewhere." She did her best to sound offhand.

Hopefully the crew wasn't privy to the plan to kill Maxim. She doubted it. The less they knew the better. Sorbacov wouldn't want witnesses. More than likely Sorbacov would have everyone killed that observed the murder aboard the yacht.

I'm not certain if he even knows I'm a kidnap victim and here against my will. He appears pretty innocent, Maxim. She didn't want Maxim to hurt the steward if it wasn't necessary.

Theodotus told me they believe your life was threatened

*and that was why there is extra security. Still. Keep that
dart gun handy.*

He came up behind the steward. "Are you all right, Miss
Solovyov? This man isn't bothering you, is he?"

"Gorya was being friendly and most helpful. He was just
checking to make certain I'm not allergic to anything."
Don't sound so scary. He went white.

I'm supposed to be scary. I'm your bodyguard.

*Do you see my cut feet and black eye? Perhaps you need
another line of work.*

*Perhaps you should do what you're told instead of in-
sisting on playing the heroine.* Maxim lifted her bandaged
foot and inspected the bloody gauze. He glanced at the
steward over his shoulder. "Where do you keep your first
aid kit?"

"Up here on the sun deck, there's one behind the bar. I
can show you if you'd like. I was telling Miss Solovyov that
I have some medical training."

"She cut her feet on glass," Maxim said.

Gorya nodded. "She told me she was a little seasick and
dropped her glass. Her eye is really swelling where she hit
the side of her head."

Nice story.

He bought it, didn't he?

*Only because you look so damn innocent. I wouldn't
have bought it for a second.*

Only because you're cynical. She yawned before she
could stop herself. Of course Maxim saw. He was looking
at the steward, but he still caught her hastily covered yawn.
"You'll need to rest, Miss Solovyov."

Her breath hissed out between her teeth. "Both of you
had better call me Airiana. I don't answer to that name. I
wasn't raised with it."

"For your own protection, as well as for your father's,"
Maxim interjected smoothly for the steward's sake.

"Whatever. Call me Airiana, please."

You could act like a spoiled rich girl. They expect it of

you. The more manners you have and the friendlier you are, the more likely it will blow your cover.

Go away. You're giving me a headache.

It's only fair. You've given me one from the moment I laid eyes on you.

Airiana burst out laughing. "Go away, both of you. My feet are fine, but if either of you are heading this way again, I would love a bottle of water. No fancy glasses, no liquor, just plain old water in a plain old bottle."

Maxim pulled a bottle from under his coat and held it out to her. *You ask and I provide.*

She resisted rolling her eyes. "Thanks, Maxim. I really appreciate it. And, Gorya, please relay to the chef that at this point, anything will be fine with me. Please allow my father to sleep through lunch."

"The security team is working at the moment," Maxim said. "They're in the sitting room and don't want to be disturbed. If there's anything you need them for, just let me know and I'll take care of it."

Deliberately Airiana made a face. "Such a fuss. Really, Maxim, you and Theodotus worry far too much."

Maxim ignored her, reaching out lazily and taking the bottle of water from her to unscrew the cap. He handed it back and turned his attention to Gorya. "I know you need to get back to the chef, but if you could show me where the first aid kit is . . ."

"Of course." The steward was all business. "Right over here." He led Maxim to the bar and reached behind him, pulling out a fairly large box.

"Thanks." Maxim nodded at the man dismissively, and Gorya immediately took the cue and hurried down the stairs.

"Why make a big deal about the first aid box?" Airiana asked. She was beginning to realize everything Maxim did was for a reason.

"I wanted him to remember I asked for it. I can use the same ploy with the captain. I'll want to get into the control room and turn this thing around. We'll need Theodotus for that."

"He won't cooperate."

"Of course he will. Your father doesn't want to die. He has a big ego, Airiana, and he's convinced himself the world can't get along without him, so it won't be a big leap for him to help us. The story will be easy enough. The team doesn't trust the contact in Colombia. Russia and Colombia are friendly, but we believe you and your father are far too valuable for certain opportunists to pass up."

"I see. Theodotus will definitely like that explanation."

"No doubt he'll come to believe it. It isn't that far from the truth. If it was known where you were, and that your father was with you, every terrorist in the world with a grain of sense would be after the two of you. You'd better believe that Evan Shackler-Gratsos is looking for you right now."

He laid the first aid kit open on the deck beside the lounger and carefully began to unwind the blood-spattered wraps on her left foot. To keep from wincing—she didn't want him to know it still hurt—she took a long swig of water. The cool liquid slid down her parched throat. She hadn't realized how thirsty—or tired—she was.

While he worked on her feet, she glanced up at the clouds. The sun was bright, shining on the water, the sky a deep blue. A few lazy clouds drifted overhead and at first she idly tried to see animals in their fluffy shapes. When she was a child she'd played that game to stop herself from noticing patterns.

Patterns were everywhere. In the clouds. In the waves. In the shadows thrown onto the deck by the sun. There was no escaping from them. She took another long drink as he applied more antibiotic cream and a new wrap.

"You're sighing."

"Because I thought we were going to get off easy, but we aren't." She watched the clouds moving above them, spinning and drifting as if they hadn't a care in the world, but inside those clouds, her fluffy animals were gone.

"No, Evan was bound to figure out who had you. He's got money, Airiana, and he's willing to use it to get what he wants. He buys people, and anyone willing to aid Sorbacov would be just as willing to help Evan. Theodotus had a plane waiting in Colombia. The pilot knew the plan was to take you from Mexico up the South American coast to rendezvous with the plane. If Evan offered him money, why wouldn't he give him that information?"

"How would Evan know who to go to for information?" Curiosity nearly took her attention from the patterns forming above her.

"The underworld is all connected," he said, starting on her other foot. "It isn't that hard to know who the major players are. Each of them is fed information through their pipelines. Some are extensive, some aren't." He gave a small shrug. "Once you're in that world and you've acquired a reputation, everyone knows what you will or won't do for money."

"Like you."

"Like me."

"So we're going to make a run for it."

He nodded. "The yacht is. We're going to bail."

She scowled at him over the water bottle. "You said no swimming. We're done with swimming. We *are* done, aren't we?"

"Circumstances have changed."

"I'm switching sides. Suddenly I feel a bout of loyalty coming on to dear old Dad. Just how bad could it be living in Russia?"

"Russia is beautiful," Maxim said. "They would welcome you with open arms."

The laughter faded as she studied his face. "But not you. Not after all you've done for your country. They'll kill you."

"Eventually. But it isn't my country killing me. It's one very powerful man."

Her heart turned over. "Maxim, you can't just accept death like you do. You have to fight this man. You're willing to fight for me. You have to be willing to fight for yourself."

He ran his fingers down the side of her face in a little caress. "Who says I'm not willing? I'm just not willing to put others in jeopardy with me."

Maxim took the cold pack from her to inspect the damage done to her face. "You're developing a wonderful shiner. When your family sees you, they're going to think I'm the kind of man who beats his woman."

Her heart skipped a beat. He probably hadn't even noticed he'd referred to her as "his woman," but right then, when they were alone and the world was quiet and peaceful, she wanted to be his.

Airiana smiled up at him. "They know what a tough girl I am. If you hit me, I would hit you back."

He picked up her hand and placed it palm to palm with his, studying the difference in their sizes. She laughed. Her hand was dwarfed by his. His fingers closed slowly around hers, one by one, almost as if he was waiting for her to pull free.

"I love the sound of your laughter," he said. "You make life a fun adventure rather than a daily job." He brought her hand to his mouth and nibbled at the pads of her fingers. "I've never done this before, you know."

Her breath caught in her lungs. Maxim wasn't given to revelations about himself. She stayed very quiet. Waiting. Hoping for more.

"Men like me have to stay alone. We can't trust anyone. Anyone could be the assassin sent to end us. We form relationships only for information. No one ever is close to us. I don't sleep when I'm near others." His mouth curved in a humorless smile. "I'm like a mole, I crawl into a hole and close it over my head if I need rest. There isn't a moment when I don't have a weapon on me and a contingency plan to escape a situation."

Airiana didn't know what to do or say, so she stayed silent, willing him to keep talking. She was hearing things he'd never told anyone else. Personal things. Reasons, of course, why he could never be with her. He didn't realize that in revealing details of his life to her, he was acknowledging she meant more to him than he was willing to admit aloud to her.

Maxim opened her fingers and pressed his mouth into the center of her palm. She nearly jumped and jerked her hand away, but managed to remain still. Deep inside, in her most feminine core, she'd felt the intimacy of his tongue stroke. Her gaze jumped to his in a kind of dazed wonder. Did he even know what he'd just done? Probably.

"I want to lie down with you and fall asleep. Just once."

As a declaration of love, it didn't seem like much on the surface, yet she felt elated, almost giddy inside with joy. She knew he wanted her physically. There was no doubt in her mind that given the opportunity, he'd make love to her. Somehow, admitting that he wanted to sleep with her seemed so much more of an intimacy.

His teeth teased at the pads of her fingers. "Someday, Airiana, if I live through all this, I'm going to do that. You'll have to leave your window open for me and I'll just slip in. You won't even know I'm there."

She would know. They both knew if he came into her bedroom, he would make love to her. And she would welcome him.

"That sounds good to me. I prefer my window open."

He frowned. "What kind of security system do you have?"

She rolled her eyes at him. The revelations were over, and he was back to being Maxim Prakenskii, all about living in a fortress. "You sound just like Levi and Thomas," she said. "If they had their way, we'd have a fourteen-foot fence with barbed wire on top and machine guns every few feet."

He frowned at her. "What's wrong with that?" His strong teeth bit down on the pads of her fingers. "I think that's a very good plan."

"You would."

"And dogs. You need a pack of very large dogs patrolling your property."

"I'd like that. We've been talking about it for a while now, but so far, no one's figured out the breed we want."

"My brother Gavriil loves dogs. I hope when he finds a safe place to settle down, he'll have several," Maxim said.

"What about you? Do you like animals?"

He shrugged, his features totally expressionless once again. "I wouldn't know one way or the other. I don't have pets, if that's what you mean. I never have had one." He let go of her hand and was up, slipping into the shadows easily, as if he belonged there.

She knew Gorya was on his way up the stairs with their lunch.

13

NIGHT appeared to fall quickly out at sea. The sun vanished, pouring liquid gold into the waters, turning the horizon orange and red in a spectacular display, and then that fast it was gone. Airiana gripped the railing hard and looked down at the dark waters. Just minutes before the ocean was bright and jeweled, sparkling even, and now it held a sinister quality, as if below the surface all kinds of predators lurked waiting for an opportunity to pull the yacht beneath the waves.

She shivered. More than anything, she wanted to go home. Sea Haven was magical and peaceful and she needed her family. She wasn't the adventurous type, no matter what Maxim might think. She lived much more in her head than others thought. Right now, Maxim had driven out the numbers and patterns and mostly she just fantasized about him.

She found it rather humiliating that she couldn't get him out of her head, although now she knew for certain that she was in his and that made it all much more bearable. If she had to suffer—he could as well.

A wave leapt up, splashing along the railing, surprisingly high, the sound like a loud slap. Across the water, in the distance, she could see lights and that was somewhat comforting. Knowing they were close to a shore—and to people—left her feeling as if there was hope that she would get home soon.

Theodotus had been just as cooperative as Maxim predicted, insisting to the captain that they turn the boat around, that he had arranged for a plane much closer than their first destination. He'd been very persuasive, and as far as she could see, the captain and crew seemed to take everything Theodotus said as gospel.

The wind tugged at her hair and brought with it news. She could feel the air stretching around her like a map, showing her the location of anyone out on the decks. She lifted one hand to tuck strands of flyaway hair behind her ear as she turned to face the two men dressed in white coming toward her.

She recognized Gorya immediately, and the man with him was the first mate, Boris something, she remembered. She sent them a small smile. "It suddenly turned very dark out there," she gestured toward the open sea. "You're probably used to it, but it's a little scary for me."

The men kept walking straight toward her and she felt her heart accelerate with each purposeful step they took.

"What is it? Is something wrong?"

"You need to come with us now," Gorya said. "For your own safety. The captain wants you off the deck."

Maxim. Where are you? They're taking me off the deck.

She stepped away from the railing, very cooperative. "Has something happened?"

"It's just a precaution, nothing more," Boris assured. His fingers settled around her arm, and she knew it wasn't just a precaution.

They were taking her prisoner. Had the security force somehow woken up and escaped? Had Theodotus?

Where are you?

Don't panic. These men work for Sorbacov, this is his yacht, not your father's, and his men reported to him. He's countered Theodotus's orders. Of course the first thing they'll do is try to secure you.

She noticed he used the word *try*. She pulled back, stubbornly refusing to move. "Please don't grab me. I don't like people putting their hands on me."

The two stared at each another, Boris obviously unimpressed with her haughtily delivered order. He didn't relinquish his hold on her.

"Gorya?" She raised her eyebrow, turning to the steward for help. "I don't mind going with the two of you, but I won't be dragged around like a rag doll."

"I don't much care what you like," Boris snapped, dropping all pretense of civility. He tightened his hold on her arm and dragged her several steps across the deck.

Airiana took three stumbling steps and let out a cry of pain as her foot came down hard. Boris paused, and she shot him in the side of the neck with her dart gun. He grunted, his mouth still forming a curse, his eyes wide with shock. For a moment he teetered back and forth and then he toppled like a giant tree, his hand still clamped around her arm.

She went down with him and lay for a moment fighting for breath. Gorya hurried to her side, still unaware that she'd darted Boris. The moment he got close, he realized something was wrong and let out a shout for help. He leapt back just as she brought up the dart gun. Rolling over to come to her hands and knees, she started to rise.

Gorya kicked her hard in the ribs, sending her sprawling across Boris's body. Pain exploded through her, but she held on to the dart gun as if it were her lifeline—and maybe it was. She kept rolling, trying to stay away from Gorya's feet. He seemed to be everywhere, dancing close and whirling away in some strange form of martial arts she'd never seen before.

He was faster than she would have believed him to be, but she should have known that everyone working on the yacht was probably highly trained in combat skills as well as their daily jobs.

Gorya kicked her repeatedly, strike after strike, always dancing out of reach, so fast she couldn't aim the dart gun. She kept moving away from him but she was running out of deck. It was only a matter of time before he landed a blow hard enough to break something.

This man is making me angry.

Losing your temper won't help. Just take aim and shoot the bastard.

She wanted to curse, but she didn't have time. Gorya nailed her in her arm, deadening it, so that the dart gun slipped from nerveless fingers.

I need to be able to bring him down.

You really need to pay more attention in your self-defense class, Maxim said.

Really? I don't think so.

She had a few defenses of her own, and Gorya's weird monkey-like dancing was making her feel a little seasick. She was tired of everyone suddenly turning from nice to enemy. She felt surrounded on all sides, and she just wanted to go home.

Airiana called to the wind to defend her. It came pouring over the yacht, fast, furious, slamming into Gorya as he rolled close to her, lashed out with his foot and retreated. The wind howled, an entity without mercy, as it struck, hitting him square in the chest, uncaring how fast he was. Uncaring how trained he was.

Gorya hit the railing hard, so hard she heard a terrible crack and a scream. The wind was relentless, sliding beneath his legs and lifting them into the air so that he teetered on the railing.

"Enough," she whispered to the wind. "That's enough."

Scooping up the dart gun, she tried to push herself to her feet. There didn't seem to be a place on her body that didn't hurt. The wind lessened its fury, but hadn't died down that much, still tugging and pushing at the steward's body, trying to get him away from Airiana.

Gorya screamed, galvanizing her into action. She forced herself to her feet. Her legs felt like rubber and she went down to one knee just as Gorya slipped off the railing into the dark water below.

She closed her eyes for a moment and knelt there, trying to catch her breath. Tears burned. She'd just killed a man, using her gifts. It was so wrong. She was supposed to use them for good, never evil. This life was madness. She couldn't imagine how Maxim had survived it and stayed sane all those long years.

She not only felt the vibration of running footsteps, but heard them as well. Maxim wouldn't make any noise. If he came to her, it would be in silence. He knew she was in trouble, so he'd be there if he could.

Tell me you're still alive, she whispered and pressed her palm hard to her thigh. She needed him. Not to save her life again, but just to hold her. Just for a minute.

She sank back onto the deck and shoved the few extra darts Maxim had given her back into the gun. Crawling, she made it to Boris's body. Dragging his dead weight was much harder than she'd anticipated and whoever was coming was close. In the end, she sank down, using Boris for a shield, trying to blend into the shadows as Maxim did.

I'm alive, Maxim assured her. *I've got a couple of them stalking me. I've already taken out two.*

I've done the same, but someone's coming.

Can you hide?

I'm trying your blurring technique. It seemed very useful. She used the air around her to build a little cocoon, wrapping herself up tight in the hopes that it would make it more difficult to spot her.

Maxim's gift of fading into the background wasn't just because he was bound to air, it was more than that, but still, she knew part of what he did was wrapping air around himself to "muddy" his image.

The captain skidded to a halt, an assault rifle in his hands. He looked furious, and ready to shoot anything that moved. She held herself very still, even holding her breath, afraid that anything at all might give her away. She wasn't certain why she found the captain so much more intimidating—maybe it was the assault rifle and the businesslike look on his face.

He spotted Boris's body and took his time, scanning the deck for trouble before he crossed to the body and reached down to feel for a pulse. He looked right at her and her heart stuttered and then began to pound. He touched Boris's neck and found the dart. He cursed as he pulled it out, once more looking around.

He hadn't seen her. Wrapping herself in layers of air had blurred her image enough that the shadows successfully kept her hidden. Reluctant to move and possibly draw attention to herself, Airiana debated whether or not to try to use the dart gun on him. Her hand already was shaking, but a small warning alarm kept going off in her head. Earlier, in the patterns she'd seen in the clouds, there had been violence, the deck riddled with bullets.

There was no sound at all to warn her, but she was suddenly aware she was not alone with the captain. Maxim had joined them. She strained her eyes looking for him, searching the darkest parts of the deck, but she still couldn't discover where he was. The captain must have his own radar because he suddenly crouched low, not more than four feet from her, the rifle ready, scrutinizing every inch of the deck systematically.

Above you. Don't move. Don't make a sound.

She didn't turn her head or tilt it, but just looked up with her eyes. Even then, with him telling her where he was, she failed to spot him immediately. When she did, the breath rushed from her lungs. He was on the ceiling of the overhang above the bar, like a spider, stretched out, using fingertips and toes to push himself like a giant spider to the very edge of the overhang.

How do you do that? Because that wasn't human. No one could hang upside down from a ceiling and not fall. That was completely defying gravity.

Air. There are all kinds of uses for air. You've never had to use them so you haven't considered them, but a large cushion of air can help hold me in position for a fairly long time. He was so matter-of-fact. He loomed over them, both her and the captain.

The captain never once thought to look up. He was on the deck, most of which was open, and it just didn't occur to him that Maxim could be overhead. She pressed her lips together tightly. She was terrified of giving Maxim away. It had been better when she hadn't known where he was. Now, it took every ounce of discipline she had not to stare at him. She feared that intensity might just draw the captain's attention.

The wind shifted, just the smallest bit, sending the gauze wraps that Maxim had removed from her feet earlier fluttering on the lounger. The captain lifted the assault rifle and sprayed the entire area with bullets.

She flattened herself against the wall, shocked at the sound of the gun as it spewed what seemed like a million bullets. She didn't think he'd ever stop. The sound hurt her ears and she couldn't stop herself from covering them.

The captain must have caught that little flash of movement and he started to turn toward her, the rifle still spitting bullets. She froze, unable to move even as the barrel began to swing around.

Maxim kicked away from the ceiling, diving headfirst, slamming into the captain hard, driving him over sideways, his hands grabbing the rifle. Airiana jammed her fist into her mouth as the two men struggled for possession of the weapon. The captain still had his finger on the trigger and tried desperately to turn the barrel toward Maxim.

She became aware of the dart gun still in her fist. Without giving herself time to think about it, she crawled forward. She had to crawl over Boris's body. Grateful that she was small, and could fit in tight places, she moved around Maxim to get to the other side of the captain.

What the hell are you doing? If I move my finger he can pull the trigger and kill you. Get the hell away from here.

She ignored the warning and kept crawling, telling herself she was a tiny spider on the deck and the captain wouldn't see her. The two men were grunting and cursing, their heels drumming at each another while both fought for control of the rifle. She pushed herself into the small space between the captain and the wall.

Damn it, shoot the bastard if you're going to. What are you waiting for?

She'd been so focused on getting to the captain's neck, it hadn't occurred to her that she could dart him anywhere. She pressed the gun against his thigh and pulled the trigger. Just for good measure she shot him again in his chest. The drug was fast acting and hit the captain hard. His eyes rolled back in his head and he went limp.

Maxim tore the rifle from his hands and glared at her. "Are you deliberately trying to get yourself killed? Airiana, all he had to do was push that muzzle toward you and squeeze the trigger."

She let the dart gun fall from her hand, drew up her knees and put her head down on top of them. Her eyes burned with tears, her throat was clogged with them. There was no way to stop them, no way to keep not just her eyes from weeping, but her entire body. She'd killed a man, using gifts meant for good. The world around her was complete madness.

Maxim felt as if she'd just delivered a wicked punch straight to his heart. He'd made her cry. Really cry. Her entire body was shaking and she'd wrapped her arms tightly around her knees, locking him out.

"I'm sorry. You just scared me, honey. It's no big deal. You're safe. I'm safe. We're good." He used his most soothing voice. She had to stop. What was wrong with him that he could be tortured and yet couldn't stand the sight of her crying? How cliché was that?

"I want to go home. Can you just take me home?"

Airiana lifted her head abruptly, her sky blue eyes wet with tears. It was worse looking at her like that than listening to her. The impact was a knife through his heart, much worse than a punch.

"I'll get you home, baby. Just stop." He reached over the captain and lifted her into his arms, cradling her against his chest. She winced as if lifting her hurt her physically. "I know it doesn't seem like it, but we're much closer to our goal."

She held herself stiff, as if she couldn't bear his touch, and that hurt worse than if she'd just slapped him. He had to give her something—a truth about himself. Something she would recognize was more than an apology. He searched for the right thing, feeling a little desperate, needing to make things right between them.

"I never considered that I might have a double standard, Airiana, but I do. I wasn't given a choice when I was taken from my family and placed in that school. There was no running away, no way to be anything but what they wanted me to be. I became what they made me."

He nuzzled her neck. Inhaled her scent. She was warm and soft and made for him. He had known that from the first time he'd researched her.

"The point, Airiana, is I had no choice. I made up my mind that, although I had to accept the hand dealt to me, never again would I be in a position where I had no choice."

She was listening to him. The tension hadn't left her body and she wasn't melting into him the way he wanted her to, but still, she was listening.

"Clearly I'm not good at explaining myself. I've never had to, nor have I wanted to. But you came along and my well-ordered world was turned upside down. Inside out. You messed with my head. I had no choice when it came to you, honey."

There. It was out. He made it sound so matter-of-fact, not at all like the fire raging in his soul. He hadn't wanted to want her. He didn't want a woman he was destined for. He didn't want a woman at all. She complicated everything. She left him with no choices—something he'd vowed would never happen again, and he was damned angry with her.

He turned her hand over and pried open her fingers, exposing her palm. His thumb brushed over the center and for a moment the two interconnected circles appeared beneath her skin and just as quickly disappeared. He sighed. "Baby, you have to stop crying. I'm trying to tell you something important and I can't think straight when you're like this." If he could have ordered her to stop, he would have.

She leaned her head against his chest and looked up at him with tear-drenched eyes. "I'm listening."

He nodded and pressed a kiss into her palm. "I have this anger inside of me, buried so deep and it never gets let out—I wouldn't dare let it out. I don't even know how to let it out anymore, which is a good thing. It just sits there, smoldering like a volcano, and once in a while it tries to surface. You changed my world, and I put you deep inside, where all that anger resides. I didn't want some slip of a woman forcing me to put my mark on her. I knew what it meant, and I knew neither of us would ever be free again, but, still, for all my discipline, all my training, I couldn't stop myself."

Airiana frowned and looked down at her palm. "I had nothing to do with that."

"A man in my position lives with absolute discipline. Everything I do or say is planned carefully. I don't have compulsions I can't overcome. That would be suicide. But I couldn't stop myself from putting my mark on you. I tied us together."

"Shouldn't I be the one angry?"

"Yes. I can concede you're right—even logical—but crazy, out-of-control emotions don't make sense, and I have never chosen to live with emotions or be dictated to by them. Until I met you. All along you've screwed me up."

Airiana finally relaxed into him completely, melting like she did, so that she felt a part of him. How could he explain to her how that felt? He was a man apart. He didn't have a woman melt into him. He didn't feel as if they shared the same mind or the same skin.

"Still, I offered myself to you and you rejected me."

He winced at the hurt in her voice. He hadn't had sex with her—something that was always calculated. He didn't want that and refused to allow his mind or body to go in that direction with her.

"I've never made love to a woman. I've had sex a million times, I won't lie, but I've never made love to a woman, and if I get that chance again, in the right time and the right place, I want it to be with you."

He kissed her palm again and brought it to his face, rubbing it along his shadowed jaw. "I know I sound a little crazy right now, but that's the way you make me feel. I just thought you should know."

He waited, holding her palm to his jaw, willing her to understand when he wasn't certain he understood what he was trying to tell her. An apology for rejecting her offer? A confession of anger because she made him feel something? That made no sense. Nothing he'd done after meeting her made any sense at all.

"You do realize I just killed a man, Maxim. I used the wind to push him overboard. I heard his back break and I don't think I'll ever get the sound out of my head. You're telling me how you feel while we're on a yacht out in the middle of nowhere and most of the crew is either dead or drugged."

"I'm very aware of those things, yes," he said.

She sighed. "Just checking that we're on the same page, because I'm a little bit upset over it all. Especially the killing part."

"Really? The killing seemed the least of it all to me. I'm upset over your crying. That just has to stop. You do it just a little too much, and I think my hair is going a little gray."

"Killing is wrong."

"Not if it's in self-defense, honey, and you were defending yourself." He was still inside. Waiting. She was turning what he'd said over and over in her mind. He needed acceptance from her.

Airiana sighed and pushed her fingers through his hair. "I don't see any gray, Maxim. Tell me the rest. I need to hear everything."

Everything made him even more vulnerable. Maybe that's what love was, and he didn't want to go there. He had no choice again. She wasn't about choices, only truth. "I don't want to love you. Not a woman like you. Loving you would be terrifying, Airiana, every minute of every day. I was terrified as a child and again, swore I wouldn't ever be as an adult—and I haven't been, no matter the circumstances—until you."

She pressed her lips together as if stopping herself from condemning him. He couldn't blame her if she did. He'd tied them together and then run for his life. The silence stretched between him, taking away his choices again. She wasn't going to give herself to him again. He understood that. She'd offered once and he'd thrown her offer back in her face.

"You're the kind of woman that consumes a man. I can't get you out of my head. I'll never be free of you. I know that already and I haven't shared your body yet." He'd slipped up and used the word *yet*. There was a part of him already accepting that he couldn't walk away from her. He could use every excuse, but he wasn't that strong.

"You make loving me sound like it just possibly could be the worst thing in the world. Worse than the life you lead now."

He winced. He supposed as a declaration of love, he hadn't done a very good job. "I suppose you could take it like that."

For a moment the storm in her eyes grew a little turbulent and he braced himself for her answer. He'd never exposed himself to anyone like that in his life. He'd never looked into his soul, let alone showed who he was to another human being. She had such power over him, and that was the problem. He didn't want anyone to have that kind of control over him.

Her gaze softened and she nuzzled his chest. "I'm going to take everything you said as a compliment. Thank you for thinking I'm worth loving, even though you don't want to love me. I can understand feeling as if you don't have a choice." She lifted her face and bit him gently on his chin. "Just remember, you aren't in this alone. You may think you are, but I'm right here with you. I didn't have a choice when you did the palm thing. I can't help being drawn to you. There are two of us feeling this way, not one."

He nodded slowly. He felt he could breathe again. His lungs actually felt raw, burning from lack of air, but the moment the storm clouds had faded from her eyes, the moment she indicated she understood, the world righted itself.

"I'll remember that, honey, I promise. You just work very hard on the crying thing. You could be the perfect woman without that little flaw."

Her eyebrow shot up. "Flaw? You might be the perfect man if you didn't actually open your mouth and speak."

The storm was back, at least threatening to come back. He could see it in her eyes. "On further thought, *flaw* would not be the correct word."

Laughter broke through the storm clouds. "Nice retraction. Can we get out of here now before something else happens? I have this really awful feeling and I don't think I can take any more killing. Or drugging. It's one thing to read about all these awful people in the news; it's another to actually deal with them in person."

"Why is it that every time you shift position you wince?"

"Gorya knew some monkey form of martial arts and kicked the crap out of me," she admitted. "There isn't a place on my body that doesn't hurt. My eye is throbbing and my feet feel like they're on fire."

His heart skipped a beat. Gorya could have killed her. She hadn't said anything to him, or cried out for help. She'd just railed at the fact that she had a difficult time darting the steward. He resisted the urge to shake her. There it was, that anger welling up because he could have lost her. She had no business being in danger. "You're a mess."

She bit his chin again, this time a little harder.

"What was that for?"

"For what you were just thinking."

"You can't possibly know what I was thinking. I have a stone face. No one reads me."

"I can read you, so stop thinking idiotic thoughts. You

kidnapped me and brought me into danger. Had it not been for you, I'd be safe at home."

"I saved you from Evan's men," he said. "That should count for something."

"Well, it doesn't. I've seen what you can do. If you'd wanted, you could have wiped up the floor with Evan's men and none of this would have happened. You were too busy taking me to meet dear old Dad, and to be honest, I wasn't all that thrilled with him."

He nodded solemnly. "That could have been a mistake on my part."

"You liked him, didn't you?"

"Yes," he conceded a bit grudgingly. "As far as I ever like anyone. He seemed genuinely interested in you and excited to meet you."

"I'm certain that he was—but for all the wrong reasons."

"Do you think you can stand up on your own?" he asked.

"I've been giving that some thought," she replied. "It depends on what we do next."

"I thought we might take this yacht in close to shore and get the hell off of it."

Her eyebrow shot up. "Off of it. That part sounds good, but close to shore is not so good. That requires getting in the water again. I have cuts on my feet, and there are sharks in the water."

"You're a little obsessed with sharks."

"I'm a little obsessed with not getting eaten by one," she corrected. She sighed, the amusement fading. She closed her eyes and snuggled deeper against him. "Do you ever get to sleep, Maxim? Because I think I could sleep for a week."

He wanted to tell her it was all right, but like Airiana, he felt alarms were going off. He held her tighter, while he went still, listening to the wind, feeling the air around them. The yacht moved slowly through the water on auto-pilot, allowing him to get a good feel for everything around them. Out in the distance there was a boat, but it was small and didn't appear to be following them. Still . . . something wasn't quite right.

He rubbed his chin over the top of her head, trying to give her a few minutes. He knew he was going to ask her to get back in the water—the one thing she was most terrified of. His every instinct was to shield her, to protect her, yet, he was going to force her back into the sea at night.

Strands of her hair caught in the rough shadow on his jaw, weaving them together. Earlier, it would have bothered him, the need to find things that would hold her to him, but right now, when he was trying to comfort her, he found the little things like those threads binding them comforted him as well.

"Thanks for listening to me, baby. I know I'm not the easiest man in the world to understand. Hell. I don't understand myself, but at least you give it a try."

"You're not that bad, Maxim," she replied without opening her eyes. "You're just a little mixed up right now. I am too. We need a minute to just stay still. Maybe if we don't move, nothing bad will happen."

He knew it didn't work like that. His alarms were beginning to affect his gut, tying him up in knots, always a bad sign. He took a breath and let it out. "I'm going to put you on the lounger and gather our things for a quick exit. I'd like to take us as close to shore as possible."

"We're really going to have to swim again, aren't we?" she asked.

He thought it significant that she didn't open her eyes or protest. She was too damned tired. "I'd give anything to keep us from having to make the swim, but it isn't safe to stay aboard too much longer. The captain had to have reported to Sorbacov, and he'll have people waiting in every harbor."

He hoped that was his greatest worry, but he feared it was Evan Shackler-Gratsos. The shipping magnate had plenty of time to send his mercenaries after them. He was certain his gut wouldn't be acting the way it was if they weren't close.

"I'm going to sleep until you say it's time to go," she announced.

He stood up in one swift move, cradling her in his arms.

"I have to take a look at you. I need to know if anything is broken or cracked. The closer we get to shore, the harder it can be."

"I doubt if anything's broken, but I can't honestly say for sure," she admitted. "I really hurt."

She didn't even sound as if she was complaining. He had to admit to himself that was one of the things he found endearing about her. She could have been a pain in the ass. He'd kidnapped her and exposed her to danger, to killing, to a human trafficking ring, even forcing her to face her worst fear—swimming in the ocean—but she didn't complain. She used humor to get her through.

He placed her gently on the lounger, not liking the rush of air escaping her lungs when he put her down, but she didn't cry out. "I'll be right back. I don't want any unexpected surprises from our captain."

"What about the other crew members?"

"I took care of them. Even the chef. No more delicious meals." He went back to slip zip ties on the captain and Boris in the event that either woke up while he was examining Airiana. Neither man appeared as if he would be waking up any time soon. She'd darted them more than once.

Maxim stood looking down at her. Her face was swollen on one side, her eye purple now from her encounter with one of Sorbacov's assassins. He found it particularly disturbing to see the bruises on her face. She looked fragile, delicate, far too innocent to be involved in such a mess.

He crouched down beside her. Her feet were bandaged but there was no more blood leaking through the gauze. He knew she was awake by her breathing, but she didn't lift her lashes. He brushed back the hair tumbling around her face with a gentle hand.

"You're almost home, baby. We're close."

She smiled without opening her eyes. "I know. I'm just resting, Maxim. I'm all right. More upset over Gorya than anything else."

"I'm going to touch you, honey, I have to get under your clothes."

She did open her eyes then, all that glorious blue hitting him hard. The impact was felt in the region of his heart. "I trust you, Maxim. You don't have to tell me that."

He pushed her shirt up over her flat belly and narrow rib cage. Already he could see the bruises coming up. The one along her left side was enormous and ugly. He felt carefully with his fingers, looking for evidence that her ribs were broken.

"I was moving when he kicked me. I didn't take the full impact," she assured.

His expression must have been frightening. Had Gorya been standing in front of him, Maxim might have beaten him to death. "I don't think your ribs are broken, you wouldn't be able to take a full breath. Still, this is going to hurt worse tomorrow."

He pulled her shirt down and opened her jeans to slide them over her slender hips. His breath caught in his throat. There was more bruising along her hip and thigh. No wonder she wasn't walking.

"I should have come here first, Airiana. I'm sorry. They came at me in force and I didn't think they would try to hurt you."

"He didn't want me to shoot him with the dart gun. He may have thought I killed Boris," she said.

He fastened her jeans. "Don't make excuses for him. If I could find him on the ocean floor I'd kill him all over again."

She laughed and then caught at her sides. "*Don't*. That hurts."

He found it astonishing that she could laugh about anything. The wind shifted, slapping at the yacht hard. The smile faded from her face and she struggled into a sitting position.

"They're here, Maxim. We're surrounded."

"I know, baby," he admitted softly.

14

ONE moment there was no sign whatsoever and then the air around them was filled with warning. Maxim knew the men had come from the boat in the distance. He hadn't detected them because they'd come at him from under the water.

He took Airiana's hand. *Don't make a sound. Sound travels at night, especially on open water. We're going to have to get off.*

He felt the protest in her mind, but she didn't voice it aloud or even to him telepathically. She nodded her head and turned on the lounger, testing her body's ability to move. She placed each foot cautiously on the deck and stood. He waited until she got her footing.

One of the men will board the yacht, stop it and let the anchor down. They don't yet know the situation on board. They think they're facing the crew as well as a security force. Once the yacht is no longer moving, the rest will come on board fast.

This isn't Sorbacov's people.

No. I'm fairly certain Evan sent his men to retrieve you.

He really is going to keep coming after me, isn't he? Even once you take me home?

He can try, Maxim said, his tone grim.

Evan could send an army, but once Airiana was back on her farm, she'd have his two brothers as well as him to look after her. One Prakenskii might fall, but not three of them. They'd make that farm a fortress.

I don't want you to move any more than you have to. You're going to need all your strength. We're going to get to the railing nearest the anchor. Can you walk that far? I'd carry you, but I need my hands free.

I can walk. Can you reload the dart gun for me?

He took the small gun and pushed in the last of the darts. *After these, the only ones I have left are lethal.*

She held out her hand for the small harness with the rest of the darts protected in the loops. He took it to mean if she needed them, she'd use them. He handed it to her silently and Airiana fastened it around her waist, securing it through the loops of her jeans.

Someone's on the deck, moving toward the control room, she said.

He'd felt the disturbance in the air as well. Air was everywhere. Evan's men definitely needed to breathe it, and there was no avoiding it. When they displaced it, moved through it, or even stood still in it, he could see their exact location, just as if he had a map laid out in front of him.

Stay low. We need to move now.

I think I should tell you I'm pretty scared, Maxim. Not of these men, I have no doubt you could take out every one of them if you had to, but I really hate the water.

I won't let anything happen to you.

Airiana knew he wouldn't, not if he could help it. She followed him across the deck, crouching as low as possible when every step she took hurt. Moving hurt. Bending low. Even breathing hurt. She hadn't seen too much evidence of him being wounded, but she was certain he was. He couldn't have gone against the entire crew and security force without having some wound. If he didn't complain, she wasn't going to either. Well, she didn't mind so much voicing her opinion on swimming in the sea at night. That was just plain common sense.

He indicated the deck and she slid down to sit with her back against the rail, waiting for whatever happened. It didn't take long. The yacht slowed even more and eventually came to a halt. The thick chain attached to the anchor fed out over the side, making certain the yacht stayed put.

Immediately, hooks came up over the railing on the deck below them as well as on their deck. Maxim dropped low, fading as he did until he appeared part of the deck itself. She remembered to wrap herself in air, to blur her lines so that anyone glancing her way wouldn't see her.

She closed her eyes for a brief moment, shaking inside, but her hands were steady on the dart gun. It wasn't just her on the deck. Maxim was there as well and he would put himself in harm's way to protect her. She wasn't going to do less for him.

Her breath caught in her throat as she saw a man in a wet suit slide onto the deck just a few feet from Maxim's head. He slid the tank from his shoulders and laid it carefully on the deck in front of him. Her heart jumped. It looked as if the tank was actually wedged up against Maxim from her angle, but the man looked toward the railing where a second man and then a third slipped aboard.

They maintained a distance apart of about six feet. She knew by the way the air moved that there were three others on the same deck with them. She took a breath and let it out.

Are you okay? Don't move, baby. They can't see us here, they aren't even looking.

He's so close to you.

The first man had stayed where he was, signaling the others to check the bar and around the lounge area. Clearly he was the leader. They talked mainly with their hands and she figured Maxim understood the signals. She wished she did. Sitting there feeling exposed and vulnerable just a few feet from one of them was one of the hardest things she'd ever done. She had to fight the urge to run continually. Twice the man seemed to look right at her.

The five men systematically and thoroughly checked the deck and every nook and cranny on it. The leader stayed where he was, covering the others. She actually felt beads of perspiration running down her body when the air was quite cool.

She held her breath when they reached the door of the den. This was the owner's sun deck and most of the rooms were devoted to his pleasure. Two men flanked either side of the door while a third stood in front of it. The leader nodded, and the man in the middle stealthily opened the door. He went through it fast, the others following.

She couldn't imagine what they thought finding so many men tied and drugged. One returned to signal to the leader. He spoke softly into a radio and then nodded his head at the man who had come out of the den.

What are they doing? Her heart pounded. Adrenaline rushed. She knew, she didn't know how she knew, but she did. The leader had just told his men to kill everyone in the den.

She heard Maxim swearing in her mind. He rose up like a wraith, right in front of the leader, his knife in his hand, slashing across the exposed throat and catching the body as it began to topple toward the deck.

Airiana didn't wait for him. She pushed herself to her feet and ran across the deck toward the open door of the den. Movement definitely attracted the eye, and she'd forgotten all about the other two men who were searching the deck. She nearly ran right into one of them and the only thing that saved her was the fact that she clutched the dart gun in her hands and squeezed the trigger point-blank into his chest, right over his heart.

The man fell heavily, his rifle dropping from nerveless hands, clattering on the deck, loud in the silence of the night. Hard hands bit at her, lifting her over the body and shoving her back away from the door of the den and down low. She recognized Maxim's scent or she would have blasted him with the dart gun as well.

We have to get in there. They're killing everyone and they're totally helpless. There were the tears again, clogging her throat. She felt desperate and a little crazy, the adrenaline surging, the fear for the unconscious men eating at her along with guilt and fury that these intruders would be so merciless.

The other assailant searching the deck faded into the shadows, but his gun burned white-hot, the flashes terrifying as he fired round after round, spraying the upper deck. Bullets hit the bar behind them and riddled the railing. Had Maxim not pulled her down, she would have been dead.

As the rifle turned away from them still spitting bullets, Maxim threw his knife. The blade hit with deadly accuracy—she didn't think he could ever miss with his knife. The gurgling sound was terrible, a death rattle she knew would haunt her. The gun continued to fire as the man dropped to the deck, his finger squeezing off rounds until the life drained completely out of him.

Maxim signaled for her to stay where she was. He shifted positions, a ghost really, a phantom of the night, gliding in deadly silence toward the open den door where two men lay prone, assault rifles at the ready.

The third man slithered onto the deck like a snake, making his way, using elbows and toes, to his fallen comrade. When he reached the fallen man, he felt for a pulse and turned him slightly, just enough to see the knife protruding from his neck. He rolled toward the railing and the darker shadows there.

He rolled right into Maxim, who had clearly anticipated the move and was waiting. She caught no more than a small movement as he cut the man's throat and was gone, blending in, moving stealthily toward the overhang. She forced her eyes to see him, to follow the movement as he became a spider, clinging to the underside of the overhang.

Her heart in her throat, she watched as he made his way across the ceiling until he was directly above the two men. A noise drew her attention toward the stairs. Hearing the gunfire, three other men had climbed the stairs to investigate. One signaled, first toward the left and then toward the right. A dark-clad man went in either direction, hugging the railing while the first covered them.

He had a direct line of vision to the open door of the den. Maxim had gone still, blending now with the ceiling.

Can you shoot him with the dart gun? You'll have to be accurate and hit him the first time. If you don't think you can, don't try.

Airiana took a deep breath, let it out and took a careful look at her target. He was using the stairwell as his cover. Most of his body lay along the stairs out of sight. Only his head and upper chest showed, the assault rifle in his arms. His head was tucked down, his eyes scanning the deck for movement.

For a moment she hesitated, but Maxim was totally exposed, and with five men searching for him, someone was bound to spot him.

She shot the one giving orders in the only real target she had that she knew would take him down—his eye. Her little dart gun was silent, but accurate. The dart hit him square in his left eye and he made a muffled sound—one that made her stomach heave. She forced back bile and watched as he slumped down.

Maxim shot the two men in the doorway with a silenced weapon, a quick one-two shot, using a silencer and adding air to muffle the sound further. He began to ease back over the ceiling, moving at a snail's pace, never hurrying, never stopping, just moving back toward the cover of the deeper shadows.

The two other men weren't aware yet of their three fallen team members. They began to circle, one moving counterclockwise and the other moving clockwise so they could cover the entire deck. Her heart in her throat, she watched as one of them paused, his attention suddenly drawn toward the bar, Maxim's destination.

Don't move, Maxim. Hold very still.

Maxim went absolutely still, clinging with fingers and toes to the ceiling overhead. Her heart pounded so loud she feared the two men on the deck would hear.

The member of the assault team went down to one knee suddenly, the movement drawing the attention of his partner, who dropped as well. Airiana studied the one who seemed to have noticed something off near the bar. She couldn't let him start spraying the area with bullets, but it was an odd angle for her. Her target would have to be his neck.

He's still uncertain, but he's watching, so stay still. Give me just a moment. She didn't have a moment. The man was suspicious, and she knew he would use his weapon. Alarm was spreading through the air and forming in the waves slapping the yacht.

Still, she took her time with her aim, feeling as though this shot was the most important one she'd ever make. She squeezed the trigger and the dart flew from her gun. It struck in his neck and he grunted, slapping at the dart as if it were an angry bee, drawing the attention of his partner.

The partner let out a yell and began firing, sweeping the deck with bullets blindly. They hit all around her, tearing up the wall behind her. Had she not been so small, she would have been hit. Maxim fired at the man, three fast shots. One must have clipped him, because the man hit the deck hard, but he rolled to cover, rapid firing as he did so.

Maxim dropped down to the deck to protect Airiana. A bullet sliced through the outside muscle of his arm, a quick kiss that burned like hell. More men were running up the steps. He had to get Airiana out of there fast, but if he left any of Evan's crew alive, they would finish what their teammates had started—murdering everyone in the den, including Airiana's father. He didn't want to have to face her if that happened.

He rolled away from her, drawing fire, and lifted his gun, spitting back a reply. They exchanged a flurry of bullets while he worked his way into position. Two more had found their way to the top of the stairs.

Stay down, Airiana, he cautioned, afraid she would draw attention back to herself.

Another bullet parted his hair just above his temple, slicing off skin and burning like a firebrand. He took his time, making his next shot count. He put the bullet squarely between the eyes of Evan's man.

He turned to see Airiana sliding more darts into the gun. *Those are lethal doses,* he reminded. *And damn it, keep your head down.*

Bullets are lethal. I'm not going to just throw the dart gun at them.

Her voice dripped with sarcasm and he found himself smiling in spite of the ferocious burning from the bullets clipping him. He'd been lucky, but if they didn't get off the yacht soon, they weren't going to make it.

He slapped a compress over the wound on his arm, sealing it and wincing when the antibiotic cream added to the burn along his raw flesh. Airiana's face was white, her eyes large and shadowed, but her expression was determined. She hadn't gone to pieces and froze. She stuck it out with him, fighting by his side no matter how hot the situation. He couldn't help admiring her.

She had a much clearer angle on the stairs than he did. The two who had come up were half lying, their heads showing just above their friend's body. He was still alive, still breathing, in spite of the drug, but rather than pull him to safety, they used his body as a shield.

If you're going to do this, baby, you have to take both of them out. A one-two shot. Go over it in your mind. Practice it there first several times. You can't make a mistake. If you don't take out the second one, he'll unload that automatic on us and we won't survive.

Don't talk to me right now, you're making me nervous.

He was silent for a moment, willing her to take the shots. If he moved, he'd draw their attention. They were going to figure out fairly quickly where they were just by the position of the bodies.

He heard the small hiss of the dart gun and saw a dart protruding from the man on the left's throat. The second dart hit the forehead of the second man. Maxim leapt to his feet and shot him twice to make certain.

He opened the first aid kit in the bar and dragged his war bag out of it, caught Airiana into his arms and raced for the rail. *Slide around to my back. Hold on tight, but don't choke me. There are more coming. We've been lucky so far, but sheer numbers are going to get us killed.*

She didn't argue, although he felt her mind go still, almost as if she didn't allow herself to think further than his command. Obediently she crawled around to his back and wrapped her legs around him and clutched his shoulders.

He went over the side, using the anchor chain as a ladder. It was slippery and he had to concentrate sliding down it to the dark waters below. Each step was treacherous, and he was very aware he held Airiana's life in his hands. He spotted the small black boat carrying reinforcements from the boat anchored a distance away.

They needed a head start. He was going to have to swim with Airiana on his back and mostly stay on the surface. The water wasn't freezing, but already she was shivering, more—he was certain—from fear not cold.

We're going in as quietly as possible. Lock your arms around my neck, but don't choke me, he cautioned again. She was terrified of the water and he didn't want her panicking. *Take a breath. We're going under. Count to forty and we'll be on our way to the surface. We have to get away from the yacht. They've got men in the water now and the moment they find us gone, they'll spread out and come hunting.*

Airiana pressed her face flat against his back, hard. She shook until her bones threatened to fly apart but she stuck with him. *I'm ready.*

He felt her fill her lungs and he slipped down beneath the water, allowing it to close over their heads as he followed the chain beneath the surface. Once out of sight, he kicked strongly, using his strength to propel them through the water as fast as he could toward shore.

He heard her counting in her mind, slow and steady, not hurried and panicked although her heart pounded against his back. When she hit thirty-nine, he angled upward. She kept counting, although he could feel her mind beginning to fight her determination.

They came up a distance from the yacht. The decks appeared to be swarming with men. He could only hope that the men wouldn't bother murdering those in the den once they discovered their quarry was gone. Evan might even have told them to spare her father for leverage.

He couldn't worry about that now. *We're going under again. Count to forty. You're doing fine.*

I'm glad you think so.

That was definitely sarcasm. Her body shuddered. She sniffed. *Damn it all. You're crying again. Woman, don't you ever stop?*

I cry when I'm stressed. Swimming underwater stresses me. You're going to have to get used to it because I'm crying all the way to shore.

He took them under. The salt water burned his wounds, but it gave him something else to curse about rather than think about her tears. That lasted for the first fifteen seconds.

You aren't helping anything by crying. Just count. That's so much more reasonable. I can't think straight with all that noise.

She dug her heel into his side hard. *Stop being a bastard. You're doing it deliberately and you've made me lose count. Now I'm going to panic for sure.*

You were on twenty-seven.

But then I had to respond to your obnoxious, self-centered remark and that took several more seconds. I'm at least on thirty-seven.

Thirty-five.

You're just guessing. I'm going to faint from lack of air.

He nearly lost what air was left in his lungs. Trying not to laugh, he surfaced a second time. The yacht was much farther away. He stayed still, treading water, calling in the fog. They needed cover. With that many men searching the yacht, they would figure out fast they were gone and come after them—and they had boats and gear.

Tendrils of grayish white drifted in, great fingers

reaching toward the yacht. The wind kicked up, pushing playfully at the fog and the water. Waves slapped over, spilling white foam. The yacht rocked. The fog enveloped the vessel in a thick blanket.

Take a breath.

She did so, drawing air deep into her lungs. Her fingers clutched at his shoulders as he went under again and kicked strongly toward shore.

Just so you know, I've made up my mind, Airiana. I think it's your complete inability to swim that's done it.

Are you purposely trying to make me lose count?

This is important and you need to hear it.

She sighed overly loud. *Seriously? Now? You're going to tell me something important while we're swimming in a dark ocean, killers coming after us and sharks circling us.*

I don't see any sharks. You're making that part up.

How would you know? You aren't paying attention. You're too busy trying to distract me from the forty-second count, which you've once again managed to do. You're going longer than forty seconds, aren't you?

Well . . . yes. But that isn't the point.

Airiana's fingers dug into his shoulders, gripping tightly. Maxim really was trying to distract her and swimming for closer to a minute—he could have stayed longer underwater—but she was too frightened. Talking to her definitely helped.

You have a point? I don't believe you.

He surfaced again, turning his head to look at her over his shoulder. Her swollen eye was black against the stark white of her face. She looked so scared he wanted to comfort her, but didn't dare. Right now he had to keep her distracted and his strange revelations could easily do the trick.

He had no idea how to talk to a woman he cared about. He had never been the most charming of agents, but at least he could talk when necessary. She pulled things out of him he didn't altogether understand, but he knew he had to be honest with her.

Just for the record, you look awful. A little like a drowned rat.

She kicked him hard enough in the ribs to make him feel it. *Don't tempt me to shoot you with this dart gun.*

You won't. He was completely complacent. *You need me to swim you out of here. And don't forget those circling sharks. You need me for protection against them as well.*

Don't think you're safe.

She leaned forward and bit down hard on his shoulder—not his injured side. He noticed she was careful of his wound.

Take a breath, honey. He'd let her rest for a moment and recover from the ever present near panic. Each time they came up and were that much closer to shore, he hoped it would be easier on her.

Is the count up to one hundred?

Sarcasm mixed with something close to a hysterical giggle. Fortunately, she had the presence of mind to keep even that between them. He took them under, swimming strongly, hoping she hadn't caught the sound of a boat sliding through the water toward them.

What were you going to tell me that was so important?

The truth. The absolute truth about us.

Is there an "us"? she asked.

It was much more difficult than he thought to reveal his feelings to her, but they were in the dark, and talking mind to mind rather than aloud. That helped. The water was warm. The dark night sky still held a million stars shining brightly over the band of mist he'd called in. The gray fog, dense and comforting, had enfolded them close, hiding them from prying eyes.

I've watched you, Airiana, with your wild hair flying and your large eyes filled with the sky, taking turns being clear and stormy. A man could get lost in your eyes. They're never the same, all that beautiful blue.

She lost count but she didn't protest. Her arms tightened around him. He felt her face press closer against his back.

You've got courage. Unexpected courage. I've never met a woman like you. I didn't know a woman like you existed, and I doubt there's more than one. You're absolutely unique.

There was a small silence. He kept swimming, hoping to move away from the pursuit.

Are you giving me a compliment? Because if you are, I take back what I said about the dart gun. You can't really say I look like a drowned rat and then say something poetic like that.

Well, just because you look disheveled right now doesn't mean you aren't beautiful. I certainly didn't say the drowned rat wasn't beautiful. He could feel the vibrations in the water, the gasses carrying to him the information of a boat coming closer.

Baby, we're going up, taking a breath and sinking fast. Do you understand? We can't chance taking our time.

She couldn't swim. He couldn't let go of her to fight mercenaries already adept in the water. They had to hide, and that meant staying underwater as long as possible.

She didn't answer him, but her fingers dug deep into his shoulders, the only thing that let him know she was as aware of the boat as he was.

He broke the surface noiselessly, got his bearings as he took a deep breath, and he sank again. The boat was gaining on them fast, although it was making a sweep of the water. Back and forth, quartering an area.

There's another one. It's a good distance away, but I can feel that one too. They're searching for me. He's not going to let it go, is he? If I go home, I'll put everyone I love in danger. That's what you were trying to say to me and I couldn't understand.

Forget what I said. What I'm saying now is that you're mine. I belong to you. It's that simple and we're going to damn well make it work. Somehow.

I thought you were all worried about choices, she reminded him.

He gave the mental equivalent of a groan. *This is my choice. And it's going to be yours. You're going to fall in love with me.*

I am? How?

It was her amusement that caught at him—that won his heart completely. Even in the midst of this terrible situation when she was in caught in her worst nightmare, she found her sense of humor.

I have no idea, he conceded. *But it's going to happen. I made my mind up about this. Maybe choices aren't all they're cracked up to be. You and I were meant to be together. I just thought it was important to tell you. I'm taking my chances with you.*

You mean warn me? As a declaration of love, Maxim, it falls a little short.

Again there was amusement in her voice. He was going to have to take them deep, making certain the boat, as it slipped through the water, was far above them. He wasn't certain what her reaction would be.

Sadly, Airiana, you're never going to get pretty words from me. You deserve them, but I don't have them in my vocabulary. I feel them, but they don't come out of my mouth, not out loud. There's something wrong with me, so you're not getting a great bargain.

You need to do better at selling yourself, Maxim.

He surfaced in the middle of thick, dense fog. The fog muffled all sound and prevented him from seeing the shore, but he could feel where they were by the patterns in the air.

Take a good breath this time, Airiana, he cautioned.

I can feel the boat approaching. They're not low in the water at all, but they're nearly on top of us, she warned.

You'll have to trust me, honey. I'm going to take us down. If you run out of air, tap my neck. I'll breathe for both of us. He knew what he was asking of her. Most people couldn't do it, let alone a woman petrified of the water. Still, he believed in her and he tried to convey the faith he had in her with his matter-of-fact tone.

Maxim? If I drown, I'm going to be really angry with you. I'll come back and haunt you. Her body shivered continuously, but her mind was determined.

Baby, if I let you drown, you won't have to haunt me, I'll be right there with you.

He slipped noiselessly beneath the water, sinking far deeper than he'd taken her before. The boat was nearly on top of them. He felt the wash of it as he sank and knew they'd just gotten under in time.

They have scuba divers in the water, Maxim. There was definitely panic in her voice.

I expected that. They have tanks, we don't. He kept his voice even and as matter-of-fact as possible. The more she panicked the less air she'd have to stay under. He swam toward the reeds rippling back and forth with the current.

I'm going to anchor us down in those reeds just ahead. We'll just sink to the bottom. We're close to shore and we're not deep here. Getting to the surface will be fast and easy.

Airiana nodded her head against his back to indicate she understood. It was dark beneath the water, but lights shone around them from several directions. She had to know what that meant.

They descended down into the reeds, and Airiana let go of him to sink into the soft powdery floor of the sea. Maxim took her hand, squeezing it to give her confidence. She clung for a moment but then turned her head, looking behind them.

Maxim spun around, drawing his knife, nearly tangling his legs in the cord binding his war bag to him. He kicked hard and met the diver chest to chest, crashing into him, gripping his arms and propelling him backward. They rolled over and over, struggling for supremacy, each controlling the weapon in the other's hand.

The diver had the advantage with his air tank. He could stay down longer than Maxim, and he knew it. Maxim felt a sudden drag on his body, and glanced down to see Airiana coming toward them. She had caught the cord of his war bag and was using it to pull herself toward the two combatants.

Maxim's heart stuttered. She couldn't swim. Was terrified of water. She had to be running out of air, but she moved right up to them, pressed the dart gun against the diver's leg and pulled the trigger.

Maxim held on to him until the body went limp. Airiana held tightly to the cord, but signaled frantically that she had to rise. He tore the tank from the diver's body and thrust the breathing regulator at her. She shook her head. He put it into his mouth to show her how to use it again. He knew she could, she'd used one before when they swam to the submersible.

She shook her head again and let go of the cord to kick to the surface. He wrapped his arm around her waist and yanked her up against him.

Don't be crazy. Breathe.

I killed that man. I can't put my mouth where his was.

He caught her face in his hands and, staring into her eyes, breathed air into her mouth, forcing it into her lungs. He gave her as much air as possible and returned to the tank so that he wouldn't get dizzy. He slipped the tank on.

I'm the one using the tank now, not him. It's my mouth on it. The next time I give you air, you take it. He used his most intimidating, commanding voice.

I will.

She sounded young and vulnerable and he felt like an ogre. She'd shown courage and he'd had to be tough with her instead of comfort her. He took her away from the area as fast as possible, sharing the air in the tank with her, moving away from the searching boats and hopefully their divers as well.

Having the tank meant they were much more mobile beneath the water. He could feel the position of the boats and divers and avoid them. They didn't have to make a straight line for shore.

Are you all right? You're being very quiet. He didn't like the silence between them. She had to be traumatized by the events of the past seventy-two hours.

She gave him a thumbs-up but she didn't reply. He didn't

like that at all. He struck out strongly for shore, towing her, the war bag and guilt. For the first time in his life that he could remember, he was terrified for another human being.

All he wanted to do was gather her into his arms and hold her, showing her she was safe with him. All he could do was force her to stay beneath the surface in the dark waters and swim with him until he felt they were a safe enough distance to get to shore and find a place to rest.

15

AIRIANA'S feet were killing her. She was bone tired. Exhausted beyond all comprehension. She couldn't think, and that had never happened before in her life.

"Your feet are going to bleed if you keep insisting on walking. Let me carry you," Maxim said for what seemed like the millionth time.

He didn't understand why she didn't want to be carried—why it mattered so much to her. She was small and she didn't have the best figure in the world. Her face looked young—although maybe not so much all battered—but that wasn't the point. She was a grown woman. It was important to her that he saw her as a grown woman as well.

She supposed that sitting down right in the middle of the path they were on would be childish. "I can walk, Maxim. You're not any better off than I am."

She'd been a bit appalled that she'd been clinging to his back while they were underwater when she got a good look at him. "But we're not passing up any more places to sleep. No matter what, we're taking the next one. I don't care if every single one of Evan's men is camped out there. I'm about to launch a mutiny."

He glanced down at her and her heart skipped a beat.

There in the moonlight, his face appeared more ruggedly handsome than ever. She was a mess. Black eyes didn't look good on anyone, and hers was swollen with an ugly cut above it. She definitely wasn't the glamorous type.

"If you're seriously thinking of mutinying, it's important that you know I singlehandedly stopped a couple of serious rebellions in foreign countries. I'm just saying you might want to rethink." His voice was droll and his fingers tightened around hers as though she might try to bolt at any moment.

She found she could still laugh, and it felt a bit like a miracle. There wasn't a place on her body that didn't hurt. Her bones hurt. She couldn't imagine how exhausted he was. She had slept a little on the submarine but he hadn't slept at all. He was bleeding in half a dozen places.

"You know, if we meet anyone, they're going to think we've been in a war," she said. "That and our clothes are wet—well, damp now." He'd blown warm air on her clothes and they were mostly dry now.

She was thankful it was a warm night. Still, she was shivering uncontrollably and her teeth were beginning to chatter.

"I'm good at talking. We'll be fine."

She sent him a look from under her lashes. "You mean you're good at lying."

He smiled at her, and his smile was worth the last hour of torture. "Excellent at it. And I'm especially adept at knowing when someone else is lying."

He'd be great to have around when she was raising the children, but she kept the thought to herself. "Maxim. I don't want to be a whiner or anything, but I have to stop. I don't care if we sleep under a bush, I have to lie down." If she didn't, she was going to fall down.

"Just ahead is another resort. I've been there before and it has a few cabanas on the beach. If I remember correctly the cabanas were set a good distance from one another. I'll be able to see anything coming at us. You can sit outside and rest while I go in and negotiate."

"So you knew where you were going all along," Airiana

said. Sometimes she wanted to kick him. Hard. "You could have just said you knew where you were going so I knew there was an actual destination instead of thinking we were wandering around lost."

His eyebrow shot up. "You thought I'd get us lost? Seriously, Airiana, this is me you're with. I always have a plan and then at least two more backup plans. I don't ever think things are going to work out perfectly, that would be ludicrous, so I have contingency plans for my contingency plans."

She did kick him. His calf felt a little like an oak tree, and it hurt her bare toes. She glared at him, certain it was his fault. "Have you ever considered communicating? Sharing your plan with your partner?"

"Did you just kick me?" He sounded shocked.

"There you go again. Your communication skills suck. Clearly I'm annoyed with you. You could at least pretend it hurt." She hopped the next three steps, keeping the blackest scowl on her face that she could, although her sense of humor was kicking in. "*Pretend* it hurt. That, at least, would give me some satisfaction."

"I'm beginning to think you were underwater too long and it's affected your brain. Stop hopping around like a rabbit. I'll have to pick you up and then you'll start with your attitude."

"I don't have an attitude, Mr. I've-Got-My-Bossy-Pants-On." She took three more steps, trying to ride on her sense of humor, but there was no more fuel in the tank. "I'm sorry. I'm going to sit down right here and wait for you to do your thing." She stopped walking and would have sunk down into the strip of sand they were crossing, but he caught her around the waist, preventing her from doing so.

"See that little patio to our right?" Maxim swung her into his arms. "I'm going to put you in a chair. You'll be in the shadows. Wrap yourself in layers of air to distort your image just in case anyone comes near." He strode across the sand quickly, blurring their image as best he could.

Working with air was easy enough if one was still, but

blurring a moving image was difficult and took concentration. Looking down at her stark white face with the swelling and bruising actually hurt. She didn't belong in his world. He cursed himself for ever bringing her into it in the first place.

Her hand came up and caressed the shadow on his jaw. "Sometimes you look so lonely and sad, Maxim, it breaks my heart."

She lifted her face and brushed a kiss across his mouth. Soft. Barely there. He nearly stumbled. His heart turned over. It was impossible not to respond to her. No matter how hard he tried, she was already inside him. There was little point in fighting it anymore, he was just thrashing around, making a fool out of himself. Love had found him in the form of a small, ethereal woman who didn't have the sense to run.

"I'm not alone anymore." He managed to get the words out around the lump in his throat, sounding more gruff than pleased. "I've got you."

She laughed softly and nuzzled his throat. "That's my grumpy man. You always have the best declarations of affection. You make me sound like a pain in the ass."

"You *are* a pain in the ass," he admitted. "But you're my pain in the ass." He toed a chair into the deepest shadows and placed her in it, leaning down, one hand on either armrest to cage her in. His eyes met hers. She looked absolutely exhausted. "Don't leave this chair for any reason. Don't fall asleep. You have to stay alert and warn me if there's trouble coming. It will be difficult, I know you're tired, but I need you to do this."

She nodded. "Do you have a bottle of water? That will help."

"I won't be long." He pulled the bottle from the war bag and then kissed her gently. "Please stay here, Airiana." His fingers found her hair of their own accord. He was so far gone that he couldn't just walk away and take care of business. He detested leaving her when she looked so vulnerable.

She touched his face. "I don't think I could move if I had to. Just find us a place to rest. I'll be fine."

"I've been here before. I can get us anything we need," he said with confidence.

He'd used the resort on three occasions over the past five years. All three times he'd been hunting and had used the resort as his base. He'd established his cover—a businessman from the United States, Max Walberg, and all three times, he'd been successful in ridding the world of three very dangerous men. One had been a Russian mobster, another a Colombian drug lord and the third had been a senator from the United States.

The three men had all died of "accidents." He was very good at slipping in and out of the shadows without being seen. And he was especially good at establishing a rapport with owners of small resorts.

His clothes were worse for wear, but they were more damp than wet thanks to the warm wind and the long walk. He entered the tiny office. The family who owned the resort actually resided there and the office was in the front of their residence. The moment he entered a bell rang.

Jorge Estrada never appeared to sleep. Maxim always arrived in the middle of the night, and Jorge always greeted him within minutes, fully dressed, alert and with a welcoming smile. Over the years Maxim had made certain to recommend the small resort to "friends," and Jorge appreciated the business. Maxim was also a heavy tipper.

"It's been too long," Maxim greeted the man. "How's your family?" The resort was a family-run business with uncles, aunts and cousins helping out. Jorge had three beautiful little girls who sang songs as they followed their mother around.

"Good. Good. But I don't have your room ready. There was no reservation." Jorge looked extremely distraught. He prided himself on his efficiency.

"What?" Maxim looked shocked. "My secretary made all the arrangements. This has been a horrible day. I got married, Jorge. I've brought my bride here for our honeymoon. I told my secretary to make certain we had the honeymoon cabana."

Jorge looked more upset than ever, shaking his head.

"We got in a car accident," Maxim added. He held up his hand when Jorge looked as if he might have a stroke. "We're both a little beat up but fine. We're just tired and hungry and now this. Do you have anything open?"

The honeymoon cabana was set apart on the beach. It was kept for big spenders, the jewel of the resort, and it was exactly what Maxim wanted. There were no other huts close, and he'd be able to see the enemy coming a mile away. He always carried money in his war bag, extra clothes and weapons, and in this case, the money would come in very handy.

"I told my wife all about the honeymoon cabana. She'll be disappointed, but she'll understand."

"No. No. You must have it, Senor Max. There is no reservation until two nights from now. I can find something else for them."

"But this works out perfectly," Max said, very happy, all smiles, pulling out his wallet and handing over a huge sum of money without so much as glancing at it. He was beaming. "We can't stay more than a couple of days. That's why it was so important to me; I've got another trip I have to make and I didn't want her upset cutting our honeymoon so short. This is great, Jorge, thanks."

Jorge handed over the key. "Are you hungry?"

"Anything would be fine, Jorge. You know me, a burrito will do the trick. Whatever you've got."

"What about your wife?"

"Anything you have will be fine."

"I'll bring you something in a half hour."

"That sounds great. Thanks." He'd established Max Walberg's easygoing personality five years earlier. The staff liked him and always went out of their way for him because he never complained and he always thanked them both verbally and with his money.

Maxim made his way back to Airiana slowly, his eyes
finding her in the darkness. For a moment, he had to stop,
love overwhelming him. It rose out of nowhere, that intense
emotion he never thought he'd feel. She was curled up like
she often did, her knees drawn up in the chair, her chin on
top of them. She was alert, just as she promised. Every few
moments she'd lift the bottle of water to her mouth and take
a sip to keep herself awake.

"Everything is set, baby," he said as he approached her.

She looked up at him and smiled. Just that. A smile. His
heart reacted with a strange twist that was actually painful.
She was the most beautiful woman he'd ever encountered—
and it had little to do with her looks.

"How far is it to our cabana?"

"*Honeymoon* cabana," he emphasized.

She lifted her head with an effort and pushed back
her hair. "Wow. My dream honeymoon. I'm looking like a
drowned rat, and you're all perfect again."

His eyebrow shot up. "Perfect? It's nice to know, when
you aren't thinking of kicking me, that you think I'm perfect."

She held up her arms, forgetting all of her former objec-
tions to being carried. She was evidently too tired to worry
about appearances. She slid her arms around his neck and
nuzzled her face against his throat.

Maxim carried her to the honeymoon cabana, his heart
pounding hard with every step. He hadn't known a man
could feel the way she made him feel. He hadn't known he
was capable of such an intensity of emotion.

The cabana was built solidly, although the roof appeared
to be straw and grass. The inside was nice, beautifully laid
out for a man like him. The windows were large for views
and he could see several quick exits should there be need.
He set her down in the center of the room and looked her
over.

He'd never felt so possessive of anything—or anyone—
in his life. In that moment, he realized his woman had less
choice than he did. He would never let her go now that he'd

made up his mind he would stay with her. He would love her with everything in him—and he would guard her with a ferocious passion that would probably drive her crazy.

"Do you have any idea what you've gotten us into?" he asked, still half angry that she could change his life in the blink of an eye.

She smiled. "Right now, Maxim, all I want to do is lie down and sleep. Can we talk about relationships later? If that's what you're referring to."

"Come here. You need to get in a warm shower. Jorge will bring food in twenty minutes and he's usually very prompt. I'll want you to stay out of sight until he's gone. I need to check your feet again, make certain there isn't sand in those cuts."

She took the two steps to him, standing in front of him, looking up with so much trust in her eyes he nearly groaned. "I used air to cushion them as we walked."

"Damn it, honey. You're killing me." He didn't tell her why. What was there to say? He'd already made up his mind she was his, and he was taking her whether he deserved her or not. Whether it was a good idea or not. "Lift up your arms, I'm going to take your shirt off."

Airiana's sky blue eyes met his. She blinked and complied with his command, allowing him to tug off the wet, salty T-shirt, revealing the massive bruises over her ribs where Gorya had kicked her. He expected her to cover her breasts, but she didn't. She just stood in front of him without a murmur while his hands dropped to the fastening of her jeans.

He had been thinking only of getting her warm, clean and in bed where she could rest, but seeing the look of absolute trust sent an unexpected rush of heat through his veins. Trust such as hers was a precious gift few ever received in their lifetime. She'd gone into the sea with him when she didn't know how to swim. She'd shot more than one man for him. He'd given her a crash course in using a tank beneath the water and she'd been terrified, but she'd done it.

Without a doubt, if he insisted on having sex with her, no matter how exhausted she was—or afraid—she would give herself to him. He could see her consent—her gift—in her eyes. She'd been showing him all along what love was and he hadn't gotten it. He had wanted to reach for it with both hands, yet he hadn't, and that hadn't stopped her from giving to him the same unconditional trust that she was giving him now.

She offered him the world, right there in her blue eyes, and he'd thrown it back in her face. His offer to her had been more of an order, a command. Her choices were gone—taken from her—almost as though, without realizing it, he was retaliating against her. He'd been arrogant, so certain he knew better than anyone else, yet truthfully, he'd been afraid to love, to have so much to lose all over again. He'd been striking out at the person who had offered him a priceless gift instead of treasuring her.

He shimmied her wet jeans down her legs, wincing when he saw the stark bruises there as well. It was a wonder she'd walked so long. He'd sustained bruises like that during fights and knew firsthand how painful movement could be.

He stripped and threw his clothes on top of hers. The resort had a laundry service and perhaps they could save the items. At the moment, he only cared about getting Airiana into a shower to get the sea off of her and then into a bed to rest.

Taking her hand, he led her into the bathroom, surprisingly luxurious for a cabana. The water was warm immediately and he tugged to bring her under the spray. When he glanced down at her, she was frowning. His heart jumped.

"What is it, honey?" he asked gently.

"You're hurt. In a hundred places." She reached up to touch his arm just below where one of the bullets had kissed him.

"Nothing fatal. That's always what counts." He forced himself to sound cheerful. She looked battered—completely battered—with bruises coming up all over her body. "If someone saw you right now, I'd be arrested for domestic violence."

She glanced down at her body, looking a little shocked. "We both look terrible. I should have checked you out instead of feeling sorry for myself, Maxim. I'm sorry. I could have at least used your first aid kit to close some of the bigger wounds."

He used the shampoo on her hair to give himself something to do besides kiss her, because he wanted to kiss her. He wanted to frame her face with his hands and taste her lips, pouring everything he ever was or ever could be into her mouth. He wanted to crush her body close to his, hold her in his arms, feel her softness melting into him and protect her with a fierceness only he was capable of. Instead, he massaged her scalp and then rinsed suds and salt from her thick platinum hair.

"I've had worse, Airiana. I might look bad, but all the wounds are fairly superficial," he assured.

She leaned into him, seemingly oblivious to the fact that they were both naked. He hadn't considered that, as tired as he was, as exhausted as he knew she was, he'd become aroused. He had far too much discipline for that, so why the hell was his body not cooperating?

Her arms slipped around his waist and she clung to him as he rinsed her hair a second time, after using the resort's conditioner. She was short, far shorter than him, and he found his shaft resting between her small breasts. Her body was soft and warm, and the spray of water didn't help. She didn't seem to mind—or notice. Maybe she was just too damned tired, but he had one hell of a hard-on and he wasn't a small man.

"Airiana?" She was killing him. He scrubbed the salt from his own hair and body. She didn't move, but stayed wrapped tightly around him, holding him to her.

"Mmm?"

He closed his eyes briefly. She sounded drowsy. Sexy. The last thing he needed. He must be far more tired than he realized to have so little discipline.

"All right, baby," he said, gritting his teeth. "We need to get you in bed."

"I'll just sleep here, thank you," she replied.

He snapped off the water with a little more force than necessary. He didn't mind if she slept on him. His shaft was quite happy in its resting place, although his brain was filling with erotic images that would have shocked his partner.

"The bed will be more comfortable," he promised and grabbed a towel to hitch around his waist and a second one to dry her off. "Jorge is going to be here any time with our meal. Let's get you on the bed. We'll drop the mosquito netting and wrap air around the bed. He knows me as Max Walberg. If someone comes by asking questions, he won't be able to describe you and he won't even consider we're the couple everyone is looking for."

She didn't answer him, and he swept her into his arms, cradling her close to his chest—to his heart. He might not be able to say sweet words to her aloud without feeling foolish, but he could feel them when she was this close to him. They had two days to recoup before the honeymoon cabana would be claimed by another couple. There was no way he was going to be able to keep his hands off of her for two days. Not and lie beside her in that bed.

She turned to the pillows the moment he set her down. Maxim took his time examining her feet before wrapping them again. He swept a cover over her body and dropped the heavy netting. Even from the bed the view was fantastic, the waves looking close as they rose and fell, white foam curling invitingly. He glanced toward the main resort to see Jorge coming.

He hadn't taken the time to stash a few weapons around the rooms—very unlike him. The sight of her body so bruised and battered really bothered him. He dragged on a shirt to hide the wounds on his own body and opened the door, towel drying his hair as he greeted the owner.

"Thank you, Jorge. We're starving." Maxim stepped back to allow Jorge to enter and put the tray on the table. He kept his hands free, although he felt fairly safe with the owner. There had never been any indication that the man was anything than what he appeared. Still, Maxim wasn't a trusting man and less so now that Airiana was with him.

Jorge looked past him to spot the clothes on the floor. "Let me take your clothes. Maria will launder those for you," he offered.

Maxim managed to look surprised, as if he hadn't noticed the wet clothes—or deliberately left them on the floor to command Jorge's attention. "Oh. Thanks." He wanted the man looking at the wet clothes on the floor of his most prized cabana and not at his woman curled up in the bed.

Jorge took the clothes, and with his happy, knowing smile left them to do what honeymooners do.

Maxim took the plate of food to the bed. He stood for a moment looking down at her. She looked far too small there in the large bed, hardly making a ripple beneath the sheet. The bruises stood out starkly on her pale skin, looking obscene to him. He sank down beside her.

"I know you're exhausted, honey, but I need you to sit up just for a minute or two and try to eat something."

Her long lashes fluttered. She opened her eyes without lifting her head. Need punched him low and wicked. Hard. And it was need. He sighed and pushed back her hair with gentle fingers. "You know I'm not going to be able to do without you. Not ever. We're bound together, you and me, for all time."

A soft smile curved her mouth—that mouth that was giving him far too many fantasies. Her blue eyes lit up. "That's so sad for you. I know you aren't thrilled."

"I've decided there might be a few perks I hadn't considered."

She laughed softly and turned over to stretch. He winced when she did, but she didn't complain. Instead she sat up, pulling the sheet up under her arms.

"I can't imagine what perks you're thinking of."

"Sex." He said it bluntly.

"I don't know a thing about sex. Not one single thing.

You're the first man I've ever kissed. I don't think you're going to be all that thrilled with me as a lover."

He laughed softly. "You really don't know a thing about men, do you? Especially a man like me. I'm quite happy teaching you how to be my lover."

He didn't want much more discussion on the matter as his body was already as hard as a rock in anticipation. Thinking about burying himself inside her hot, slick channel, surrounded by her soft body, was doing things to his own body he'd never experienced before.

Every seduction had been calculated and planned for a specific reason. The women were targets—or he had been one. Either way, the act of sex had been just that. He had a certain expertise, taught, and used when necessary, but his emotions had never been involved. In his own way, he supposed he was as much a virgin as she was—which was laughable.

"I'm going to marry you, Airiana." He set the plate between them and handed her a fork. "Jorge's wife, Maria, is an excellent cook. Eat."

She pressed her lips together, taking the fork slowly, her blue eyes regarding him steadily. "That's it? You declare you're going to marry me and then tell me to eat."

He shrugged. There wasn't really much more to say. Clearly she wanted more, but that was all he had. As far as he was concerned, it was all there was.

She sighed. "I feel like kicking you again, Maxim. I fear you're going to have bruised shins for the first twenty years or so that we're together."

Relief flooded him. He hadn't even known he'd been holding his breath. It was strange to him how he was absolutely confident in every area of his life aside from with her. Airiana shook him up inside. Caused chaos in his well-ordered mind.

"Eat," he ordered again. His voice came out gruff, maybe even a little harsh, and that earned him another look from under her long lashes.

She took a bite of the burrito. A very small bite. One couldn't even consider it an actual bite, more like a delicate nibble. He had the sudden urge to shake her.

"You might consider that I'm a lot bigger than you are, honey, when you decide to defy me over something so ridiculous as eating."

Her fork stopped midway to her mouth. "Defying you? Seriously? Maxim, I feel sick to my stomach, but I'm eating because you asked me to and I wanted to please you. I'm taking small bites to make certain I don't throw up. Stop being an arrogant jackass. I'm not really in the mood for it. Sometimes it's cute and funny and even appealing. Right now, when my stomach is lurching and I hurt like hell, it isn't at all attractive."

He didn't get past that she was eating because she wanted to please him. There was something about loving another person that eluded him, and it was right there in front of him. Airiana did things for him that she wouldn't normally do—and she did them to please him.

He touched her hair. In the warm air it was slowly drying into wild, untamed waves and even a few curls over her head. "I'm sorry, baby. I'm just worried about you. I tend to react with . . ." he trailed off.

"Arrogance? Anger?" she suggested.

"Maybe both. When I can't control something I probably react with anger, although honestly, it's buried so deep I'm never certain if that's what I'm really feeling. Anger is an emotion we're not allowed for many reasons. It isn't safe."

"This school you attended was pretty messed up, Maxim." She took another bite of the burrito and chewed thoughtfully. "Everyone feels anger once in a while. It isn't healthy to keep it buried."

"My anger would be like unleashing a volcano, and that wouldn't be good for anyone."

He watched her swallow the small bit of food, and for some inexplicable reason, the movement of her throat tight-

ened his body even more. He was afraid he might end up
with a permanent hard-on if he didn't claim her body soon.
The sheet dipped just a little, revealing the small creamy
swell of the tops of her breasts. Without thinking he reached
out and tugged at the sheet until it dropped down to her
waist.

She sat very still, holding her breath, her gaze jumping
to his. He smiled to reassure her and then realized he probably looked like a wolf about to devour her.

"I'm only looking at what's mine," he assured her. "You
need to sleep. But I like looking."

Her breasts rose and fell when she drew in her first deep
breath of air, filling her lungs. Her nipples were rosy and
peaking under his scrutiny. Temptation in the form of a
woman. He couldn't help himself. One hand caressed her
left breast, a brush with the pads of his fingers. She was
warm and every bit as soft as her skin looked.

A current of electricity ran from her breast to his groin.
The charge sizzled through his veins, a rush of intense heat
that flooded his body. His cock jerked, drawing her attention to the bursting fullness he couldn't hide beneath the
towel cinched around his waist. He didn't want to hide his
reaction to her.

"Do you think you'll actually fit?"

He closed his eyes for a brief moment trying to hold on
to sanity. It was the last thing he expected her to ask. Especially in a curious, I'm-so-intrigued tone.

"I think you were made for me," he assured. "I'll take
good care of you, Airiana, always. A man should prepare
his woman, and I have no doubt I'll find that task very pleasurable. I think I could eat you like candy and never get
enough."

She blushed. The color surged into her face, down her
neck and into her breasts. He felt the heat beneath his ex-
ploring fingers. She didn't pull away from him, not even
when he tugged on her nipple gently. Heat flashed in her
eyes, desire pushing at the exhaustion. He wanted her with

every breath he took. It was going to be a long, excruciating night with his body on fire and no relief. That was certainly a first for him.

"I can't eat any more, Maxim, I'm sorry," she said. She put the fork down and looked around a little helplessly. "I don't have a toothbrush."

"The resort always has a little supply of things in the bathroom, including toothbrushes. Not a cheap one either." He'd used one of their toothbrushes he'd taken with him to kill a man who had ambushed him in his hotel room in Cairo. He thought it best not to mention that fact to her. "In the second drawer. There's toothpaste as well."

Her face lit up. "Thank you. My mouth will be forever in your debt."

"I like that idea," he said softly, contemplating the possibilities. She hadn't moved to make her way to the bathroom, and he realized she was sitting very still under the assault of his fingers. He hadn't stopped caressing her breasts. He enjoyed the shiver running through her body when he tugged at her nipples. She was definitely very sensitive. The idea of teaching her the things he liked was becoming more pleasurable by the moment.

He ran his fingers from the tip of her breast, lightly down her bruised ribs to her navel. Because he could. Because she was his. Reluctantly he dropped his hand. "Go brush your teeth, baby. You need to sleep before I change my mind."

She slipped out from under the sheet, a slow process when every muscle hurt. The tiny curls just above the junction of her legs were every bit as platinum, gold and silver as the hair on top of her head. He had to resist touching her there—and it wasn't easy. He would have followed her to the bathroom to ensure she didn't fall, but his body was too hard and painful to walk. He managed to set their meal aside on the end table before slipping the towel from his body and lightly circled his shaft, wanting to give himself relief, but knowing it wouldn't help.

He found himself smiling. She made him feel so alive.

He wasn't alone in a hotel room, or a cabana or the cabin of a ship. He wasn't alone traveling the world, going back time after time to empty apartments he'd rented in several different names. She knew his true identity. She saw him; the man that he wanted to be—could be—was deep inside where no one else could ever go.

"I could maybe help."

Airiana stood beside the bed, looking at the thick length of him. This time he could see the apprehension in her eyes. He almost loved that as much as the curiosity, because she was so willing, even in spite of her anxiety, to please him. Was that love? Unconditional surrender? He wanted to know. More and more it mattered to him to find the right path with her.

"Not tonight, honey, although you can't know how much I want to take you up on that. I have to protect you, even from myself. You need care tonight. Rest. Not more physical activity, as much as it pains me to say."

"I want you to be able to sleep, Maxim. You haven't slept in days."

"I sleep. I've taught myself to sleep whenever possible."

He pulled back the sheet and waited for her to climb into bed. There was no resisting caressing her firm, rounded buttocks. He had a great appreciation of her shapely backside. She didn't pull away from him at all, rather pushed back into his hands while he kneaded and massaged the firm muscles.

"Lie down, honey," he instructed a little gruffly.

She was just too much of a temptation. His body refused to settle down, even when he willed it to. That had never happened to him before. He found it oddly unsettling and yet exhilarating.

Airiana complied with his command, and he pulled the sheet over her. They had never really turned on any of the overhead lights. The moon was up and light spilled into their cabana. He didn't like lights at night. People could see in and he couldn't see out.

"At least lay down, Maxim. I know you said you can't

sleep with anyone in the same room, but I've gotten used to you being close and I don't want to be afraid."

He stretched out beside her, pleased she wanted him close to her. She moved subtly, enough to press her body close to the heat of his. Strangely, the small action made him far more comfortable.

She fell asleep almost immediately, and he turned to curve his body around hers protectively. Propping himself up on one elbow, he indulged his need to memorize every sweet line of her face. His body slowly settled now that she was asleep. He found himself just watching her, drinking her in.

16

MAXIM became aware of movement close to him. His hand tightened around the butt of his pistol beneath his pillow—an automatic response—just before awareness told him where he was and who lay beside him. He was curled around Airiana's body, her breast nestled in his open hand. He felt her nipple against the exact center of his palm.

He found himself smiling. He had a gun in one hand and a breast in the other. That had happened exactly seven times throughout the night—but he'd slept beside her. He'd actually gone to sleep with another human being beside him. Elation filled him. Airiana was magical. She represented everything good he'd never dared to want or dream about having.

He had only known pain. Loss. Heartache. Betrayal. He trusted no one, and no one trusted him. He had been alone for so long, existing in a shadow world where he was nothing but a ghost. He would have died in those shadows eventually without ever knowing what love was.

He breathed her into his lungs. His mouth moved against her temple and all that soft hair tumbling around her face slid over his jaw. Her skin tasted like love. Her hair felt like it. When he looked at her, his armor, always in place, always formidable, had cracked. Crumbled. Fell away.

He had promised himself he would never feel like that helpless boy, ripped apart by the loss of every single person he loved. He wouldn't love. Wouldn't feel. No one could ever hurt him like that again. How had she slipped past his every defense? How had she found that tiny piece of his soul he kept hidden from the world?

She stirred and he slipped his arm around her waist, wanting her to sleep as long as possible. He needed a little time to assess the intensity of his feelings for her. So strong. Overwhelming really. There was no way to hide from the emotions building with every minute spent in her company.

He hadn't known he was vulnerable. Now, it was too late. He had said he had no choice, and maybe the truth was, there never had been one, not when it came to Airiana, but he knew his conscious choice would be her. He would be risking everything. *Everything*. His life didn't matter that much to him, but his heart . . . his soul . . . those mattered, and she owned them.

He had watched her the entire time they were together, and a man like Maxim noticed everything. He knew her every move. The little faces she made when he annoyed her and the sudden flashes of humor or temper. He had never considered what it would be like to have a partner, someone to watch his back, and he certainly would have laughed if someone had told him this little slip of a woman would be the one he would always want with him.

He pushed back strands of blond hair spilling into her face. Her eye was several shades of purple and still looked a little swollen, but the seawater had helped, taking some of the raging fire out of it. Her feet were healing a bit as well. She seemed to be able to heal fast and he was grateful for that.

She regretted killing the men she'd been forced to kill. He wondered what it would be like to be that innocent. He knew what those men were like, what they were capable of. There was no redemption—nor did they want it. The men he hunted and the ones associating with them were the dregs of society. They made up the harsh underbelly where it was kill or be killed.

Maxim breathed her in again, taking her deep. She was already tangled tightly inside of him, and there was no getting her out. He couldn't run. He couldn't hide. He had to face the fact that love had ferreted him out. He hadn't been prepared so there was no way to combat it. The emotion stole up on him and like the truest arrow, pierced his heart until he knew there was no recovery.

Her lashes fluttered, those long, feathery lashes that drew his attention immediately to her eyes. He bent to brush kisses along the lids. Her eyes were gorgeous, such a startling blue, and could deepen or lighten in color depending on her mood. He had to admit the storm clouds swirling at times were well worth stirring her up.

A man had to wonder if her passion ran as hot as her temper. Or if that habit she had of giving herself so generously would be there in her lovemaking. His body had flared to life the moment he had awoken, her breast in his palm. He shifted, sliding his thigh between her legs, careful to keep his movements gentle. One hip and thigh carried bruises from her encounter with Gorya.

There was something extremely sensual and decadent about sliding one's skin along a woman's soft skin, especially her inner thigh. His body hardened more, his blood rushing to fill his aching shaft with a hungry demand. He pressed close to her buttocks, nestled there between her soft, firm cheeks, warm and aching with a pleasure he'd never known.

"Maxim?" Her arm reached behind her to circle his head. "You slept." It was a question and a statement.

He brushed kisses over her eyes and down her nose to the corner of her mouth. "I've never slept so much in my life. Lying beside you is amazing." He kissed her, tangling his tongue with hers, thrusting inside her mouth to get the taste of hers that drove him mad and kept him coming back for more. The taste he dreamt about and had on his tongue when he wakened.

She pushed her body tighter against his, kissing him back with the same generosity she showed in everything

she did. She just gave herself to him. Completely. Her trust
was like an aphrodisiac pouring into his mouth and down
his throat. Heat surged. Rushed. Electricity crackled and
sizzled. He wanted her until every cell in his body ached
and demanded.

He rolled her under him, on her back, still kissing her,
trying to stay gentle when he felt like a tiger about to devour
its most alluring prey. Her hands slid over his shoulders,
touched one wound lightly and slipped to his biceps. Just
that whisper of her touch on his body inflamed him more. He
wanted her to touch him everywhere. He needed her touch.

Right now, he wanted to know every curve and valley.
Every shadow. Intimately. Her body had been given to him,
into his care, and his job, as he saw it, was to care for every
aspect. He kissed his way to her chin, her throat and then
down to the swell of her breasts.

Her breath came in a ragged, shocked gasp as his mouth
closed over her breast and drew it deep, his tongue lashing
her nipple. Teeth scraping. Her body arched. Pushed into
his. So responsive. So perfect. She made a little sound in her
throat and his own body answered with hot blood raging in
his veins.

He indulged himself as he never had before, taking his
time, using his teeth to tug and his tongue to ease any sting,
his hands shaping and kneading. She fit in his hands. Her
perfect little body, all woman, curved and soft and belonging to him. He realized he'd be ferocious in his possession
of her. No other man would ever come near his woman or
her body. And no one would ever harm her.

He kissed his way over her breasts down along her injured ribs to the dip of her sweet belly button just waiting
for him to explore. Her little noises drove him wild, and
now her body writhed under him.

"You're mine," he whispered against her soft skin. He
kissed her belly, right where his child would grow someday.
He had choices, and his choice was to claim her. To keep
her. To let her teach him all about love. Enough that he
could share that love with children.

Her eyes met his. Even with one slightly swollen, her intense blue gaze moved him. He couldn't speak. Couldn't move. His entire body felt paralyzed with need for her. She shook him up so that the world tilted for a moment, and he held her close, waiting for the intensity of his emotions to settle.

Show me, Airiana. I want to learn how to love with you. I'm not going to run away. I honestly didn't know I was hiding myself away, but I don't want to be alone anymore. He couldn't give her the words aloud. He just couldn't. But he could say them in his mind to her. He could kiss her firm belly and swirl his tongue over her delicious skin.

I know everything there is to know about sex, but not about love. I want to love you, to show you I can be counted on. I'm not going to bolt the moment things get rough.

She reached up and pushed back his thick hair. "I know that about you."

He wanted her to know everything. To know her trust and faith in him would never be a mistake. *I'm tenacious and relentless. I'm capable of being there for you under any circumstances and I always will be. You'll never need to worry that I'll want another woman.*

"I've always known you were a man of your word and once you gave yourself to someone, it would be forever. For always. You have too much integrity to do anything else, Maxim." Her fingers slid lightly over his nose and traced his mouth.

The things he'd told her about himself were all true. He knew once she belonged to him he would hold on to her with everything he was, but he had to trust her that she would accept that flaw in him.

She slipped her arms around his neck and pressed her body close to his. "I'm not going to hurt you, Maxim. I just want you safe. You'll be safe with me."

He allowed himself a small smile. "There's nothing safe about being with me, Airiana, both of us know that, but if you're really willing to take the chance, I'm willing as well. Are you really looking at me? Do you see me?"

She nodded slowly, her eyes holding his. "I see you better than you see yourself. You want out, away from these men who send you all over the world, but you're so afraid everyone you love will be taken if you escape. You're a good man. A brave one. But you're far too protective of everyone."

He knew he had been attempting to protect his heart and the small slice of a soul that was left inside of him. If he loved her and lost her . . . He groaned and lowered his forehead to hers, still looking into the deep blue of her eyes. "Be certain, Airiana. I'll never give you up." It was already too late—love had found him and it was already wrapped tightly around his heart and had entered his soul.

"You're *my* choice, Maxim."

"It won't be easy loving me." He could at least admit that to her. Warn her. He would hold too tight. Make her crazy with his arrogance. Expect her to follow his every dictate. He had the feeling his shins were going to be black and blue a lot.

Her soft laughter vibrated through his body. "Did you really think I didn't know that about you?" She took his hand and brought it to her mouth, her tongue sliding over the center and then up his finger. Gently she bit on the pad of his middle finger, her teeth scraping back and forth. His breath left his lungs when she sucked his finger into her mouth.

"You must really like a good challenge," he said, hardly able to draw air into his lungs. Her mouth, so tight around his finger, gave him the same sensation around his cock. She nearly drove every sane thought from his head. Thunder roared in his ears.

Her tongue wrapped around his finger, stroking along the pad until his only thought was to bury himself deep inside her and relieve the building pressure. He withdrew his finger, and for one moment reveled in the knowledge that he would be teaching her how to please his body with her mouth and tongue.

He had that privilege. That pleasure. He kissed her.

Gently. Tenderly. He hadn't known tenderness and certainly hadn't known he was capable of such a thing. Possession welled up. Need. A dark craving that spread through him like a firestorm.

He nipped her chin with his teeth, lavished more attention on her breasts until she was once again writhing beneath him, arching up to give him better access. He wanted her with every breath he drew. She was more precious to him than his gift of air. He stroked his hand down her body possessively, from beneath the soft rise and fall of her breasts to the triangle of curls guarding her treasure.

His hands caressed her inner thighs as he pushed her legs apart and wedged his hips between them to keep her open to him. "You're going to lie very still for me," he instructed. "No matter how difficult it is, you're going to do that because I want you to. I want you to feel everything I'm doing to you."

He lifted his head to look into her deep blue eyes. Fear skittered there. Just a small edge for the unknown, but he saw the trust. She bit her lip and nodded her head.

"Say it, for me, baby. Tell me you'll hold still for me, even if you're afraid. You'll trust me."

She licked her lips with the tip of her tongue. "I trust you, Maxim. I gave my body into your keeping a long time ago. You just didn't know it."

He didn't wait. He'd already waited too long. He simply bent his head and tasted her. All that sweet, creamy honey waiting for him. He knew what she'd be like, totally addictive. He already craved her and he hadn't even had the chance to devour her—until now. He needed to eat her like a bowl of wild honey.

His tongue lapped at the heated liquid dripping there as if from the very center of the honeycomb. She cried out, a soft little shocked cry that only spurred him on. He drew more liquid out, his hands holding her flower open to him. His teeth found that small bud and teased while he suckled.

Airiana bucked, although she couldn't go far, and her small, whispered apology only added to the excitement and pleasure as he took his fill. He wanted her slick and hot, so slick he wouldn't hurt her when he entered her for the first time. He had no illusions that it would be perfect for her.

He used one finger to feel her tightness. Her muscles resisted for a moment and then opened enough to allow his entry. She gasped and pushed against the mattress, her body shuddering with the effort to keep her promise to him.

"Maxim, it's too much. I feel like I'm going to fly into a million pieces," she whispered, her voice strained.

Her head tossed on the pillow, her hair wild. He loved the way she looked, her body flushed, her lips parted, eyes a little dazed. The way his hands looked so large and dark against her white skin and small bones made him feel his power all the more.

"It isn't too much, honey, this is the way you're supposed to feel. Let yourself go. Give yourself completely to me. All of you. Everything you are. I'll catch you."

He lowered his mouth again, and she screamed, a cry of shock and pleasure. He held her still when she could no longer keep herself from pushing into him, need driving her now.

That's what he wanted—that mindless hunger that would allow his entry to be much more comfortable. He knelt between her legs and positioned the head of his cock at her entrance. She was so hot, he could feel that welcoming heat before he even lodged himself inside her.

Her eyes widened as he pressed forward. She gasped at the burning, stretching feeling she hadn't expected. Her channel was slick and hot, just as he'd planned, grasping at his invading shaft, nearly strangling him she was so tight. Her body gave way reluctantly, opening like a flower, but slowly, and unwillingly.

"Stop. You're too big." Panic was in her voice. In her eyes.

He stopped moving but didn't withdraw, just held himself there, her body surrounding him with the most exquisite feeling he'd ever known. Her gaze clung to his. He refused to allow her to look away.

"I'm not too big, Airiana. You were made for me. That mark on your palm told both of us you were. It's your first time. You're a little scared, but in a few minutes, the pleasure will take over. You have to relax. Take a couple of deep breaths and feel me inside of you. It's where I belong."

She pressed her lips together as if to keep from contradicting him, her gaze still clinging to his as if he was her lifeline. He was her everything, she just didn't know it quite yet. He gave her another moment and slipped in another inch. His hands held her open to him and he caressed her soft skin with his thumbs, but she couldn't move. Couldn't writhe around or buck hard against him.

He didn't dare allow her to inflame him anymore than he already was. He wanted her so much. Everything in him demanded he take possession, that he bury himself deep. The roaring in his ears was too loud, the fire raging too strong. He'd never been out of control before, certainly not during sex. Now, more than any other time, he needed discipline and control. He wanted her first time to be wonderful, not painful and frightening.

Another inch set him against her firm barrier. Panic set in, he could see it in her eyes, but she still didn't fight him, or demand again that he stop. He felt his cock grow even more, swelling with hot blood, as her body, stretched around him, gripped him with burning silk. He grit his teeth, fighting to stay in control when his body was going up in flames.

"Look at me. Keep looking at me," he ordered. He waited until her eyes cleared. He surged forward, a hard thrust, driving through the barrier and seating himself deep.

Airiana gasped, a small cry escaping. Tears swam in the blue of her eyes. He held himself very still, allowing her to get used to his invasion, used to that full, tight, stretched feeling.

"We're good now, honey," he soothed. "I'm sorry that hurt."

She nodded, her gaze clinging to his. Again, all he saw

was trust, and it was humbling. He hadn't given her that much reason so far to really enjoy sex. He was more determined than ever to love her, to show her love.

He waited until he saw the pain recede from her eyes before he moved again, a long leisurely surge, watching her closely the entire time. Her breath caught in her throat and her eyes went wide.

"That's it, honey, just relax and let me do the work. It's going to feel good. I can promise you that." It had to feel good to her, because her scorching hot, liquid honey surrounded him, held him tightly, the friction sending streaks of fire racing through his bloodstream to center in his groin.

He set a smooth, easy rhythm, watching her intently, touching her mind with his to ensure she wasn't in any pain. Once her expression cleared he guided her response with his hands, bringing her body up to meet his.

He saw the moment the sensations went from too tight and too stretched to pleasure. He'd never forget that moment or the expression on her face—or the way her gaze jumped to his in startled shock. In awe. Almost reverent. He increased the pace, still careful of her, needing to take her to a place of pure pleasure.

Her little panting gasps drove him wild. Her ragged breath became a counterpoint to his own. The sound of their bodies coming together added a depth to the music he heard in his head along with the roaring in his ears and the thunder in his veins.

His control was slipping fast. She was hot and tight and felt as if she'd sheathed him in tangles of living silk. He began to thrust harder and deeper, driving them both up again and again to the very brink, the friction turning into a fiery crash of pleasure consuming him.

He clenched his teeth as flames licked at his thighs, his balls, his belly and then centered in his groin. She gripped him, milked and squeezed, surrounding him with sheer pleasure. He'd been taught a million ways to please a woman, but he'd never had the experience of a woman trying to please him.

Her shy, untutored responses pleasured him more than all the experienced women he'd ever been with. He lost himself in the sensations welling up, gripping her tightly, taking her past the point he should have, but he couldn't stop.

Maxim?

Her voice quivered just a little, bringing out his every protective instinct. *Stay with me, baby. I'm right here. Let yourself fall. I'll catch you.*

I can't.

It wasn't going to be perfect for her. As a first time, it wasn't bad, but she was just too small and tight, and he couldn't stop his body's reaction to her scorching sheath and her innocence. He gave himself up to the fire, allowing the flames to consume him. He felt like the phoenix, dying in one fiery ecstasy of death and rising again reborn into something altogether different. Or maybe he just wished for different.

Her body trembled, but she didn't fall with him. She didn't soar. He was supposed to be the best at sex, so trained no woman could ever resist him, and the one woman who mattered the most, that meant everything to him, had a painful, unfulfilling experience. What the hell kind of lover was he?

"I'm sorry, baby, I'd never experienced making love. Just sex, and there's a hell of difference—or maybe it's just you. I'll do better next time."

He kissed her over and over, knowing he couldn't take any chances and do a better job that moment, but he would before the day was out. "I know that wasn't the best for you, Airiana, but it will definitely get better."

"It's better than that? Because I thought it was pretty good."

"Believe me, honey, I can do much better for you." Thank God she was so innocent and had no clue. She still looked at him as if he was the greatest man in the world when he definitely didn't deserve it.

Maxim held her to him, rolling, still buried deep, but

pulling her body on top of his so he didn't crush her. She lay with him, sharing the same skin, trying to recover her breathing. He could feel her heart pounding right over his.

"Was I terrible?" she asked, turning her head so she could look up at him.

"No. You're . . ." He searched for the right word. "Extraordinary. I had no problems, as you could tell. It was you who didn't get the full benefit of what we can do together."

She sighed. "You don't have to say that to me. I know I don't have any experience. You've probably been with all kinds of women who knew exactly what they were doing."

He stroked his hand over her silky hair. "My emotions weren't engaged, Airiana, with anyone else. Not one time. Of course the bodily function was pleasurable, it's meant to be, and I was definitely trained to ensure that, but my emotions were never involved. I never loved someone or wanted to please them because of the way I felt about them."

"There's a difference?" She frowned, trying to puzzle out if he was telling her the truth or not.

"I won't lie to you, honey. I lie to the rest of the world, but not you. If we don't have truth and trust between us, we don't have anything." His fingers slipped from her hair to the heated silk of her bare skin. "You give yourself generously and that's more than half the pleasure right there. You give me your complete trust, and that's a gift beyond any price. More than that, you *want* to please me."

She pressed a kiss against his chest. "Of course I want to please you. I just don't really know how yet. But I will, Maxim," she added adamantly. "I'll learn."

"Putting your partner's needs and desires above your own is what makes an extraordinary lover. You trust that I'll do the same for you." He moved subtly, enjoying the scorching hot silk of her sheath surrounding him. That little action sent a series of shocks vibrating through him.

"Of course I trust you," Airiana said. "I gave myself to you, didn't I? I wouldn't ever do that if I didn't trust you."

"Trusting me is one thing, honey; giving yourself to me the way you did is something altogether different." He bunched her hair in his fist and brought it to his mouth. "But what do I know? I might be the expert on sex, but you're the expert on love. I'll teach you what I know about sex and you can teach me about love, because I really want to know. This one was my fault because I couldn't control myself. That's never happened before."

"I'm fine with trying again," she assured with a small smile that twisted at his heart. "And I really love the fact that I can make you lose control."

He wanted to make her lose control. To give everything to him. "I want to be a good husband to you, not the overbearing ogre I'm fairly certain I'll be."

She laughed, a sweet, melodic, unexpected sound that sent vibrations through his shaft and melted his heart. It didn't take much for her to wrap him around her finger. She always seemed to react with unexpected amusement.

"Ogre?" She lifted her face and scooted up his hips just enough to frame his face with her hands.

His body left hers and he immediately felt abandoned. His first instinct was to bury himself deep inside her again, but he didn't want her to be sore. He could see the blood and seed on her thighs and that kept him sane enough to stay still.

"Do you honestly think I'd put up with an overbearing ogre? I'm not built that way. I think enough of myself to refuse to be mistreated in any way. And now I've got four children—if they'll have me—and I have to set an example for them."

He sighed. There would be no talking her out of those traumatized children. Truthfully, he would have found a home for them, provided for them and watched over them—without them knowing, of course. Airiana was the hands-on type.

"Honey, you do realize that the oldest girl is only a few years younger than you." He chose his words carefully. "She may be too troubled for someone so young."

"I'm a good ten years older, Maxim, and I have you." She gave him a brilliant smile and pressed kisses along his jaw. "You're old enough and intimidating enough for them to respect anything you say."

"What if they don't want to stay? They're from Italy. They may want to go home."

"Then we'll see to it that they find a good home there. I think we're the right people to help them, but of course I'd never make them stay with us if they didn't want to. Our farm is a magical place—a place of healing. You wait and see."

"We've been gone a few days. They may have forgotten all about us." He didn't know if he was hoping for that or not. Sometimes when he closed his eyes he could see all four of the children staring at him, and they'd looked at him as if he was a hero—a savior—which he was *not*.

"Right now, my sisters have taken those children under their wing. Judith has probably made each of them their own healing kaleidoscope—she's amazing and can sense just what a person needs. Lexi's got them working the farm with her and Lissa's cooking up a storm with them. Who knows? Rikki might even have given them a ride on her boat. And she doesn't let anyone on her boat."

"Counting you, that's five out of six. What's the sixth one doing for them?"

She closed her eyes and snuggled close to his throat. "Blythe. She'll mother them, just like she does all of us. She'll be the one to call a counselor and persuade them to go. She'll make certain they have clothes and everything else they need."

"Benito will be in his element with five women and his sisters doting on him," Maxim said. "He'll definitely need a firm hand. He's got a temper, that boy. And guts."

"He's like you were when you were young, isn't he?" Airiana asked softly. "He reminds you of yourself."

Knots formed deep in his gut. He refused to give into the temptation to throw his hand over his eyes and shield himself from her brilliant blue gaze. Sometimes she saw too much. Looked too deep.

He didn't reply. Couldn't. He just lay still, waiting for the moment to pass.

"Maxim?" She bent her head to press a series of kisses along his chest as if she knew imparting personal information was nearly impossible for him at times. "Benito is special, just as you are. He's got your generous, protective heart and he'll want to guard it, just the way you do."

"He'll want to kill, Airiana. Don't kid yourself. He's burning up with rage. Rage at what they did to his family and rage at what they did to him. There's so much rage inside you don't dare let it out."

"You're a good man, Maxim," she whispered against his throat. "Benito will be like you and that's just fine."

He shook his head, unable to believe she didn't see that side of him when she saw so much, the cold-blooded rage that allowed him to move in darkness, in the shadows and exist where depravity, greed and perverted sickness lived. "I don't want him to become a killer, or a man afraid of ever having a family and someone to love."

"That's why it's so important that he stay with me . . ."

"With us," he corrected. He'd taken the step out of the shadows by binding his life with hers and he wasn't going back. "It's important he stay with us."

Her blue gaze collided with his. "With us," she corrected. "On the farm. Sea Haven has a special quality about it. You'll see, Maxim. Unless you're bored out of your mind. I don't know how exciting life there will be for you."

"With four children? With you?" He gave her a small smile, his hands cupping her firm buttocks. "I think I'll be just fine. Let's get you into a bathtub. I'm not going to be able to keep my hands off you much longer and I don't want you sore."

"I thought I'd just go to sleep right here," she announced, a lazy, slumberous note in her voice.

His body tightened all over again. It didn't take much. She was soft and warm and melting into him. "I know. A bath first though, and then food. I thought we'd get a message to your sisters and let them know we're coming in."

She lifted her head, her face lighting up. "Talk to them? I'd love that."

He shook his head. "It wouldn't be safe to talk to them yet. Evan is going to have his people monitoring the phones."

She frowned. "Can he do that?"

"He's a billionaire. He can do anything." Cradling her in his arms, he sat up. "Listening in on conversations is easy enough. Private investigators do it all the time. For someone like Evan Shackler-Gratsos, it would be a piece of cake."

He set her on the bed and padded into the bathroom barefoot, pausing to study the outside around them with care. He'd left the windows open, using the wind to sound the alarm if anyone came close, but still, he always checked visually. He stayed alive because he never took anything for granted.

He started the bathwater, making it hot. She thought getting home was going to end their problem, but he knew Evan would never give up. It was possible Uri Sorbacov, in Russia, would continue to try to acquire Airiana as well. He had no idea if she was capable of re-creating the project she'd started as a young girl, but everyone else seemed to think she could, and that made her a target.

He weighed the pros and cons of bringing her back to the farm as the tub filled. The children had been through enough trauma, but he couldn't make a decision based on what was best for them when he had no idea if they were even still there or would want to stay.

He had three brothers residing in Sea Haven—if he could count his youngest brother, Ilya. Ilya's life had been so different from his and the others'. He'd been mostly used for legitimate work, and that had kept him—so far—off any hit list. For certain Stefan and Lev would help him keep Airiana and the others safe.

From what he'd seen of the farm, they could protect it fairly easily with enough money to buy the necessary equipment to turn it into a small fortress. He had money, and he suspected both Stefan and Lev did as well. It was never that difficult to acquire money when one stayed in the shadows and was smart about it.

If they ran together, he could protect her. She would learn how to fade into the background, how not to be seen or call attention to herself, but what kind of life was that for her? She didn't belong in his world.

"Maxim."

Airiana touched his hip and just the small brush of her hand sent his emotions spilling through him. He framed her face with his hands and looked into her eyes—those eyes could sweep him away with all that blue.

"You're a damned miracle, Airiana. You don't even know it."

She brought her hands up to curl her fingers around his wrists. "I know you're a special man, Maxim, and I want to be with you. Tell me what's wrong. I can take it. I've not let you down once. Talk to me."

He kissed her. He was best talking to her with his body. He could show her he loved her with his body much better than he could find the words a woman needed to hear. He was going to risk everything for her. He had to. There it was, the choices he always had thought were so important. He had no choice when it came to Airiana, yet she would be his choice every time.

When he lifted his head, her eyes had gone a brilliant sky blue, just the way he loved them. He swept her up again and put her in the large tub. The honeymoon tub had enough room for both of them and he slid in with her, sinking down into the hot water.

"I love the way you kiss me, Maxim," Airiana said. She leaned her head back against the porcelain, regarding him steadily. "But you still have to use your words. What are you worried about?"

He laughed. Out loud. She was priceless. She sounded like a little schoolmarm giving him a gentle lecture. "Use my words? Did you really just say that?"

"You're not getting out of this. We're a team, and we're talking about spending our lives together. We have to be able to communicate with each other."

He reached out and snagged her hand, knowing his eyes

had gone flat and cold. Cold rage erupted for just one small moment, flaring through him with lethal intent. "Baby, we're well past the talking stage. We are going to spend our lives together. What the hell do you think we've been doing here, other than communicating? You made a promise to me. You're not going to back out because I'm not the prize you thought I was."

She didn't move, her gaze fixed on his face. He'd spoken in a low tone, each word distinct and biting. A slow smile curved her mouth. She gave him a look filled with so much love, her gaze soft and her smile generous, moving him like nothing else could. The anger was gone as if it had never been. Everything in him that felt wild and dangerous, settled. She was his. He saw it on her face, in her eyes, in the sweet curve of her mouth.

"Maxim, I'm not ever going to run off and leave you."

His heart turned over. He was hers forever. Always. He turned her hand over, his thumb sliding over her palm, the exact center so that the two rings came briefly to the center. So small, and yet she held him right there. In her palm. She was wrapped tightly around his heart.

"I've given myself to you. All of me. Wholly. I know how to do that, and I'm not afraid. I know you'll always be here for me," she said softly. "You have to believe the same thing of me."

17

MAXIM sighed and brought her hand to his mouth, pressing kisses into the center of her palm. "I'll get the hang of relationships, Airiana. I'm learning, it just seems I'm on the slow side."

He scraped his teeth back and forth over the two connecting rings. Hers. His. Those rings, a strange phenomenon of the Prakenskii men, had sealed their fate together. He had run like a rabbit from her in his mind for far too long. He wanted choices and felt as if that had been taken from him so he'd been a child throwing a tantrum. Now he not only accepted that Airiana was his first and only choice, but that he was a very lucky man.

"When a man who has never had anyone finds a woman like you, Airiana, he can't help but hold too tight. How could he not? Losing you would rip out what's left of my soul—and God help me—there isn't much left." He made the confession looking at her palm, at the rings, not at her face. He already knew what her expression would be.

Airiana had more compassion in her little finger than most people did in their hearts. She would understand. She probably understood him better than he did himself.

"You aren't going to lose me. I'm not the running type.

If you get too far out of hand, believe me, Maxim, I'll be sitting you down and we'll be having the talk."

He kissed her open hand much more intimately, pressing his tongue into the very heart of her palm. He looked up quickly, wanting to see her eyes go wide with shock. She felt the intimate kiss deep in her very core—another wonderful phenomenon given to the Prakenskii men and their women.

Her lips parted in a little round *O* and she pulled her palm away from him. "That could get us in trouble."

He laughed softly. "Or keep you in line."

She examined her palm. "Does it work both ways? Can I do that to you?"

A groan escaped before he could stop it. The thought of her mouth so intimate on his body was enough to make him as hard as a rock all over again. "Yes. But please don't. Not yet. I'm really trying to be a decent man here. You need to rest and have some food. We've got all day before they come for us."

A shadow moved across her face. "Come for us? Do you think they're going to find us? Which ones? It's seems like everyone's after us."

"Evan's men? Sorbacov's men? It's all the same." He shrugged. "If they come here looking, Jorge won't point them in our direction. We're honeymooners, and he's known me for several years. No, I meant Stefan . . . Thomas and Levi," he corrected himself.

She sent him a quick, amused glance from under the sweep of her lashes, most likely remembering his first reaction to her knowing he was a Prakenskii. He had to remember to use his brothers' new identities when talking to them or referring to them.

"Thomas and Levi are going to come here?"

"If I ask, they'll come. With the two of them here, no one is going to stop us from getting home. Jorge keeps a small private airstrip for his guests and they'll be able to bring in a plane. We can take it back to the Little River

Airport." He made up his mind. With his brothers, he could protect her better.

She brought up her knees and hugged them, an action he realized she did when she was nervous. "I want to go home more than anything, Maxim. You know I do, and it's all I think about . . ." She sent him a shy look. "When I'm not thinking about you. But I don't want to put the people I love in danger."

"I think they're already in danger whether you're there or not. If Evan gets his hands on any one of them, you'd attempt to give yourself up for them."

"Attempt?" She raised her eyebrow.

"I wouldn't allow you to be so foolish." He caught her chin when she would have protested and looked into her eyes, wanting her to know he meant every word he said. "I can't be anything but who I am, Airiana. I'll always protect you, even from yourself. You can't expect less of me. Sometimes you aren't going to agree with my decisions, but when it comes to your protection, you aren't going to win any arguments."

Airiana chewed on her lower lip while she turned over and over in her mind his declaration. He was obviously stating a fact to her, one she had to think about. She knew he would be dominant and a little overbearing at times, but she saw into him and knew he was a good man who would always put her first. She hadn't quite thought that part all the way through. Putting her first meant sometimes he would decide what was best for her, rather than talking it over.

She let her gaze drift over him. He would never be considered handsome, he was far too rough-looking for that, but she loved his face. He was all hard planes and angles, scars and a perpetual five-o'clock shadow. His eyes were hooded and reminded her often of a predatory bird watching prey from a lofty height. His shoulders were wide, his chest thick, and there wasn't a place on him that didn't ripple with muscle when he moved. He exuded absolute confidence in everything he did—except when it came to her.

Even now, on the outside he appeared calm and implacable, his expression set in stone, but she could feel him holding himself very still. He would never be as sure of her as he would want to be and that would cause him to react in ways that she might not like.

"I can see patterns in the air, in the movement of air," she said. "Just as I can see mathematical equations, I can see patterns. You're there in those patterns, Maxim. The love you feel for me runs deep and true. I can count on it, like the sun rising in the morning and setting in the evening. It's always going to be there. Do you see in patterns? Can you see me in them?"

He would hold too tight until he could believe she would always be his. That was inevitable.

"I see them, Airiana, but this isn't about whether or not you're going to run off because you don't like a decision I make. This is about you knowing I'm going to make them. You aren't always going to be comfortable with who I am and what I need."

She shivered, suddenly aware the water was cooling down. "I understand." She did. She didn't have to like it, but she understood.

Maxim wasn't going to change because he had found love. He had been trained from childhood to prepare for danger and to expect it. He would guard what he had with ruthless implacability, and all within his household, those he loved, would listen to him when it came to matters of safety. She would be able to temper him only so much.

"I'm getting cold and I'm suddenly starving." She stood up.

He slid his hand up her leg, unable to help himself, caressing her inner thigh. "Stay right there for just a minute, honey. I can't get over your skin and how soft it is. Wet like this, you're so damned sexy I'm not certain I'll be able to wait."

She placed one hand on his shoulder, bracing herself as

he stroked her thighs, each caress taking him closer to her inner heat.

"You're so amazingly responsive to me," he said. "Even when I didn't do the best job for you." His fingers stroked her satin thighs. The air was warm and he wrapped her up in a cocoon of it, drying her body while he held her there. "I think all my training just went out the window with you. You make me feel . . . . alive."

Airiana pushed her hands into his hair, massaging his scalp and letting thick strands of hair run through her fingers. "Almost from the moment I saw you, I wanted to do this. Well, not when you were carrying me over your shoulder into the helicopter. Then I wanted to stab you through the heart," she said, precisely honest.

He laughed. A roaring laugh. A belly laugh. A laugh he'd never thought could come out of him, and he didn't recognize it at all. Startled, he dropped his hand and stared at her with a small accusing frown. "I don't even recognize myself anymore. Are you capable of putting a spell on me? I have gifts, maybe you have some I didn't know about."

Airiana leaned down and pressed a kiss on top of his head before stepping out of the bathtub. "Of course I put a spell on you. How else do you think I could get you to fall madly in love with me?"

Her soft laughter teased his body—or maybe it was her words. He laid his head back against the porcelain tub and closed his eyes, savoring the sound of her moving around. There was something soothing and comforting about having a woman do small, intimate things such as brush her hair or teeth with her man in the room. No one had ever teased him. No one had ever made him laugh.

"You know, baby," he murmured without opening his eyes, "you've given me far more firsts than I ever thought possible. I think I really did die when we made love and rose from the ashes a better man."

She circled his neck from behind, something he would never have allowed anyone to ever do. "You've always been a good man, Maxim. I'm crazy about you."

He laid his hands over hers, staying very still, working to keep the lump in his throat from getting larger. "Or just crazy, but that's all right, if it means I get to keep you."

He turned his head to look up at her. At once his heart stuttered in his chest. She had a look of absolute love on her face. Airiana didn't hold back her feelings or conceal them behind a stony expression. She just gave. Generously. He reached back and circled her head with his arm, bringing her down to him.

His mouth found hers. Demanding. Filled with his kind of love. Not at all like her gentle unconditional but passionate caring. He was hard edges and so was the love he had for her. He was always wholly focused and very possessive. He was dominant and overbearing and his kiss was the same, pouring his need and hunger into her, taking her response and holding her captive.

Airiana simply gave herself generously. He felt as if he was a beast she had to continually tame. In her quiet, humorous way, she somehow always managed. She'd reassured him many times she wasn't going anywhere. She'd given her body to him, she'd followed him time and again, trusting him to lead her, and yet at times, like now, when his love was too much, too overwhelming, he needed to crush her to him, hold her so tight she was imprinted on his skin.

Damn you, Airiana, for making me feel like this.

He waited for her condemnation. Her mouth was gentle beneath his, her tongue sliding oh so sensually alongside his. That rush—that fire—spread through his veins and electricity crackled between them.

Her mouth was perfect under his, her taste wrapping him up in addiction. He craved her the way others might drugs. The depth of his feelings shook him. The passion and love mixed together inside him, welling up like a volcano, consumed him.

Still kissing her, he turned, standing, taking her with him, lifting her and walking her backward until she was pressed tightly against the wall. He couldn't stop, even when he told himself to. There was no controlling his need for her.

Put your legs around my hips. I have to be inside you right now.

His kisses were burning hot now, feeding the terrible fire that refused to be sated. He needed the flames she provided, that hot, wet core of her surrounding him and taking him into her.

Airiana circled Maxim's neck with her arms, linking her fingers behind his head. He had her trapped between his powerful body and the wall, her feet off the ground. He was enormously strong, and she could feel the tension in him, the urgent hunger riding him hard. She should have been afraid. He could do anything he wanted to her and she couldn't stop him. Instead of fear, there was need and hunger rising just as strong to meet his. She craved his touch, the way his hands felt on her body, the way he was so desperate to have her. She reveled in the fact that his body trembled for hers. That she could make him feel this way about her—that he actually lost his perfect control around her.

Maxim made her feel as if she were the most beautiful, sexy woman in the world and no one else could ever satisfy him. It was a heady feeling as well as a powerful aphrodisiac. His hands and mouth were everywhere, rough and insistent, a dangerous combination, but one that only added to her pleasure.

She loved the feel of him out of control. How could she not when he was all about control and discipline? His mouth moved over hers, down to her breasts and back up to her lips. His teeth and tongue were everywhere, inflaming her senses, bringing her to a fever pitch of need.

I'm not sorry in the least that you feel this way for me, Maxim, I love that you do. I feel the same for you. She wasn't going to apologize.

Airiana had grown to care for him, respecting and admiring him and then actually falling in love. It wasn't the intensity of their situation or because he'd saved her—she knew that with certainty. She loved who he was. Even the man who was still a little angry that he fell so hard and fast for her. Maybe he'd always have flares of anger when his love for her overwhelmed him, but she could live with that. What woman wouldn't?

He bit her breast, gently sending darts of fire to her sheath. She nearly convulsed with pleasure. He'd taken the temperature up so much further this time and she loved it. His hand went between her legs, fingers pressing deep to feel her readiness.

I can't say, at this moment, that I'm sorry either, he answered.

He lowered her slowly until she could feel the large head, burning hot and velvet soft pressed tightly at her entrance. So hot. So big. She wiggled her body just a little, trying to get him to speed up. Her body felt overheated and achy. Tension built rapidly, gathering in her very core, a need and hunger only he could assuage.

Don't move. Let me do this. This time, you're going to go up in flames with me.

She thought she *had* gone up in flames with him. His voice, so commanding and tyrannical, should have annoyed her, but instead, his tone sent a thrilling shiver down her spine. She tried to comply, trusting he knew better than she did what would feel the best—and she wanted to feel that amazing pleasure again.

He pressed her body down over him, so that he entered her with exquisite slowness, his shaft pushing through her soft petals, forcing her open to him. Once again there was resistance and burning, a stretched, full feeling, but this time, it was accompanied with a streak of lightning that burst through her mind like a firestorm of sheer pleasure.

She panted, trying to hold still until he'd filled her completely. His thickness seemed to stretch her impossibly, but beautifully. His length took him so deep she was afraid he might lodge on her stomach before she was fully seated on him.

When she was completely on him, he held her there, allowing her body to adjust to his size. He nuzzled her neck.

See, Airiana? We fit. We're perfect together.

She wanted him moving. Fast. Hard. She could feel the urgent need in him rising to devour him, and she wanted to go there with him. She threw her head back and lifted her body at the urging of his hands. The ride up was breathtaking.

She moved down again on his long, thick shaft, tightening her muscles and squeezing to create as much friction as possible. She was learning slowly, little by little, just how to please him. She could feel his body shudder in reaction, the swell of his cock even more inside of her. She tried slow circles as she moved up and down, a slow ride designed to make him insane.

Damn it, woman. You're killing me. He sounded harsh, his eyes hooded and heavy with the intensity of his desire.

He grit his teeth and caught her hips in firm hands, taking back control in one swift movement that robbed her of the ability to breathe. He began surging into her, over and over, hard, deep strokes that sent her into the wall, a counterpoint to his hammering body. Each thrust sent flames sizzling through her body. Tension coiled and grew. Heat turned scorching, searing her. Blood rushed through her veins and roared in her ears.

He didn't stop. He was relentless, forcing her beyond all comprehension of lovemaking. Her body just wound tighter and tighter, accepting the wild pounding, helpless to do anything but catch fierce fire and burn with his.

I can't stand it, Maxim. It's too much.

She'd thought that the last time, and this was far more. Everything about the situation was more and she knew she'd be forever craving this man and what he could do to her body. She felt her body gathering itself, her temperature soaring. Her breath came in ragged gasps and she became aware she was chanting something that made absolutely no sense, a litany of pleas.

You'll stand it. This is us, Airiana. You and me. Just like this.

His body was incredible, his strength beyond anything she'd imagined. His hands were hard on her buttocks, driving her up and down. Her inner muscles squeezed and gripped, the friction growing hotter and wilder. She hadn't thought it possible. Earlier she'd felt every bruise she had, now there was nothing but sheer glorious pleasure coiling to the point she was afraid she might lose her sanity. Fear skittered down her spine. How could she feel like this with him and if something happened and he couldn't settle . . .

Let go, baby. That's all you have to do. Just let go for me.

She was terrified. If she did and her body went up in flames, what would be left? She would be his on his terms, not her own. All along she'd been the one giving herself to him, but this was different. This was a complete takeover. She would need him. Crave him. Be lost without him.

Airiana. I said to let go. Let yourself go and trust me to catch you.

Her body responded to his command even when her mind was still questioning her sanity. She felt the first swelling ripple and she heard herself scream as the orgasm overtook her. It hit strong and hard, taking over her body from her breasts to her thighs, sweeping her up in a tidal wave, a tsunami of emotion and sensation all wrapped together.

Her orgasm was so strong that she took him with her, clamping down on him like a vise, milking the seed from him, so that jet after jet rocketed deep inside her. She actually felt the hot splashes like brands burning his essence into her for all time.

She clung to him, hearing his hoarse gasp of her name, feeling his body shudder against her, his fingers digging deep into her while their bodies rippled with life and rocketed with an intense pleasure that was shocking.

She wrapped her arms around his neck tightly and held on as if he was the only sanity in a world gone mad. Tiny stars burst behind her eyes, and she fought to get one single breath into her burning lungs. "I'm never going to be the same, am I?" she asked him. "Never. I'm lost somewhere inside you. Or you in me. It's like we melted together, and now I don't know where I am without you. How did that happen?"

Airiana sounded so lost his heart turned over. "You're safe with me, honey." He leaned her into the wall so his rubbery legs could hold them both. "That's exactly how I feel about you. I don't know how or why the connection is growing stronger between us, but it is."

"You can't get any better than that, Maxim, or I'll die. Seriously. I don't think my heart can take it."

He rubbed his chin on top of her head. "There's so much more, Airiana. We're only getting started."

"I don't think I can walk. Can you? Because one of us has to man up, and it isn't going to be me. Physically and emotionally I'm totaled. You scare the hell out of me."

He laughed softly, tightening his arms around her. "That's my line, not yours."

"Not this time. I need to go to sleep and dream about you again. A girl's fantasies, not a woman's. You're too much for me." She bit his shoulder hard.

He laughed again, a strange sensation that told him he loved her stronger than ever. He carried her back into the bathroom and set her down. "I'm going to arrange for breakfast, some clothing for you and a ride home."

She leaned against the sink, staring up at him with her blue eyes. They looked a darker blue, more turbulent, and just a little dazed. "I can't walk. I don't think I'll ever walk right again."

He frowned, suddenly concerned. "Did I hurt you? I was a little rough for your second time. I'm not a gentle lover, although I tried, Airiana."

"I don't think it has anything to do with how rough or gentle you were. Quite frankly, I love the way you make love to me, rough or not. It's your size. I think I've got permanent skid marks inside."

"I'll run you another bath."

"Put some bath salts in it. I saw some under the sink. By the time you come back with breakfast, I'll be feeling fine again." She gripped the counter as if she might really fall down.

Her eye was still swollen, although he'd saturated her body with air each time he woke throughout the night to promote better and faster healing. The bruises still stood out against her skin, but he expected that. Even with a healing session or two, the bruises would have to run their course. He just hoped the pain was gone.

He ran her bath while she twisted her hair into some intricate knot that women liked to do before getting into the water. The bath salts were in packets, and gave off a lavender scent when he poured two into the deep tub.

He'd been too long without recon and was a little nervous about leaving her, but she was far safer in the cabana hidden away. Evan's men had to be searching for them. The Greek didn't much care for his men failing him, and he'd especially be angry after losing his entire crew and two of his best customers and having his ship boarded by the coast guard. He had guns and drugs aboard as well as evidence of a human trafficking ring. He'd be livid.

"Don't use the phone," he cautioned.

"You already explained that wouldn't be safe," she pointed out, sinking down into the hot water. "Seriously, Maxim, I do have a brain as well as a good memory."

She sounded annoyed with him. He was all right with that as long as she listened and did as he told her. One phone call would bring the enemy down on them in a heartbeat. He just needed a few minutes to send an alert to his brothers on their private site. They used it rarely, but all of them checked it often.

Airiana watched Maxim take a brief shower, just rinsing off, and then pull on clothes. She was grateful he was leaving her alone for a few minutes. He took up space in every room—a lot of space. She was used to alone time and she was fairly certain he was as well.

Whenever he was near, she saw more patterns than ever in the air around him. He exuded danger. If she hadn't known he was a Prakenskii, she certainly would have known he was lethal to his enemies, just by the way the air displaced around him. His aura was dark, colors swirling beneath the darkness, but the inky black layer on top was nearly impenetrable.

She took her first breath of air without him in what seemed like days. She wanted him. She'd practically thrown herself at him, and she had no complaints. She just needed—space. He was wonderful. Magnificent. She felt so ordinary in comparison, yet he didn't view her that way at all.

Still, he was bossy. He often got a look on his face that told her if she didn't comply with his wishes, he had no problem with just picking her up and forcing her to do as he said. She wasn't exactly a "yes" person. She understood him and his need to keep her safe, but that didn't mean it was easy—or would be easy—when they disagreed.

She sighed and splashed the water at the other end of the two-person tub. Life with Maxim wouldn't be boring, although he might think it was. That was another thing she needed to consider. What if the farm was just too quiet for him? He was used to a high-octane way of life and one could get addicted to that. He could leave her for long periods of time. She had no doubt that he would come back to her—but how would she handle that?

She shrugged and carefully washed her legs and feet. She would have to. She wouldn't give him up. If leaving periodically was what he needed, she would find a way to adapt. He would have to find ways to make it up to her, to make himself invaluable around the farm, so everyone missed him when he was gone and welcomed him home.

Airiana wasn't the type of woman to go into something with her eyes closed, not after the disaster of her childhood school. She'd been so eager to learn, to explore every possibility she could that she hadn't taken the time to see what was happening around her. She hadn't considered the effect of her absence on her mother. Had she been paying attention to the warning signs, her mother might still be alive.

She hadn't gone into her relationship with Maxim without giving it a lot of thought. She knew what kind of man he was, but she knew, once the connection had grown into a telepathic form, that he was extraordinary. He might not ever see himself that way, but he would be loyal and unswervingly faithful. He would always try to make her happy. She could see that in his character, through his mind, as well as looking at his aura and the patterns in the air surrounding him.

She sighed again. He would be a bear when they disagreed and it was inevitable that they would. She pushed her hand idly through the water, glancing out the window. Clouds drifted across a startling blue sky. Her body went still. The clouds rolled gently, forming patterns impossible not to read. There was love there, but there was danger and violence swirling in and out of the love.

She closed her eyes, hoping and praying she was wrong. The mathematical equations swirling in the clouds told her the violence and danger surrounded her, that it didn't belong to Maxim nor was it between the two of them.

She took a deep breath. "All right then," she murmured aloud. It wasn't over just because she was going home.

She let out the water, stood up and quickly dried off. If she returned to the farm, she'd be bringing trouble to everyone she loved. The children waiting there might even be taken back to the life they'd escaped.

I can feel your unhappiness, Airiana. Talk to me.

She had reached out to him without even being aware she was doing it. He had to be close to the cabana. She didn't have much time if she was going to keep them all safe. Hastily she rummaged through his war bag and found the jeans she'd been wearing when he'd kidnapped her. They had a comfortable, homey feel to them as she pulled them over her hips.

This isn't going to happen. I'm looking at the same patterns, if that is what has you spooked.

I'm not taking trouble home with me.

Yes, you are—I'm going with you. There was a trace of humor in his tone. *They all have a better chance with us there. We can control the situation. If we're not there, how can we protect them?* "You're panicking for no reason, honey." He stepped into the cabana, his broad shoulders filling the doorway.

She paused in the act of pulling on her shirt. Was she panicking? "He's really going to send his men after me again."

"I figured he would. You're valuable to him and he isn't going to give you up so easily. Men like Evan Shackler-Gratsos tend to feel entitled to whatever they want. Anyone standing in his way will be mowed down. He doesn't mind selling children and murdering them afterward. He'll come after your family to get you."

She dragged the shirt over her head. "How can we stop him?"

Maxim smiled at her. "That's my girl. Now you're thinking again. We've got the advantage at the farm."

"How is that?"

"My brothers. We'll be ready for him this time."

"What if he doesn't give up and keeps coming at us?"

"Can you fix this weapon they all seem to want?" He leveled his gaze at her.

She bit her lip and shook her head. His gaze didn't waver. She let out her breath. "I don't know. Maybe. Probably. But I don't make weapons, not for any country. I'm not going back into that life."

"Not even if your mind is going a little crazy with inactivity?"

"I keep it active."

Maxim smirked at her, but left it alone. He walked all the way into the room, placed a small pile of folded clothes on the end of the bed and took her hand. "Let's go outside.

It's beautiful. The waves are rolling gently and everything is an amazing shade of blue. We've got our own little private strip of beach. I'll wrap us up in air to protect us from anyone spying."

She went with him, liking the feel of her hand in his. He made her feel safe and loved. It was that simple. The woven chairs under the shaded table were comfortable and she sank into one, still feeling a little shaky.

Maxim leaned down and kissed the top of her head. "Do you have any idea how many times I've sat outside in a beautiful place and never managed to see it? Until you. Waking this morning with your skin next to mine changed everything for me. I never thought I'd ever have the chance to have a home of my own."

He dragged his chair around to place it next to hers, so they could both easily view the ocean as it rose and fell. Dolphins chattered and leapt out of the water in a joyful dance, almost as if they could hear Maxim.

"The point I'm trying to make is, I'll protect our home and family with everything in me. I know its value far more than most men. Evan isn't going to take a single family member from us. It doesn't matter how long or how often he keeps coming at us, he won't get any satisfaction. We'll close ranks and protect our own."

"Judith travels. Rikki dives."

He nodded. "I understand that and we'll do the best we can to make arrangements to keep them safe, but sometimes they'll have to compromise."

Her gaze jumped to his face. "You meant that for me."

"Airiana, you're the main target. You'll need someone—preferably me—with you at all times until this is over. You'll have to be realistic about what your life is going to be like. You have a gift and everyone wants it. I can't protect you if I'm not with you."

She nodded. "I'm not going to argue with you. I've seen what Evan's men are like. And I'll convince my sisters."

"Levi and Thomas will take care of Rikki and Judith.

They'll see to it that both women cooperate, but Levi tells me that Lissa and Blythe may be our biggest worries. Lexi stays on the farm most of the time anyway except for her trips to the farmer's market. We can handle that."

Her breath caught in her throat. "You talked to Levi? Today?"

He nodded. "Everyone is okay, and they were relieved to know you were okay and with me. The children are very quiet, he says, and are anxious we return. They don't trust anyone enough to talk about what happened. As far as they can tell, the children really don't have any relatives. Levi and Thomas have shored up the paperwork and are giving the children histories with us. If anyone tries to trace them they won't be able to."

Airiana felt the burn of tears and quickly blinked them away. Home seemed far away. Maxim had actually spoken with Levi. "Are they coming to get us?"

Maxim nodded and took her hand. "They'll be here today. We just have to relax and wait for them. They'll land at Jorge's private airstrip and fly us home."

"It feels as if I've been gone a year," Airiana said.

He rubbed her fingers over his jaw. "Jorge is bringing the food, honey. Why don't you slip inside and wait for him to leave." He kissed her hand. "I like Jorge. I think he's a good man, but he has a family to feed and to protect. I'm not going to risk trusting him with your safety. Evan's men will be spreading money up and down the coast, eager to pay for a sighting of you. If Jorge never catches a glimpse of you, there's no risk of temptation. I'd really hate to have to kill him."

Airiana obeyed instantly. She understood. Maxim liked Jorge, but if Jorge betrayed them and put her in danger, Maxim would kill him in a heartbeat. She retreated to the cabana, wrapping her arms around herself, happy to know she would be going home in just a few hours.

She danced around the room, unable to contain her excitement. She was going home to her family. Things might still be up in the air and frightening, but she'd have her sisters around her to help and she knew, from experience, that when they were together, they were formidable. Now, with three Prakenskiis as well, she felt they had every chance of being successful in fighting off their enemies. She was going home.

18

AIRIANA was crying again. Maxim leaned on one hip with deceptive laziness and watched his woman while she sobbed. The five women around her hugged and kissed her repeatedly. He studied each one as a potential threat to his relationship with Airiana.

Lexi, the youngest, was too sweet for her own good. She showed signs of intense trauma, much like the children he'd sent to the farm. She was a pretty girl, with too-old eyes and delicate, soft features. Her hair was a deep auburn and would burn bright in the sun. She was definitely an earth element, and from what he understood, she ran the farm. He found just looking at her made him feel protective—the younger sister he'd never had. He had the feeling she would be on his side. There was far too much compassion in her than was good for her.

Blythe was the oldest and clearly the one the others turned to and listened to the most. She was tall and blond with shrewd eyes and a runner's lean body. She had looked him over carefully when they'd arrived, and even now was sizing him up. She was a potential problem if she thought he might hurt Airiana in any way; otherwise, she would reserve judgment. Clearly she had gifts, but he couldn't see them, he couldn't feel the tie that bound elements together, yet there was something subtle there he couldn't quite comprehend. She was a question mark to him.

Rikki was different and definitely would have a difficult time with him, but not necessarily because he was with Airiana. He knew from what his brother had told him that she was autistic and had a hard time adjusting to change, yet he watched her with the children and she seemed open to them. She was the water element, and a very strong one, according to Levi. She was fiercely independent, but very loyal to her sisters. She would come to accept him, he was certain, as long as he didn't push the relationship on her. She would have to accept him in her own time.

Maxim had absolute confidence in every area with the exception of personal relationships. He had no real experience. He was a young boy when he'd been taken from his family, and his training had been drilled into him. He'd been a loner, and even now, in this circle of close-knit people, two of his own brothers, he felt like an outsider.

He kept his gaze fixed on Airiana. He knew her better than he did his brothers. She was the only person in the world he really knew—the only one who saw him. He willed her to look at him, make some acknowledgment that she was as aware of him as he was of her.

He couldn't take his eyes off of her, afraid if he blinked, she'd vanish without a trace, like everything else worthwhile in his life had done. His palm itched, but he wasn't going to use that connection between them, it wouldn't be fair to her. She was holding on to her sister, the one with flaming red hair.

No doubt that was Lissa, the fire element. She was the one he would have to be careful around. She would defend her sisters with her last ounce of breath. She was fairly small, but in her case, he didn't think for one moment it was a handicap. He could see she was especially close to Airiana and blamed herself for not being home when Airiana was kidnapped. She hadn't yet asked for details—how he'd come to be involved—but she would soon.

Benito leaned against the other side of the door and crossed his arms over his chest, regarding the women as well. "She's happy to be home," he observed.

Maxim nodded. Benito had a houseful of sisters. He would know why women cried all the time. He made certain his expression was sheer stone. The boy saw far too much.

"What do you think, Benito? Have you and your sisters decided what you want to do?" He needed to take his mind off his insecurity and focus on something that mattered—like the four children. "You've been here long enough to get some kind of idea what it would be like. Is it too different from where you grew up?"

Benito shrugged, trying to look both nonchalant and tough at the same time. "The girls want to stay, so we stay." His dark eyes bored into Maxim. "You're staying, right?"

Maxim jerked his chin toward Airiana. "She's home for me. So yes, I'm staying." He bared his teeth at Benito. "That means I'm in charge."

Benito made another casual shrug, and Maxim's heart turned over. That shocked him—having a physical reaction to another human being other than Airiana. The boy was trying so hard to be grown up. He didn't know the first thing about kids, but he could see Benito's struggle. There was a man's cold rage deep inside him and yet a boy's much more sensitive emotions. The kid was struggling to hold back the tears and keep his head up.

"I can live with that," Benito said. His voice sounded a little strangled, and he couldn't keep the relief from showing on his face. "Too many women around here. They're trying to make me see a counselor. A woman. I'm not talking to any woman."

Maxim frowned. "You'd rather talk to a man?"

Benito's expression changed swiftly to outrage. "That's never going to happen. I don't need to talk to anyone about anything. My sisters can go."

"Benito," Maxim said softly, searching for the right thing to say, wishing he had more wisdom. "Your parents were murdered. They weren't killed in a car accident. Ricco murdered them for the specific reason of acquiring you children. Your younger sister was murdered by a depraved madman."

Benito ducked his head. "I know."

"See all these women?" Maxim gestured around them at the women who had gone from crying to laughter. "Each of them had a loved one or loved ones murdered. My parents were murdered. That ties us all together in a weird way. We understand one another where other people don't have a hope in hell of knowing what we've gone through."

Benito ducked his head and scuffed the floor with the toe of his shoe. "Yeah. I got that."

"Talking to someone helps with the grief and anger and the guilt. We all feel guilty for something we had no control over. Guilt is a strange thing, Benito, it eats you alive. So does misplaced shame."

The boy's head snapped up. His eyes blazed fire. "I'm *not* talking about anything *ever* with any man or woman."

Maxim wanted to pull the boy into his arms and hold him tightly. Instead, he shrugged lightly. "It's up to you what you talk about. But going to the counselor and talking about your parents is a smart idea."

He needed Airiana more than ever. He was so out of his depth with this boy who looked at him with something close to hero worship. He was no hero and no one for a boy to admire. He cleared his throat and nodded at Judith. She was the spirit element and she was married to Stefan, his brother, although Stefan was now Thomas Vincent. "What's she like?"

Judith seemed to be a happy person and her laughter could make everyone in the room want to laugh with her, but she kept sneaking glances at him and frowning. He didn't like the feeling that she saw more than he wanted her to.

It wasn't like he was a great prize to look at. He was rough, and it showed in the lines of his face and the ice cold of his blue eyes. There was no getting around the scars on his body or hands. He looked like what he was, and it was unrelenting. He didn't have Stefan's sophistication or Lev's ability to charm.

"She's all right. She let us all make a kaleidoscope." There was a small thread of hidden excitement in the boy's voice. "That was cool. She's an artist and does a lot of paintings." The thread grew stronger, although clearly Benito tried not to give away his interest.

"She's a good artist," Maxim agreed. "Her paintings are shown all over the world. I understand she restores art as well. I've always thought that was a really cool process. Did you know that about her?"

Benito nodded. Now his eyes had gone bright. "She took us through her studio and explained how it's done to us. My sisters were annoying and she had to stop."

Maxim shrugged again. "Fortunately she lives here on the farm, and from what Airiana tells me, everyone goes to each other's homes when they want. I'm sure if you want to understand art restoration, she'll talk to you without your sisters."

Maxim looked over at Airiana. Her gaze jumped to his face and he found himself falling into her blue eyes. Yeah. He could live here and take care of the kids with her. The boy needed a firm hand or he'd turn out just like Maxim. He smiled at her.

They've had to call Jonas Harrington and inform him I'm back. He'll be showing up soon and he's a cop. Are you ready to meet them all?

That's a silly question. There's six of you and only one of me.

But you're a badass.

The laughter in her voice warmed him. She had a way of tying them intimately together with just a few words. Where he had no clue what to say, she always seemed to find the right thing.

"I'm crazy about that woman," he admitted to Benito. "There's danger in separating yourself from everyone, not wanting anyone to see inside of you where you're vulnerable. We know the world isn't safe and perfect like the fairy tales. But if you let it eat away at you, when that one comes along, that woman you know is going to make your world for you, you won't see her, because you're too busy hiding. I almost missed my chance with her."

"We're going to live with *you* and *Airiana*, aren't we?" Benito blurted hastily as the women crossed the room toward them. "All of us. Together in the same house."

Maxim realized that was the burning question Benito had had on his mind all along, but hadn't known how to work it casually into the conversation. He feared they would all be divided into the other women's homes.

"If that's what you want. But Benito, once you've decided, there's no going back. Airiana and I will be your parents. What we say goes."

Benito tried to hide his relief. "I can live with that."

"So can I, but we'll have a lot of women to take care of. I believe in being prepared for anything. I'll want you to learn."

Benito stood straight, his chest out. "I want to learn. No one is ever touching my sisters again."

Airiana came to him, holding out her hand. She smiled at Benito. "Have you picked your rooms yet?"

Maxim closed his fingers around hers and pulled her beneath his shoulder. Her sisters were right behind her, surrounding them. Levi and Thomas grinned at him, knowing how uncomfortable he was in the spotlight. He was introduced to each woman, and he'd assessed the situation correctly. Lissa was going to be the holdout. She was polite about it, but she was extremely reserved.

Still, he felt power in the air. It was unmistakable. Surrounded by them all, with Judith and Blythe close to bolster the other elements, he felt the ripples in the air, as if it were impossible to contain so much energy. He glanced at his brothers. These women were a force to be reckoned with when they were together.

Thomas nodded, and Maxim relaxed just a little more. It wouldn't just be the three Prakenskii brothers protecting the farm and everyone on it, these women could protect themselves if need be. It was only a matter of getting them into that mind-set. He knew having the children there would help. Women had a tendency to protect children when they might not protect themselves.

"Thank you for bringing Airiana back to us," Blythe said. "I don't know how we can ever repay you."

Maxim tightened his fingers around Airiana's. "I rescued her at sea, on board a ship. That makes her mine. The same with the children. Isn't that right, Rikki?" he asked, drawing in the water element. "That's payment enough, finding a family."

The sisters turned to Rikki. She nodded her head slowly. "He's right." A slow smile lit her face. "That's how I got Levi. The sea's been good to us, hasn't it?"

Maxim nodded, feeling very lucky that he'd had the chance to include Rikki. She was more open than ever to including him in their family. Before the women could ask any other questions, Lucia came in, holding tightly to her sisters' hands. Nicia gave a soft cry when she spotted Maxim and raced to him, startling him. The child flung herself at him, wrapping both arms around his leg. Lucia and Siena stood uncertainly just a few feet away.

Airiana beckoned them into the circle. She wrapped her arm around Lucia. "Have you seen our house yet? Did anyone show you?"

Blythe cleared her throat. "Um. I should have said something. We let them choose where they wanted to stay, and they decided it was better to be in the house that would be their permanent home. Lissa's been staying there with them."

Lissa flashed her first smile. It was directed at Lucia, not Maxim, but still, he took it as a good sign. "And you know what a stellar housekeeper I am."

"Oh, dear," Airiana said. "Is the house still standing?"

Lucia gave her a reassuring smile. "I kept up with everything, although Benito helped me with the laundry . . ."

"I did *not*," Benito denied. He actually looked embarrassed. "I don't do women's work."

Blythe choked back a laugh. Judith covered her mouth. Rikki looked confused. Lexi did laugh openly. Lissa just shrugged. "I try not to either, Benito. I'm with you on that."

"*Don't* encourage him," Airiana reprimanded. "Laundry is anyone's work, *not* gender specific."

"Still," Lissa said. "No one wants to do it, so if you can get away with saying a specific gender has to do it, more power to you. Personally, I think it's man's work myself."

Benito snorted his derision, loud and clear, glaring at his sister at the same time.

"I *meant*," Lucia clarified, "that Benito helped me figure out the English directions and how to use the machine."

Benito looked mollified. He crossed his arms over his chest and regarded his sister with a little less outrage.

"I've had to do my own laundry for years," Maxim said. "When you're in my line of work, you don't send it out or trust anyone else to do it." He hoped that would give Benito food for thought.

"Lissa is a really good cook," Lucia defended.

Even Benito nodded his head. Lissa smiled at them, but turned to Maxim, her eyes wide and innocent. "Just what kind of work are you in?" she asked. "And why were you wandering around on that horrible ship?"

"Lissa," Airiana hissed at her, directing the thread of sound through the air directly at her sister. "Not in front of the children."

Maxim was proud of Airiana's ability to use a stream of air to deliver sound. It was a difficult trick to master, yet he wouldn't have known she spoke to her sister except that he was in her mind about to ask her how honest she wanted him to be. They hadn't discussed their story at all. He had the feeling Airiana would insist on being very straightforward with her sisters—and that wouldn't win him any friends.

He realized he was still afraid of losing her—afraid somehow they would persuade her that he was no good for her.

"What's important here," Airiana said, "is to understand

the ongoing threat to all of us. A man, we believe his name is Evan Shackler-Gratsos—who was the brother of the Greek shipping magnate Stavros Gratsos, who died out at sea just off Sea Haven recently—thinks I can help him create a weapon that he can use to blackmail every country with. He's going to keep coming after me. Maxim felt that it was safer for all of you—and me—to be here on the farm. He thought with all of us and Thomas and Levi, we had a better chance together than apart."

"That name keeps popping up here in Sea Haven," Blythe said.

Airiana nodded. "He isn't going to stop. Maxim and I can leave if all of you would feel safer."

Benito and Lucia shook their heads, looking as if they might burst into tears. Nicia clung tighter to Maxim's leg. The youngest child, Siena, put her thumb in her mouth.

"We don't want to go," Airiana said, assured them. "But we want all of you safe."

"How would that keep anyone safe?" Levi asked. "If he doesn't find you here, all he has to do is snatch one of your sisters and you'd come out of hiding to exchange yourself for them."

"You can't leave," Lexi said. "I mean it, Airiana. You can't go. I vote no, you have to stay here." She would have sounded firmer if her eyes hadn't welled with tears and her chin hadn't quivered.

"Absolutely not," Lissa said. "I'm with Levi on this. We can protect you here now that we know he's coming back. And your Maxim will be very handy to have around," she conceded. She studied his face and then her gaze suddenly flicked to Levi and then Thomas.

Maxim saw her catch her breath and then her face paled. She pressed a hand to her stomach as if she might suddenly feel sick. *She just recognized me, that I'm a Prakenskii. Why would that upset her?*

Why do you think? She's not stupid. Four of seven brothers have settled here. Remember, Ilya is here as well, Airiana pointed out. *We were actually talking about how we didn't want any other brothers to show up because that meant one of us could fall.*

You mean fall madly in love? His voice purred deliberately with satisfaction.

She sent him a look from under her long sweep of lashes. Madly *is a good word.*

"Thomas and I want you to stay," Judith said, looking at her husband for confirmation.

"Of course you have to stay," Thomas said.

Rikki bit down on her lip and rocked back and forth. Levi casually put his arm around her shoulders. "I want you to stay. I think we're better together than apart," Rikki said.

Blythe nodded her head. "I say you stay."

Airiana looked at the children. "You have a say in this as well. We're a family. All of us. We came together because we are stronger together. We empower one another. But all of us have a vote."

Nicia tightened her arms around Maxim's leg so he knew if he took a step, her little legs would come off the ground. She wasn't about to let go. "Stay." That was the only word she said.

Maxim reached down and picked her up, holding her in his arms. She'd lost her twin sister and her parents, and already at her young age she'd been through an ordeal beyond most people's comprehension. The child buried her face in his neck and he was lost. If he could have, he would have gone back to the ship and killed Prince Saeed all over again. This time it would have been a hell of a lot slower.

"It's going to be all right," he murmured to her. "I'm here now."

Benito put his hands on his hips. "We all want you to stay here. If we're going to be a real family, then we need to be together."

"I agree," Lucia said. "And so does Siena."

Siena looked from Maxim to Airiana and nodded her head vigorously.

"Then we're going to need to lock this place down,"

Maxim said. "It has to be a fortress. All of you are going to have to sacrifice some freedom in order for everyone to be safe."

"I want to get into my house and have a cup of tea before Jonas gets here," Airiana said. "And we need to visit with the children and make certain they have everything."

"We also need to know what's on all the paperwork," Maxim said. "This Jonas, will he be asking about the children?"

"It's possible," Levi said. "He's a good friend of Ilya's. He's as cooperative as he can be under the circumstances. He may not believe the paperwork, but if it's in order, he won't question it. We've worked up a good story for the kids."

"I helped," Lucia said proudly.

"She did," Thomas said. "I'll let her tell you all about it. Get your cup of tea and settle in, because Jonas said he'll be here soon. His wife was in labor and he's waiting until the baby is born before he comes, but he is coming."

"Hannah's in labor?" Blythe said. "Libby must be back. Hannah would have sent for her." She glanced uneasily at the others. "That means they'll all be coming back. Ilya and Joley won't be far behind Libby."

Maxim raised his eyebrow at Airiana.

The Drakes. Elle Drake was undercover looking for the head of the human trafficking ring, and Levi was undercover for Russia as well. She was taken prisoner, and from what I understand, it was horrible. Levi couldn't save her, and everyone is afraid Elle's husband will not be very accepting about him being in town. He's friends with Jonas and Ilya. Airiana filled him in on their worst fears quickly. *We don't want to have to move, but the Drakes are very powerful here.*

Because they were using telepathic conversation rather than speaking aloud, Maxim felt her genuine fear. He bit back his first response. She knew the family she spoke of—he didn't—but he knew undercover work and the choices—

none of them good—that often came with that work. If Elle Drake had been undercover she knew the risks, and she would understand Levi not breaking cover.

We'll cross that bridge when we come to it. Right now, we have to take care of these children, give them a sense of safety even when we know it isn't safe.

Airiana nodded. "I can't wait to get a real cup of tea. I'll see you all tomorrow morning. I'm home and safe. Thank you, Thomas and Levi, for coming to get us and for getting the children for us."

"No problem." Levi sent Maxim a look, one that said they'd be meeting when the women were in bed. He was back to sneaking off in the night.

Airiana's house was larger than he expected. From the outside, it didn't seem as if it would be so spacious. It was two stories, with her bedroom and bathroom on the upper story. That was fine when one was single or married with no children, but putting Benito downstairs without supervision was just asking for trouble.

The boy had an eye for security. There was no doubt about that. He'd insisted his sisters take the two back bedrooms and he'd taken the front one. Maxim knew the boy's mind. They looked at one another and Maxim nodded his head in silent approval. The kid was looking out for what remained of his family. Maxim would have been doing the same thing.

"We'll work on the house security," Maxim said aloud, acting as if he was talking to no one in particular, but he was reassuring Benito. Benito was terrified of losing the ones he loved, and Maxim knew that feeling all too well.

Airiana went through the rooms to make certain the children had what they needed. Blythe and Judith had supplied them with the essentials. "I'll have to take you shopping, to get clothes and comforters and blinds you want in your room."

Nicia and Siena shared a room and Lucia had her own. Clearly both little girls had been sleeping in Lucia's room with her. Maxim suspected that Benito had lain across the doorway in the hall after they went to bed at night. It was something he would have done at that age.

His heart went out to the boy. Already, little Nicia and Benito had a hold on him so strong he didn't think he could easily break it. He hadn't considered that he might love the children as well as Airiana. He thought he was only capable of loving one person. His woman. Now, he had an entire family, and they were going to take his life over. One didn't ever walk out on kids who had suffered such trauma.

They settled in the large sitting room while Airiana put on the teakettle. Nicia and Siena took the chair next to him, while Lucia and Benito sat across from him.

"How is it you can speak English so well?" Maxim asked Lucia.

"Our grandmother on our mother's side was from the United States, so Mama wanted us to know both Italian and English. We grew up speaking both languages," she answered.

"Papa sent us to a private school," Benito added. "We were required to know Italian, of course, but also English, French and German."

Airiana had come back into the room silently and taken a chair on the other side of Siena and Nicia.

Their parents had to be wealthy. They're too well educated. Look at them, Airiana. Aloud he had to ask. "Do you have family alive? Aunts? Uncles? Your grandparents?"

Lucia shook her head. "Not anymore. There were no aunts or uncles on either side, and we never knew my papa's parents. They died a couple of years after I was born. Mama's mother passed away last year. I never knew my grandfather."

Maxim wasn't surprised. The children would have wanted to go to a relative once they'd been rescued. They'd made it clear on the ship that they had nowhere to go, but he had to be certain.

"You do know that if we change your identity in order to keep you in this country with us, you probably won't be able to claim the inheritance from your parents. If we take you back, the chances of us getting you are slim to none," Maxim said. "That's a reality, and one I can't get around. I can look into it if you want me to, but we'll be running a risk that we'll be found out. Right now, everyone thinks you died aboard that ship."

"Like Sofia," Nicia said, and began to cry. She ran across the room to fling herself into Lucia's lap.

Siena began to cry as well, but Lucia's lap was already occupied. Airiana picked her up and cuddled the little girl. She rocked her back and forth gently.

"I'm sorry about Sofia," Maxim said. "I know it's hard, Nicia. She's where no one can hurt her now."

"I want to be with her," Nicia said.

Maxim's heart beat overtime. *What the hell does that mean? What am I supposed to say? Surely she isn't talking about suicide.*

She's a little girl who lost her parents and her twin sister, Maxim. It's natural for her to want them back, to want to be with them.

At least he could breathe again. He wasn't going to be great at parenting. He'd rather shoot someone when he heard Nicia cry than try to figure out the right words of comfort. Shooting was easy. Talking, not so much.

"Of course you do," Airiana said. "I miss my mother every day. I want to be with her too. But we're going to be a family, and we'll love and support one another. Maybe we can help each other not miss the ones we've lost so very much."

"We don't want the money," Benito said, glaring at his sisters as if they might contradict him. "We're going to stay here where it's safe."

"Will you really let us stay here?" Lucia asked. She looked as if she was bracing herself for bad news as she rocked her sister soothingly. She looked to Airiana for the answer, not Maxim, which he found telling. She knew Airiana belonged on the farm, that this was her house and the others on the farm were her sisters. Airiana had the power to make them all leave.

"We want you to stay with us," Airiana said. "I was kidnapped and taken aboard that ship too. I think we're all in this together. If Maxim hadn't rescued me, I'd be in as much trouble as all of you. My sisters might not have told you, but we're not sisters by blood. We weren't born into the same family, but we chose one another. We choose to be sisters. We call ourselves sisters of the heart."

"I'm not saying that girly stuff," Benito declared. "I'm not being a brother of the heart or anything like that."

"Benito." Maxim just said the kid's name. He used his low tone, the one that said he wasn't messing around. "Don't be disrespectful to Airiana. I wouldn't like it and neither should you. She's ours. Just as your sisters are. We take care of our own, and we respect our women."

Airiana stirred as though she might say something but stopped when he sent her a quick reprimanding glance. *He's too much like me, honey. This is necessary. He needs to respect you from the beginning because I do. He has to learn what he values. We're already close to losing him.*

She didn't question him and he was grateful. He continued to pin Benito with his gaze, leaning forward to make certain the boy understood. "I'll be teaching you things that can kill, Benito. I have to know you'll have the right values and discipline to know when and where to use the knowledge I give you. You have to make up your mind either to be a good man or a bad one. No one else can do that for you. Your family is sacred. The women have the right to your respect. They are not less than you and they will never be. Do you understand what I'm trying to tell you, because this is your first very important lesson when it comes to living your life. Not only was Airiana telling all of you something important, she was also sharing a particular painful experience."

Benito nodded his head slowly. "I'm sorry, Airiana. I didn't mean to be disrespectful." He held his chin up and looked her in the eye. "Please tell us what you were about to say."

Airiana bit her lip and took a breath. *He's wonderful.*

Truly wonderful after all he's been through. He's trying to be a man, and clearly he trusts you when he doesn't trust anyone else.

Benito had suffered horribly in that cabin, all the while knowing Galati would kill him after all that had been done to him. He also knew his sisters would be sharing the same fate. Maxim had come along like a hero in a movie and rescued him. It didn't surprise him that Benito looked to him when his world had crashed down. Nicia, the same thing, but he was surprised by Lucia and Siena's reaction to him. He would have thought they'd be more suspicious. He figured Benito had talked him up.

"As I was saying, everyone on this farm has a connection. Each of us has had a family member or members violently murdered. Some have had experiences similar to yours and can understand what you're going through. We help each other when the nightmares come and the memories are too close. We've formed our own family, every bit as tight as one that has a blood connection," Airiana explained.

The teakettle whistled shrilly and she stood. "Lucia, we'll form our family and learn to be rely on and trust one another. We'll hit a few snags, but we'll work it out. My sisters and I bought this place together, and we learned to talk things over right away. We don't let things fester. We have regular family meetings. Some things, like martial arts and learning to shoot a gun, will be mandatory."

She made a face at them over her shoulder as she made her way into the kitchen. "Not everyone embraces the lessons, but we all agreed we needed to learn to protect ourselves. You will too. In matters of safety, we defer to the experts. That will be Maxim, Levi and Thomas or Lissa. Lucia, you're in your teens, that won't always be easy to do, because at some point you'll have school friends and want to do normal teen things and they'll squash some of your activities, but you have to understand that safety for everyone is important."

I know that was difficult for you to say. He couldn't help the laughter in his voice. Now that they had children, Airiana was much more conscious of their security.

Ha, ha, ha. I was talking about them. I'm trying to get Benito and Lucia to really think about things before they make a rash decision to stay in the United States with strangers when maybe there is someone in Italy they would be more comfortable with. I don't want them to go because I think they need us, but it really has to be their decision.

She was giving the children a choice. He was all about choices. He believed in choices, but damn it all, they were kids. What did they know? They could screw up their entire lives with the wrong choice. *Don't drive them off by being so negative. It won't be that bad. It's not like I'm going to lock them up.*

"We're staying," Benito reiterated in his firmest voice. "Right, Lucia?"

Lucia ducked her head, but Maxim caught the glitter of tears. When had he become such a wuss? The child was killing him, just like Airiana. She'd been so brave and tried to take care of her brother and sisters. She had to be scared to death. He remembered that feeling all too well when he'd been taken from his parents and brothers by force.

"Lucia," he said softly, and waited for her to look at him. When she raised her large, dark eyes to his, he nodded his head solemnly. "I give you my word, I won't go anywhere. Airiana and I will give all four of you a home and a family. We'll make this farm safe and fun and a place where you can grow up. We can't change what happened to you and your brother and sisters. We can't bring back your parents or little Sofia, but in time, we'll be a real family and we'll love one another."

Airiana came into the doorway, nodding her head, leaning her hip against the doorjamb. "You can always depend on us. I give you my word as well. I know you have no reason to trust us, but that's the best we can do to reassure you. You either feel the truth or you don't."

Lucia nodded. "I want to stay. I feel safe here. I know

what you said about the danger, but I still feel safe. I just want to go to sleep for a while and not be terrified."

Maxim stood up and went to her. He dropped his hand on top of the girl's head. "I'm home now. No one is going to get past Benito or me."

"They killed Papa," she pointed out.

"Your papa was a good man. I'm mean, honey. I hunt men like the ones who killed your papa. They won't get past me."

Is it a good thing to tell them that?

It's the truth, baby, whether you like it or not, that's who I am.

19

JONAS Harrington arrived at eight o'clock in the morning, and he didn't come alone. It was the second man Maxim studied. Harrington looked like a man who could handle himself, but it was the other one introduced as Damon Wilder that Airiana was afraid of. Anyone she was afraid of wasn't welcome in their home, as far as Maxim was concerned, yet she smiled graciously and opened the door to allow both entry.

Maxim slipped into the background, blurring his image just enough so that when he went completely still, he all but disappeared.

"Jonas," Airiana greeted. "The children aren't up yet. Apparently they haven't been sleeping very well and now that we're home, they can actually rest."

Maxim winced. She'd used the word *we're* and Harrington was quick on the pick-up. His eyes scanned the room and then moved through it a second time much more slowly, as if sensing they weren't alone. He spotted Maxim standing just in the shadows across the room where he had a clear shot to either man.

"I understand, Airiana," Jonas said smoothly, "but you can understand the urgency of our business. You were taken from your home, and not too long after, the children arrived, and then we got a message that you were safe. We also understand that a ship was discovered, one with dead men strewn from one end to the other and evidence of human trafficking in the luxury cabins. Strange though, a couple of the cabins were wiped down so there were no fingerprints, no evidence of who had been there." While he talked in his easygoing manner, Jonas Harrington looked directly at Maxim. Unlike Damon, Jonas didn't take the seat Airiana offered. "Who's your friend?"

Airiana's gaze flicked to Maxim. She smiled, her bright, loving smile that always melted his heart. He didn't step from the shadows. Airiana started toward him.

Walk around the chairs. Don't get between us.

She looked startled but obeyed him. When she got to his side, she put one hand on his arm, instead of taking his hand. He was grateful to her for that. She learned fast.

"Jonas, this is my fiancé, Max Walberg. Max, Jonas Harrington, our local sheriff, and his brother-in-law, Damon Wilder." Airiana performed the introductions.

"Don't get up," Maxim said to Damon in as gracious a tone as he could manage. Damon had started to rise. His limp was very pronounced, and Maxim wracked his brain for information on the man. The name was familiar, and it only took seconds for him to recall that Damon Wilder was the United States equivalent to Theodotus Solovyov. "It isn't necessary."

Maxim stepped forward as Jonas put out his hand toward him. The moment he came out of the shadows, he saw recognition on Harrington's face. The man knew he was a Prakenskii. His first instinct was to kill him, the second was to remember this man knew his youngest brother. Somehow the two men were friends. If he could recognize Maxim, he had to know about Stefan and Lev.

"Max Walberg, is it? Strange, but you look very Russian to me."

Jonas took his hand in a firm grip, but didn't indulge in

petty games to see who was stronger and that told Maxim he was even more dangerous than he appeared.

"My grandmother on my mother's side was Russian," Maxim said smoothly. "I had no idea it showed."

Jonas nodded and stepped back to allow Maxim to precede him to the cluster of furniture. Maxim didn't move.

Airiana smiled up at Maxim as if unaware of the undercurrent. "Would you mind terribly getting the coffee? Jonas will drink tea, but he does love his coffee in the morning, at least that's what Blythe tells me."

Clever woman. I'm marrying a genius, aren't I? She'd given him the perfect excuse to move away from the men without turning his back.

Absolutely you are.

You don't need to know whether another man prefers coffee or tea.

Her laughter drifted through his mind, a sweet melody that relaxed him as he glided to the door. "Either of you take sugar or cream?"

Both Jonas and Damon shook their heads. Airiana smiled at the two men as she dropped into a chair. "It's good to be home. I understand Hannah had the baby last night."

"A very stubborn baby," Jonas clarified, his first genuine smile spreading across his face. "Libby delivered, but it took nearly all night. Hannah called her when she first started having signs of labor and Libby managed to make it back fairly quickly. I think Tyson hired a private jet. Sarah was there as well, so it was quite the event."

"Congratulations. Is Hannah all right? Boy? Girl?" Airiana prompted.

The way the house was built, the sitting room flowed into the kitchen. The large archway leading to the kitchen allowed occupants to be part of the conversation in the sitting room. Maxim was grateful for the design as he could easily keep an eye on Airiana. He doubted that either man was there to harm her, but with Wilder coming along for the police report, he knew Airiana was very uneasy.

"We had a boy. We haven't decided on a name yet, but we're working on it. Hannah is fine, but very tired."

"That's so wonderful, Jonas," Airiana said sincerely. "I'm happy for you."

Jonas leaned toward her. "Thank you, Airiana. Now tell me what the hell happened."

Maxim winced at the tone. The man was good. Chit-chat. Put her at ease. Then go all commanding on her. The teakettle whistled. "Tea in a moment, honey," he announced unnecessarily to give her a chance to collect herself. He shouldn't have worried.

Airiana sank back into her chair. "Can you believe my birth father had me kidnapped? I've never laid eyes on the man. I didn't even know he actually existed, let alone who he was. It seems my mother met him when she attended the Moscow Institute of Physics and Technology. You know the story, it happens all the time. He was married. She was young, and he was a superstar in physics. They had an affair, and I was the result."

It was Damon who leaned forward, his gaze intent. "Who is your father, Airiana?"

"Theodotus Solovyov."

"Of course." Damon all but rubbed his hands together. "That explains so much. A brilliant man, Jonas. Absolutely brilliant. You inherited that from him, Airiana."

Her smile faded. "My mother was brilliant. Whatever my father is, he's nothing to me. He was willing to turn me over to the Russian government even when I told him I was a citizen of the United States and I wanted to come home."

Maxim came in with coffee for both men. He handed the steaming mugs to them and then moved behind Airiana's chair without sitting down on the pretense that he had to get the tea for her. He brushed a kiss on top of her head.

Are you all right? I can ask them to leave . . . politely.

Her gaze jumped to his face and he saw the love there. Amusement filled his mind. *Politely? Did you plan on shooting bullets at their feet?*

Of course not. Chucking them out the window is a much better solution. No possible hard feelings that way.

She reached up to stroke his fingers and he realized she did need comfort. Talking about her birth father was difficult after all she'd been through. She had to have mixed feelings. He took her hand, his thumb sliding gently over her inner wrist in a slow caress. *I'll get your tea and be right back, baby.*

She nodded, and he slipped away. Her gaze collided with Jonas's.

"The man moves like a cat. Your fiancé. How long have you two known each other?"

"Max? It's been about two years, on and off. He travels a lot, so we mainly corresponded at first." Airiana delivered their cover story like a pro. Her tone even held the ring of truth.

"And he's related to the children? They're from Italy."

She nodded and lowered her voice as if the children might overhear. "It was such a tragedy. Their parents and a sister were killed in a car accident. They have no other relatives, so of course Max and I will take them in. Neither of us expected a ready-made family, but we're both happy to have them."

"I see." Jonas's tone indicated he thought she was feeding him a line of bull, but the paperwork Lev and Stefan had created was impeccable. Max Walberg was the only living relative of the four children.

"Why did your father decide to kidnap you?" Jonas changed tactics. "Why not pick up the phone and call you?"

"I asked him that very same question," Airiana said. "He claimed he wanted to get to know me, but I pointed out that kidnapping me wasn't a very good beginning."

Maxim handed Airiana a cup of tea and sank into the chair beside her. "Solovyov believed a man by the name of Evan Shackler-Gratsos had sent his men to kidnap her. He's a billionaire. He inherited everything from his brother, but prior to that he was the head of a worldwide motorcycle gang. He's suspected of murder, drug and human trafficking as well as arms dealing."

"How would you know all that?" Jonas asked.

"I worked, until a few days ago, for the government, and we were tracking Shackler-Gratsos." He was careful not to say which government. "We were tipped off by a man deep in his organization that he was planning to grab Airiana, so we were already rushing to protect her. Her father's men got to her before Shackler-Gratsos."

Airiana gave a delicate little shiver. "It was very disconcerting to know that my own father had arranged to have me kidnapped. And amazing to have Max be the one to come to my rescue."

"How handy that you knew each other ahead of time," Jonas said, without managing to sound sarcastic. He flicked a glance at Airiana, who calmly took a sip of tea and regarded him with a small smile.

"Isn't it though? I was lucky that he recognized my name and immediately found me. I think if Theodotus had managed to get me to Russia, I would never have gotten home."

"Where did Max find you?" Jonas prompted.

"I was on a yacht just off the coast of Mexico. My birth father told me his idea was to take the yacht to Colombia, using the time for us to get to know each other, and there would be a private plane waiting to take us to Russia."

"What happened to your face? And your feet," Jonas added with a little frown.

Maxim liked him better for that frown. Clearly the sheriff was not a man who liked seeing bruises on a woman.

"There was a Russian aboard, a man named Gorya. I think he was the steward. I had already cut my feet on a glass Theodotus threw—he was a little angry with me—and I went out on the deck to get away from him. Gorya and I got into an altercation and he punched me." She consolidated the attacks, one from Gorya and the other from Sorbacov's assassins.

"He didn't just punch her," Maxim added. "She has bruises all over where he kicked her as well."

"Why would he do that?" Damon asked, looking shocked. "He dared to touch the daughter of Theodotus Solovyov? That could get him imprisoned."

"Or killed," Jonas added, looking at Maxim.

"I was very uncooperative."

Jonas frowned. "I don't understand. Did they expect you would want to go to Russia after being kidnapped?"

Airiana sighed and put her teacup down. "They wanted me to do something for them. They *expected* me to do it. If I didn't cooperate, my father indicated, although he didn't say it outright, I would be forced."

"And this Gorya was their enforcer?"

Airiana shrugged, unwilling to lie outright. *Misleading using the truth is one thing, but I've never been good at lying.*

You're doing great, honey. And you aren't lying. That's exactly what your father expected from you.

Airiana pressed her thumb into the center of her palm as if her palm itched. Jonas's gaze immediately followed that small, subtle motion. Maxim couldn't help but admire the man. He was good at his job. More, Maxim was certain his sheriff's job wasn't where he'd gotten his training.

"Why had you suddenly contacted me, Damon? We lived in the same town for a long while, yet you never came near me." Airiana suddenly went on the attack. "Did you expect me to believe that on the very day I was kidnapped by Theodotus Solovyov for his government it was just a coincidence that you made an appointment to see me?"

"What I have to talk to you about is of vital importance," Damon said, "but it is also classified and I can't discuss it with anyone else present."

"That's really too bad. I have no interest in anything classified or anything my fiancé can't hear. Are there any other questions you need answered, Jonas? The children will be waking up soon."

Maxim could have told her Benito was already awake and listening to every word.

"You're putting me in an awkward position," Damon said.

"I know. I'm sorry, but I can't help you."

"Can't? Or won't?"

Airiana let her breath. "I don't know. Is the threat real?"

Damon shoved his hand through his hair. "I can say, in the abstract, that yes, it is. I could use your help."

Before Airiana could reply, Maxim put his hand over hers, to stop her. "If she agreed to try to help you, would your government help in any way possible with her protection? Give us license to do the things necessary here at her home to protect her family? You know as well as I do, that if she does this thing, she'll be a target."

I'm already a target.

So why not get what we need with the government's approval. If we give them a list and they agree to everything, you'll know just how valuable you really are to them.

Airiana couldn't breathe with the rush of adrenaline pouring through her veins. To work again. To talk to people who could brainstorm with her. The thought was just as intoxicating as it was frightening. She could get caught up in that life all over again and neglect the people she loved.

"I have Max. And the children. They need me."

"We can reduce your work hours, and a good part of it can be done from your home once it is secure," Damon said. "I'm certain you'll have every cooperation to make you and your family safe."

Airiana bit her lip. She glanced at Maxim. "I have to think about it, Damon. I was being honest with you when I told you I didn't know if I could help you. It's been a long time since I've done any work."

"On paper maybe, but in your head . . ." Damon trailed off.

"If I do this, Max has to come with me as my bodyguard."

"No." Not from Damon, but from Jonas. "He can't."

Damon shook his head. "Jonas, anything is doable. We'll make it work. She's too important to my work to close any doors."

"I don't care what his paperwork says, Damon. I don't care if the investigators pronounce him American of the year. He's Russian and his loyalties are to Russia."

"I have no ties to Russia," Maxim stated. "Every bridge is burned. I brought Airiana home. My loyalties are to her."

Jonas jumped to his feet and paced across the floor. "I can trust your word because I know who you are, but not for my country's security. Airiana, you have to understand, no one, not even you, can take that chance."

"I am Max Walberg, a citizen of the United States. We're going to be married as soon as possible and this will be my home. I'm becoming a father to four children and hope to have many more of my own, but above all, I will see to Airiana's protection."

"That's the deal, Jonas," Airiana said. "Apparently my father is a famous Russian physicist. If you question Max's loyalty, you're going to have to question mine."

Jonas swore and turned away from them to stare out the window. "Do you have any idea how complicated this situation is becoming? The Drakes are all returning. With them will come Elle and Jackson. Now this. I feel like I'm walking through a damn minefield."

"He's going to make another try for her, Harrington," Maxim said softly, watching the man. His hand was never far from his weapon and the sheriff knew it, but it hadn't stopped him from expressing his frustration.

"Who? Her father?" Jonas spun around.

Maxim shook his head slowly. "The Russians might try again for her, but somehow I don't think they will. No, Shackler-Gratsos. He won't come himself. He'll send mercenaries. He's angry. Shackler-Gratsos doesn't like to be thwarted by mere mortals. He feels entitled to anything he wants. And he wants Airiana."

Damon sucked in his breath sharply. "It's him. He's got to be the one behind . . ." He trailed off.

"That's what Theodotus thought as well. The Russians were threatened." Maxim wasn't employed by either government anymore and not bound to silence. He wanted Damon, at least, to take the threat to Airiana's safety very seriously.

"What makes Airiana so important to all these people?" Jonas asked. "To you, Damon?"

"My brain," Airiana answered, a shade sarcastically. "The girl's got a brain."

Jonas stopped his pacing abruptly in front of her chair. "Have I ever given you the impression that I think less of you because you're a woman? Or that I think women aren't as intelligent as men?"

Airiana shook her head, looking slightly ashamed. "No, of course not, Jonas."

Jonas shot Damon a hard look. "It isn't you I'm upset with, Airiana. It's the situation. I came here to take a report on a kidnapping and my brother-in-law asked to come along. It didn't occur to me that he had any motive other than concern for your well-being. I don't like being used. Airiana has clearly been through hell, Damon, and now you're insisting she do whatever it is she does for you. What makes you any different than Shackler-Gratsos or her birth father, who, by the way, should be thoroughly ashamed of himself."

Damon sat back in his chair. "I guess I think of us as the good guys."

"So does every other country. I'm a patriot, but I don't like bullying or threatening women for any reason. Shouldn't she be protected whether or not she does whatever it is you want her to do?"

"Of course. If the situation wasn't so dire . . ." He broke off, and shook his head.

"Is it?" Airiana took a breath and let it out. *What if Evan has already developed a weapon? But then he really wouldn't need me, would he? But if he has it . . .*

If he has, could you counter it?

She shrugged. *Maybe.*

You explain to Wilder and Harrison that I already know what this is about while I take care of our child who has big ears.

Airiana nodded and waited until Maxim excused himself and left to go down the hall. "Theodotus talked in front of Max. He already knows everything."

The breath hissed out between Jonas's teeth. "Great. The Russian knows. The Greek knows. I'm the only one in the dark, and I'm the one who has to sort all this out."

"He wouldn't do that," Damon said.

"He would if he expected Max to be killed—which he did. That's the reason for my cut feet and Gorya punching and kicking me. When I realized they were going to kill Max after he rescued me from Evan's men, I tried creating a diversion so he could get away."

"So Evan's men actually were the ones to kidnap you," Jonas said, sinking once more into his chair.

"The Russians believe he or his brother kidnapped a physicist, a man by the name of Dennet Laurent, and gave him what little they had of a project I'd started when I was a child. My mother fed the information to Theodotus. He was working on it as well, using my work as a platform."

"So that's how they got their hands on it," Damon said. "We suspected your mother of selling the information, but there was no real evidence of it."

"She gave it freely to my father. She was proud of her daughter, not betraying her country. Theodotus had a wife who had many lovers, and one of them worked for Shackler-Gratsos. He was able to use her to get the work Theodotus was doing and they turned that over to Laurent, or at least that's who Theodotus suspects Shackler-Gratsos had taken prisoner."

"Certainly Dennet Laurent is one of the few who could have figured the weapon out," Damon agreed. "Everyone wondered what had happened to him. He disappeared without a trace."

"It wasn't a weapon. It was never supposed to be a weapon," Airiana said. "It was a useful tool to help countries get food. To help farmers with their crops. To stop global warming."

"You're talking about controlling the weather," Jonas said. "That's what this entire thing is about."

Airiana nodded, ignoring Damon's groan of frustration. "I found patterns I could use to predict hurricanes and droughts. Even tornados. I envisioned expanding the results in order to go into each area where the weather affected what was happening on the ground, long droughts for instance, and being able to make it rain."

"Haven't they already tried that?"

"I'm not talking about seeding clouds, Jonas. What if I could actually change the weather patterns and make it rain naturally. Remove one component so the hurricane won't make it to land. Stop two cells from forming a tornado. Think about all the good that could be done," Airiana said. "But no, instead of helping starving children, each person who has seen the projections immediately thought of it in the context of a weapon."

"That's not entirely true," Damon contradicted. "I was using your platform with the idea of the same thing—until we got the threat. We didn't know which terrorist had the capability of changing the weather, and everyone was scrambling around trying to find a countermeasure. The request is nearly impossible to meet and we're running out of time."

"Except," Maxim said, walking back into the room, "the fact that Evan tried to acquire Airiana, which means he may have run into the same glitch Theodotus and you did, Wilder." When Damon raised an eyebrow, Maxim shrugged. "It isn't that difficult to figure out that your work wasn't completed. You wouldn't be here if you'd been able to complete the project."

Jonas shot Maxim an amused glance. "He's got a point, Damon."

"Clearly Theodotus couldn't finish it either," Maxim added. "I can't imagine that Laurent could when the two of you couldn't do it."

"We can't take that chance," Damon said. "A weapon like that in the hands of a madman could virtually wipe out countries. He could be trying to get Airiana because he doesn't want her working for anyone else."

"He would have killed her," Maxim said. "He needs her. Shackler-Gratsos kills anyone who gets in his way. He never has to get his own hands dirty, and there's never evidence to connect him. He may have owned that ship filled with guns, drugs and women and children he knew would be murdered, but he's far away and will show outrage that such a thing occurred on one of his vessels. He can manufacture evidence against the captain and make himself look like a victim."

"You know a lot about him."

"I knew a lot about his brother. Less about him. He wasn't raised with his brother. The mother took Evan and fled to the United States, hiding from his father. His father was a billionaire with a far reach. There were all kinds of rumors about him but no one could ever prove anything. He was a cruel man and being his son couldn't have been easy, especially after the mother left," Maxim said.

"Now you're talking about his brother, the one killed off the coast here," Jonas said.

"There was some speculation that Stavros had his own mother killed when he found her. He'd grown as cruel as his father and he'd never forgiven her for leaving him behind with the father. He took whatever illegal activities his father had started to an entirely new level. When he died, Evan inherited everything."

"You certainly know a lot about these men," Jonas said.

"I told you, we've been after them for some time. Their human trafficking ring is probably the largest worldwide. Evan's mother came here with him and she met and fell in love with a man in a motorcycle gang."

"They call them clubs," Jonas said.

Maxim showed his teeth. "They can call themselves anything they want. In the end, it's all the same. Evan didn't grow up with the privileges his brother had, but the genetics held true. He thrived in the biker world of drugs and arms dealing, eventually rising to the top to lead them."

"So now this man controls a major biker gang that has chapters all over the world, as well as his brother's business," Jonas said. "He's the one all of you believe has this weather weapon?"

Maxim nodded. "He'll be sending his men after Airiana. Anyone trying to stop him will be killed. That's what he does. That's who he is. Inheriting the money only made him more powerful."

Jonas looked to Airiana. "What do you think? What do you want to do?"

Maxim was surprised at Jonas's reaction. Everyone else had tried to force Airiana through different means to do what they wanted; Jonas was asking her what she wanted. His opinion of the man rose.

Airiana moistened her lips. She glanced at Maxim.

What is it, baby?

All the theories they have to date, using hot spots, isn't going to do much good. It sounds good, but it won't work. Unfortunately, I don't think I can make my project work for anyone else. I didn't realize I could manipulate air and shift warm spots into areas where it's needed.

You aren't telling me what's wrong.

I don't want to do anything that would hurt you. Of course I want to see if I can make it work, but not if it would make you unhappy.

Why would that make me unhappy? He'd never had anyone worried about whether or not he'd be happy or sad. It was a new experience and one he wasn't altogether comfortable with.

I'd want to work for the U.S., and you love your country as much as I love mine. I can't guarantee if I did find a way to make it work, that it wouldn't be used as a weapon.

I'll always love Russia, honey, but this is my home and this will be my country. I can never go back. In fact right now, Sorbacov is dispatching hit men to find and kill me. You do whatever it is that will make you happy.

"Damon, I'll work with you," Airiana decided. "But from here on the farm. I'll put together a secure room. That way I know Max can watch over the children at the same time he's watching over me. I've got four children who need someone to guide them. That has to be my first priority, but I'll do the best that I can to help you."

Damon nodded. "Thank you, Airiana. I know it isn't easy thinking about coming back after all that has happened. I wouldn't have asked if it wasn't important. Even if Shackler-Gratsos doesn't have the work completed, it would be nice to have a countermeasure in place just in case it ever happens."

"I'll give you a list of supplies we'll need," Maxim said. "To beef up security around the farm."

"When do you think Evan is going to strike at you again?" Jonas asked.

"He won't wait long. He can't. He has to know either Russia or the United States is going to protect her. Even with a good team of experienced mercenaries, he'll know his chances of acquiring her will go down drastically if we have her under wraps," Maxim said.

"I'll make a few calls," Damon added. "My people will come out and secure a room for you to work in. Do you have any ideas where you want your workroom set up?"

She glanced at Maxim. "I have one. There's a basement below us, in the ground actually. It's like a big bunker. I wipe it clean every now and then just in case."

Damon gasped. "You *destroy* your work? Are you crazy? Airiana, you have one of the greatest minds on the planet. It was bad enough that you hid yourself away, but to have been working all this time and periodically wiping it out is just insane."

"I refuse to make weapons for anyone. I want to do something about children starving to death. I don't want to send a hurricane to Italy or Greece or tornadoes to the Middle East just because I don't like their politics."

For the first time Damon actually looked excited. "I'd love to see what you've been working on. Talking to you would be . . ." He trailed off, looking at his brother-in-law. He gave a little shrug. "Sarah is great and she understands me, and Libby's husband, Tyson, listens, but Airiana actually thinks like I do."

"She doesn't want to make weapons, Wilder," Maxim pointed out.

"Neither do I, although I do see the need to protect our country."

"You work for the Defense Department," Maxim said. "One would think they would expect you to come up with weapons for them."

I understand what he means. Sometimes my brain goes into hyperdrive and I can't slow it down and I make myself crazy trying to stop it. Having someone else to talk to, someone like me, could be wonderful. I loved the school I was in for that reason. I was surrounded by others who continually thought up new and exciting ideas and how to implement them.

Yeah. He got that. He didn't have to like it though. He wanted to be her—everything. He didn't want her to have to need anyone else, not even for her peace of mind—especially not for her peace of mind. He nodded slowly. She would spend a lot of time with Damon Wilder and they'd have long, animated conversations she would never be able to have with him.

Maxim.

There it was again. Her soft voice, just saying his name in that tone. So much love washing over and through him with just one word. His gaze jumped to hers. He sank into the blue sky. There were no drifting clouds, only the intensity of her love. His heart reacted like it always did, a slow somersault that left his throat raw.

You'll be with us. Remember. You're my bodyguard. I won't do this if you don't want me to. You're far more important to me. The children are more important. I learned the hard way about the things in life that matter. That's you. The children. My sisters and Levi and Thomas. All of us here. I don't need to do this.

She was so generous in her love and trust of him. All along he had wanted her to show him what love was. Real love. There it was laid out in a neat gift-wrapped package for him. She would give up the thing that made her mind calm. He felt her excitement at the opportunity to work with a man like Damon Wilder, but because he might be uncomfortable with it, she was ready to say forget it. That was love. How could he show her less?

Maxim shook his head and leaned down to brush a kiss across the top of her head. *You work with this man, baby. It will help you when you think your mind is too chaotic. I want you to do it. I'll be with you every step of the way. When the talk gets too boring, I'll go play with the kids.*

Airiana burst out laughing. *You're just trying to get me to underestimate you, Max. I'm fairly certain you'll be able to understand most things, if not everything we say. How do I know this? Because you understood the concept when Theodotus was talking to me. You didn't need any explanation and you grasped the severity of the situation immediately. You can pretend you don't understand, but my guess is, beneath all that rough warrior skin lies a brain much like mine.*

Maxim nodded. "So bring in your people to secure her workroom immediately. I'll get the list of supplies to you by noon. I want to consult with Levi and Thomas first just to make certain I'm not overlooking anything."

Jonas made a sound of pure derision. "The urchin diver and the art gallery owner? They'd know all about security, now wouldn't they?"

"Jonas, that was so sarcastic," Airiana reprimanded. "You know very well both Levi and Thomas know this farm better than Max could possibly know it." She raised her gaze to Damon's. "Now that I have children, and won't be helping out so much on the farm, we'll need to talk salaries."

20

MAXIM woke with the moonlight pouring through the bedroom window. Beside him, Airiana's eyes snapped open and she glanced out the window as well. He felt the instant tension run through her body. He put a hand on her to keep her calm. Siena and Nicia had both climbed into the bed and he didn't want them to wake up and cry.

He sat up slowly, making certain not to shift his weight too fast and risk waking the two little girls. Lucia lay on the floor wrapped in a blanket a few feet from Airiana's side of the bed while Benito lay on his side. He hadn't expected all four children to be joining them at night—*every* night. They definitely needed a sign as well as a lock on the door or they'd never get any privacy in the bedroom.

During the day the children spent their time with Judith doing art projects or Lexi on the tractor or inside the greenhouse. Benito hung out with the men and Lissa trying to learn everything as fast as he could about weapons and turning his body into a weapon. The boy was like a sponge, soaking up every bit of information as fast as he could. He learned quickly to be respectful of Lissa's skills. Maxim had learned respect for her as well, although he still knew little about her.

Daytime was the only time Maxim could sneak off with

Airiana and seduce her. Fortunately there were many places on the farm they could go and be undiscovered. Their house was just not one of them. True to his word, Damon had men rebuilding Airiana's workspace, making it soundproof and totally secure. Maxim was going to be very grateful for that room if the children insisted on sleeping with them every night.

He didn't have the heart to force them to go back to their own rooms once they showed up. All of them suffered terrible nightmares, particularly Nicia. She seemed to do better when she was close to him. Lucia and Siena clung to Airiana. Benito was Maxim's shadow. He'd even had to take the boy aside and give him "the talk" about how he needed alone time once in a while with Airiana. That had bought him a few small reprieves, but Benito seemed to need to be as close as possible to him too.

They're here, Max.

I know, baby. We'll be fine. Everyone knows what to do. Levi and Thomas will know, just as you do. Lissa too. Thomas will get word to Lexi and Blythe. Let's get the children to safety.

His one concern was Benito. The boy had a burning thirst for revenge and he had taken very seriously to heart the lecture Maxim had given him—particularly the part about protecting his family. Maxim woke him first. He put a finger to his lips.

"They've come for Airiana, just like we figured they would. I need you to help me take the girls down to the safety of the secure room. It's been ready for a few days, and Airiana's work is put away." She'd been locking it up to be safe in case they needed the room for the children.

"I'm ready," Benito whispered.

He not only looked ready, but eager as well. Maxim nodded. "Good. Once we're down there, I'm going to lock you in with the girls . . ."

"*No.* No way. I'm coming with you. I can shoot a gun."

"Right, you can. I need you to protect the girls. I can't do it, Benito, so I'm counting on you. I'm giving you a pistol, but if you leave that room, you'll leave them unprotected. I have to know I can rely on you."

Benito's face was a study in war. Part of him believed Maxim and the other part was certain he was being tucked away somewhere safe while the enemy came.

"I don't have time to argue. Either you're going to help me with this or you're not. I'm counting on you to be a man." Maxim pushed a whip of command in his voice, as well as a touch of impatience.

Benito squared his shoulders. "You can count on me. No one will get through that door to take them again."

Maxim nodded in approval. "I'm going to take the two little ones down the stairs. Watch my back for me. Let Airiana and Lucia down in front of you."

Benito pushed out his chest. "You got it."

Maxim nodded to Airiana and she gently woke Lucia while he scooped up the two younger girls. They moved together as a group through the house, in darkness, down the stairs to the basement below. No one spoke, but Lucia's breathing was too fast.

Maxim settled the two younger girls on one of the loveseats in the corner of the room where Airiana liked to put her feet up and stare off into space, presumably thinking. More often than not, they ended up making love, which he told her gave her even more to think about.

He caught Lucia's hands and looked into her eyes. "No one is going to hurt you or the girls or Benito again. You'll be safe here. Don't panic. You didn't panic on the ship, and there are a lot more of us to stop them this time. Just sit down here and read a book or try to sleep. Benito will shoot anyone coming through the door if they don't identify themselves properly."

She took a deep breath and nodded. "I want a gun too, Max."

"Sweetheart, you've only had two lessons, and the last time I took you out on the range, you shot just about everything *but* the target. It isn't safe yet. You'll get it down, but let's wait so no one accidentally gets hurt."

"Levi told me to practice more and I should have listened." She blinked back tears. "He showed me before you did, but I didn't like it."

"Lexi doesn't like it either, honey. That's all right. We're going to be fine. I need you to look after the little ones just in case they wake up. There's a small bathroom off of this little sitting area." He held out his hand to Airiana. "We have to go."

Airiana kissed Lucia. "We won't be long, honey," she promised.

Benito held out his hand. "The pistol."

Maxim pinned him with steely eyes. "Don't shoot anyone unless you have to, Benito. And don't leave this room. Once I'm hunting, I'll kill anyone I come across and you don't want to be out there."

Do you think we should say arrest? Shouldn't we try to arrest them?

Maxim wasn't going to dignify that with an answer. He wasn't a cop, and these men had come to his home to take his family from him. He'd lost one once before, it wasn't happening twice. He shot her a quelling look and she smiled at him.

So sorry, Mr. Badass. It was just a suggestion.

"Let's get out there. Benito, the code word is *nutmeg*. If that word isn't given, shoot. Do you understand?"

Code word? Nutmeg? *Are you kidding me?* It was all she could do not to roll her eyes. Nutmeg *seems to be a favorite code word for you.*

He has to feel important. I don't want him trying to follow us. These men Evan sent are top players. They know what they're doing and they'll be well equipped. Which is where you women come in. Thomas and Levi tell me you can handle yourselves when you're together. I need a good distraction while we pick them off.

Benito nodded, his dark eyes going fierce. "I understand, Max. I won't let you down."

Maxim couldn't help himself, although the gesture startled both him and Benito. He leaned down and brushed a kiss on top of the boy's head. "Keep them safe. Lock this door behind me."

Airiana followed Maxim up the stairs to the ground floor. The men Damon had sent had brought with them the supplies Maxim, Levi and Thomas had insisted they needed. It had been Maxim who had built the secret door into the side of the house where the bushes grew high and wild. He'd carved out a small pathway through the bushes were they couldn't be seen from anywhere on the property.

They rendezvoused with Airiana's sisters in the small bunker prepared in the center of Airiana's garden, just to the left of the gazebo. All of them had practiced for this moment hundreds of times, although only a few days had passed since Airiana and Maxim had come home. The men had worked them hard, not allowing anyone to go to work or do anything but go over the steps they would take when threatened.

Even if Evan's men tried to burn down Airiana's house, the spacious room in the basement would, in theory, still stand and the children would survive. Airiana hoped they wouldn't have to test that hypothesis. She greeted each of her sisters with a hug. Lexi shivered, but she stood her ground.

"We've got this," Airiana told Maxim. "Be safe. Go do whatever you need to do, but don't let anything happen to any of the three of you."

Maxim caught her face in both hands and kissed her hard. Leaving her wasn't the easiest thing he had to do, but these women all had enormous gifts. Each woman alone was a force to be reckoned with, but together, they made a frightening force. He stared into her blue eyes for a long moment, noting the gathering storm there.

Airiana wouldn't hide herself away, not when someone was threatening her family. Not when these men worked for the man who had sent the children to his ship to be abused and murdered.

"I love you," he said. The words came out husky, a voice he'd never used before, maybe even a little harsh. He'd never said them before, but he needed for her to know.

She reached up and pulled his head down to kiss him a second time. "I love you right back. Now go. And be safe."

"Yes, ma'am." Maxim left her to it.

Airiana turned her face up to catch the slight wind. At once the map of the farm sprang into her mind. The enemy had come in from three different directions. *One group, at least five—I think I'm getting five—is coming in from the back entrance near the irrigation pond.*

Judith linked them all together, the six women and the three men.

I can confirm that, Thomas said. *I'm moving in that direction now.*

How close are they to the pond? Rikki asked.

They're approaching it now, Airiana said, feeling the displacement of air near the pond's end. *They're close to the small group of flowering trees we planted last year.*

Thomas, stay on high ground, Rikki advised. *Judith, remember Levi, Thomas and Max are out there when you and Blythe give us a boost. Don't be heavy-handed.*

I'll do my best. You know when we're all working together it can be hard. Blythe will need to keep us toned down.

Airiana glanced up at the sky. Clouds drifted slowly above them, but with a little bit of heat she managed to pull water from every source into the clouds. Rikki lifted her hands, her fingers tapping into the air as if she might be tapping the keys of a typewriter. Airiana moved behind her, back to back, her own hands going up. The wind picked up, rushing toward the back of the property, back toward the pond.

Maxim was shocked at the authority in Rikki's voice. She was captain of her boat and she took it seriously. Apparently she was captain when she decided to wield her water talent as well. From his vantage point on the roof of Airiana's house, he could see Thomas crouched near a small grove of trees, waiting to do his part.

The wind hit the surface of the water, dipped low, and three geysers shot into the air, spinning fast, dancing across

the pond, rising higher and higher. The twisters jumped
from the pond to land, spinning madly, picking up debris
along the way as they moved across the land now.

The sight was a little disconcerting, even though Maxim
knew what the women, as elements, were capable of. The
twisters looked malevolent—alive—and bent on destruction. They raced toward the five intruders in silence while
more formed in the water, springing up like mad, whirling
soldiers.

Dozens more leapt from the surface of the water, spinning madly, bending toward the mercenaries as the group
approached the far side of the pond. In order to get to Airiana's home they would have to walk close to the spinning
tops of water.

"What the hell?" the leader snapped, holding his fist up
to still everyone's approach.

Airiana, where are the others coming in? Levi demanded.

Airiana turned her attention from providing the propul-
sion of wind to the waterspouts back to the map of the farm,
checking for displacement. *Another group of five is coming
in from the main entrance. They're about halfway past
Rikki's house heading to Judith's.*

I'll take them, Levi said. *And the last group?*

*They're dropping down from above, right into the clear-
ing where the gazebo is. Right in front of us. Max, are you
under cover, they should be able to see you.*

The men dropping on ropes from the helicopter were too
close to the house and the hidden children. It was all well
and good to give young Benito a gun, but he had no business actually shooting anyone. Airiana glanced toward the
house, afraid for Max, afraid for the children.

I've got them, Maxim said, his voice as always calm and
confident. *They're in the helicopter, Airiana. Bring in the
wind and slam it hard into their left side. Hard enough to
spin them if you can. You know they won't be able to see
me. I'm the shadow man. I'd do it myself, but I'll need to be
ready to take them out from here.*

Don't get overconfident, Levi said.

Maxim laughed softly. *You take care of your little band of mercs and I'll take care of mine, baby brother. Lissa, are you ready? When Airiana brings in the wind, give me some fire, breathe it right through the helicopter.*

Can you do that? Airiana asked, startled. She'd never really considered what Lissa could or couldn't do with fire.

Of course. It's all about energy and igniting the gasses in the air, Lissa replied.

Lexi, I'll need you to keep the men near Judith's occupied while I get into position to pick them off, Levi said, ignoring Maxim.

No problem, Levi. Lexi slipped her palms about an inch beneath the soil, listening intently. *I've got them. Stay above the little dip Judith has near her arbor. Tell me when you're clear. Blythe, Rikki needs Judith to boost her while Airiana is directing the wind. Can you give me a little extra power?*

Blythe never spoke of her gifts. She was a Drake, not an element, but she had power, and they suspected it had to do with unifying all of their gifts, not in the same way as Judith did, but in a much more subtle way. She soothed them all and yet could empower them as well. She seemed to be a melting pot of several gifts.

I'll do my best, Lexi, Blythe promised.

Lexi pulled her hands from the soil, doubled them into two tight fists and angled her punch toward Judith's home, mapping out the path of the tremor in her mind. She hit the ground hard, a one-two punch that sent a small ripple through the earth. As it moved toward the group of five men, the ripple spread and picked up speed. It shook the earth beneath the mercenaries, knocking them off their feet.

One fell to the right of the group, almost under Levi's nose. The man rolled, clutching his automatic weapon as if that would save him. Before he could come back up on his feet, Levi was on him, hooking him around the neck and snapping it fast, leaving him where he lay and scooting away. *One of five,* he reported.

Airiana concentrated on the helicopter. Maxim had said to bring the wind in hard from the left, to slam it into the stealthy helicopter. She took a deep breath and called the wind to her. She felt the rapid buildup of power—of energy—suddenly aware of the roiling gasses in the air around the helicopter. Sparks crackled around the rotor blade and body of the craft.

The wind slapped at the helicopter, swatting it like a bug, nearly knocking it from the sky. At the same time, the helicopter rocked wildly from side to side, the buildup of electricity in the air tangible. The sparks surrounding the craft and the ropes burst into flames. The wind fanned the flames so that the helicopter appeared to be a ball of orange-red in the sky. The ropes caught fire.

Maxim rolled from the low side of the roof, directly over the spot where the first of the team had landed after fast-roping down as the rope above him burst into flames. Maxim waited until the man began to rise cautiously and dropped directly on him, wrapping his legs tightly around the man's neck, driving him back to the ground as he snapped his neck. Immediately he rolled into the brush and scooted forward toward the next target he had marked.

Above his head the helicopter spun like a top, throwing one of the men to the ground while the other three slid down their ropes fast to give the pilot time to try to find a place to land the burning craft.

Hit him again with the wind, Airiana, drive him out to sea, Maxim commanded as he came up behind his next mark, his knife in hand. He drove the blade deep, one hand over the merc's mouth to keep him silent until the life drained out of him. *Two down. They won't get into the house, Airiana, I promise you that. Lissa, can you make your way around toward me?*

Lissa was much smaller than he was, so slight she barely made a shadow on the ground. She was dressed in dark clothing and had tightly braided her hair. Maxim had watched her closely during their numerous training periods and she had skills when it came to combat. She was absolutely calm in any situation he or one of his brothers had thrown at her.

I'm making my way toward you now, coming in from the south. Are you in position to take the man crouched in the flower bed? Lissa asked.

I'm in front of him. There's no way to get on him without being seen. I can't risk the gunfire yet, it would alert the other teams, Maxim said.

He won't be able to see you in a couple of seconds, Lissa assured.

A stream of bright orange-red flames crackled and danced in the air, a fiery whip extending from the helicopter to the ground. The whip lashed at the spot where the third mercenary had crouched low, cradling his weapon, frantically looking around with his night goggles to see what, if anything was coming at him.

The whip suddenly went white-hot, a dazzling display lighting up the ground as if it were a lightning bolt, blinding the team members wearing night vision.

Maxim was on the third mercenary immediately, moving with blurring speed, using his body weight to control the weapon while his blade sank into the man's heart and his hand covered his mouth. The man died staring at him. For a moment, he recognized Maxim. Maxim had seen him a few times over the years, always for hire to anyone who would pay him, uncaring what the job was.

Maxim lowered the body silently to the ground and slid into the shadows. *That's three. Lissa, you've got one to the right of you. Don't move, I don't want him to fire his weapon. Just ease down to the ground, keeping every movement slow and I'll work my way over to you. We'll trap him between us.*

Maxim tried not to worry about the woman, but he'd called her out of the safety bunker, knowing she would be the best one to get onto the roof to watch over the children. If necessary, he knew Lissa would kill to protect the others. Killing up close was far different than from a distance. It would bother her, but she'd be able to live with herself.

The children had to be protected on the off chance that whoever was running the operation had a couple of others waiting until everyone else was occupied. They could sneak in and supposedly grab Airiana or the children. That's what he would have done—sacrificed the pawns to get the queen. Lissa was his best bet against that possibility.

I need a little help controlling these waterspouts, Rikki said. *I've got too many of them. Thomas, stay back until I know I've still got all of them under control.*

Airiana threw the wind at the helicopter, doing her best to hurl the craft out over the ocean. She didn't want a forest fire or the thing crashing on someone's home. The moment she saw that the helicopter, now engulfed in flames, was over the ocean, she turned back to help Rikki.

The spouts were everywhere, a virtual army of water surrounding the five mercenaries coming at them from the back side of the property. The men knelt, watching the water dance around them. One held his hand out experimentally and touched it to his mouth. They looked relieved that it was only water.

I'm moving into position. Can you cut off the one flanking them? He's dropped back about six feet from the others? Can you be that precise? Thomas asked.

Rikki gave the telepathic equivalent of eye rolling. *Seriously?* She could do anything with water. She had already planned to start twisting the tops of the waterspouts together to form a tunnel around the men.

You're such a show-off, Blythe teased.

Rikki closed her eyes, feeling the water heavy in the air now. Judith fed her power slowly, but it wasn't really necessary. Every drop of water for miles responded to her, she could feel it, the drops all interconnected. She had to be careful that she didn't call in the seawater as well. She manipulated the twisting spouts, so that several left the ground, cushioned by the air Airiana sent under them.

I'm in position. Drop them, Thomas commanded.

Rikki did so easily, the spinning spouts landing solidly

between the four men and the one who had dropped back. The four men were completely surrounded by walls of water so thick it was impossible to see through them. Thomas struck hard and fast, coming in from the mercenary's left where the strongest pull on the water was.

He struck with his fist, a punch of enormous strength against the artery in the neck, paralyzing the man momentarily. He eased him to the ground as his knife bit deep, twice. He laid him almost gently on the ground and moved back into the shadows.

One down from the backup team, Thomas reported. *Rikki, push the water inward on the left side.*

Rikki did and the wall of water, all the spouts merging completely, revealed one, soaking-wet mercenary. The man spun around, trying to get the water off his goggles to see. It was already far too late. Thomas rose up like a monster from a horror film, his knife slashing deep, hitting arteries on the way, even as he yanked the weapon from the man's nerveless fingers. The blade buried deep in the mercenary's throat. He lowered him to the ground.

That's two, he reported as he rolled through the wall of water to the other side of the three men left.

He caught a glimpse of the remaining three. They had become aware of their missing companions and had gone back to back. He continued his roll until he was in the heavier brush. The moment they examined the bodies, they would know they weren't alone.

Can you push them toward the irrigation pond? Thomas asked. *Subtly though, but keep them moving. I don't want them to have the chance to spray the area with bullets.*

Judith, pull back the power altogether, Rikki said. *I'll handle this, you help Levi.*

Rikki maneuvered the wall of water closer to the three men huddling in the center. They inched away from it. The water had built into a powerful fall that was endless, soaking the ground and creating a muddy mess that sucked at their boots. One ducked his head and tried to go through it upright. The force of the water drove him to the ground. His buddies grabbed his boots and pulled him free before the water could bury him in the mud.

Lexi, Rikki said, *can you help me saturate the ground with water? I'm calling it up from underneath, but if we can stop them from moving, as long as Thomas is careful, we can contain them there.*

Sure. Lexi plunged her hands in the earth, feeling for the ebb and flow of the earth's song. The melody connected with the blood in her veins, and sang through her body until her heart beat with the same rhythm.

Lexi felt for the disturbance in the earth toward the back of the farm. Water was pounding down, saturating the ground. She shook her hands gently, mixing the dirt with her fingers about an inch or so beneath the soil. At once the earth responded to her call.

The ground beneath the three mercenaries shifted subtly, turning to soup, trapping their legs in the mucky goo. The water shifted directions, hitting them in the face, effectively blinding them.

Be careful of the ground, Thomas. It's highly unstable, you could sink with them, Lexi warned, *or get stuck.*

Thomas slid on his belly, dispersing his weight across what essentially had become quicksand. He moved slowly and deliberately, not drawing attention to himself. The mercenaries had other things to worry about. Each of them had realized they were sinking and had laid their bodies as flat as possible on the surface, dispersing weight as Thomas had.

They probably wouldn't have sunk any farther than their waists, but the combination of spinning water towers and sinkholes had shaken them all. He didn't want them back on their game. He killed the man nearest him with a quick thrust of his knife through the back of the neck. As he started to move away, the closest man suddenly turned his head.

He's got me, he's targeting me, Thomas said, rolling, trying to use the dead body for cover.

Roll toward the irrigation pond now. Roll now! Lexi slammed both fists hard into the ground, her heart pounding in her throat. She saw Judith turn toward her, her face going white.

A deadly jolt ran straight from Lexi's fists, picking up speed and strength as it raced underground toward the sinkhole. A crack opened just a few yards from the pond and continued like a lethal snake, widening as it ran toward the two men.

One had lifted his rifle, finger on the trigger, spraying the ground through the veil of water Rikki tried to keep up to protect Thomas as he rolled away from the unstable ground. The crack opened the earth below them. Both men dropped down, water pouring in on them. The crack undulated and then receded, drawing back, the ground beneath closing as if it had never opened.

Thomas! Thomas answer me! Judith cried.

Thomas rolled over and stared up at the sky, his heart pounding. He'd seen the women in action before, but each time they came together, the power seemed unbelievable. *I'm fine,* mi angel caido.

Lexi sank back on her heels and pressed her hand to her mouth. *I'm going to be sick. I'm sorry, Judith. I didn't know what else to do.*

You saved my life, little one, Thomas said. *Thank you. You did the right thing. That's all five. Give me a minute and I'm heading your way, Levi.*

I forgot Levi, Lexi wailed. *Levi, are you all right?*

I'm trailing after my four. They're trying to rendezvous with the two Maxim has left. Give me a minute. Maxim? Did you get that? Three more headed your way. They're all trying to converge on your home, Levi reported.

I see them, Maxim confirmed. *Lexi, quick thinking. Thanks for keeping Thomas alive, we all owe you one. I tried to muffle the sound of gunfire coming from the back side of the property, but everyone here is on alert now.*

Same with this group. I'm taking the one on the right. He's coming straight at me, Levi said. *The others have passed. Lissa, can you do another flash for me. Bright and hot.*

Maxim felt his heart stutter. Lissa was trapped, lying perfectly still with one of the mercenaries only a few feet from her. She was small and fit nicely beneath the shrub, but if he had looked down at his feet, he would have seen her. If she moved . . .

No problem, Levi. Count down to three. It's coming.

Maxim wanted to tell her to stop. He could only hope the man practically standing on her hand would be just as blind as the one Levi had targeted. The whip of orange and red flames danced through the sky, lashing toward the ground close to the garden, gathering energy as it snapped down toward earth. Suddenly it went white-hot, so bright the entire ground was illuminated.

Maxim cursed under his breath as the mercenary close to Lissa tore off his goggles and threw them, his hands going to his eyes.

Levi came at his target from behind, taking him fast, using his strength to break the man's neck, drop him and roll out of sight. *That's two. Don't mistake me for one of them, Maxim. I'm trailing after them.*

Maxim pushed his knife back into the sheath and pulled out his pistol. He was too far away from Lissa to use a silent kill. The mercenary close to her was bound to look down for his goggles.

The moment the flash of light was gone, the mercenary spun around, to look behind him. Lissa rolled out of the brush toward the man, evidently just as aware as Maxim that there was no way she could remain undetected. Her legs shot smoothly and precisely between the soldier's legs and she rolled, bringing him down. Fire raced up and over the ground, long ropes of it, wrapping around the rifle so that the mercenary had no other choice but to drop it.

Lissa's blade flashed for a moment in the moonlight and then it was gone, buried in the enemy's chest. She rolled away, coming to her hands and knees. She looked as if she might be getting sick.

Lis? Get the hell out of there, Maxim commanded, hoping his voice alone would snap her out of it.

The man's partner, a few feet ahead, swung his head around and spotted Lissa. Maxim shot him through the head twice before he toppled to the ground. The sound of the two bullets fired one after the other galvanized Lissa into action. She sprinted across the garden to the shadows of the house.

Maxim covered her as the other three men Levi was tailing burst into the garden. He beckoned to Lissa to keep running. She used him as a ladder, leaping into the air, one foot finding his hand, then his shoulder before she gained the roof.

All five down, he reported.

Not only had they built three bunkers, two of which still needed work, but they had added blinds on the rooftop as well. They hadn't had a lot of time to prepare, but they'd made the most of it.

Maxim swung onto the roof beside Lissa. *Do you have a gun?*

She nodded, scooting toward one of the blinds to cover the back of the house. She looked very pale, but determined.

Airiana, they're close to you. No one make a sound. Not a movement. Stay low. We're in a gun battle now. Weave the air around the bunker, make it dense and tight just in case a bullet travels that way.

If I do that, we can't help you, Airiana protested.

Maxim spotted Thomas converging from the south. Levi came in from the west, still behind the three remaining mercenaries.

Max! Two more. Two more. They're behind the house, right behind, at the window already, Lissa hissed.

Of course. The sound of gunfire had been the signal to bring in the last of Evan's team. These two men were the elite, the ones who were not considered expendable. Evan believed they could get the job done.

Go, Levi said. *Thomas and I have got this.*

Maxim caught another glimpse of Levi coming up behind one of the mercenaries, locking an arm around his throat and using the man's weapon to shoot the second one as he turned. Thomas knelt and took aim on the third man, firing as the mercenary turned back, firing his rifle in an effort to kill Levi.

Levi sank his blade into the man he held as a shield. *All five gone.*

The moment Levi gave the report, Airiana burst from the bunker and raced for the house. There would be no stopping her. Maxim couldn't blame her either—he was feeling a bit desperate himself. Benito had a gun and he would fire it if somehow the two mercenaries managed to get through the door to the secure room in the basement, which would be nearly impossible. Still, their children were in danger.

Maxim leapt from the roof almost in front of Airiana. She skidded to a halt. He threw her a hard look, one that should have intimidated her, but he realized Airiana didn't intimidate all that easily.

Thomas is entering through the back window, right behind them, Lissa reported.

Levi is taking the front, Judith added.

We're going in through the new entrance, Maxim stated, still glaring at his errant woman.

She held out her hand for a gun. He gave her the pistol and drew his Glock, waving her to stay behind him. He went in silently, easing the door open to feel the air patterns.

They're upstairs, in the main bedroom. They're moving in standard, two-man formation, clearing every room, he told his brothers.

Please don't get blood in my bedroom, Airiana said.

You're such a girl, Thomas teased.

Maxim, can you close the door on them? In, say, that small recreation room just between the kids' rooms? Levi asked.

What are you thinking? Maxim asked.

Let them make their way there. You and Airiana close off the room and suck the air out.

They can break out the windows, Maxim reminded.

Exactly, they'll get the hell out of your house. Thomas and I will be waiting for them, Levi said.

Not a bad idea.

Don't want that sister of mine to be upset over a little blood, Levi teased.

Hey! Have you ever tried to get blood out of something? Anything? It just doesn't want to come out, Airiana justified. *And the children don't need to see anything like that in their home.*

Both Thomas and Levi laughed at her, an affectionate, gentle laugh that helped to ease the tension. Maxim and Airiana waited while the two mercenaries made their way back down the stairs and cleared the first bedroom, Siena and Nicia's room. It took only a few minutes and the two men were back in the hall before slipping silently into the recreation room that separated Lucia and the younger girls' bedroom.

Together, Maxim and Airiana slammed the door closed, and sucked the air from the room. The two men reacted exactly as Levi predicted, throwing a chair through the window the moment they couldn't breathe, and diving through to the yard below them.

Thomas and Levi were on them immediately, two shadows, dealing death. *All clear,* Thomas reported.

Maxim once more felt the air outside to make certain no other enemy was near. He put his arm around Airiana. *Everyone is safe. I'll call Damon and let him know we need a cleanup crew out here now. It's been a long night. Thank you. All of you.*

We're just protecting our own, Blythe said.

Maxim glanced out the window to see Thomas with his arm around Judith, and Levi holding hands with Rikki. Lissa and Blythe were on either side of Lexi as they walked toward Lexi's home. No one looked at the bodies scattered around the garden.

"It's over," Airiana said softly. "Thank God."

Maxim didn't reply. It would never really be over, not until Evan Shackler-Gratsos was dead and gone, but there was no real way to get to him—yet. They'd just have to keep building up their security and watching over one another.

"What was that password I gave to Benito? The boy's so trigger-happy he might shoot us both," Maxim said. "You know, baby, we can't let them out until the cleaning crew has removed all the bodies."

"Max"—she shook her head—"they're probably scared to death. You're so . . . bad."

"They're sleeping in our bed at night. I'm desperate."

She laughed softly. "If I'm honest, I have to say, so am I, just a little bit, but we have to go reassure them."

"This parent thing is killing me," Maxim said.

21

MAXIM woke with the moon shining on his face. He could hear the children breathing softly, surrounding him, a familiar sound he was beginning to enjoy. His body was hard and uncomfortable, almost painful. He shifted his gaze to look down at the woman tucked beside him.

She was awake and she had her open hand pressed to her mouth, her blue gaze on him while she licked and bit and even sucked on the exact center of her palm. The breath slammed out of his lungs as he felt her tongue on his cock, curling around him, her mouth hot and moist and the edge of her teeth ever so gently nibbling down his shaft.

What the hell do you think you're doing, woman?

Waking you up. I'm feeling neglected. You do have a job to do and you've been falling down on it recently. You promised I'd always be happy.

We're surrounded by the enemy. He pointed out the obvious, feeling a little desperate. *Children everywhere and they won't leave us alone! Not for a minute.*

Be inventive.

He glared at her. She just smiled and slipped from the bed, and padded on bare feet across the room to the window. She had to skirt around Lucia, but she made it without waking any of them. She was dressed in thin shorts and a tank, neither of which could possibly keep her warm, but allowed her to be modest in front of the children in their bedroom. Airiana flung the fire ladder out the window, gave him a seductive smile, and climbed out.

Maxim lay there for a moment, a smile on his face. His woman was wonderful. Crazy. Ingenious. He was madly in love with her, there was no doubt about it. He breathed deep, trying to get his cock to cooperate. If it would just ease up a little, he could follow her, because right at this moment, if he moved, he was certain precious parts of his anatomy would shatter.

There was no stopping his smile. Airiana was teaching him how to enjoy life. She was just plain fun. Her laughter was contagious, and when he was overbearing with the children, she managed to turn the situation into something altogether different. He still couldn't figure out how she did it without undermining his authority, but it didn't matter, he'd get it eventually, and in the meantime, she had his back.

He sat up carefully. He wore only a light pair of sweatpants, and his chest was exposed, with all the scars as well as recent wounds.

"Wow," Benito said. "That's so cool. You never told me you had all those scars."

"Shh," Maxim cautioned, putting a finger to his lips. "I'm going out for a while. You watch over the girls, but if I catch you sneaking out after us, I'm going to shoot you. Really shoot you. And scars aren't that cool, so do what I say."

Benito laughed. "Airiana wouldn't like you telling me you're going to shoot me."

"Probably not, but that won't stop me from doing it. Stay here." Maxim rose and carefully skirted around Lucia. "And stop threatening to blackmail me. There's an entire forest out there, kid. I'm not afraid to use it."

Benito laughed again. Maxim liked the sound. The children rarely laughed, and he couldn't really blame them.

They were still getting to know one another, trying to form a family, and in the middle of it all, they were securing the farm as fast as they could, which meant workmen coming and going continually, disrupting them.

He grinned at the kid as he slipped out the window. "You're coming along, Benito. I'm proud of you."

His last glimpse of the boy told him he'd said the right thing for a change—the kid lit up like a Christmas tree.

Halfway down the ladder Maxim jumped to the ground, landing in a crouch, pausing to listen to the sounds of the night and let the air tell him exactly where she was. He didn't really need it, she'd left a trail of flower petals for him to follow. The woman was a romantic at heart—a good thing when he didn't have a romantic bone in his body.

The soft petals were silvery white, and she'd strewn the path liberally so he had no trouble finding his way to the gazebo. He saw her through the screens, standing with her back to him, staring out into the forest, surrounded by dozens of lit candles. Her fall of platinum hair looked like spun silver and gold tumbling down her back. He knew how soft that silky fall really was.

The thin shorts clung to her bottom as lovingly as material could possibly cling. Her bare legs looked firm and strong, her muscles clearly defined. He took his time looking at her, drinking her in, allowing the intensity of his love to wash over him.

She turned then, her eyes meeting his through the mesh of the screens. For a long moment, she held his gaze, and then she smiled at him. He loved every single feature on her face, from her large eyes, small straight nose, to her full, generous mouth. Her cheekbones were high and her lashes very long. When she smiled, he was fairly certain the sun rose in the sky.

Maxim stepped up the two brick stairs and opened the screen. Airiana gestured, her arms wide, indicating the setup waiting for him there in the gazebo, the mattress on the floor, the scented candles and the bottle of oil. She'd planned every detail, arranging their secret getaway.

"The boy has binoculars," he greeted her, because if he said anything else, the lump burning in his throat might find a way to reach his eyes. He had wanted her to show him what was love was, and she was continuously doing so.

She laughed softly. He felt that soft melodious sound go down his spine just like the touch of her fingers, and his entire body came alive. There was something about her that made his spirit soar high, and it always disconcerted him.

He cleared his throat. "You gave them to him and I remember I was adamant that it was a really bad idea."

"He loves them," she pointed out, laughing.

"He spies on everyone."

She stepped close to him and ran her hand up his bare chest, from his flat belly to his left nipple. "He's you, Maxim, and we have to shape him carefully. He needs to become the man you are. We can't lose him. The binoculars occupy his mind right now." She leaned forward and pressed a kiss into his belly button.

His breath caught in his throat, his fist bunched in her hair. "He's a shadow, and one of these days I'm going to accidentally step on him."

Her tongue teased his flat stomach, teeth nipping here and there. "You already love that boy."

"I love all of them, but they need to stay in their own damn beds," he growled. "We put them to bed every night and they just keep getting up and coming in, one by one like they have little strings connecting them, and they all wake up at one time."

"Nicia only feels safe when she's with you. She needs time, Max," Airiana said, her hand coming up to nuzzle his burgeoning cock through his sweats while her mouth continued its foray over his belly.

A savage ache invaded, his cock so full and hard he could barely catch his breath. His hand cupped the back of her head as she pressed little butterfly kisses down his belly, driving the air from him so that even his lungs burned. Her hands dropped to the waistband of his sweats, slowly untying the drawstring.

You've gone very quiet, Max.

That soft laughter in her mind sent more blood rushing through his veins, hot with excitement. Whatever she had planned, his body was more than ready for.

I knew we had a problem with the children invading our private space, so I created another one. I've wrapped the gazebo in a weave, Benito's binoculars can't get through, and I've made us our own private bedroom. We might not be able to sleep together out here, but I can love you all I want.

There was purring satisfaction in her voice as his sweats dropped to the floor with a single tug. He stepped out of them and kicked them away. Her hands cupped his sac, fingers moving gently over the velvet smoothness.

I love the way you feel. Your body is as hard as a rock, yet so easy to touch.

She stroked and massaged as she leaned into him to find the smooth head of his cock with her tongue, licking at the pearly drops there as if she might an ice cream cone. He threw back his head, closing his eyes, giving himself up to the slow, fiery burn of her mouth sheathing him.

A sound escaped her throat, a moan of satisfaction, and the note vibrated through his shaft, sending flames dancing through his entire body, radiating out from his cock to every nerve ending he had.

Have I told you how much I love you, Max? I wake up each day in your arms and can't believe how lucky I am to have you.

Her mouth was heaven. Hot. Tight. Wet. She curled her tongue around his shaft, found the sensitive spot beneath the lip of the head. His fists tightened in all the silky hair tumbling around her face, pulling it back. He wanted—no needed—to see her. She looked so beautiful with her mouth stretched around him and her blue eyes looking up at him with so much love.

He'd never considered that he would ever have a family, let alone a woman who would so generously give herself to him. She made these little sounds of joy, of satisfaction, as if giving him pleasure gave her so much more. Each time she made those throaty, sexy notes, rockets went off in his head, through his body, teasing at his full cock until he thought the top of his head might come off.

She drew him deep into her mouth and then slowly released him, moving back up his shaft only to vary the speed so there was no way to catch his breath. Streaks of fire raced from his groin to his brain. He felt his control slipping.

Airiana, he warned.

I've got you, baby, she said softly, *you're safe with me. We're alone here. We're safe. Let yourself go. Give yourself to me.*

His heart went into overtime. What if he was too rough? Too much for her? Did something she was afraid of? To just give in and let his body and mind go to that place freely, without restraint or worry . . .

Airiana. Was he telling her yes? No? To be careful of what she wished for?

Her mouth tightened around him, she suckled and then did the strange thing with her tongue that practically sent him into another realm.

Give yourself to me, Max. Don't hold back. I don't want you to. I want all of you. I want you to belong to me the way I belong to you.

He closed his eyes and let go, giving himself up to the sheer glory of her loving mouth and hands. It was like leaping off a cliff and free-falling, the exhilaration mixed with joy and trepidation. His hips began a gentle thrusting, taking him deeper into her tight, hot mouth.

Twice he held himself there, feeling her throat constrict him, watching her eyes, watching the sultry, smoky heat that only added to his building need. She'd lit a match to a stick of dynamite. He could see no fear or reluctance in her at all, only hunger, a deep hunger that matched his own.

He gave her just enough time to catch her breath, but she never fought him, never did anything but love him, accepting his rougher side as if every stroke gave her joy. He couldn't believe a woman could be so utterly generous.

He knew he wasn't going to be able to last much longer and he wanted the night with her. She deserved the night with him. With great reluctance, he began to withdraw. She suckled much stronger, frowning a little around his cock, if that was actually possible.

Baby, enough. We've got the night and I need to give back to you.

This is your night. I'm giving it to you. My gift. I want this. I want this night for you, Max.

This is for me, Airiana. I need to be inside you, sharing your skin. He did. He wanted to feel surrounded by her—to lose himself completely in her. He wanted to give her as much—or more—pleasure as she was bringing to him, because no man could have such a woman and not want to keep her always.

He took his index finger and gently inserted it into the side of her mouth, breaking the seal she had on his cock. *Come here, honey. I need you right now.*

He didn't wait for her consent, he knew he had it. It was in the soft melting of her body, her eyes, so filled with love he was certain he didn't deserve. It was in the generosity of her mouth when she brought him nearly to his knees.

Maxim lifted her into his arms, finding her mouth with his. His kiss was ferocious, demanding, much rougher than he had ever given her. He forced her head back to allow him to explore her mouth the way he wanted, taking his time, devouring the faint peach flavor that was essentially Airiana.

She moaned softly, kissing him back, her mouth open to his, her tongue sliding along his tentatively, but giving him everything he insisted on. She had given herself to him and he was taking what belonged to him. Her mouth was soft and hot and sheer paradise. He could kiss her forever and never tire of it.

He kissed her over and over as he laid her on the soft

bamboo sheets she'd covered the mattress in. One hand found her right breast while the other spanned her throat. His appetite was voracious, insatiable, he could never get enough of kissing her. His hand cupped her soft breast, just holding the slight weight in his palm because he could. He felt her shiver. Her breasts were so sensitive, and he loved that about her. His fingers began to roll and tug on her nipple to bring it to rapt attention.

He didn't allow her to catch her breath, he breathed for her, his lungs to hers, sharing their breath, exchanging it. He transferred his attention to her other breast, but already, the sweet peach taste in her mouth had made him hungry for her feminine essence, all that hot honey he knew was spilling out of her in welcome for him.

Maxim kissed his way down her throat to her breasts, pausing to suckle and nip with his teeth, hard, stinging nips his tongue laved and soothed. He continued his travels along the underside of her breasts and along the bruises on her ribs, now mostly healed.

She felt so small, giving him a heady feeling of power. Every kiss, every nip, his hands stroking and caressing left her panting, gasping, begging for more. She was vocal, letting him know by every gasping, ragged breath, every thrash and turn of her head, her bucking hips and writhing body, that she belonged solely to him—that she enjoyed everything he was doing to her.

His hands went to her thighs and she shivered as he parted her legs and blew into all that heat. He loved the fire in her. It was all his. All for him.

This is mine. For me. He stated the fact, for the first time believing it.

All yours, she agreed. *I gave myself to you almost the first day I met you.*

I'm giving myself wholly to you, Airiana. As messed up and as far gone as I am, I'm yours and always will be. He meant his declaration from the bottom of his shredded soul.

He bent his head to her as he lifted her hips. His mouth

settled over her and she screamed, the woven air around the gazebo containing the sound, keeping her cries of pleasure for his ears only.

He took his time devouring her, wanting every drop of her honey, using his tongue to draw it out, suckling strongly, teasing her taut little bud until she was writhing and pleading with him, until his own body made its savage demands.

He moved up and over her swiftly, not waiting for her body to adjust to his size, but surging into her with one, long brutal stroke, burying himself as deep as he could possibly go so that he was surrounded by her. Her feminine sheath gripped him tightly, so tight he felt the scorching hot burn he'd been waiting for.

She was a vise surrounding him with living, moving silk, the walls of her channel hotter than hell as they grasped at him. It took her body a moment to accommodate his size, and just as she was relaxing into him, he set a ferocious pace. He thrust into her over and over, gripping her hips, yanking her legs over his shoulders so he could get deeper, so he could feel that moment when they were one. When her soul connected to his.

It was beautiful. Perfect. He was never going to stop. He pounded into her. Her soft moans and breathless pleas began to rise into a crescendo. Still, he didn't stop. Her ragged breath and gasping cries became a counterpoint to each hard thrust.

Sweat beaded on his body. There was a fine sheen on hers. The night air wrapped them up in warmth. The scent of her candles mingled with the scent of their lovemaking, a heady aphrodisiac.

Now, Airiana, come apart for me. He made it a command. *I want everything you are. I'm giving you everything I am.*

Her muscles tightened around his, clamped down so hard that, for a moment, the sensation was close to pain, but then her body gripped and milked, a hard fist of silk surrounding him, drawing his seed into her. He felt the eruption like a hot jet of fuel, spurt after spurt filling her, while around him her body rippled with life, and that cleansing fire stormed through both of them.

He allowed himself to rest on her for a moment before wrapping her tightly in his arms and rolling over so he wouldn't crush her. He couldn't bring himself to separate from her and she lay on him, her cheek on his chest, over his heart.

"I love you, Maxim. I do. Thank you. I needed . . . you."

He stroked her hair. Maybe he could never give her the words out loud that she needed to hear, but he could say them with his body, whisper them intimately into her mind. He would always belong to this woman. He would always treasure her and care for her. His fingers tangled in all that silk.

"You know we're not finished out here, not by a long shot."

"I was hoping you'd say that. I brought some wonderful peppermint oil. It's quite edible, and when one puts it on interesting places . . . well . . ." She trailed off, laughing.

He loved her laugh nearly as much as he loved her.

Keep reading for an excerpt from the next
exciting Carpathian novel by Christine Feehan

DARK BLOOD

Available September 2014 from Piatkus Books!

SOUND came to him first. A low drumming beat growing louder. Zev Hunter felt the vibration of that rhythmic booming throughout his entire body. It hurt. Each separate beat seemed to echo through his flesh and bone, reverberating through his tissue and cells, jarring him until he thought he might shake apart.

He didn't move. It was too much of an effort even to open his eyes and figure out what that disturbing, insistent call was—or why it wouldn't go away. If he opened his eyes he would *have* to move, and that would hurt like hell. If he stayed very still, he could keep the pain at bay, even though he felt as if he were floating in a sea of agony.

He lay there for a long time, his mind wandering to a place of peace. He knew the way there now, a small oasis in a world of excruciating pain. He found the wide, cool pool of blue inviting water, the wind touching the surface so that ripples danced. The surrounding forest was lush and green, the trees tall, trunks wide. A small waterfall trickled down the rocks to the pool, the sound soothing.

Zev waited, holding his breath. She always came when he was there, moving slowly out of the trees into the clearing. She wore a long dress and a cape of blue velvet, the hood over her long hair so that he only caught glimpses of her face. The dress clung to her figure, her full breasts and small waist, the corset top emphasizing every curve. The skirt of the dress was full, falling over her hips to the ground.

She was the most beautiful woman he'd ever seen. Her body was graceful, fluid, an ethereal, elusive woman who always beckoned to him with a soft smile and a small hand gesture. He wanted to follow her into the cool forest—he was Lycan, the wolf that lived inside of him preferred the forest to the open—but he couldn't move, not even for her.

He stayed where he was and simply drank her in. He wasn't a man clever words came easily to, so he said nothing at all. She never approached him, never closed the distance between them, but somehow, it never mattered. She was there. He wasn't alone. He found that as long as she was close to him, the terrible pain eased.

For the first time though, something disturbed his peaceful place. The booming beat found him, so loud now that the ground lifted and fell with an ominous, troubling thump. The water rippled again, but this time he knew it wasn't the wind causing the water to ring from the middle of the pool outward. The drumbeat throbbed through the earth, jarring not only his body but everything else.

The trees felt it. He heard the sap running deep in the trunk and branches. Leaves fluttered wildly as if answering the deep booming call. The sound of water grew louder, no longer a soft trickling over rocks, not a steady drip, but a rush that swelled with the same ebb and flow as the sap in the trees. Like veins and arteries flowing beneath the very earth surrounding him, making its way toward every living thing.

You hear it now.

She spoke for the first time. Her voice was soft and melodious, not carried on the wind, but rather on breath. One moment she was on the other side of that small pool of water, and the next she was sinking down into the tall grass, leaning over him, close to him, her lips nearly skimming his.

He could taste cinnamon. Spice. Honey. All of it on her breath. Or was it her skin? His Lycan senses, usually so good at scent, seemed confused. Her lashes were incredibly long and very dark, surrounding her emerald eyes. A true emerald. So green they were startling. He'd seen those eyes before. There was no mistaking them. Her bow of a mouth was a man's perfect fantasy, her lips full and naturally red.

The booming continued, a steady, insistent beat. He felt it through his back and legs, a jarring pulse that refused to leave him alone. Through his skin, he seemed to follow the path of water running beneath him, bringing life-giving nutrients.

You feel it, don't you? she insisted softly.

He couldn't look away. Her gaze held his captive. He wasn't the kind of man to allow anything or anyone to ensnare him. He forced his head to work—that first movement that he knew would cost him dearly. He nodded. He waited for the pain to rip him apart, but aside from a little burst through his neck and temples that quickly subsided, the expected agony never came.

What is it?

He frowned, concentrating. The sound continued without a break, so steady, so strong and rhythmic, he would have said it was a heart, but the sound was too deep and too loud. Still, it was a pulse that called to him just as it called to the trees and grass as if they were all tied together. The trees. The grass. The water. The woman. And him.

You know what it is.

Zev didn't want to tell her. If he said the words, he would have to face his life again. A cold, utterly lonely existence of blood and death. He was an elite hunter, a dealer of death to rogue packs—Lycans turned werewolves and preying on mankind—and he was damned good at his job.

The booming grew louder, more insistent, a dark heralding of life. There was nowhere to hide from it. Nowhere to run even if he could run. He knew exactly what it was now. He knew where the sound originated as it spread out from a center deep beneath him.

Tell me, Hän ku pesäk kaikak, what is it you hear?

The melodic notes of her voice drifted through his pores and found their way into his body. He could feel the soft musical sound wrapping itself around his heart and sinking into his bones. Her breath teased his face, warm and soft and so fresh, like the gentlest of breezes fanning his warm skin. His lungs seemed to follow the rhythm of hers, almost as if she breathed for him, not just with him.

Hän ku pesäk kaikak. Where had he heard that before? She called him that as if she expected him to know what it meant, but it was in a language he was certain he didn't speak—and he knew he spoke many.

The drumbeat sounded louder, closer, as if he were surrounded on all sides by many drums keeping the exact beat, but he knew that wasn't so. The pounding pulse came from below him—and it was summoning him.

There was no way to ignore it, no matter how much he wanted to. He knew now that it wouldn't stop, not ever, not unless he answered the call.

It is the heartbeat of the earth itself.

She smiled and her emerald eyes seemed to take on the multifaceted cut of the gems he'd seen adorning women, although a thousand times more brilliant.

She nodded her head very slowly. *At long last you are truly back with us. Mother Earth has called to you. You are being summoned to the warrior's council. It is a great honor.*

Whispers drifted through his mind like fingers of fog. He couldn't seem to retain actual words, but male voices rose and fell all around him, as if he were surrounded. The sensation of heat hit him. Real heat. Choking. Burning. His lungs refused to work, to pull in much-needed air. When he tried to open his eyes, nothing happened. He was locked in his mind far from whatever was happening to his body.

The woman leaned closer, her lips brushing against his. His heart stuttered. She barely touched him, feather light, but it was the most intimate sensation he'd ever experienced. Her mouth was exquisite. Perfection. A fantasy. Her lips moved over his again, soft and warm, melting into him. She breathed into his mouth, a soft airy breath of clean, fresh air. Once again he tasted her. Cinnamon. Spice. Honey.

Breathe, Zev. You are both Lycan and Carpathian and you can breathe anywhere when you choose. Just breathe.

He was not *Sange rau.*

No, not Sange rau, you are Hän ku pesäk kaikak. You are a guardian.

The breath she had exchanged with him continued to move through his body. He could almost track its progress as if that precious air was a stream of white finding its way through a maze until it filled his lungs. He actually felt her breath enter his lungs, inflating them.

I'm not dreaming, am I?

She smiled at him. A man might kill for one of her smiles.

No, Zev, you're not dreaming. You are in the sacred cave of warriors. Mother Earth called the ancients to witness your rebirth.

He had no idea what she was talking about, but things were beginning to come back to him. *Sange rau* was a combination of rogue wolf and vampire blood mixed together. *Hän ku pesäk kaikak* was Lycan and Carpathian blood mixed. He wasn't certain what or where the sacred caves of warriors was and he didn't like the word *rebirth.*

Why can't I move?

You are coming to life. You have been locked away from us for some time.

Not from you.

She had been with him while he was locked in that dark place of pain and madness. If there was one thing he knew for absolute certain, it was that she had been there. He couldn't move on, because he hadn't been able to leave her.

He remembered that voice, soft and pleading. *Stay. Stay with me.* Her voice had locked them both in a sea of agony that seemed endless.

Not endless. You are awakening.

He might be waking, but the pain was still there. He took a moment to let himself absorb it. She was correct, the pain was subsiding to a tolerable level, but the heat surrounding him was burning his body. Without the air she'd given him, he would be choking, strangling, desperate.

Think what body temperature you wish. You are Carpathian. Embrace who you are.

Her voice never changed. She didn't seem impatient with his lack of knowledge. Before, when she was a distance from him, she hadn't been aloof, she simply waited. Now she felt different, as if she expected something from him.

What the hell? If she said to think about a different body temperature other than the one burning his flesh from his bones, he could give her that. He chose a normal temperature and held that in his mind. She spoke to him without words, telepathically, so she must be able to see he was doing as she asked.

At once, the burning sensation ceased to be. He took a gasping breath. Heat filled his lungs, but there was air as well. He knew her. Only one woman could speak to him as she did. Mind to mind. He knew her now. How could he have ever forgotten who she was?

Branislava.

How had she gotten trapped with him in such a terrible place? He sent up a small prayer of thanks that he hadn't left her there. *She* had been the one to whisper to him. *Stay. Stay with me.* He should have recognized her voice, a soft sweet melody that was forever stamped into his bones.

You recognize me. She smiled at him again and he felt her fingers brush along his jaw and then go up to his forehead, brushing back strands of hair falling into his face.

Her touch brought pleasure, not pain. A small electrical current ran from his forehead down to his belly, tightening his muscles. The current went lower, coiling heat in his groin. He could feel something besides pain and, wouldn't you know it would be desire?

It seemed absurd to him that he hadn't known all along

who she was. She was the *one* woman. The *only* woman. *The* woman. He'd known women, of course. He'd lived too long not to. He was a hunter, an elite hunter, and he was never in one place long. He didn't form attachments. Women didn't rob him of breath or put him under spells. He didn't think about them night and day. Or fantasize. Or want one for his own.

Until her. Branislava. She wasn't Lycan. She didn't talk much. She looked like an angel and moved like a temptress. Her voice beckoned like a siren's call. She had looked at him with those unusual eyes and smiled with that perfect mouth, inciting all sorts of erotic fantasies. When they danced, just that one unforgettable time, her body had fit into his, melted into his, until she was imprinted there for all time, into his skin, into his bones.

Every single rule he'd ever made about women in the long years he had lived had been broken with her. She'd robbed him of breath. Put him under her spell. He thought of her day and night and fantasized far too much. He wanted her in every way possible. Her body. Her heart. Her mind. Her soul. He wanted her all for himself.

How did you get here? In this place?

It alarmed him that he might have somehow dragged her down into that sea of agony because he'd been so enamored with her. Could a man do that? Want a woman so much that when he died, he took her with him? The idea was appalling. He'd lived honorably, at least he'd tried to, and he'd never hurt a woman who hadn't been a murdering rogue. The idea that he might have taken *this* woman into hell with him was disturbing on every level.

I chose to come with you, she replied, as if it were the most normal thing in the world. *Our spirits are woven together. Our fate is entwined.*

I don't understand.

You were dying and there was no other way to save your life. You are precious to us all, a man of honor, of great skill.

Zev frowned. That made no sense. He had no family. He

had his pack, but two of his pack members, friends for so many long years, had betrayed and tried to murder him. He was mixed blood now and few of his kind would accept him.

Us all? he echoed. *Who would that be?*

Do you hear them calling to you?

Zev stayed very still, tuning his acute hearing to get past the heartbeat of the earth, the flow of water beneath him, reaching for the distant voices. Men's voices. They seemed to be all around him. Some chanted to him in an ancient language while others throat-chanted as the monks from long ago had done. Each separate word or note vibrated through him, just as the heartbeat of the earth had.

They summoned him just as the earth had. It was time. He couldn't find any more excuses and it seemed no one was going to let him vegetate right where he was. He forced himself to open his eyes.

He was underground in a cave. That much was evident immediately. There was heat and humidity surrounding him, although he didn't feel hot. It was more that he saw it, those bands of heat undulating throughout the immense chamber.

Great stalactites hung from the high ceiling. They were enormous formations, great long rows of teeth of various sizes. Stalagmites rose from the floor with wide bases. Colors wound around the columns from the flaring bases to the pointed tips. The floor was worn smooth with centuries of feet walking on it.

Zev recognized that he was deep beneath the earth. The chamber, although enormous, felt hallowed to him. He lay in the earth itself, his body covered by rich black loam. Minerals sparkled in the blanket of dirt over him. Hundreds of candles were lit, high up on the walls of the chamber, illuminating the cavern, casting flicking lights across the stalagmites, bringing the muted color to life.

His heart began to pound in alarm. He had no idea where he was or how he got there. He turned his head and instantly his body settled. She was there, sitting beside him. Branislava. She was truly as beautiful as he remembered her. Her skin was pale and flawless. Her lashes were just as long, her lips as perfect as in his dream. Only her clothes were different.

He was afraid if he spoke aloud she would disappear. She looked as ethereal as ever, a creature from long ago, not meant for the world he resided in. The chanting swelled in volume and he reached for her hand, threading his fingers tightly through hers before he turned his head to try to find the source—or sources—of that summons.

There were several men in the room, all warriors with faces that had seen too many battles. He felt comfortable with them, a part of them, as if, in that sacred chamber, they were a brotherhood. He knew their faces, although most he'd never met, but he knew the caliber of men they were.

He recognized four men he knew well although it felt as if a hundred years had passed since he'd seen them. Fenris Dalka was there. He should have known he would be. Fen was his friend, if someone like him could have friends. Beside him was Dimitri Tirunul, Fen's brother, and that too wasn't surprising. The brothers were close. Their last name was different only because Fen had taken the last name of a Lycan in order to better fit in during his years with them.

Two figures stood over another hole in the ground where a man lay looking around him just as Zev was. The man, in what could have been an open grave, looked pale and worn, as if he'd been through hell and had come out the other side. Zev wondered idly if he looked the same way. It took a few moments before he recognized Gary Jansen. Gary was human and he'd waded through rogue wolves to get to Zev during a particularly fierce battle. Zev was very happy to see him alive.

He was familiar with Gregori Daratrazanoff. Usually Gregori wasn't far from his prince, but he hovered close to the man who struggled to sit up. Gregori immediately

reached down and gently helped Gary into a sitting position. The man on the other side of the "grave" had the same
look as Gregori. This had to be another Daratrazanoff.

On the other side of Gregori, a short distance from him,
stood two of the De La Cruz brothers, Zacarias and Manolito, both of whom he knew and who had joined with him
in a battle of some kind. The actual facts were still a little
fuzzy. A third man stood between them.

In the center of the room were several smaller columns
made of crystals forming a circle around a bloodred formation with what looked to be a razor-sharp tip. Standing beside it was Mikhail Dubrinsky, prince of the Carpathian
people. He spoke very low, but his voice carried through
the chamber with great authority.

Mikhail spoke in an ancient language, the ritual words
to call to their long-gone ancestors. *"Veri isäakank—veri
ekäakank."*

To his absolute shock and astonishment, Zev understood
the words. Blood of our fathers—blood of our brothers. He
knew that was the literal translation, but the language was
an ancient one, not of the Lycans. He had been born Lycan.
He had heard the language spoken by Carpathians down
through the centuries but he shouldn't have understood the
words so clearly.

"Veri olen elid."

Blood is life. Zev's breath caught in his throat. He *understood*. He spoke many languages, but this was so ancient he couldn't have ever learned it. Why was he
understanding it now? Nothing made sense, although his
mind wasn't quite as foggy as it had been.

Branislava tightened her fingers around his. He turned
his head and looked at her. She was so beautiful she took
his breath away. Her eyes were on his face and he felt her
gaze penetrating deep. Too deep. She was already branded
in his mind. She was coming far too close to his heart.

*"Andak veri-elidet Karpatiiakank, és wäke-sarna ku
meke arwa-arvo, irgalom, hän ku agba, és wäke kutni, ku
manaak verival,"* Mikhail continued. The power of his

voice rang through the chamber, raw and elemental, bringing Zev's attention back to him.

Zev interpreted the words. "We offer that life to our people with a blood sworn vow of honor, mercy, integrity and endurance."

What did that mean? This was a ritual—a ceremony that he felt part of—even though he didn't know what exactly was going on. The appearance of Fen and Dimitri was reassuring to him. The longer he was awake, the more his mind cleared. The two were of mixed blood, although both had been born Carpathian.

Mikhail dropped his palm over the very sharp tip of the dark red column. At once the crystals went from dark red to crimson, as if Mikhail's blood had brought them to life.

"Verink sokta; verink kaŋa terád." Mikhail's voice swelled with power.

Zev saw sparks light up the room. He frowned over the words Mikhail had uttered. "Our blood mingles and calls to you." He was mingling his blood with someone of power, that much was obvious from the way the columns throughout the room began to come alive. Several gave off glowing colors, although still very muted.

"Akasz énak ku kaŋa és juttasz kuntatak it."

Zev interpreted again as the columns began to hum. "Heed our summons and join with us now." The columns throughout the room rocked, the multicolored crystals illuminating, throwing vivid, bright colors across the ceiling and over the walls of the chamber. The colors were so dazzling, Zev had to shade his sensitive eyes.

Crimson, emerald, a beautiful sapphire, the colors took on the strange phenomenon of the northern lights. The humming grew louder and he realized each took on a different note, a different pitch, the tone perfect to his ear. He hadn't noticed that the columns appeared to be totems with faces of warriors carved into the mineral, but now they came to life, the color adding expression and character.

Zev let out his breath slowly. These warriors were long dead. He was in a cave of the dead and Mikhail had summoned the ancient warriors to him for some purpose. Zev had a very bad feeling that he was part of that purpose.

"Ete tekaik, sayeak ekäakanket. Čač3katlanak med, kutenken hank ekäakank tasa."

Zev swallowed hard when he translated. "We have brought before you our brothers, not born to us, but brothers just the same."

Zev had been born Lycan and he'd served his people for many long years as an elite hunter who traveled the world seeking out and destroying rogue wolves who preyed on mankind. He was one of the few Lycans who could hunt alone and be comfortable and confident doing so. Still, he was Lycan and he would always have the need to be part of a pack.

His own kind despised those of mixed blood. It mattered little that he became mixed blood giving service to his people. He'd been wounded in hundreds of battles and had lost far too much blood. Carpathian warriors had more than once come to his aid as they had done this last time.

Zev looked up to find Fen on one side of him and Dimitri on the other. The two De La Cruz brothers stood with the stranger between them.

Gregori and his brother stood on either side of Gary, who now was getting to his feet with Gregori's help. Zev took a breath. He would not be the only man sitting on his ass while the others stood. He was getting up or would die trying.

Zev let go of his lifeline, and the moment he did he nearly panicked—another thing men like him didn't do. He didn't want her to disappear. His eyes met hers. *Don't you leave me.*

She gave him a smile that could allow a man to live for the rest of his existence on fantasies. *We are tied together, Zev. Where you go, I go. Only the ancients can undo a weave of the spirits.*

Is that what this is about? He wasn't certain he wanted to continue if it was.

Not even the prince can ask for such a release. Only me. Or you.

She gave him the information, but he had the feeling she was a little reluctant. That suited him just fine. He wasn't willing to relinquish his bond with her just yet.

Fen, I don't have a stitch on and I want to stand up. I'm not going to lie in this grave like a baby. For the first time he realized he was absolutely naked and Branislava had been beside him the entire time holding his hand; even when his body had stirred to life she hadn't run from him.

At once he was clean, and clothed in soft trousers and an immaculate white shirt. He struggled to get to his feet. Fen and Dimitri both reached for him at the same time, preventing him from falling on his face and making a fool of himself. His legs were rubber, refusing to work properly. For a Lycan that was embarrassing, but for an elite hunter it was absolutely humiliating.

Mikhail looked over at him and nodded his approval, or maybe it was relief at him being alive. Zev wasn't certain yet if he was relieved or not.

"Aka sarnamad, en Karpatiiakak. Sayeak kontaket ŋamaŋak tekaiked. Tajnak aka-arvonk és arwa-arvonk."

"Hear me, great ones. We bring these men to you, warriors all, deserving of our respect and honor." Zev translated the words carefully twice, just to make certain he was correctly interpreting the prince's discourse with the ancient warriors.

Gary, standing between the two Daratrazanoff brothers, straightened his shoulders as if feeling eyes on him. Zev was fairly certain that somehow, those spirits of the dead were watching all of them, perhaps judging their worth. Colors swirled into various hues and the notes blended together as if the ancient warriors questioned the prince.

"Gregori, és Darius katak Daratrazanoffak. Kontak ŋamaŋak sarnanak hän agba nókunta ekäankal, Gary Jansen, hän ku olenot küm, kutenken olen it Karpatii. Hän pohoopa kuš Karpatiikuntanak, partiolenaka és kontaka. Sayeak hänet ete tekaik."

"Gregori and Darius of the great house of Daratrazanoff claim kinship with our brother, Gary Jansen, once human, now one of us. He has served our people tirelessly both in research and in battle. We bring him before you.'

Zev knew that aside from actually fighting alongside the Carpathians, Gary had done a tremendous amount of work for the Carpathians, and had lived among them for several years. It was obvious that every Carpathian in the chamber afforded him great respect, as did Zev. Gary had fought both valiantly and selflessly.

"*Zacarias és Manolito katak De La Cruzak, käktä enä wäkeva kontak. Kontak ŋamaŋak sarnanak hän agba nókunta ekäankal, Luiz Silva, hän ku olenot jaquár, kutenken olen it Karpatii. Luiz mänet en elidaket, kor3nat elidaket avio päläfertiilakjakak. Sayeak hänet ete tekaik.*"

"Zacarias and Manolito from the house of De La Cruz, two of our mightiest warriors claim kinship with our brother, Luiz Silva, once jaguar, now Carpathian. Luiz saved the lives of two of their lifemates. We bring him before you."

Zev knew nothing of Luiz, but he had to admire anyone who could stand with Zacarias De La Cruz claiming kinship. Zacarias was not known for his kindness. Luiz had to be a great warrior to run with that family of Carpathians.

"*Fen és Dimitri arwa-arvodkatak Tirunulak sarnanak hän agba nókunta ekäankal, Zev Hunter, hän ku olenot Susiküm, kutenken olen it Karpatii. Torot päläpälä Karpatiikuntankal és piwtät és piwtä mekeni sarna kunta jotkan Susikümkunta és Karpatiikunta. Sayeak hänet ete tekaik.*"

"Fen and Dimitri from the noble house of Tirunul claim kinship with our brother, Zev Hunter, once Lycan, now Carpathian. He has fought side by side with our people and has sought to bring an alliance between Lycan and Carpathian. He is of mixed blood like those who claim kinship. We bring him before you."

There was no mistaking the translation. Mikhail had definitely called his name and indicated that Fen and Dimitri claimed brotherhood with him. He certainly had enough of their blood in him to be a brother.

The humming grew in volume and Mikhail nodded several times before turning to Gary. "Is it your wish to become fully a brother?"

Gary nodded without hesitation. Zev was fairly certain that, like him, Gary hadn't been prepped ahead of time. The answer had to come from within at the precise moment of the acting. There was no prepping. He didn't know what his own answer would be.

Gregori and Darius, with Gary between them, approached the crystal column, now swirling a dull red. Gregori dropped his hand, palm down, over the tip of the formation, allowing his blood to flow over that of the prince's.

"Place your hand over the sacred bloodstone and allow your blood to mingle with that of the ancients and that of your brothers," Mikhail instructed.

Gary moved forward slowly, his feet following the path so many warriors had walked before him. He placed his hand over the sharp tip and allowed his palm to drop. His blood ran down the crystal column, mixing with Gregori's.

Darius glided just behind him in the same silent, deadly way of his brother, and when Gary stepped back, Darius placed his palm over the tip of the bloodstone, allowing his blood to mingle with Mikhail's, Gregori's, Gary's and the ancient warriors who had gone before.

The hum grew louder, filling the chamber. Colors swirled, this time taking on hues of blue, green and purple.

Gary gave a little gasp and went silent, nodding his head as if he heard something Zev couldn't. Within minutes he stepped back and glanced over to the prince.

"It is done," Mikhail affirmed. "So be it."

The humming ceased, all those beautiful notes that created a melody of words only the prince could understand. The chamber went silent. Zev became aware of his heart beating too fast. He consciously took a breath and let it out. The tension and sense of anticipation grew.

"Is it your wish, Luiz, to become fully a brother?" Mikhail asked.

Zev took a long look at Zacarias and Manolito. The De La Cruz brothers were rather infamous. Taking on their family as kin would be daunting. Only a very confident and strong man would ever agree.

Luiz inclined his head and walked to the crystal blood-stone on his own, Zacarias and Monolito behind him. Clearly Luiz had not been wounded. He was physically fit and moved with the flow of a jungle cat.

Zacarias pierced his palm first, allowing his blood to flow down the stone, joining with the ancient warriors. At once the hum began, a low call of greeting, of recognition and honor. Colors swirled around the room as if the ancients knew Zacarias and his legendary reputation. They seemed to greet him as an old friend. There was no doubt in Zev's mind that the ancient warriors were paying tribute to Zacarias. Many had probably known him.

When the humming died down, Luiz stepped close to the stone and pierced his palm, his blood flowing into that of the eldest De La Cruz. Manolito came next and did the same so that the blood of all three mingled with that of the ancient warriors.

At once the humming of approval began again and the great columns of both stalagmites and stalactites banded with colors of white and yellow and bright red.

Luiz stood silent, very still, much as Gary had before him, and just as Gary, Luiz nodded his head several times. He looked up at Zacarias and Monolito and smiled for the first time.

"It is done," Mikhail murmured in a low tone of power that seemed to fill the chamber. "So be it."

Zev's mouth went dry. His heart began to pound. He felt tension gather low in his belly, great knots forming that he couldn't prevent. There was acceptance here—but there could also be rejection. He wasn't born Carpathian, but Fen and Dimitri were offering him so much more than that— they stood for him. Called him brother. If these ancient warriors accepted him, he would be truly both Carpathian and Lycan. He would have a pack of his own again. He would belong somewhere.

The feeling in the great chamber was very somber. The eloquence of the long dead slowly faded and he knew it was time. He had no idea what he would do when asked. None. He wasn't even certain his legs would carry him the distance, and he wasn't going to be carried to the bloodstone.

"Is it your wish, Zev, to become fully a brother?" Mikhail asked.

He felt the weight of every stare. Warriors all. Good men who knew battle. Men he respected. His feet wanted to move forward. He wanted to be a part of them. He was physically still very weak. What if he didn't measure up in their eyes?

You aren't weak, Zev. There is nothing weak about you.

Her voice moved through him like a breath of fresh air. He hadn't realized he was holding his breath until she spoke so intimately to him. He let it out, braced himself and made his first move. Fen and Dimitri stayed close, not just to walk him to the bloodstone, but to make absolute certain he didn't fall on his face. Still, he was determined it wouldn't happen.

With every step he took on that worn stone floor he seemed to absorb the ancients who had gone before him. Their wisdom. Their technique in battle. Their great determination and sense of honor and duty. He felt information gathering in his mind, yet he couldn't quite process it. It was a great gift, but he couldn't access the data, and that left him even more concerned that he might be rejected. Somewhere, sometime, long ago, he felt he'd been in this sacred chamber. The longer he was in it, the more familiar to him it felt.

As he approached the crystal column, his heart accelerated even more. He felt sheer raw power emanating from the bloodstone. The formation pulsed with power, and each time it did, color banded, ropes of various shades of red, blood he knew had been collected from all the great warriors who were long gone from the Carpathian world, yet who, through the prince, could still aid their people. Mikhail understood their voices through those perfectly pitched notes.

Fen dropped his palm over the tip of the stalagmite. His blood ran down the sacred stone. The colors changed instantly, swirling with deep purple and dark red. He stepped back to allow Zev to approach the column.

Zev wasn't going to draw it out. Either they accepted him or they didn't. In his life, he couldn't remember a single time when he cared what others thought of him, but here, in the sacred chamber of warriors, he found it mattered much more than he wanted to admit. He dropped his palm over the sharp tip so that it pierced his skin and blood flowed over Fen's, mingling with the one who would be his brother, and with the great warriors of the past.

His soul stretched to meet those who had gone before. He was surrounded, filled with camaraderie, with acceptance, with belonging. His community dated back to ancient times, and those warriors of old called out to him in greeting. As they did, the flood of information through his brain, adhering to his memories, was both astonishing and overwhelming.

Zev was a man who observed every detail of his surroundings. It was one of the characteristics that had allowed him to become an elite hunter. Now, everything seemed even sharper and more vivid to him. Every warrior's heart in the chamber from ancient to modern times matched the drumming of the earth's heart. Blood ebbed and flowed in their veins, matching the flow of the ancients' blood within the crystal, but also the ebb and flow of water throughout their earth.

Dimitri dropped his palm over the crystal and, at once, Zev felt the mingling of their blood, the kinship that ran deeper than friendship. His history and their history became one, stretching back to ancient times. Information was cumulative, amassing in his mind at a rapid rate. With it came the heavy responsibility of his kind.

The humming grew loud, and he recognized now what those notes meant—approval, acceptance without reserve. Colors swirled and banded throughout the room. Those ancient warriors recognized him, recognized his bloodline, not just the blood of Fen and Dimitri who claimed kinship, but his own, born of a union not all Lycan.

Bur tule ekämet kuntamak. The voices of the ancestors filled his mind with greetings. Well met, brother-kin. *Eläsz jeläbam ainaak.* Long may you live in the light.

Zev had no knowledge of his lineage being anything but pure Lycan. His mother had died long before he had memory of her. Why would these warriors claim kinship with him through his own bloodline and not Fen and Dimitri's? That made no sense to him.

Our lives are tied together by our blood. They spoke to him in their own ancient language and he had no trouble translating it, as if the language had always been a part of him and he had just needed the ancients to bridge some gap in his memory for it all to unfold.

I don't understand. That was an understatement. He was more confused than ever.

Everything, including one's lifemate, is determined by the blood flowing in our veins. Your blood is Dark blood. You now are of mixed blood, but you are one of us. You are kont o sívanak.

Strong heart, heart of a warrior. It was a tribute, but it didn't tell him what he needed to know.

Who was my mother? That was the question he needed answered. If Carpathian blood already flowed in his veins, how was it he hadn't known?

Your mother's mother was fully Carpathian. Lycan's killed her for being Sange rau. Her daughter, your mother, was raised wholly Lycan. She mated with a Lycan, and gave birth to you, a Dark blood. You are kunta.

Family, he interpreted. From what bloodline? How? Zev knew he was taking far longer than either Gary or Luiz had, but he didn't want to leave this source of information. His father never once let on that there was any Carpathian blood in their family. Had he known? Had his mother even known? If his grandmother had been murdered by the Lycans for her mixed blood, no one would ever admit that his mother had been the child of a mixed blood. The family would have hidden her from the others. Most likely her father had left his pack and found another one to protect her.

The humming began to fade and Zev found himself reaching out, needing more.

Wait. Who was she?

It is there, in your memories, everything you need, everything you are. Blood calls to blood and you are whole again. The humming faded away.

"It is done," Mikhail said formally. "So be it."